JUST FRIENDS

HALEY PHAM

SIMON &
SCHUSTER

London · New York · Amsterdam/Antwerp · Sydney/Melbourne · Toronto · New Delhi

First published in the United States by Atria Paperback, an imprint of Simon & Schuster, LLC, 2026
First published in Great Britain by Simon & Schuster UK Ltd, 2026

Copyright © Haley Goodman, 2026

The right of Haley Goodman to be identified as author
of this work has been asserted in accordance with the
Copyright, Designs and Patents Act, 1988.

3 5 7 9 10 8 6 4

Simon & Schuster UK Ltd
1st Floor
222 Gray's Inn Road
London WC1X 8HB

For more than 100 years, Simon & Schuster has championed authors and the stories they create. By respecting the copyright of an author's intellectual property, you enable Simon & Schuster and the author to continue publishing exceptional books for years to come. We thank you for supporting the author's copyright by purchasing an authorised edition of this book.

No amount of this book may be reproduced or stored in any format, nor may it be uploaded to any website, database, language-learning model, or other repository, retrieval, or artificial intelligence system without express permission. All rights reserved. Enquiries may be directed to Simon & Schuster, 222 Gray's Inn Road, London WC1X 8HB or RightsMailbox@simonandschuster.co.uk

Simon & Schuster Australia, Sydney
Simon & Schuster India, New Delhi

www.simonandschuster.co.uk
www.simonandschuster.com.au
www.simonandschuster.co.in

The authorised representative in the EEA is Simon & Schuster Netherlands BV,
Herculesplein 96, 3584 AA Utrecht, Netherlands. info@simonandschuster.nl

Simon & Schuster strongly believes in freedom of expression and stands against censorship in all its forms.
For more information, visit BooksBelong.com

A CIP catalogue record for this book
is available from the British Library

Paperback ISBN: 978-1-3985-5676-8
eBook ISBN: 978-1-3985-5677-5
Audio ISBN: 978-1-3985-5678-2

Interior design by Davina Mock-Maniscalco
Chapter opener art by Michaela MacPherson

This book is a work of fiction. Names, characters, places and incidents are either a product of the author's imagination or are used fictitiously. Any resemblance to actual people living or dead, events or locales is entirely coincidental.

Printed and Bound in the UK using 100% Renewable Electricity
at CPI Group (UK) Ltd

Praise for *Just Friends*

'It is IMPOSSIBLE to believe that this is Haley's debut novel! *Just Friends* is a heartwarming second-chance story that contemporary romance fans will adore. An absolute must-read!'
Lynn Painter

'Champion of reading Haley has written a beautiful, sensitive second-chance romance that her millions of fans are going to love. I was reminded of the warmth and heart of Emily Henry. *Just Friends* is so assured and confident it's hard to believe it's a debut. Haley is a big new talent for the genre'
Mhairi McFarlane

'Haley Pham's debut novel, a second-chance romance set in a seaside town, is a sun-drenched delight. *Just Friends* explores grief, vulnerability and the power of forgotten dreams. I could not stop turning the pages, following Blair and Declan's flight toward each other, and love'
Amanda Eyre Ward

'In this debut novel, Haley Pham explores first love and second chances with a tender gaze. Not shying away from the raw emotion that accompanies grief, Pham handles both love and loss deftly and with a kindness that will leave readers warm and smiling by the final pages'
Emma St. Clair

'A moving story of first love finding its way home. Utterly delightful'
Rachel Catherine

*For Ryan, who made my life
a romance book before I discovered them.*

Hi Reader pops,

If you're reading this, that means you are holding the first printing of my first book. That automatically shoots you up to OG status, and that can never be taken away from you. But on a real note, THANK YOU. Thank you for giving my writing a chance. Thank you for your optimism and support. Especially to those of you who have been following my writing journey before I ever even announced the title or the plot! By picking up Just Friends you are making my dreams come true. So once again, thank you.

♡ Haley Pham ♡

Chapter 1

"The fear part only come when it's love," Aunt Lottie would always say in the kind of broken English others noticed but I never did. "The kind of love that burrow so deep, it transform you. If you lose it, it feel like losing a part of yourself, too."

That feeling is personified in my stomach right now, and not in the way I expected her advice to come true—about some boy, about Declan. Instead, that full-bodied, love-fueled fear was stirring awake because of her.

"I just want to warn you. Things will look a little different when you get here." My mom's voice fills the car speaker.

"I know. It's— That's fine. I'll be there in twenty. Love you, Mom," I say in a rush, finger hovering over the red button.

She sighs like mothers sigh when they know they can't protect their daughters from inevitable pain. "Okay, then. I love you more, sweetie. See you soon."

The call ends, and I swallow hard, readjusting my grip on the steering wheel. A two-lane highway stretches before me, kissing a steep cliff that slopes toward waves that crash against the shore.

As I drive through the tunnel that transports you from vast, open skies to a town that feels too cozy not to be fiction, I force myself to perceive its beauty like the travelers who flock here every summer might. An overhang of trees makes it seem like the town is wearing a beret, and flowers in bloom seemingly all year dot the quaint cottages that look like they're built by fairies.

A few turns later, I'm nearing my childhood home—or more specifically, The Great Aunt Lottie's house—but I want to make a stop first. Perhaps it's further avoidance of what I'm scared to find when I arrive, but I veer left toward the picturesque downtown square regardless.

There's one local bookstore in Seabrook, California, and it's only open during the busy tourist season—which seems to be now, judging by the crowds. I have to yield to a conglomerate of pedestrians almost every ten feet. Dads wearing fanny packs are followed closely behind by kids wearing waffle crewnecks screen-printed with the name SEABROOK, melting ice cream cones in hand.

Scoring an unlikely parking spot in front of the bookstore, I brace myself before pushing open the heavy oak door to Seabrook's Books and Nooks, knowing the odds of running into someone I know from childhood are extremely high.

JUST FRIENDS

The comforting aroma of vintage paper wafts toward me as I step in, and my shoulders drop. A bookstore is the first place my feet take me in every town, even the town I know every square inch of. Just as I predict, I'm only three strides into the romance section when my suspicions become a reality.

"Oh my gosh," a familiar voice starts, "Blair?"

Slowly, I rotate on my heel to see a girl peering around the bookshelves. She wears oversized square glasses and a messy bun, and she's awaiting my response. It's a relief that I recognize her.

"Hey, Rosie," I say with a wan smile.

We were never close in high school, but she was always sweet. Sat in the back of class, smiled at me in the hallways.

"What are you doing back? I thought you were moving to New York City or something." She waves nonspecifically with her hand into the ether as she fully emerges from around the corner.

At first, I'm astonished by her forwardness. Perhaps I've forgotten how much four years can change about a person, but Rosie was particularly known for her *lack* of speaking.

"Uhh, well." My hand scratches the back of my neck. "My aunt is sick actually. Came back to spend some time with her." I drop my hand and try a smile to show her she doesn't need to feel awkward for asking.

"Oh gosh, Blair, I'm so sorry. I didn't—"

Before she can continue stammering, I fill her in on the details she's probably wondering about, or maybe I do it in an attempt for it to feel real.

"It's okay. Stage four lung cancer. Came out of nowhere and has progressed quickly." I say it like I'm describing the weather, trying to dismiss the rising emotion in my chest.

"But it will be fine," I tack on.

That was good, I decide. Instead of trying to scurry around unnoticed I actually let Rosie in on something in my life. I try to not regret it as I look at the pained expression on her face, half sympathy and half panic, unsure of how to respond to something so grave.

Rosie just nods with a grimace as she looks down at her twiddling fingers, which I take as permission to turn around and end this painfully unpleasant experience for both of us, finishing my journey toward the romance section.

There's a book I just finished on my Kindle last night I want a physical copy of. Frivolous, I know, but I'm unwilling to restrain myself from any hit of dopamine right now. I'll take any ounce I can get to prepare me for what's to come.

Usually, pulling into the smooth cobblestone driveway of Aunt Lottie's house feels like exhaling. Today it feels like forgetting how to breathe. There's a roundabout that loops in front of the sprawling mansion. Smooth brown-gray stucco sits under sloping wooden roofs, as if the house were built from the nature surrounding it. Contemporary glass windows adorn the sides, but the curtains are all drawn, making the pit in my stomach open wider.

Childhood memories of Lottie chasing me through the garden flood my mind. I try not to choke on the thought of her weakened body laying inside.

My great-aunt Lottie fled Saigon as it fell and was taken over by communists. She told me the story in detail of how she picked up and left everything she knew at age twenty, boarding a boat that was meant to hold two hundred people, but became one thousand. Desperate and grief-stricken, the people forced themselves onto the boat, trying to take hold of their last option out of the country as their homes vanished behind them.

Food had to be rationed, and even so, there wasn't enough to go around. She described the bunk bed she lay atop of, hidden in a lower level of the boat, trying not to move, trying not to think, for the seven days it took to arrive at a small neighboring country.

From there, she waited months for a sponsor in America to host her arrival, and it came in the form of a generous family in Orange County. In her adult life, she stumbled upon the small town of Seabrook, California, and fell in love with the beaches lined with cypress trees and moss-covered thatched roofs. She settled down before tourists discovered it, and opted to open a convenience store instead of finishing college in a language she barely knew. That convenience store expanded to two locations, which later became seven.

Lottie understood what it was like to be ejected from the life you knew. So, when my mom and the five-year-old me showed up on her doorstep, fleeing from an abusive husband, *my father*, she let us take refuge inside her home. And eventually, inside her heart. I take a deep breath and bolster myself to see the women who raised me waiting inside.

As I enter, my body takes note of the eerie silence before I can register why it feels so blue. Lottie is missing from her spot by the window, where she's usually whistling a tune or reading her newspaper.

I call out, "Mom? Lottie?"

"Up here!" my mom yells from above.

I sprint up the winding staircase to Lottie's bedroom. When I walk in, I try to hide my shock at seeing Lottie propped up in a mechanical hospital bed, wearing one of her beautiful floral dresses.

My eyes dart to my mother's. She smiles at me encouragingly, opening her arms as I run toward them.

Her comforting scent wraps itself around my heart and squeezes as I squeeze her.

"Hi, Mom," I breathe into her neck, "I missed you."

"Missed you too, sweet pea."

Turning to the mechanical bed, I bend down.

"And Lottie!" my voice pitches upward, hoping to raise the obviously somber mood. "How are you managing to look so gorgeous in this dinky bed?!" I kick it playfully, trying to disguise my unease as I take in how wrong she looks in a hospital bed.

A mild laugh bubbles out of her, eyes twinkling as her shoulders shake up and down gently.

"Come here, my sweet girl." She reaches out to my head to bring me down, giving me her famous sniff kiss—a kiss on the cheek that starts with a deep inhale and ends with a smooch. The ridiculous sound of her aggressive inhale on my cheek always makes me laugh.

"Congratulations on graduating, con." She uses the Vietnamese word for child lovingly. "I am so proud of you."

Her voice sounds weaker, bringing tears to my eyes before I can stop them.

"Now"—she waves her hand in my face—"no crying for me, con. I've had a happy life. Everything I could ever want is right here in this room." I look behind me at my mom standing in the corner with a pained expression on her face, trying so hard to be stoic for my sake. "You don't let this drag you down, okay? I'm comfortable here. I want you to go enjoy! Enjoy life!"

Even after living here for fifty years, she has an accent that perseveres. I will never stop loving the sound of it. Speaking her life truths to me in fragments or dropping the *s* on plural words.

No matter how much pain she is experiencing, I know she will go to lengths unknown to keep it hidden from me. She and my mom have always been this way. Encouraging me to be strong, forge on, despite the circumstances.

I give her another hug, aware that this frail body beneath me contains all the love I felt in my childhood, and is now being ravaged by cancer.

"I love you," I whisper brokenly into her ear. I wipe my tears with my hands before taking a seat in a chair set up beside her. But the second I do, Lottie chastises me.

"No, no, con! Don't sit here with me. You finally back home. Go explore."

I squint as I try to catch her darting eyes.

"Lottie, don't be silly—"

"Baby," she croaks. "I'm not joking. Please, go enjoy this beautiful day. I'm not going anywhere."

I still at her words, unsure how to respond.

"Shoo! Out you go!" She waves her hands theatrically until I stand. "Keep going!" She doesn't relax until I'm halfway out the door.

"Okay, okay," I concede in a weak voice, peeking my head through the door one more time. "I love you."

"I love you too, con. Now, go have some fun."

Chapter 2

Two weeks ago I got *the call*. If you've ever gotten "the call" in your life, you'll unfortunately know what I mean. The one that creates a before and after in your story, bookending each side. Whatever you had been doing prior to it becomes so hilariously insignificant in comparison to the words coming through the phone speaker.

I was sitting on an ocean-aged bench overlooking Malibu's choppy waves when the podcast I was listening to was interrupted by "Hopelessly Devoted to You" wailing in my headphones. My phone was ringing, a photo of my mother's effervescent smile and dark hair filling the screen.

JUST FRIENDS

"Hi, Moooom!" I drawled with faux lethargy.

"Hi, baby. Is now a good time?" My mom's usually light, sugary tone was pulled taut. The tension in her voice stiffened every muscle in my body, causing me to shift to a straighter position on the bench.

"Yeah, what's going on?"

"It's Aunt Lottie. I just wanted to let you know we decided to put her on at-home hospice care. The cancer progressed way faster than any of the doctors saw coming so we've made the difficult decision to quit treatment and . . ." Her voice trailed off as my ears began to ring.

My body felt like it was tilting internally, an air of unreality coating me. My fingers tingled and my vision darkened at the periphery.

A memory of Lottie dancing around the kitchen in one of her floral printed maxi dresses, singing "The Butterfly Song" in Vietnamese, waltzed across my mind.

"Kìa con bướm vàng, Kìa con bướm vàng!" She would sing to me with her eyebrows raised and skirt fluttering around her as she seemingly floated over the wooden floor. I would sit there in a fit of giggles, completely enraptured by her beauty. Her voice felt like a safe cocoon. She was a second mother, a grandmother, and a best friend, all in one beautiful, tiny body.

"I-I'll come home as soon as possible, Mom. This is top priority to me. I'll get someone to—" My mind sputtered as I tried to work out the logistics of leaving college when there were only two weeks left until graduation, of abandoning the consulting job I had lined up in New York.

"No, baby. I want you to graduate first. Don't worry about us just yet. She's comfortable here; the nurses come twice a week. Just work out how to come here for the summer if you want to, okay?" my mom said, tone placating my panic.

"I will be there for sure. There's nowhere else I'd rather be," I emphasized, promising with no concrete plan of how. But didn't at-home hospice care mean death was approaching?

My mom has always been worried about overstepping—the complete opposite of a stereotypically overbearing mother. At times, she's too polite in her attempt not to overstep, and it feels like I could drift away from her and Lottie and never hear from them again if I wasn't the one to tug on the rope, pulling them closer to me. I couldn't rely on my mom to emphasize how dire the situation was. Lottie could be at risk of dying tomorrow and Mom would still encourage me to go to New York City and not worry about it.

Now, two weeks after the call that derailed my life, my massive luggage bobbles violently up the cobblestone walkway that leads to the guesthouse.

I could have spent my visit home in my untouched bedroom, but the thought made my skin crawl. There was nothing like a childhood bedroom to make you feel like the years you've spent trying to progress have been erased.

If Lottie's compound was an island, the guesthouse would be like a lighthouse perched on a rocky cliff. As a kid, the short walk made me feel like a character from *The Hobbit*, trekking up the cozy pathway that led to the smaller structure with its curved wooden door.

But I don't see any of it as I pull my belongings behind me. My body feels numb from shock. Seeing Lottie for the first time after the call was even worse than I conjured in my imagination. The last time I saw her she had been sick, yes, but she was still moving about the kitchen like she was floating beneath her floral dress.

Pushing open the wooden door of the guesthouse, the comforting musk of old clothes and fresh sheets greets me. My gaze snags on the wooden coatstand in the corner. An aged yellow bucket hat hangs from the top rung. Memories flash through my mind of the beach trips Lottie took me on when she had a day off managing her convenience stores. She'd help me build "hot tubs" in the sand, transporting ocean water to our man-made hole and sitting in it like lobsters in a pot. The memory feels like a hand reaching through my chest, squeezing my heart uncomfortably. I fight to take a deep breath and drag my bags all the way inside. I have a sinking feeling the sensation will only become more prevalent in the future.

I cross the small bedroom to the bathroom, lined with jade-green tile, turning the shower handle to its hottest setting. As I wait for the water to heat up, I scan the layout of the bedroom, trying to appreciate the coziness of the beautiful room rather than feel the pit of dread rising in my stomach.

A glimpse of my reflection in the seashell-encrusted mirror causes me to do a double-take.

My body looks deflated, like it's had a head start processing the news before my mind got to the starting line.

I tousle my curtain bangs and wipe the tears from beneath my tired eyes. My phone buzzes. I pick it up to find a Google calendar reminder for three months from now: "Ernst & Young Start Date." My shoulders tense. I delete the reminder and throw my phone on the bed and then step into the shower's comforting heat.

I was offered the consulting job I had been gunning for my entire time at Pepperdine. Up until the call about Lottie's health, I was prepared to move to New York City and buckle down for the next few years of twelve- to fourteen-hour workdays, excited by the prospect of finally working toward my goal.

"Do you have, like, an NYC bucket list?" Faye, my best friend from college, asked me one night.

I blinked at her and said, "What do you mean by . . . bucket list?"

"Like, aren't you envisioning the cute outfits you'll wear to work every day and the sexy dive bar you'll get drinks at where you might spot a celebrity?" she said, eyebrows raised in anticipation.

But the question stumped me. Landing this consulting gig wasn't about enjoying my work, having a vibrant social life, or living in a big city. Those all paled in comparison to the expression I imagined on my mother's relieved face as I delivered her the news: "You can retire."

Leaving Seabrook had always been about getting the best job possible so that I could relieve my mom from working behind the cash register at one of Lottie's convenience stores. But more than that, I wanted to buy her independence. Her life had been about supporting me for so long, I wanted to pay her back. I wanted to see her carefree enough to hang out with friends or consider dating someone again. To simply do something because she *wanted* to. Not because she needed to for me.

But here I was, job deferred.

Which was fine, of course. There was nowhere I'd rather be than with Lottie. But simultaneously, it felt like I was abandoning my mom. She would never see it that way, because she'd never ask for my help in the first place. Her life was about making sure I could live mine. But I wanted to make mine about making sure she could live hers.

I let my mind wander to my friends' more promising first days out of college. Faye moving her clothes into a walk-in closet, kissing her new husband on the cheek before ushering him out the door to make enough money for both of them. And Roshi, receiving congratulations from relatives as she announced the prestigious law school she got accepted to.

JUST FRIENDS

Their futures are unfurling while mine feels like it's snapping backward: Freshly moved into a tiny house at the back of a mansion I had no merit in earning, back to square one in my hometown. The irony is jarring. My friends are the mansion. I am the guesthouse.

I shut the water off and yank a pink towel from the rack, hastily drying off and ready to exit the guesthouse not long after arriving. Sulking wouldn't get me closer to my dream of letting my mom finally retire, and Lottie wanted me to spend the day outside. So, if I couldn't pursue the job I wanted, it was time I found one here in Seabrook. Descending the cobblestone steps and brusquely turning onto a wide road, I stride toward downtown where small businesses thrive during the tourist season. Somewhere, someone will surely hire me.

One of the things I missed most about home was the ability to walk everywhere. Within seconds, I remember why Seabrook is called "a storybook come to life." The way the trees, seemingly as old as time, hunker down into the earth with muscular roots and weave through roads. A choir of birds sings as squirrels dart from branch to branch. Houses and shops lack street numbers, so hand-painted wooden signs offer names to reference instead. "Bristle & Brine," reads a swinging sign to a boutique with robin's-egg-blue-painted shutters.

Three blocks into the city, I lock eyes with my target—Seabrook Coffee House. A more recent addition to the city square, the name is a far cry from unique, but the shop itself makes up for it.

The white cottage house is nestled in a courtyard, led to by a brick street. Lush greenery hugs the roof like a sweater.

As a child, I would hide behind the abandoned house's bushes while playing tag with the local kids. Now, as a newly graduated adult, I swing the creaky red doors open to beg for a job.

A short, blond-haired girl peeks over the register at me and gives me an excited grin. She looks like she just celebrated the birthday that made her old enough to work here.

"Good morning! What can I get ya?" she says with a sunny smile.

An odd amount of shame creeps into my voice as I reply, "Morning! I was actually checking to see if you guys were hiring." Perhaps seeing that I'd be coworkers with a high schooler after completing my degree at a prestigious university is what triggers it.

It's just for the summer, I tell myself, making sure to liven up my expression so this cheery-faced girl doesn't receive the brunt of my postgrad crisis.

The girl's eyebrows crinkle like she's trying to soak up the totality of my face before snapping out of it and blurting, "Yes! Let me just go ask the manager real quick!" I furrow my brow as she scurries to the back like a small mouse.

My ear unintentionally catches the sound of Sunny Teenager informing the manager that "a girl" is here looking for a job. There seems to be a tense exchange, whispered questions and responses, but I can't hear what they're saying.

The manager is facing her, his broad shoulders blocking my view, but the sun beams through the window and highlights his jagged cheekbone. From the back, his hair looks messy in a way that suggests he was too busy to put effort into styling it.

The conversation between Tense Manager and Sunny Teenager ends, so I turn away sharply, hoping they don't catch me eavesdropping. I'm facing the window, pretending to look outside, when I hear his footsteps approaching.

A calm, deep voice sounds off behind my left ear. "Excuse me, ma'am?"

The sound makes me time travel while standing in place. I spin around, still suspended in the second of shock, where my brain screams improbability.

My eyes finally land on him and the floor of my stomach becomes a faulty elevator.

The person who felt more like home than my house did, the one I spent twelve formative years with, the name that became too painful to think about after disappearing without saying the word *goodbye*, is standing in front of me.

More to myself than him, a subconscious breath of a word rasps out of me, *"Declan."*

His pupils dilate in response. Or am I imagining things?

Apart from the tiniest twitch of his strong mouth, his jaw stays locked in cool concentration. He seems unmoored, maybe more resigned to see me than shocked by my presence.

Why is he unfazed?

Everything about him is familiar in an instant, and yet, wholly different.

Declan has the face of someone who only becomes more interesting the longer you look at him. I instantly get lost surveying his recent developments. In the four years since I've seen him, his face has stretched tight over the angular planes of his cheekbones. A speckling of stubble dots the slant of his jaw. New lines are etched into the grooves beside his eyes. But the dimples, the freckle on his bottom lip, just slightly to the right, and the freckle on his neck, slightly to the left, are still perfectly in place.

"Blair," he responds in a clipped tone and a simple, albeit slightly awkward nod, before shoving the application into my hands and spinning around to walk away.

As he does, I notice something that wasn't there the last time I saw him. A subtle limp.

Chapter 3

My fingers navigate to Roshi's number the second I step foot out of the coffee shop. Distant chatter fades as she answers the phone.

"Hey, Blink. How's Seabrook life treatin' you?" Her voice is a slow, laid-back drawl.

I'm out of breath as I answer, "Roshi."

"What! What? Don't use that voice! It scares me." She snaps out of her typically affable demeanor in an instant.

"I. Just. Saw. Declan," I grind out, word by word.

There's a moment of silence that stretches for so long, I remove the phone from my ear to check if she got disconnected. I'm grateful the speaker is away from my ear because she screams, "WHAT?? *THE* DECLAN RENSHAW!?"

"Yes!" I cry, relieved to finally have someone else say it back to me.

My eyes. On Declan Renshaw. Four years after the accident.

"Where did you see him?" she asks. "Just out on the street or something?"

"No, he's the manager of some coffee place. I was applying for a job there before I knew he worked there, obviously!"

"What was his reaction?" she demands.

"I don't even know. It was so weird. He didn't look shocked to see me at all. His face was like this . . . black hole. Just completely devoid of emotion. And then he shoved the job application into my hands and stalked off to the back room like he had something else to deal with."

"What!?" Roshi squeals. "That's all? He didn't say anything about it being . . . *you*?"

"I mean, he said one word before disappearing, and it was my name. That's it. I guess I also only said one word too, but . . ." I trail off.

"Hmmm," she hums. "He's gotta be affected by seeing you for the first time after all these years though. Right?"

I huff out a breath, the question is exactly the thought I've had looping through my mind since it happened.

How could he ever move past everything we experienced together? There was the fight but, weren't we more than that? And how we ended . . . how was he so unbothered by it?

"Wow. Very strange indeed," she says quietly, seeming to ponder the strangeness of it alongside me. "Are you still gonna apply for the job?"

"Yeah, I mean, I need a job with overtime hours. Plus . . . is it bad that I kind of want to work there? To get some sort of closure or something? The last time we spoke . . ." I hesitate. How we ended isn't something I've ever shared with anyone. It certainly wouldn't paint me in the best light.

"Yes, of course that makes sense!" Roshi insists. "I'd be in that coffee shop every day until that man gave me answers."

"Yeah. Right," I intone, choking down a morsel of guilt. "I'm gonna apply."

Conflict, to me, might as well be synonymous with death. But this is Declan. I can't help my curiosity now that I know he'll be in that coffee shop a few blocks away from me every day. Plus, the odds of him hiring me are low anyway.

After catching up with Roshi, I return to the guesthouse, charging up the uneven cobblestone, and let myself into the cool air-conditioning. Throwing my phone on the bed, I rip my suitcase open in search of running clothes.

Adrenaline and ancient, teenage-level angst are still pumping through me. My thoughts won't calm on their own, but I can force them to by demanding they focus on the essentials only. Breathing. A beating heart. Obsession and heartbreak won't have room in my body anymore once I start running.

I throw the arch door open, lock it behind me, and jog out onto the street, turning right instead of left to hit the forest road instead of the town.

The sound of my cushioned shoes hitting the black tar road becomes the metronome for my thoughts to stay on beat.

Never, in all my hours spent pondering Declan's whereabouts, did I consider the coffee shop three blocks from my childhood home. It felt like spending years trying to break into a laptop, only to find out the password was password.

When we lost contact I continued to believe he went to play football for a D1 college. Simply for following the trajectory he was on, being watched by agents who kept their eye on rising stars, surely, once he healed, he could take his pick of any college team.

Maybe I'm oblivious to how much damage the accident caused, but Declan (and his mom, yes, I checked) hadn't left a single social footprint on the internet, much to my dismay. Other than a single photo posted to Declan's Instagram account, which created more questions than answers. Still, I'm shocked to have finally found him, back home, managing a coffee shop.

As much as I try to resist it, a memory from six years ago forces its way to the forefront of my mind, taking center stage. If the memory's job is to make sure I never finish getting over him, I don't think I ever started.

Six Years Ago: Summer

"Just run like five yards and then look over your shoulder, and I'll throw you the ball." Declan is trying to coax me into the idea of pretending to be his wide receiver. It's the summer before our junior year and he's antsy to start practice with his new team. We're facing off in the middle of Seabrook High's empty football field, a rare misting of dew coating the perfectly grass-green turf beneath us.

"I don't think you're understanding me," I retort. "I have never been good at running with my legs and simultaneously using my arms."

Declan stares back at me with a disbelieving half-smirk, so I forge on.

"Let alone using my eyes to track the ball at the same time. It's not happening."

"Okay, fine. I'll tell you a secret." He throws the ball as high as it will go and lets it hit the top of his head on the way down. I flinch when it lands, but he doesn't react in the slightest. It topples to the ground and bounces side to side like a fish out of water before settling.

"Wh— How did you—"

"This is a fake football," he supplies, reaching to pick it up off the ground. "It's made out of foam." He squishes it, showcasing how easily it molds to his grip.

"Oh." I blink twice. "And why do you, two-time state champion quarterback, have a fake football?"

He looks down, flipping the football-disguised piece of foam in his hands. One stray lock of brownish-blond hair flops over his forehead.

"Because I wanted to practice with you."

"So . . ." My eyes narrow. "You only bought it to play with—"

"Yes," he says with force. "With you specifically. So, you have to at least try to run a few yards and catch it now that I've confessed that."

The admission does something I don't want to name to my chest.

"Seems fair. Hurry up then." I clap my hands together before breaking into a sprint. Mostly so he can't see the blush creeping up on my cheeks at the thought of him going to the store and buying a foam football just to spend this mundane summer evening playing catch with me.

I have no gauge for how far five yards is so I sprint until I hit a white line and then look over my shoulder. To no one's surprise, by the time I turn around the ball is flying toward me faster than my eyes can communicate to my arms to respond.

Declan laughs when the foam football hits my face. It kisses my nose before bouncing off in a cartoonish arc. It's too squishy to hurt, so I descend into self-pitying chuckles, coming to a stop and letting my arms hang limply at my sides in defeat. Meanwhile, Declan peels over at the waist in a fit of full-on cackles.

I stand there watching him with my lips pressed together in an ironic, self-evident display of pity, overstating how correct my previous objections to this idea were. I'd have the nerve to actually be annoyed if he didn't look so cute laughing.

It's like his face can't take the weight of his joy, so it has no choice but to crumple beneath it. Lines bracket his mouth like parentheses, and a specific spot above his cheek is creased down with nowhere to go. After another second, he collects himself, pushing off his knees to stand up straight and walk over to me.

His face becomes my entire view, obscuring the damp blades of fake grass and the bright yellow field goal post.

"I told you! "I wouldn't have been able to catch that ball if my life depended on it."

"Are you okay?" he tries to say through leftover laughter, still filtering itself out of his body.

"Yes," I reply, deadpan. "I am fine. But unfortunately for you, I don't think I'll be a good partner with whom to practice your throws. Just like I predicted."

"With whom, huh?" he volleys, eyebrows rising in that challenging way that sends a tingle of awareness up my spine.

"Mm-hmm. With whom indeed." I nod defiantly. "I think

I'll stick to reading my books. Sixteen-year-olds casually overthrowing kingdoms, etcetera."

"Right. But can't you do that and continue being my football partner?" At my stony look he adds, "Please?," eyebrows tenting upward in a pitiful plea.

"I don't think I'll be much help training you to become a good quarterback if your practice buddy can't catch any balls. Good or bad throw? Won't matter. They'll all land right here." I point to the tip of my nose.

In a shocking display of affection, Declan grabs my wrist from my face and says, "No, come on. No football buddy would look half as cute as you did when it hit your face."

My heart thuds double time as soon as the word cute escapes Declan's wide mouth. We might have known each other since before we could string multiple sentences together, but it didn't change the fact that Declan was turning into a boy who made me wonder what I looked like from his point of view.

He was no longer suffering from the awkward stage. He shed his thick, black-framed glasses and developed a throatiness to his voice that made my mind wander while he spoke. Long gone was the five-year-old boy I met on the strawberry farm who was too mousy to speak. Now, he led football teams. He carried himself with authority and ease. If my thoughts had unnoticeably drifted from normal, friend-like thoughts into territory like this, did his too? Did he consider how I had been changing?

Cute.

It wasn't a fair word in this context. It had too many possible meanings and potential margins for error.

Cute, like little-sister cute? Pathetic, helpless cute? Or cute, like . . . the type he'd want to kiss-cute?

JUST FRIENDS

My brain manages to contemplate all those thoughts in one held breath. Finally, I exhale, realizing he's still gripping my wrist and awaiting a response. So, of course, I go with a tight, sardonic "Sure" before breaking into a sprint again. I clap my hands like an overeager penguin while I wait for him to throw the ball.

His face softens with a satisfied smile. "Atta girl," he says in a low voice. He launches the ball at me again, and this time I catch it, but my eyes are squeezed shut, so I topple over, falling onto my butt and then rolling over my shoulder as if the misty turf had a downward tilt. It was perfectly level.

Finally, I open my eyes to see Declan's shoes.

"First of all," he starts, crouching down to get in my line of sight, "you should be proud of yourself."

I croak out a scoff that comes out louder than intended. "And why's that?"

"Look down." He gestures at me with a nod.

I look down to find the football safely held in my arms despite the backward shoulder roll I survived.

"You protected the ball at all costs. Which is pretty much the number one rule. I think you might be better at this than you think." He says it like a proud coach.

"Huh. Well, would you look at that. Now, help me up please. I think I've done my job."

Declan stretches his hand toward me to grab, so I do. But instead of using it to pull myself up, I tug down with all my strength.

"Oof, what are you—" He chuckles, allowing me to drag him down to the turf beside me. Emphasis on "allow," because I know he could have resisted my weak pull if he wanted to. I, however, am realizing I'm not capable of the same when it comes to him.

He faux tumbles, careful to avoid hitting me with his sprawling limbs, and then settles onto the bright green turf next to me, leaning back on his elbows. Declan always looks like he's been lounging somewhere for hours before you've happened upon him, even if he just arrived in the position a second ago.

"What was number two?" I fish.

"Hmm?" He breathes through his nose, tilting his head at me.

"You said 'first of all,' and then never told me what was second of all."

"Oh. Right." He nods and looks up at the sky. "Forgive me for forgetting my next point. A little birdie took my kind offer for help and dragged me down with her."

A laugh escapes me, chest feeling warm at the easy camaraderie I've always shared with him. He runs a hand through his hair, gaze fixing on the empty bleachers. I wonder if he's imagining them filled.

"Come on, what was it?" I nudge my elbow into his side.

"Okay, fine. I was going to leave off on my compliment, but if you wanna force my hand, you force my hand."

I'm staring at his frame, shoulders wider than they were a year before, hair longer, still waiting for his response. He stills and looks back at me. But then his eyes seem to drift to something slightly above my head. I'm confused until he reaches out to smooth down my hair. It must have looked like a bird's nest from all my tumbling.

"I was going to say," he starts, voice gravelly as his hand slows on its path down my head. I feel his fingers on the crown of my head all the way down to my toes. "You looked like a baby bird getting shoved out of the nest for the first time trying to catch that ball." He delivers the words slowly, tone drier than the desert, so it takes me a moment to process the words.

"Oh my gosh!" I squeak, pushing his hand off my head in exasperation as I realize I've been caught in a bit. "And here I was waiting for the next compliment."

He laughs with his head down, the perfect display of a delighted boy who has pulled off his joke.

"Mm-hmm," I hum. "But let's consider if this is the insult you think it is. Birds must be pushed out of the nest at some point to fly, and plus, they can be cute." I clamp my lips shut. I've accidentally referred to myself as cute in the most roundabout way possible. "What bird species are we talking here? Duck?" I ask in an attempt to clear his memory of it.

"You? A duck?" he muses, looking me up and down like he's considering the thought. "Nah. Not a duck."

"Okay. Not a duck girl. Noted. How about a flamingo?"

"Oh, definitely not a flamingo."

"Why not a flamingo? They're sophisticated. And pink."

"Have you seen a flamingo's face up close?" he retorts, looking taken aback.

I rack my memory. "I don't think so."

"Well, it's definitely not the look you're going for. They're like the lawyers of birds." He shudders and I cough a shocked laugh. "You would be more of a . . ." He runs a hand along his jaw, pretending to be deep in thought.

I stare at his outrageously sarcastic expression, eyes looking up like the answer is just beyond his reach.

"Oh! I got it!" He snaps and points at me. "A blue-footed booby. That's what you looked like."

"A what?" I sneer. "Did you just call me a booby? What is this? Seventh grade?"

"No, no, no! A blue-footed booby," he says, slower this time, elongating every word.

"Oh. Duh. A blue-footed booby," I repeat as if it's suddenly obvious.

I stare at him with a blank expression. He stares back with a satisfied grin.

"AND WHAT IS THAT?"

"They're these birds that have blue feet who walk funny and do a weird little dance when they're trying to find a mate," he continues, unfazed by my outburst.

I arch my brows in suspicion at the word mate.

"It was mostly just the blue feet and clumsy part that I was referring to," he clarifies, pointing to my feet, which are donned in baby blue high-top Converse.

"Ahh, I see. I'm a blue-footed booby," I conclude, nodding my head in faux understanding. "Of course, you would know a bird like that, you nerd."

He shrugs with his arms up like, "Don't shoot the messenger."

If Declan hadn't been blessed with football quarterback genes, his mental Rolodex of fun facts would've land-locked him in the nerd category at school immediately. No one gets away with knowing that much information about a niche bird species without looking like that.

"Funny little dance though? I'd pay to see that," I continue.

"You don't have to. Wait here. I'll show you." He pops up and sprints over to our pile of belongings at the beginning of the field, digging for his phone under his crewneck, and then sprints back to me.

I watch over his shoulder as he maneuvers to YouTube and types "blue-footed booby mating dance" into the search bar. He clicks on a National Geographic video and turns his phone horizontally for me to watch as two birds stand awkwardly beside each other, picking up their absurdly aqua-colored feet and putting them back down. They really are bright blue.

Declan chuckles and then points at the screen. "Watch. If that wasn't enough, they start showing off their wings. And even better, if they really wanna win them over, they offer the females a gift. Like a little pebble or a stick."

I watch as a white-bellied bird tosses the tiniest pebble you've ever seen into the other bird's line of sight. And that's all it takes I guess, because next thing you know the female joins in and starts dancing with him.

"Awww, that is too cute," I coo behind his ear.

A text drops down on his screen, interrupting the video. I try not to read it but the text is in all caps so it's kind of difficult to avoid. There's a guy's name and the words "DECLAN! ANSWER YOUR PHONE! ARE WE SCOOPING, OR NAH?" underneath it. He quickly swipes it away and says, "Oops. Sorry about that."

"No, it's fine. Looks like they really need to reach you."

"Oh, it's nothing. Some of the new teammates are going to Murphy's Drive-Thru tonight."

"You should go!" I say, even though it makes my heart dip into my stomach as I do.

But only the normal amount of disappointment when you're having fun and don't want it to end, of course. It's not because if we stop hanging out now, I'll have to spend the hours before normal bedtime warding off replays of each scene of our day in painful detail. Overanalyzing each moment and then overanalyzing why I'm overanalyzing our friendship and if it means I'm starting to develop feelings that would ruin it.

"No, no really, it's fine. I don't want to," he insists.

"Oh right. I forgot you bought this entire ball for me." I

hold up the foam ball, trying to make a joke out of the situation, but the tops of his cheeks turn pink and I realize what I've said has too much truth. I'll be thinking about that particular shade of pink for days to come.

He bought a foam football to play with me alone, and is still here when he could be getting burgers with his teammates.

I scramble to my feet and mumble something about needing to get more practice in if I want to stop looking like a blue-footed booby. I try to move past how off-balance the sight of his embarrassment throws me.

That night, as I crawled into bed, sore from exerting myself on the empty football field, my phone lit up with a single text from Declan.

> Good work out there, Little Bird.

I drifted off to sleep with a dumb smile on my face. My dreams were filled with birds with hilariously bright cerulean feet, dancing and offering pebbles to win each other's affection.

Chapter 4

My feet trod down the uneven stone-paved sidewalk. The gentle morning sunlight flits in and out of tree branches, illuminating the leaves seemingly from the inside out. Some of the branches have moss that look like the Lorax's fingers draping down lazily, and from certain hills, I'm high enough to see the ocean glittering in the distance. As I near downtown Seabrook I forget where I'm headed and am momentarily put at ease.

I reach for my phone and swipe to the camera to check my under-eye bags.

I stayed up late last night by Lottie's bedside, trying to

scribble as many stories as she could remember into my journal. Stories of her arriving in America, starting her convenience store without knowing any English, and within a year, throwing parties so large with the local customers and out-of-towners, her house looked like a parking lot. Her words, not mine.

I felt like a time traveler, looking at her, knowing she was still here but wouldn't be for much longer. Knowing that the image of her, thirty pounds underweight, laying on a hospital bed in her bedroom, would mar my mind for countless days after this one. This tired, disfigured version of her felt like some sort of cosmic glitch.

The only thing keeping me from turning around was Lottie's insistence that I enjoy my day and the thought of helping my mom. My concealer is doing its job for the most part, and my dark, short hair and curtain bangs are behaving, so I swipe out of the camera app to check the time—thirty minutes until my interview at the coffee shop I somehow managed to schedule. Peppy Teenager answered the phone when I called and confirmed the interviewer would be the manager, Declan.

I'd come home only a handful of times during college and not once did I see a glimpse of him. Not even his car. Or his mom, Gwen. Maybe it's because I flinched away from any opportunity to leave the house, insisting that my mom needed company working her shift at the convenience store (but only from the back room), or that Lottie needed help with her litany of plants around the house. "Oh, they're already watered? Perhaps the junk drawer needs a pass-through again!"

The first year was especially difficult. The wounds of Declan's and my separation were still fresh. Coming home was like walking through a city full of land mines. Street names weren't just street names. They were the titles to bittersweet memories. Late nights spent talking in Declan's car, playing me songs from strange, obscure bands he had recently discovered. Him looking over at me in the dim streetlamp's glow, waiting urgently for my face to give away my reaction. I loved that about him. How he loved watching me experience something he'd discovered on his own.

After three blocks, I turn onto the narrow brick road and hesitate on the landing before the coffee shop's red French doors. There are so many ways this interview could go and I have not a single clue as to how Declan will choose to acknowledge me. Will he treat me as his best friend of twelve years who became more? Or like a regretted past, pretending we're no more than strangers to each other?

Blinking twice and pushing through the doors, I utilize a muscle I've honed well, compartmentalizing an emotion until it is small and tuckable, and then shoving it into the deepest recesses of my mind. Right now, what I need is for a coffee shop manager to hire me for the summer. That is all.

Do it for your mom, I tell myself.

The coffee shop has a steady stream of customers placing their weekday orders. Sounds of metal cups being picked up and set down echo from behind the counter. Names are read off lattes at a tiny bar. Peppy Teenager seems to be chief of taking orders, her kind voice trilling as she greets customers. She's smiling with the excited glow of a new job's responsibilities still intact.

My eyes scan the small shop. It's previously house-shaped bones are charmingly obvious. The barista's bar sits at the back of the house, extending to various mid-century seating options: leather chairs, deep couches, and a half-built bar overlooking a window to sit at.

There seems to be some construction going on in an alcove

to the left, pieces of raw wood resting against the wall. A refraction of light on the floor causes me to look up.

Eclectic . . . birdhouses are hanging by nearly invisible strings from the wooden beams on the ceiling. They look handmade, random wheels and gears decorating the outside of each one.

It's as if Dr. Seuss and Einstein collaborated on a coffee shop in a wealthy town.

Glancing around to the left, I'm startled to find Declan already standing right beside me, as still as a statue.

"GAHOH-Oh-gosh." My body jolts like a boomer being shown one of those videos of a baseball flying straight at the camera. "I'm sorry, I . . ." I clutch my chest and descend into awkward mumbling. "I didn't see you there."

He stares down at me. Face unmoving.

"Ms. Lang?" he asks, feigning sincerity.

Ms? Really? That's how we're going to play this?

"You can call me by my first name."

His expression remains the same. "Please, if you'll follow me."

I try not to stare as I watch him walk casually to the back corner of the coffee shop. His limp is well hidden within his ability to act like he doesn't carry a singular care in the world. Despite my efforts to treat this as a simple job interview, this is my first time seeing Declan after the accident. Seeing the repercussions of what that night did up close makes my heart constrict, and I contemplate if I can do this. *Why did he suffer alone? Why wouldn't he let me in?*

"Please." Declan's eyes flit up to mine. "Have a seat."

My lips form a thin line as I try to get comfortable in the metal chair. My back is as straight as a ballet dancer's, hands folded in my lap. I try to wear the expression of a trustworthy potential hire.

Declan clears his throat. "So, tell me a little about yourself." He mimics my clasped hands and sits back in his chair, face blank.

I blink twice in rapid succession. *Tell me a little about yourself?* There is not a single human on planet Earth who knows more about me than this boy. Well, man, now. I did no part of my growing up without him standing by as a witness. Of all the ways I imagined our first conversation going, this one never made the list.

"Tell me a little bit about yourself?" I repeat back to him, voice emphasizing what I think of the question.

It's been two seconds since the interview began and I've already forgotten to behave like someone trying to get hired. Perhaps unprocessed grief, over this current situation and Lottie's, beckons me to act the way I do. Because in a swift moment of poor decision-making, fueled by the disbelief that any of this is really happening, I decide to up the ante on his weird game of pretend. I can act equally as naive and unaware if that's how he'd like to handle this.

I compose my face into a well-poised mask. The goal is manic pixie dream girl. The execution is probably more resentfully-bitter-immaturely-obsessed.

Regardless, I start, "Well, I was born and raised in Alberta, Canada. My parents have been happily married for thirty-five years. When it was time for college, I decided traveling the world would suit me a bit better instead, and now my travels have landed me here in Seabrook." I smile with dead eyes, displaying as many teeth as possible. At his silence I continue, "This town is *such* a well-kept secret, huh? Better keep it up before the men in suits find it. If they saw how beautiful this hidden gem of a place is, they'd be marching in with their blueprints and drills in an instant!" My voice pitches up, saccharinely sweet, eyebrows tented in faux sincerity.

Declan's face contorts slightly, but he manages to neutralize before anyone around us is able to recognize anything other than an ordinary interview taking place. That years of unspoken tension are being dug up in code. His gaze bores into my soul. He does not move an inch. I study his expression, trying to read if he's perturbed at all, or if he's been so thoroughly over me that this act won't rile up an ounce of emotion. He clears his throat again.

"What three words would your closest friends use to describe you?" He keeps his head down, never looking up from the page in front of him.

"Hmm, my closest friends?" I repeat, as if I need clarification.

He nods once, lips pressed tightly together.

"Are we talking college friends? I made some great friends in college. Or— Oh, you mean high school? Or, no, sorry, you meant middle school?" I scrunch my brows in faux confusion. Picturing Roshi and Faye bowled over in howls of laughter when I tell this story later is the only thing getting me through.

Finally, I see his face give away the slightest twitch. I'm annoying him. His mask is slipping. "Any. Any friends. It doesn't matter."

"Alright then. If I had to guess, they would probably call me loyal. Loyalty is huge for me. I'm sure it's an overused declaration, but when I love someone, I truly would not let *anything* stand in the way of us ever again. I would stick by them forever." I punctuate the words and watch them land with the intended impact on his face. "Well, as long as it is up to me, of course," I add.

Declan remains still. I chalk it up to my imagination, but I swear I see a hint of confusion flicker across his face.

After a moment he seems to remember to speak. He jolts, gesturing with his hand for me to continue. "Two more words, please."

"Oh, right, excuse me." I pretend to be deep in thought. Looking up toward the left. "Maybe they would also deem me straightforward and a concise communicator. If something has happened or feelings have changed, I'd rather come out and say exactly what I mean rather than . . . well, I don't know. I suppose maybe some people would rather not say anything at all."

Declan looks down at this. He knows enough about me to realize what I've said is completely false. I am a conflict avoider. An emotional black hole. Emotions come to me to be smothered by denial and a list of actionable solutions.

He gets up suddenly and begins gathering his things. The rustle of papers jars me. "Well, I think that will conclude our interview, Ms. Lang. I'll be in contact soon."

I'm left halfway standing as I stare at his retreating back. My mouth is partly open in response as I watch him bear his weight onto his right leg and walk away.

Chapter 5

"Four years ago, I practically spit in Declan's face that I didn't need him. And now? I'm hoping he hires me at the coffee shop he manages? I mean, are you kidding? He couldn't have written a better gotcha moment himself," I say to Roshi's and Faye's bobbing heads on my phone.

"Blink," Roshi starts. "There is absolutely zero reason to feel embarrassed. If he's the manager then he probably could have refused giving you an interview in the first place."

"Yeah. Or he took it just to rub it in my face," I retort.

"Wait," Faye chimes in. "Why is he working at a coffee shop? Wasn't he going to be a professional football player?"

JUST FRIENDS

Her question makes my skin feel too tight in an instant. I try to school my face but there's no use. My imagination has imitated memory so many times I can't tell the difference anymore.

A moment of shock and then darkness. Waking up in a hospital room.

"He stopped playing his senior year. Couldn't anymore. But I don't know how he ended up back in Seabrook. I thought he'd still be in college in some random state," I reply, voice shaky.

"Yeah, well, didn't you just shoot yourself in the foot by lying in the interview? Don't you actually need this job?" Roshi says.

Faye raises her eyebrows like, "Good point."

"Guys, he's not gonna hire me. He clearly wants nothing to do with me if that was our first conversation after all this time," I respond.

"Yeah, that. Or he was just as shocked to see you as you were to see him?" Roshi suggests. "By that standard he could assume that you want nothing to do with him after the way you acted."

I stare at her wine-red curls on my screen.

"Fair point," I say. "I guess we'll just have to see, won't we?"

"I guess we shall," Faye intones, regal as always.

"Welp. Faye, keep your eye out for a delivery. You should be getting something by today," I announce.

"Blairy, stop, you shouldn't have!" she squeals.

"Oh, please. Don't thank me yet. You might think it's hideous," I joke, deflecting her excitement.

"Ohhhh, you're the sweetest. If it's from you I'll love it no matter what." Faye blows kisses from her hand to the phone screen and I pretend to dodge them.

I ordered a customizable kitchenware set from Etsy with her new initials engraved on them. Faye's boyfriend of two years proposed the spring of our senior year and they eloped in France before spring break was over. (She always joked that a "ring by spring" was the ultimate goal of college. She of all people was much too attractive to make that joke. And apparently, it wasn't one.) Her now-husband landed an engineering job that would bring enough income in for both of them, regardless of whether she chose to work or not. She has informed us over innocuous champagne-fueled giggles that she will be choosing the latter.

Roshi rolls her eyes in the box that hovers beside Faye's. "Ugh, I wish I were a housewife right now. If any of you would like to memorize the contents of my Civil Procedure textbook for me before school starts, let me know."

"Pass," I say.

"Yep. Hard pass," Faye says.

We all became close after our first week at Pepperdine University, but much to our disappointment, our lives have diverged onto vastly different paths since our last day living together in our Facebook Marketplace–furnished apartment.

Roshi got accepted to Harvard Law School. Faye moved into an apartment with Stephen in Virginia. And when I was supposed to go to NYC for my consulting job, we planned multiple trips to see each other, our new states just a skip and a hop away. But now we had zero dates on the calendar, reduced to seeing each other's faces on a phone screen.

Roshi clears her throat, looking solemn suddenly. "Um, so, how's Lottie doing?" she asks, saying the words quickly.

"Oh." I wave my hand, discomfort fueling the movement. "She's uhh— She's been better," I say, lips pressing together in an awkward line.

JUST FRIENDS

Roshi and Faye nod in unison, eyes downcast. There's a moment of tense silence. *Anddddd this is exactly why I don't discuss these things*, I think to myself.

"Well, let us know if you need anything, Blink," Roshi says, finally ending the weird lull in the conversation.

"Yes, please let us know!" Faye adds.

"I will," I say, knowing it's a lie.

Roshi's use of my nickname causes the genesis of our friendship to spring to mind. A week before my freshman year at Pepperdine, I forced myself to go to a mixer to meet some other kids my age, but of course, I was terrified. It was my first time being away from the tiny beach town of Seabrook where everyone was familiar and every corner was a safe haven of lush forestry and sandy cobblestone walkways.

The dark house was filled with sweaty bodies bopping to unintelligible mumble rap. My shoes stuck to the floor. The event had to be held off campus at an unofficial frat house to comply with alcohol codes on campus. I couldn't have been further from my comfort zone.

I was pretending to fiddle with the drinks in the kitchen when a guy who had an uncanny side profile to Declan walked past. The disheveled blond-brown hair. The way he took his strides, elongating each one like he had to get the most out of each step. I was still fresh with hurt after our inexplicable separation. My whole body felt like an open wound.

The fight. The accident. His subsequent silence.

I froze, staring at his doppelgänger walking past me with my eyes wide open, looking like I'd seen a ghost. That's when Roshi walked past.

She waved a hand in front of my face.

"Oh my gosh, blink!" she yelled. "Your eyes are gonna dry up and fall out!"

I did finally blink, and my eyes readjusted to the tiny girl standing before me, box-dyed cranberry hair and nose ring glinting in the low light.

"Are you okay?" she asked. The sincerity in her voice made my shoulders fall.

"Uh, yeah." I shook my head and tried a laugh to make my weird behavior seem like a fluke. "Just thought I saw someone I knew."

"Ooooo! You like them?" she guessed, wiggling her eyebrows as she looked at the boy I mistook for Declan. "Come on, I can introduce you to him!" She grabbed my wrist, but I quickly shut her down.

After the way things ended with Declan, I vowed to be alone. Maybe it was pride, but I spent most of my childhood believing I could prove my mother wrong. *All men leave at some point.* It was the motto I spent countless nights overhearing her preach during late-night conversations on the phone or with Lottie in the living room when I was supposed to be sleeping. "It's just not worth it," she'd say, clucking her tongue. "All men leave or fall out of love at some point. You just have to accept that and move on." She would say it flippantly, like becoming a single mother was just something to be expected. *That's not true. It can't be*, I remember thinking as a naive child. But my absent father and ghost of a childhood friend would beg to differ. She was right, and I felt stupid for ever believing I could prove her wrong.

After I vehemently shut Roshi down, removing her hand from my wrist and explaining my vow of boy-dating celibacy, she stopped.

"Okay, Blink . . . no worries. Honestly, that's kind of a power move with the whole short-haired, doe-eyed beach-girl look you've got going on," she responded, leaning backward with her hands up. The movement made me chuckle. *This girl is going to be trouble*, I remember thinking. "I'm Roshi, by the way." She stuck her hand out for me to shake, which was oddly formal in this environment.

I hesitated, then smiled and took her hand, shaking it like it was an oath.

"I'm Blair."

"Cool name! No *e* at the end like in *Gossip Girl*?"

I nodded my confirmation.

"Sick." She nodded, satisfied. "Mind if I still call you Blink, though?"

That was four years ago. We're no longer the tiny, fresh-faced freshmen bopping around Pepperdine like scared chihuahuas, but she never stopped calling me "Blink" after that first night.

"Okay, welp. I've gotta go bury my face back into these law prep books," Roshi says from the screen in the present, holding up a thumb and smiling with dead eyes.

"Yeah, I've gotta go too. I have a chicken potpie to toil over before Stephen gets home tonight. And before you roll your eyes, Rosh, it's harder than it seems. Making sure the filling cooks without burning the crust is no joke," Faye whines, lifting her eyebrows to indicate her sarcasm.

"Alright, guys. Talk soon," I respond.

After our FaceTime ends, my lock screen illuminates. The image stares up at me, taunting. It's a screenshot from one of my favorite movie scenes at the end of *Lady Bird* when she's walking down the streets of New York City. She has tears streaking down her face, but she just keeps walking, not really sure where she's trying to go.

She turns onto Waverly Place and Washington Square Park and then is lured into a cathedral from hearing the choir inside. After a moment, she leaves the church and calls her mom. Her relationship with her mom couldn't be more different from mine, but there's something about the way that movie captures the city. She's young, confused, still unsure of where she'll go, but she's there, and she's ready.

That's how I always pictured New York would be for me. A clean slate. An objective bystander with open arms. Uninterested in where you came from or why you had come. Just a place to be alone, unbothered by the disappointments of relationships, giving you the space to find independence for yourself. A guaranteed way to ensure my mom's future. I let myself stare at the phone for another beat before slamming it facedown on my desk and standing to leave. There's only one reason I'm here instead of New York City right now.

I knock on the door of her bedroom before coming in. She smiles up at me. It is weak, but her joy at seeing me is apparent all the same and I feel bad for the mental debate I had a moment ago.

"Hi, Lottie," I whisper, smiling back at her and bending to give her frail frame a hug. Her cashmere sweater is soft on my cheek, and I breathe in her scent as deeply as I can. It's been consistent since my childhood, and I've never found one more comforting.

It's the smell of her skin, maybe the detergent on her clothes. The tiniest bit floral, bold and warm. Impossible to re-create. A dose of panic seizes me at the thought of her scent disappearing with her.

"Guess who I just ran into at the coffee shop?" I wag my brows up and down, hoping to make the mood feel jovial. As if I were coming home and catching her up on my life like nothing was abnormal.

"Who, baby?" She croaks out the nickname I've always had in her deep smoky voice.

"Declan freaking Renshaw. He's the manager of the place apparently." My lack of curse words is habit from my mom telling me it was "unladylike" to swear.

My great-aunt gasps. It's the largest reaction I've seen her capable of since laying in this hospital bed. "Oh, honey," she says, a mixture of hope and empathy in her eyes.

"Mm-hmm," I nod as she reacts.

"What did you say to him? How long has it been?"

"It's been"—I look up at the ceiling as if I've lost count—"about four years now. But I was trying to apply for a job there, you know, *before* I realized he was the manager of the place. And then he was the one who interviewed me and I lied to him in every interview question just to see how he'd react." I roll my eyes. "He already knows the answers. And they seemed a little personal anyway. Something tells me he got to choose the questions himself as manager." I try to joke, but Lottie's demeanor turns serious.

"Did you ever apologize to that boy? You two should have a conversation about why he stopped speaking to you, sweetie."

"Oh, Lottie. It's not that simple." I brush the hair off her forehead and continue stroking her head gently in a manner I hope is comforting.

She continues looking at me and it bores into my soul. Despite being unable to get out of this bed, she is not going to let me off the hook. There is not a single emotion I could hide from this woman.

"Isn't it a little ironic to try and have a conversation with someone about why . . . they didn't ever want to involve themselves in conversation with you ever again?" Lottie looks unfazed by my attempt at avoidance.

"Con," she says in her lovingly stern voice. "How old were you when that happened?" She says it as a question, but it lands more like a statement. A reminder made to communicate the irrationality of the teen years.

"Seventeen," I say, dragging the word out like I was reduced to that age again. "But don't you think if he wanted to contact me all these years he would have? We were best friends since we were literally five years old. Who just ghosts someone like that when you live in the same town?" My voice rises regardless of how much I've said that line.

"What that boy went through was very traumatic, sweetie. You can't assume you would do anything different if you were in his position. You don't know what it's like," she says, hard as steel and somehow the gentlest woman in the world.

I sigh through my nose, realizing my great-aunt is speaking from experience, to have your health come into question suddenly and without warning. She hasn't invited any family members or friends to visit her since starting at-home hospice care. Even her sisters or women she's been best friends with her whole life. When I plead with her to tell me why she doesn't want to see them, she gives clipped responses.

"I don't need them to see me like this, baby!" Her accent peaks when she says "baby." "Let their memory of me be healthy. That is who I was. I don't want them to remember me like this."

Her words tighten my chest like a bodice being sewn through my lungs. I'm convinced the only reason she allows me to be here is because my mom "forgot" to tell her I was coming home for the summer. And even so, she's forced me to leave after I visit her in the morning and doesn't let me sit by her side until the sun is setting. But I still notice each time she grimaces in pain and tries to hide it.

Last night, her hospice nurse was giving her a shower when I overheard her whimpering in pain. Within seconds of her first cry, Lottie's hushed voice pleaded with the nurse through the thin bathroom door: "Can you tell my Blair to leave? I don't want her to hear this." Then, I heard the nurse protest, worried for Lottie's safety alone in the shower. But Lottie didn't relent. "Please. Leave me. I will be fine. Tell her to go." My throat constricted. I didn't know what was worse. Hearing her cry for the first time or her weak voice as she begged the nurse to make me leave. I wasn't supposed to hear that. It was heart-wrenching that her prevailing concern amid her groans of pain was about my experience. Even if she was suffering, she'd do anything in her power to make sure I wouldn't. Especially on her behalf.

I understand wanting to be strong for the ones you love. I even understand that Lottie thinks it's more loving of her to protect me from seeing her decline. But doesn't love go both ways? What is love if not the desire to be there during someone's lowest moments? What use does it have if we refuse to let the people closest to us share in our suffering when it matters most?

It goes to show I have no idea what being in her position is like. Lying on this mechanical bed all day and night. Knowing your healthy body and all you enjoyed with it is behind you.

We move past the topic of Declan and onto our usual non-talk, which has become everything to me. I'm overly aware that every casual conversation is from a diminishing handful. As usual, her advice has left me with no defenses and much to ponder.

When I unlock the door to the guesthouse, I find myself unable to shake the memories that come flooding back. Looking into Declan's eyes for the first time in years, if only for a brief moment, reignited emotions I thought I had successfully reasoned my way out of. Lottie's refusal to let her family see her in this condition reminded me of the door separating Declan and me four years ago. I wanted to be by his side, but he didn't want the same. I always wanted to give him more than he wanted of me.

"Don't put too much stock in people, con. They can disappoint you." My mom's offhand advice burrowed into my hardwiring. Funny how it was never the life lessons they spent hours lecturing you on that stuck. It was her split-second reactions that formed how I viewed people. It was our circumstances, even. Absent father. Tired, single mother. The conclusion, naturally: Sharing wasn't safe. Opening up was a risk the emotionally unintelligent made. And, of course, people always leave eventually. If they haven't yet, it's because you just haven't gotten to that part of the story.

Eight Years Ago: Freshman Year

Declan and I escape the bustle of students leaving school and start along our well-worn path toward our homes. It takes us along the town's cobblestone streets, past the local stores and coffee shops, and ends with a stroll near the ocean's edge. Close enough to hear the sound of waves crashing on the shore.

"—but I don't know if Coach will approve my idea. It would be risky, but I think it would be really worth it." Declan's voice is the melody we walk side by side to. "Just picturing the look on my dad's face if we won the game and I got to tell him those routes were my idea?" He shakes his head with a wistful look. "It would be priceless."

I chuckle at his boyishness. It's refreshing after a long day of school.

Declan's phone buzzes in his pocket and he pulls it out. Looking at the screen he says, "Oh. Speaking of my father. He must have heard a ringing in his ears."

His previously light demeanor seems to fade as he reads the text on his phone.

"Everything okay?" I ask.

"Uh, yeah. I just—" He runs his hand down his face, blowing out a breath. "Sorry. It's just—classic Randall stuff. Nothing is ever enough for the man." He uses his father's first name like they're less close than they are.

"What happened? What did he say?"

"It's nothing new. He's just lecturing me on the chores I didn't do to his liking, and then there's a list of items I need to help my mom with, and on top of all that, he's sending paragraphs about how we need to have a serious chat tonight about the importance of every game leading to championships. As if I'm not already spending every waking hour stressing about that while trying to keep my grades high too."

I go quiet at his frustration. Despite my efforts to fight it, I feel a twinge of jealousy that his father cares enough to bother him so much.

"I'm sorry," I mumble. "He only asks so much of you because he believes in you, though. Right?"

"That's one way to look at it," Declan scoffs. "It just never ends with him. Right when I think I've finally done enough to earn his approval, he gives me a list of critiques instead."

"Maybe he seems harsh, but I think he's proud of you. Even getting a long text like that shows he spends tons of time thinking about you. I wish I had that." I add the last part without thinking.

JUST FRIENDS

Declan pauses and turns to look at me. "Is this about something else?"

He looks into my eyes like he's noticing my fragility for the first time. It catches me off guard and I find myself unable to respond.

"I know we never talk about your dad, but we can," he offers.

I'd avoided discussing my dad with Declan for years now. Early on in our friendship, he came over to my house and asked if my dad was at work. I told him, "No. I haven't seen him in a while." And that was that. He never brought it up again, and neither did I. The longer we went without discussing it, the harder it seemed to start.

At my silence, Declan steps toward me.

"Are you okay?" He places a gentle hand on my arm. "You don't have to if you don't want to, but I'd love to know more about your dad if you're comfortable talking about it."

That one simple statement made me feel a lifetime closer to him. Sometimes, Declan simply being who he was felt like a character attack on everyone else. He just existed and in comparison, everyone paled. People were an average amount of friendly or thoughtful, and then Declan came around and convicted them all of mediocrity by being the type of friend he was to me.

Everyone in Seabrook knew I lived with my mom and great-aunt, but no one ever asked where my dad was. I came to the conclusion that they didn't care to find out. Or that if they did ask where my father was, the explanation would reveal some character flaw I had no control over. I felt I owed Declan the truth simply for being the first person to ask for it.

"Yeah, uh. I'm comfortable talking about it. I mean, I think it's about time you finally knew the full story." My heart leaps to my throat.

Declan's eyebrows soften with tentative hope, and the look is so sweet that it feels possible to go on. We wordlessly agree to start walking again. I let my thoughts race back to the night that changed everything for my mom and me.

"Keep in mind, I was probably four and a half years old. So, everything is pretty fuzzy," I start, too nervous to glance over at him. I see him nod in my peripheral vision. "It was nighttime, and I remember hiding under my covers because I heard screaming in the kitchen. Or, I think it was my dad screaming at my mom, mostly. That went on for a while. And then the front door slammed, and it was silent."

Declan doesn't speak but I can feel his gaze on me. I keep mine pinned to the exact point where the ocean meets the sky, not really seeing as I continue.

"Sometime later my mom crept into my bedroom and made me pack some things in my tiny, pink, sparkly suitcase. And then we were on the highway in the middle of the night."

I rush through certain parts of the story. The insignificant things are the most vivid in my memory. Like telling my mom I was scared of the dark from the back seat, so she offered her hand for me to squeeze while she drove. I could still remember the way her eyes flickered to me through the rearview mirror every few seconds. "Do you remember your great-aunt Lottie's beach house?" she asked. "We're going on a little vacation there for a little bit, okay?"

"We drove over to Seabrook and here we are. Just me, my mom, and Lottie, as you know," I finish quickly, trying to sound upbeat.

I leave out the subsequent events. The ones that really made an impact. Like when two months in I started to realize it wasn't just a spontaneous trip to Lottie's beach house. Or the conversations I overheard from upstairs when my mom would rant to Lottie about how my father promised she'd never have to work a day in her life, and yet, here she was, living off the kindness of her aunt and taking care of me alone.

How I'd ask my mom if my dad wished me a happy birthday or wanted to see me, and she would roll her bottom lip into her mouth to nervously bite while she figured out how to let me down gently.

Or when I was six and my mom was trying to juggle working at the convenience store. She couldn't afford summer childcare, so I'd sit in the back room of the store on an upside-down crate and watch her work all day. She tried to hide it, but she had this nervous, always-about-to-burst energy about her.

"Do you remember all those summers that I hung out at your house in elementary school?" I tack on, the warm memory alleviating the knot forming in my throat.

"Of course I do. Those were the best summers," he says, voice low and smooth like a gentle caress on the back of my neck.

"That was such a huge help to my mom." I nod, head bouncing with too much force. "I don't know if you ever knew that, but you and your family played such a big role in us being able to stay here."

The goal is to distract myself from getting emotional about my father leaving, but the memory of Declan's mom making us warm chocolate chip cookies while we sat on their huge living room couch and watched TV shows is more threatening. I don't even remember talking to him that much. We'd just sit side by side in silence while we devoured the entire plate of cookies, and at some point, my mom would pick me up after work.

"Gosh, that's horrible," he says while shaking his head.

It was Declan's first time hearing the events that led up to me sitting on his couch those first summers. I could see the information unspooling in his mind. And for some inexplicable reason, I feel shame creep in. It was my first time having to say the words out loud to someone else. Words explaining how easy it was for my dad to never see me again. Technically, it was my mom who left him. But he stayed gone every year after, which felt like a leaving in itself. Showing Declan I was unwanted by my own father felt like a risk—what if it made him start looking for reasons not to want me too?

He stops walking and puts a hand on my shoulder, spinning me toward him. "Thank you for telling me that, Blair. And I don't know if I'm allowed to say this, but I think your dad is a certified idiot."

I cough a surprised laugh, the tension exiting my body with it.

"I'm sorry. I probably shouldn't have said that. But—" He looks away, lips pressing together. "You guys didn't deserve that. At all. And now you're turning into this amazing person, and he doesn't get to witness it. I mean, how much dumber could you get?"

My eyes have tears forming, and yet I huff another shaky laugh.

"Oh, wait," he says. "Sorry. I wasn't going to call him stupid again. My bad. But you know what I mean." This is the most high-school-boy response of all time, and yet it's really working for me. He goes on, almost like he's talking to himself as the story sinks in. "He doesn't know how much you like dystopian books. And writing your own stories when you should be paying attention in class. And that you're really, really bad at math. But I do. So, he's the unlucky one in this situation. Not me. And not you."

He emphasizes the last two words with an urgency I've never heard in his voice. I can't form words. Can hardly force my eyes to meet his. But when I finally do, we both just stare at each other, like we're both suspended in this moment, neither of us wanting to burst the rare bubble we've entered.

He throws his arms around me and pulls me into his chest. With my head squished up against the warmth of him, I hear the faint thump of his heart beating. Or maybe it's my own. The hush of the ocean persists in the background, harmonizing with the subtle rise and fall of our heavy breaths.

He pulls back sooner than I'd like and we keep walking. I wait for the shame of opening up to creep in, but to my surprise, it doesn't.

"By the way, I'm still sorry for how your dad treats you," I say abruptly.

Declan tilts his head at me with a slight smile. "Thanks, Blair. That's nice of you."

I nod at him. "I still find myself wishing I had a dad who pestered me with his expectations sometimes." I chuckle to distill the potency of that confession. "But I see how hard he is on you and that sucks."

"Trust me, I don't think you'd wish for it after experiencing it for a week."

I look down at my Converse as we walk down the street.

"No . . ." My voice is flimsy as I try to straddle truth and levity. "I think I would still trade situations with you if I could."

"Really?" Declan asks.

"I mean, yeah? I don't mean to make your relationship with him sound *easy*, but at least you have a relationship to struggle with."

He looks out at the middle distance in thought. A hardness creeps into his eyes.

"He doesn't just, like, 'expect a lot of me.' He practically does not and will not love me unless I get perfect grades and win every football game so that I can get into an Ivy League school and go to the NFL one day. Every time he's up late at night working, he reminds me that he's making sacrifices for me to live *my* dream. But . . . the dream was his to begin with. I love football, don't get me wrong. But if he thinks I'm talented enough for the NFL, schools will hand me free rides. Money wouldn't be the problem. It's just a nice scapegoat for his addiction to work, claiming it's all to make his son's dreams come true."

"Okay, but you *do* live up to all of his expectations. You're a freshman in high school and there are already college coaches interested in you. That's unheard of," I retort, arguing an opinion I didn't know I had.

He scoffs. "That's my point. I do everything right, and it's still not enough. The goalpost moves the second I reach it, but I just keep running to the next one. It's pathetic."

Our eyes scan each other's faces, trying to understand how we got here so fast. The sound of our footsteps punctuates the tense silence.

"It's not pathetic," I say in an attempt to diffuse the tension. "It makes me feel evil for craving my father's attention after knowing how much he hurt my mom. But it's just like you said. You can't just stop craving your father's approval. But at least you'll get the reward of his love when you accomplish those things. I have to succeed because my dad *isn't* here to take care of my mom. And I still won't earn the reward I really want," I finish, voice low. So much for diffusing the situation. A tear threatens to make itself known but I harden my face in resistance.

The side of his mouth falters and I can't tell if he's sad or angry. He looks at me for another moment, a thousand expressions passing over his face like a sped-up time lapse. Finally, he mumbles, "I'm sorry, Blair. If it means anything to you, I'm here."

It feels like my chest truncates with the unexpected warmth of his words.

"I'm sorry too, Declan. I shouldn't have said that—I'm saying things I don't know anything about." I press my lips together.

His eyes soften and his shoulders relax. Mine do too. We stare at each other while we wordlessly unfurl our white flags.

"I'll like you even if you don't make it to the big leagues. If that's any consolation," I say.

His expression is wary for a moment, but then my dry tone lands and a grin blooms across his face. He releases a disbelieving chuckle and pulls me into his chest. His voice rasps softly by my ear and I have to force myself to keep still. "I know. That's why you're my favorite."

Chapter 6

"Are you sure I can't help you out around here for a little bit?" I ask my mom's retreating frame.

"No, con. I'm fine. I don't need any help," she replies, voice stern. She disappears, entering the front of the convenience store again.

I exhale through my nose, trying to temper my reaction to the answer I've heard my entire life. "I don't need help" was probably in my mother's top ten phrases. And it was worse seeing her sweaty brow with hair plastered to her forehead as she ran from the front of the convenience store to the back with a notepad in her hand, scribbling numbers for restocks and math for the shocking amount of cash-paying customers.

She flies through the swinging back door again, eyes darting around at the boxes of extra stock sitting on the floor.

"I applied to a coffee shop, but I just figured that you would finally accept help here since Lottie is . . . ya know." My eyes fall from hers, unable to finish the sentence.

She exhales and removes the glasses from her face. "Lottie and I don't want you to be burdened by her sickness, honey. You heard her. She wants you to enjoy your life. Don't worry about the convenience stores. We'll figure it out."

I nod despite my disagreement. Does she think she's been successful at hiding her stress? She's in over her head going from running a cash register to overseeing seven stores at once. But I drop it. There's no use. The world could be collapsing and she'd swear she was fine until the rubble trapped her under it.

She rummages around her desk and then scurries back to the front, so I return to the laptop bouncing on my knees. I'm sitting on an upside-down red crate. My spot since before I could remember.

The back of this store is as familiar to me as my childhood bedroom, late nights spent waiting for my mom to finish her shift, just enjoying the company of being near her, even if we didn't say a word. We might not have discussed our emotions, but we loved each other. That much was known.

I switch agitatedly between job listings for consultants— absolutely nothing open for the job I had already secured at Ernst & Young. When I gave them the news that I'd be moving home for the summer, they agreed to defer my offer to September, but it feels like a precarious bet, hoping they don't give away my position to a willing, fresh-faced graduate in the meantime.

Biting my nails, I open my email, not sure what I'm hoping to find. But, sure enough, illuminated at the top of my inbox is a subject that reads Seabrook Coffee House—Job Application. I lurch off the crate like a firecracker has gone off beneath me, fumbling to keep hold of my laptop as I reorient myself. I click it open, and my eyes race to scan it, but there are only two lines of text. Zero greeting. It simply says:

> Your application to work at Seabrook Coffee House has been approved. Please arrive promptly at 7:50 a.m. this Friday to begin training.
>
> -Declan
> House Manager

I got the job!
Wait. So Declan hired me . . . I think a second later, with a mixture of relief and surprise.

If he's the manager, doesn't he have the final say? Couldn't he have easily sent a cold email expressing his refusal, left off his moniker, and wiped his hands clean of me like he seemed like to want to? What was his angle in hiring me, knowing he'd be forced to be near me?

Does he . . .
No. I force myself to stop before finishing the thought.

I picture his cold, unwavering expression boring into me across the coffee shop's table as he asked me to tell him a little bit about myself. The way his face twitched a nearly imperceptible amount when I described myself as *loyal*. Maybe I read into it. Or maybe I still knew his tells.

Does he want closure too? Is this an excuse to be near me?

And there it is. The thought I can't help myself from wondering, no matter how naive it makes me feel. It was this exact type of thinking that got me into this mess in the first place.

"Okay," my mom interrupts my flurry of thoughts, walking into the back room. "Work is done for the day! Let's go home to Lottie," she says with a smile.

I slam my laptop closed in haste and try to reorient my face to a neutral expression.

"Sounds good!" I force out.

On Friday morning, I steel myself and walk through the red French doors, waiting for someone to notice my arrival and intercept me. Peppy Teenager is nowhere to be found. Neither is Declan. I pretend to look busy at the lid and straw station before the front door is kicked open. Four cardboard boxes are stacked on each other, carried inside by carpenter-style pants and work boots. The legs and cardboard boxes come to a stop in front of me. My breath catches in my throat as the boxes are set at my feet, a disheveled-looking Declan appearing from behind them.

"Oh, hi, Blair," he breathes, seeming to recalibrate at the sight of me. He drags his eyes from my shoes up to my face with a pained expression.

At least he's upgraded from "Ms. Lang" to "Blair" again.

"Oh! Glasses?" I say, shocking myself with the comment.

Declan looks down at me, chest heaving slightly beneath his shirt as he recovers from the exertion. "What?"

His hair is damp at the ends, gathered over his forehead, grazing the tops of his glasses. I haven't seen him wear them since middle school.

"Oh. Sorry, it's just that . . . you're wearing glasses," I state like an idiot, standing with my finger pointed at them.

His eyes flick away for a moment, probably searching for an escape route. He presses his lips together before looking at me again. "I'm . . . sorry?"

"No. Sorry—I'm sorry. Never mind. I don't know why I—" Someone please hit me over the head with an espresso machine.

"Um," I try to recover. "I'm here for training?"

"Oh, yes. Harper will be training you," he says, leaving the boxes and striding behind the counter.

"Harper!" he yells toward the back of the coffee shop. "One moment, let me find her."

I nod and gesture with my hands that he is free to go searching. My gaze travels upward, snagging on a birdhouse hanging from the ceiling that was not here the last time I was. This one looks like a hand-carved, miniature version of the fairytale cottages downtown: a sloping roof, curved door, and circular window. There's the faint sound of twinkling, and as I squint, I notice the silver metal wheels attached to the side are spinning. I've never seen decor like it in a coffee shop. I've never seen *anything* like it. I mentally pocket the image to analyze later.

Declan comes shuffling back, looking perturbed.

"So," he starts, looking anywhere but me. "Harper just got a call that her cat has been throwing up since she left for work this morning. She's rushing home to take him to the hospital right now."

"Oh no, okay, uhh," I stammer. "Should I just come back tomorrow or?"

"No," he interrupts. "No. That won't be necessary. I'll just train you." Declan presses his lips together again.

"Okay, sounds good." I nod.

It doesn't look like he wants to train me, I think to myself.

In fact, he's avoiding eye contact with me like I'm the source of a disgusting sewage problem. Too disgusting to face head-on or you might just get a whiff.

Finally, at my silence, he looks at me.

I look at him.

"Do we start out here or . . ."

"Yeah. But not looking like that." His eyes dart around my face, skimming over my body and up again so quickly I almost chalk it up to my imagination. And then he spins on his heel and walks to the back room. Is my outfit inappropriate for training?

My mouth is agape as I try to reconcile what just happened. But after a second, Declan explodes from the back again, brushing through the double doors with an apron in his hand, a stern look coating his face. I would pay someone money to paint the expression I must be wearing right now.

"Put this on." He sticks his arm out to me, a white apron fisted in his tanned hand. My gaze momentarily snags on the new veins and muscles in his forearm before I snatch the apron from his grasp. Four years has done great things for this man's forearms.

"Oh. Thank you," I mumble.

As I fit my head through the top and start tying a knot behind my back, I look up to find Declan studying me like I'm a puzzle he needs to solve. Making eye contact is an improvement, at least, but I hate the way I physically feel the difference in how he looks at me now. What was once intimate is now replaced by something cold, hard, with the tiniest hint of inquisitiveness. Like he doesn't understand me anymore, but he wants to. Or maybe that's just wishful thinking.

"Come over here." He spins around, gesturing with his arm to follow. "We'll start on the basics."

Something about this feels like a skit. I'm the one who taught him how to drink coffee in the first place. I messed with every coffee gadget great-aunt Lottie would order to the house. I taught myself how to make Frappuccinos, which graduated to cappuccinos, and then became an obsession with experimenting with weird flavors in my lattes.

"First, make sure this device is placed here to measure how many grams of beans fall into the grinder," he says, talking to the bean grinder instead of me.

"When it hits eighteen, stop it. Tamp it down, ninety-degree angle with your elbow, then fit it into the espresso machine." He flicks on the machine and we stand rigid beside each other, staring, just waiting for the water to trickle through the puck of coffee grounds.

I bravely flick my eyes toward him to find that he's concentrating on the coffee machine like it's about to give birth to his first child. My lips press into a thin line before looking back at what I realized was my dream espresso machine growing up.

It has wooden handles and a moss green coating. I know exactly how much it costs from years of tracking the prices across multiple websites on Black Friday sales. This one is professional grade though, quadruple the size of one made for home use, parading four different spigots. There's a silver wheel from what looks like the inside of a deconstructed watch on the side of the machine, exactly like the one on the birdhouses hanging above our heads. Very interesting.

The espresso drips out in a luxurious bronze stream, filling the shot glass beneath it. When the scale hits 36g he swings the lever shut to stop the flow of water.

"For a latte you'll add about this much milk." He holds it up to my eye level to see, which is quite below him.

JUST FRIENDS

I scoff before remembering myself. We did this exact same dance as kids, except I was the one saying those words to him.

He pauses, a momentary hitch in the brusque presentation he's been performing like he's remembering it too. To recover, he gets busy adding ice, a lid, and a straw. I'm about to grab the ocean-wave-themed plastic cup from him to take a sip when he says:

"Ahh!" He holds up a finger to pause me, still avoiding eye contact.

He grabs a syrup labeled Marshmallow Madness and pours a more-than-healthy amount before putting the lid back on and stirring. You're not supposed to add the syrup after the ice, I think before realizing what I'm looking at.

This was my favorite latte to make every day my senior year of high school. I read about a girl in a cozy, fall-themed book who loved marshmallow-flavored lattes. Almost zero coffee shops carried it, especially in our small town, so I had to order a special syrup online to make my own.

My hand trembles as I take the latte from him, giving away any semblance of cool I had a moment ago. Suddenly, his light green eyes are poised on mine as he waits for my reaction, looking eager for the first time. I take a sip, eyes unmoving from his. It tastes exactly like I used to make them.

Exactly.

Are my pupils dilating? Are his?

The latte falls from my lips but our eyes remain locked.

And as if to taunt me, last night flashes through my mind. I fought the urge to do something I hadn't reduced myself to in years. But I lost the battle, opening Instagram and typing Declan's username into the search bar. It was the exact same as it had been for the past two and a half years.

One photo, the only one on his entire feed, posted my

sophomore year at Pepperdine. It was burned into my brain at this point. It was a perfectly framed, picturesque shot, clearly taken at a wedding based on the opulent display of flowers and the form-fitting suit molding his body. Where is this? Paris? Italy? I had wondered countless times.

Declan's arm was fastened around a beautiful lanky blonde wearing a silky red dress. Her head is tilted into the crook of his shoulder, smile beaming from ear to ear like she might just explode from happiness. His face is poised in his typically confident smile, standing tall. It was radiant without looking effortful, and it pissed me off every time. I'd try to click on her profile, but there was no tag.

He had moved on with this girl. I tortured myself with the thought, rewinding and replaying it the second it ended. She was stunning. Exactly who you'd picture standing next to a man like him. I'd wept pathetically over the photo, deleting my search history over and over again, just to repeat my actions the next day. Like a dog returning to its own vomit.

Did you ever check up on me? I wonder as I stare at him from behind the marshmallow latte.

You know that look movie characters get on their face when they realize it's the beginning of the end? That they're the idiot hurtling toward some inevitable conclusion?

"How is it?" he asks, eyes bright with expectation.

"Yeah," I nod. "Good. Really good."

That was me. Hurtling toward an immovable end. I was going to get answers from him this summer. Perhaps by osmosis alone. And I was already bracing for impact.

Five Years Ago: End of Junior Year

I'm almost to the school's exit when a perturbed-looking Declan darts in front of me without warning.

"Oh my gosh!" I jump back and clutch my collarbone. "What were you doing in the janitor's closet?" I whisper-yell.

"Shhhhhh." Declan scurries beside me and grabs my elbow as he drags me through the double doors. "You're gonna think I'm horrible," he says in a conspiratorial voice. His eyes ping-ponging around the parking lot.

"I already think you're horrible."

"Rude."

"Kidding. Tell me."

"The school is exploding with promposals right now. *Three* of my teammates just got asked. All with one of those elaborate posters with some unoriginal pun, like, "Will you TACKLE prom with me and be my number #1 fan?" Declan mimes gagging. "I think a group of girls banded together and decided they'd be the ones to ask the guys this year. So, we need to leave. *Now*."

My head yanks backward with raucous laughter. "You've got to be kidding me."

"*Blair*. Keep your voice down." Declan ducks his head at the sound of my cackling like it will draw everyone's attention, throwing his letterman over my shoulders to hide me. "Not funny!"

"I'm *sorry*," I say in exasperation through his huge jacket sleeves covering my face. "It's just too classic."

"What's too classic?" he demands, still preoccupied with scanning the huge lot like we're in *The Walking Dead* and will have to dodge rabid zombies soon.

"You and the trail of drooling girls you need to run away from," I screech, throwing my hands up.

I've somehow become so trained at acting like I'm separate, when in reality I am a part of that crowd, and the thought of being just another girl at the back of the line makes my chest feel too tight for my heart and lungs.

Without realizing it, I had envisioned us going to prom together. More so for the simple fact that we did everything together. But if this was how he was reacting to the most beautiful girls at our school chasing him down, what made me think he'd want to go with me? And yet, I still felt a morsel of hope that he would.

"Oh crap," Declan exclaims, pushing me forward with half his jacket draped over my shoulder. "They're coming."

"Who?"

"I don't know! Squealing and giggling girls with poster board!"

My legs try to match his pace but I'm holding him back. We're only halfway through the parking lot and the group of three girls are gaining on us.

"Well," I start, voice tight. "Which one would you rather go with?"

"What?" he sputters.

"Out of all of them, which would you rather go with?" I demand.

"The question itself is faulty, how am I supposed to answer that?"

"What do you mean?"

"What do *you* mean?"

For a moment, we both forget the plot and stop walking, turning to face each other like we're about to duel.

"What do you mean 'what do you mean?'" I spit.

"I mean," Declan huffs a breath, looking behind us at the group of approaching girls and then back to me, leaning in to whisper something by my ear. "The question doesn't make sense because I'd rather go with you."

Warm fireworks explode beneath my skin. If I could sparkle from the inside out, this is what it'd feel like.

I can't help it. The brightest smile I've ever smiled detonates across my face.

"Well, you should've just said so sooner," I whisper back into his ear before theatrically falling on one knee.

"Blair, what are you—" he protests, but the slightest tug at his lips gives him away. He approves of the plan.

I crane my neck up, balancing my hands on my bended knee. "Declan Renshaw!" I shout at the top of my lungs, making sure the three girls hear every word. "Will you make me the happiest girl in the world by going to prom with me?"

He stares down at me, and for a horrible moment I think I've misread the situation. But then he straightens and shouts back, "Yes! It would be my honor!" He plays along perfectly, overemphasizing the musical quality to each word as if we were eighteenth-century lovers, a dopey grin on his face.

Declan cups a hand over his face so that our audience won't see as he mouths *Now get up!* Laughter punctuates each word.

So I do.

We keep walking through the parking lot, clenching our fists to stop the threatening laughter from bubbling out. When we finally make it to our cars, we turn around to find our suspicions confirmed. The group of girls has dissolved. Probably right after our timely performance. He silently pumps his fist in celebration.

"What would I do without your quick wit and ridiculous, unwavering commitment to bits?" he says when they're out of hearing range.

Bit? I think, foolishly.

I mean, it was one for their sake, but what if it wasn't for mine?

"Hah!" I choke out. "It's unimaginable, really."

"Truly," Declan agrees, raising his eyebrows before opening his car door. "But, hey. We do need to follow through and go to prom together. Or else we'll be found out for the liars we are. And nobody likes a liar." He raises his shoulders like *what can ya do?*, then disappears behind his car door, slamming it shut.

Chapter 7

After my first day of training at the coffee shop, I walk the short distance back to my childhood home. It is beautiful as ever, with tall multipaned windows and ivy-covered walls standing at attention. But it feels different. Like there's a thick atmosphere surrounding it. An eerie sense of brevity that is about to pop. And not in the mysterious or sexy way *temporary* could sometimes seem, like a summer fling or a nice car you're only renting, but in the way that everything about life as I knew it was about to change.

The usually chirpy birds seem to hold their breath as I walk up the cobblestone driveway.

There's a van I don't recognize parked outside, and I think my body knows it before my mind catches up. When I walk into the house, my biggest fears are confirmed. Medical-looking bags are thrown next to the shoe rack by the door, evidence of nurses nearby.

I take the stairs two at a time to reach Lottie's bedroom faster. When I turn the corner, the sound of Lottie's breaths rattling fills the room. It was like loose change was clanking around a metal box in her chest. I'd never understood what "death-rattled breathing" meant until now. And I found it cruel to find out. I already feared the countless nights I would be awake, the sounds of her death echoing endlessly in my mind.

I look at my mom's distressed face as she kneels next to Lottie, her fingers gently stroking Lottie's weathered hand. She presses her lips into a thin line and looks across the bed toward the woman standing in the corner. Lottie's usual hospice care nurse is checking her vitals, but there is a woman wearing a pantsuit I have never seen before. Without speaking, I know she is my personal Grim Reaper. The person they send you when your loved one is reaching the end.

She notices my entrance and motions to speak, but the thought of her delivering words I could never unhear makes bile rise up my esophagus. Tears cloud my vision, making her an indecipherable blob until I manage to mumble "I'm sorry," before running from the bedroom, down the stairs, and heaving over the sink.

Nothing comes up, but the sobs rack their way through my chest and into my throat. My breathing is so sporadic it forces me to cough. I keep trying to suck down air, trying and failing. I begin dry heaving, the force causing me to double over at the hips. Still, nothing comes up. I wait in anticipation for my diaphragm to stop contracting. It does, and when my vision clears, I notice the bowls in the sink I was hunched over.

It feels so cruel that life as I knew it was ending. The woman who was another mother to me was dying, and I had dirty dishes in the sink. Where was I expected to find the energy to care for the details of my life when the main one had been irreversibly altered? Shouldn't the world slow, the frivolous tasks of life disappear, while the tectonic plates of my life shifted?

Shouldn't they assign me a pass for today? For the next seven hundred "todays"?

My "todays" would never look the same, but the dishes were still dirty.

After the woman in the purple pantsuit leaves, I drag my feet back into Lottie's room. My mom looks at me like I'm fragile. And as much as I hate it, I'm starting to realize she's not wrong.

"Come here, sweetie," she says. "Please sit."

Lottie's uneven breathing sounds like snoring. Some of the pauses are longer than normal, so long I think it might be her last, until another abrupt croaking snore bubbles out and unnerves me further.

"She's not in any pain," my mom says. "They started the morphine drip this morning because . . ." She trails off, looking away.

I've never seen my mother cry, and I hold my breath, waiting to see if today would be my first. But then she looks back at me, eyes clear, and says, "It was time, sweetheart. She doesn't feel a thing right now, but she might be in this state for a few days before fully passing."

"Wait, so," I start. "She won't . . . wake up again? This is it?"

My mom simply presses her lips together, dipping her head in a gentle nod. The tiny movement rips my heart in two. My conversation with her last night was the last one I'll ever have, I realize with startling force.

I feel horrible for crying again, but I can't control the way my shoulders collapse inward. I fall into my mom's arms, making a guttural sound I don't recognize as my own, and clutch her to myself as tightly as possible without hurting her. I have never been more grateful that she is still here.

She pets my hair over and over again as she whispers, "It's okay, sweetie. Let it out. It's okay." She holds me until my breathing calms, and when it does, I poke my head up from her shoulder, wipe my tears, and build up the courage to look down at Lottie's face. Her mouth is pitched open at an unnatural angle, and a bowl of water with a sponge sits next to her for my mom to moisturize it every now and then.

Despite the chest-rattling and snoring sounds, she looks serene. Peaceful. I didn't make a conscious choice to move toward her. I only realize I'm situating myself under the sheets with her as it's happening. My sock-clad feet brush against her calves as I slide down beside her, laying on my side and draping my arm across her chest. I cry into her shoulder, feeling selfish doing it. She is dying, and here I am, sobbing all over her. I take her hand and fit it into mine. Her stiff fingers move as I lead them, and they stay put in mine like we're holding hands. Just like we used to. The sight of them interlaced makes me sob harder into her shoulder.

"I love you, Lottie," I whisper into her ear. "I love you so, so much. You've always been a second mother to me. I love your calm presence and your sweet smile. How you laugh when I tell you about dumb book plots. Everything about you made me feel so loved. Makes me feel so, so loved," I correct, voice breaking. "Thank you for letting my mom and me live in your house all these years. For becoming a home yourself. You've always held us up. But you don't have to anymore." My voice is garbled as I choke out the words. "You can let go now, Lottie. You can rest now. Thank you for everything. Go. Be at peace. I will see you there soon." I kiss her hand, and my tears flow down our intertwined fingers. My vision is blurred by them, so I close my eyes, rest my head. Laying my head beside hers is the last memory I will ever make with her. I fall asleep, and when I wake up, it's to an entirely different world.

Chapter 8

The funeral arrives with a suddenness that feels rehearsed. Why does the funeral attendant seem so casual holding the door open for me? Does he hold doors open for people like me to walk into the worst day of their lives every day? Did the guests receive the funeral invitation like they were receiving a coupon in the mail? Did they dress in all black and practice the grimace they'd give me when they saw me walk in?

A woman in her late fifties stares at me as I walk into the funeral home. She offers me a look she should have practiced in the mirror a few more times. The lines creasing her mouth point so far down, it feels like she's doing a bad impersonation of a sad clown hired for a kid's party. I find it hilarious and have to wipe the smirk off my face lest someone catch me having an inappropriate reaction to this horrific day.

I force myself to remember why I'm here. It's the day my second mother happens to be the one lying in the casket.

There's a spot for me at the very front, so with effort, I try not to chuckle as I walk down the aisle, and more strangers offer me bad impressions of clown faces.

Perhaps, somehow, in some strange stress response, my mind is coping by making jokes about the situation. Protecting me by creating a sort of hazy denial bubble to float in. Incredulity, more accurately. But I don't think Lottie's friends would understand that on the day of their grieving, so I try my best to make my pressed lips look like an attempt at holding back tears rather than hysteria.

I take my spot on the crushed velvet pew and smooth down the skirt of my favorite black dress. I've never imagined I'd need to wear it to an event like this. My mom gives me a pained smile beside me, then faces forward for the start of the service. The hilarity of the event dies down—poor choice of words, I know—when Lottie's friends start to give speeches. They tell inappropriate story after inappropriate story about her glory days, drinking to the point of embarrassment, and hooking up with boys at their high school. It angers me to a degree I can't recognize.

My great-aunt Lottie was not the rambunctious socialite they are making her out to be. She was patient, an ever-constant, nonwavering source of love. Her disposition was careful, her movements steady and composed.

She had the most unique sense of quiet confidence I have ever witnessed. She didn't need to speak; she could just be present in a room, and it was enough to put me at ease. Her favorite activity was watering her plants, for crying out loud.

Whoever they're speaking about at the podium is not someone I knew. But the gregarious sounds of laughter tear through the room regardless. When everyone is finally laughing at the funeral, I no longer am.

I look to the back of the room to start planning my escape when my eyes catch on a tall figure standing in the doorway. My breath skips like a dusty record. I hate that I know exactly who it is by the stance alone. Declan's gaze snags on mine as readily as a three-pronged ring catching a thread in a lace dress. He bores into my eyes with a kindness that pisses me off. It somehow communicates a multitude of thoughts through the fifty feet of space, rows of chairs, and laughing bodies between us. The type of look that is only possible through years of shared history. And somehow, infuriatingly so, he has the uncanny ability to look at me with genuine care without the stomach-roiling pity that usually comes with it. Who told him about the funeral?

I stand up abruptly, apologizing to my mom for knocking her knee, before bowing my head as I stalk toward the exit.

I plan on keeping my head down as I brush past Declan on my way to the bathroom. I should know by now plans like that never work when it comes to him. He can predict when I'm about to run. He's seen it happen before. With five feet remaining before I plan on speeding past him, he disappears behind the door.

Where is he going?

I clear the door he was just leaning on and turn the corner to find the restrooms. And there he is, standing in front of them.

Of course, he guessed my next move.

"Blair," he says, voice barely above a breathless whisper.

"Excuse me," I demand, trying to move past him.

He places his hand on my shoulder, so light it feels ticklish through my sleeve.

JUST FRIENDS

"Come on. I know you don't have to use it," he says.

I rear my head back. "And how do you know that?"

He tilts his head in response, and it communicates more than I want it to.

Because I know you, he doesn't have to say.

I shake my head. The embarrassment of leaving the funeral during speeches and now being intercepted by the last person I'd want to see feels like a physical attack. If we're going to have any conversation right now, it isn't going to be within hearing range of these maddening speeches.

I spin around, march toward the exit sign at the back of the funeral home, and throw open the doors that lead to an empty parking lot. The cool breeze gives me some relief, but my head is still spinning. I sit on the closest thing I can find—the parking curb.

"Blair, wait," Declan's voice comes from behind me, but I don't look. I can hear the sound of his uneven steps as he approaches, and then he sits beside me on the curb. An errant tear threatens to escape, so I keep my head bowed in hopes that he won't see it.

"I know your friends weren't able to make it. And I know we're . . ." He breathes in deeply before continuing. "I just wanted to be here."

"How did you know my friends weren't able to make it?" I snap my head toward him, stunned.

Roshi and Faye weren't able to put their lives on hold on such short notice to come to the funeral. The flight plus the road trip makes Seabrook quite the trek to get to, and with their exciting new lives ramping up at full speed, there just wasn't any way for them to come. Still, though, he's never met them. Did I mention them at the coffee shop?

"I . . ." he stammers, and it catches me off guard. This man has never been one to stammer. Even at the age of twelve, he spoke with a conviction that was borderline funny.

"I didn't see them in the front row next to you," he explains. "So, I figured."

That doesn't begin to skim the surface of how he would know this. I tilt my head to the side like a dumbfounded golden retriever. Minus the golden part.

"You stalked my Instagram, didn't you, Declan Renshaw?" I guess.

I'm aware of my eagerness to revert to humor to avoid the reality of today, but I smile a mischievous smile anyway.

"Yes. I stalked you, Blair. Is that actually shocking to you?" He smiles at the pavement. His voice sounds confident, but I can tell he didn't mean to reveal this information to me. He's witnessed me stumble through countless friendships throughout my adolescence. So, his awareness of Roshi and Faye feels good. Like a stamp of my growth since him.

"And did you like what you saw?" I prod. A lightness I haven't felt all week enters my body.

Declan shakes his head and lifts a hand to run it through his hair. He's smiling bashfully, looking caught in an act he didn't mean to expose.

"Of course I liked what I saw." His tone is so matter of fact that I feel my heart thrash jaggedly against my rib cage. He looks at me, letting the silence of what he's admitted to stretch on. Is it a challenge I see in his expression? To confront what he's just admitted to?

"Are you still with that girl?" I blurt the question, unable to handle his piercing stare any longer.

His eyebrows furrow. "What girl?"

"You're not the only one capable of using Instagram," I state dumbly, looking away. I can't believe I'm saying this right now.

JUST FRIENDS

"Shelby?" he says, voice dipping and coming back up.

I shrug my shoulders. "Is that her name?"

He begins to laugh.

Oh gosh. He's laughing at me.

"Look, I didn't mean it in any way. I'm happy for you if—"

"No! No," Declan says between fits of laughter. His shoulders bounce up and down, head shaking. "No, please don't be happy for me. We're not dating."

He wipes a literal tear from his eye from laughing so much and I want the ground to swallow me whole. "Shelby is my cousin."

"Oh," I mumble. I've never felt dumber.

It was his freaking *cousin*.

All these years, I was jealous of his COUSIN.

"I only posted that because the bride, my *other* cousin, forced us to under their wedding's hashtag for some competition they were having," he clarifies, waving his hand. "Otherwise, I don't really use . . . social media."

He seems ten years older with the way he describes posting photos online. *How did he get so much older?* That's kind of the only thing time does, I remember stupidly. That is why I'm sitting here, at Lottie's funeral. The thought makes my stomach turn inside out, skin getting hot and then cold all over.

"Well, sorry for thinking you were dating your cousin. And . . . thanks for being here. I better get back inside." I wipe my hands on my dress as I stand and stalk back toward the entrance.

Today is not the day to be mulling over what his words mean, or why he even showed up in the first place. I resume my journey back inside. I don't hear his footsteps behind me.

Five Years Ago: Senior Year

"Break a leg!" I call out as Declan runs onto the field. It's the start of our senior year, and though our home turf is humble in size, the anticipation buzzing through each student for the first game of the season could power the largest nearby city. Declan brought us to state championships the past two years. If he does it again, he'll be the first quarterback from our tiny beach town to win three in a row. He is single-handedly putting Seabrook on the map to those who don't vacation here in the summer. I've made my way to my usual spot on the cold metal bench at the top of the bleachers, giving me the perfect view of Declan talking animatedly to his huddled team.

JUST FRIENDS

He's the only player with his helmet off, wisps of damp chestnut brown-blond hair curling at the base of his neck and behind his ears. I'm mesmerized by the cool determination on his face as he riles up the team. The hard set of his jawline, his Adam's apple bobbing as he shouts, swiveling his head to meet each player's eye.

The first state championship he won was his sophomore year, which was enough to draw expectant eyes on him. The pressure has only increased since to keep up with that so-called potential.

This was only high school, but high school led to college, which led to the NFL. Declan had his mind set on the life he could achieve after college before kids in high school knew what classes they were taking that year.

The start of his ambition could've been credited to his dad forcing him to train at a young age, but eventually, the lines between his father's demands and his own desire to win were blurred. Perhaps only being loved when he achieved was a form of training in itself. Now, he did exactly what his father wanted for his life without having to be told.

Declan finishes his speech to the team and they clap each other on the back while shouting "BREAK!" They disperse throughout the field like bees leaving the hive, jogging, stretching, or getting water before the game begins. But Declan stands still, helmet in hand, as his eyes begin scanning the crowd. They find mine in impressive time.

I wonder if he also had that subconscious meter, working at all times regardless of my efforts to silence it, that scanned a room for his presence. I always seemed to know where he was. His face softens when he spots me, the tension melting from his eyebrows like butter melting in a warm pan. Like, if he hadn't found me in the crowd, it would have crushed him.

He waves at me and I try to stifle the giddiness that swims up my chest as I wave back. He winks before putting on his helmet and running into position. It reinforces everything I've been feeling (and trying with effort not to name) that's been shifting in our friendship since this past summer.

I try to wipe the idiotic grin off my face. The game has begun.

As I watch, mesmerized by Declan's ease on the field, I find my mind sifting through memories of the past summer when we spent every second together that he wasn't training. I've replayed them so many times, combing through each frame for new hints or clues, there must be grooves permanently engraved into my brain.

Starting with prom at the end of junior year: us swaying to the sound of The Cars singing their contemplative lyrics, "Who's gonna pick you up when you fall?" Forfeiting our dismissive, playful demeanors for heated silence. As if we were trying to communicate something through sight alone. "Who's gonna pay attention to your dreams?" The sentiment stuck in my mind as I stared into Declan's soft green eyes.

It was something big. So big that it felt too scary to acknowledge quite yet.

But then, nothing. Heated stares dissolved with the turn of his head. Almost moments became nothing moments.

He had so many opportunities to end this nauseating friendship purgatory. But he never did. So, I guess it wasn't purgatory for him, just normal life. One he enjoyed, where he kept me as his friend and nothing more.

He must have felt something, but I was never going to find it in me to break the tension first. The thought of losing him forever over emotions he didn't reciprocate sounded worse than swallowing glass. So, I bowed my head and kept my wrists devotedly together, forever caught in his invisible grasp.

I blink and the crowd of students erupts into a cacophony of cheers.

Declan threw a game changing pass.

We have this game in the bag now, but it doesn't diminish the frenzy we feel as a collective, watching the team with your school's name dominating the field.

Declan removes his helmet and I'm entranced by the sight of his puffy maroon lips, swollen by his mouthguard, and the errant strand of hair dripping sweat over his forehead. There was nothing more attractive than watching someone lost to what they loved doing most. The full-bodied focus, paired with the comfortable ease with which they maneuvered in their expertise. It could be underwater basketweaving, but if they were passionate, it was intoxicating to witness.

Finally, it's the fourth quarter. Declan runs back onto the field with the offense, huddling in a tight ball before yelling a series of words, and they scatter into their positions.

"DOWN. SET. . . ." Declan pauses a second longer before calling "HIKE!"

And the ball is in motion, hurtling from the center and into Declan's palms.

My leg bounces uncontrollably, and a pointed glance from the girl beside me causes me to grip my knees to keep them steady.

"Sorry," I mumble.

She just nods, looking back toward the field.

"Come on, Declan. Come on," I murmur under my breath.

Declan makes eye contact with a wide receiver farther

down the field. Throwing it from where he stands would be a fifty-five-yard pass across the field.

Almost half the football field.

There's no way he could make it. He glances toward the opposition, checking if anyone is close to tackling him while he decides who to throw to.

He makes a face of resolve, and there's something about it that I just know. He's going to attempt the half-field throw. He's insane. There are NFL quarterbacks who wouldn't be able to complete that pass.

A millisecond passes as he grinds his lips together, pulling his arm back as far as it will go before launching the football with all his weight. It soars so high for so long that everyone seems to hold their breath. Our wide receiver continues running full speed toward the end zone, tracking the football with unrelenting concentration.

It lands perfectly into his hands. And he's so far from any defenders that he casually strolls into the end zone, slamming the ball down and roaring in pure ecstasy.

The game-winning touchdown.

Every single person in the bleachers jumps up, including me. The commotion is so sudden it feels like an earthquake.

"YESSSSSSS!" I join the crowd, fists pumping in the air.

"SEABROOK! SEABROOK! SEABROOK!" they chant.

The screams of joy ripple through the crowd as the realization dawns on them. Declan might lead us to the state championships for the third year in a row.

Everyone stampedes down the metal stairs at once, charging onto the field to lavish the football players with praise. My eyes furiously scan the turf for one person. There are so many bodies cheering at once. It adds to the commotion filling my head. There's blood pounding in my ears. But I have no one to share my joy with until I find him.

Find him. Find him—my body thrums with energy.

The bleachers have cleared out, so I'm left standing alone, using the vantage point to look for Declan.

I spot him.

He's the only one standing still amid the maelstrom. People are running back and forth, pumping their fists, picking up teammates in bear hugs, and putting them back down. Cheerleaders' pom-poms are cascading in formation.

But Declan is standing still, looking at me. It feels like a lock clicking into place when our eyes meet. A wordless understanding.

I sprint down the stairs as fast as my legs will take me, and I'm immediately thrown into the crowd, shoulders bumping into me at my eyeline.

I push through and run toward him. The smile overtaking his face cheers me on. It's the kind of smile that bubbles up and can't help but take over your entire face, demanding to be seen.

The satisfied relief etched into his body language at the sight of me feels rewarding in a way I can't describe. The feeling of being equally wanted in a place you already craved to be.

He stretches his arms out for me to leap into.

So I do.

I jump, arms wrapping around his neck, the shoulder pads of his uniform giving me purchase, and my legs follow suit, wrapping around his middle. He spins me in a circle, and our breathless laughter bursts into each other's necks. His warm breath tickles my ear as he slows, and for a moment, I panic, knowing that when I look at him from this position, something substantial will have changed between us. The tectonic plates of our friendship are shifting. Whatever happens next will be the aftershock.

I pull back to look at him, and instantly I just know. Maybe it's the mixture of longing and hesitation in his eyes. Maybe it's the excitement of having just won the game or the sounds around us dimming our better judgment, but somehow, we both come to a silent agreement. He leans in, not giving me a second to hesitate.

Our lips meet, and the crush of them together sends shock waves through my entire body. Having imagined how his lips would feel beneath mine a thousand times only adds to my elation.

It's happening. It's finally happening, I think.

He pulls away slowly, seeming to savor the moment equally as much as he disbelieves it's happening. I actually giggle; the sound is light and giddy, like a child's surprised delight at seeing bubbles for the first time—a sound I've never heard come out of me. He responds with a low chuckle, vibrating the dense air between us.

My feet find the ground, and I stare up at him. My cheeks must be burning crimson. I've wanted this for so, so long. And if anything, the first thing I feel is vindication; it wasn't just me feeling the spark—I wasn't the only one harboring hope for a future where we were more than just friends.

"How long," he breathes, urgency in his tone.

"What?"

"How long, Blair," he begs.

"Yes." I laugh.

"What?"

"Yes, Declan. This whole time. Yes, to all of it. Every year. Every single year I've known you." I know he's asking how long I've liked him. I know because it's the first thing I wondered when he pressed his lips to mine.

I feel giddy with the relief of it. Of saying it aloud and seeing his pleased face staring back at me. He's so beautiful.

He crushes his lips back against mine, as if he can't stop himself now that it's been allowed. We laugh, pulling apart. I feel like I'm in a dream. Like my head is floating off my shoulders, bubbles rising to the top and releasing with a satisfying fizz.

"Why now?" I can't help blurting.

He understands the question instantly. "Because." He looks away, wiping a hand through his sweaty hair, and then back at me again. "Because I can't—I really don't want to mess this up, Blair. If we start, I don't want us to end."

It sounds like he's thought about that sentiment a thousand times before confessing it. And I understand the feeling so deeply, I don't know how to communicate it in words.

I readjust my grip on the back of his neck, making sure he hears me when I say, "You won't mess this up." I shake my head. "If the goal was to make sure you didn't ruin this friendship, I've already done that a thousand times in my head."

The smile I was hoping for creeps onto his face, starting from the corners of his lips as he realizes my meaning.

Confetti pops from canisters beside us with a loud CRACK, and colorful pieces of paper rain down on us gently—a piece of pink confetti sticks to my cheek. Declan looks at me like I might disappear if he looks away. Like, if he's not careful he might wake up to find that this was all a dream. He lifts his hand. The movement is slow, tender, as he brushes the confetti off my cheek, holding it between his fingers like a trophy.

"Let me take you on a date," he says.

"What? A date?" I stall, still not believing this is finally happening.

"A date," he confirms.

"Yes." I nod vigorously, like an army sergeant commanded it.

He smiles, his dimple deepening. The freckle on his bottom lip catches my attention.

I finally kissed that freckle, I think to myself.

"Tomorrow. I'll pick you up at seven p.m. Wear clothes you don't mind getting dirty."

"Yes," I say again.

My brain is barely functioning.

"We won't mess this up," he says, like he's trying to convince himself.

I shake my head. "We won't," I insist, and pray to God that it's true.

Chapter 9

"You guys know the drill. Lots of tourists will be dipping in and out this summer, so we need to be a well-oiled machine. If we all do our part, none of us should feel overwhelmed," Declan says to the small crowd of coffee shop employees, of which I am one now.

Declan never said more words than the exact amount necessary to get his point across, and it was apparent he treated being manager like leading a football team. He rattled off tasks and updates, and although firm, the staff seemed to enjoy him. The surety of his commands, efficient and precise without sounding harsh, forced me to note the ways he'd grown since our high school years.

"Harper, you can teach the newbie how to make this month's specialty drink."

I'm so distracted, I almost miss the fact that he referred to me as "the newbie."

"Got it!" she says, red gingham bow bouncing in her ponytail as she nods.

Declan's eyes glaze over me as he continues going over roles like I'm an employee he barely recognizes. It's been one week since the funeral and I'm back to work, unable to stand the emptiness of the house.

I glance away from him, angry at myself for wishing he would look at me like he used to. Or at least like he was the same person who showed up unannounced at Lottie's funeral.

Roshi and Faye sent sweet messages of condolence, but they had a rushed undertone. "Reach out if you need anything!" with no questions of how I was doing or actual action of calling to check on me.

I don't think they understood how close I was to her. Most people don't grow up with their great-aunt, I realized. Most of all with one as special as mine. In Lottie's absence, I felt something new inside of me. A craving to be comforted in a way I never felt I needed before.

In fact, I always prided myself on being self-sufficient. Often, I couldn't relate to wanting to discuss the details of my life like they were entertaining beats to hit in conversation. It felt good knowing I didn't need to externally process anything in order to get through it. And yet, here I was, entire body aching with the tenderness of an open wound. My internal dialogue screamed "LOTTIE IS GONE" every five seconds, like it'd just received the news and needed to inform me for the first time.

JUST FRIENDS

And in a confusing new development, I felt like I needed a sounding board to process this new reality. The last thing I wanted was to feel alone in it, but standing in this crowd of coworkers I didn't know with my ex–best friend avoiding my gaze, I did.

Declan claps and the team scatters in a multitude of directions, getting busy with work. I blink, trying to remember what I was supposed to be doing. There's a tap on my shoulder. I turn around and am met by a blinding grin.

"Hi! I know we kinda met when you came in for a job and I'm also the one who scheduled you for your interview over the phone, and I was supposed to train you, but my cat was puking so I couldn't." She finally sucks in a breath. "But I wanted to formally introduce myself. I'm Harper," she finishes, sticking her hand out for me to shake.

"Hi," I reply numbly, taking her hand. "I'm Blair."

She stares at me for a moment, spidery lashes reaching her eyebrows.

At my blank expression, she continues. "Okay, well, I'm supposed to teach you this month's specialty drink." She picks up a hand-painted sign near the register and holds it up for me to see.

"This month's drink is a hazelnut banana latte, with whipped cream and vanilla wafers on top." She cups her mouth and leans in. "The manager likes 'em sweet!" I look behind her where the manager stands, an empty cardboard box in his hands.

An odd rush of jealousy flashes through me without warning. I was the only one who knew Declan liked sweet coffees. The realization that other people have learned his habits is shockingly painful.

"Okay, so for the hazelnut banana latte you're going to . . ."

Harper explains how to make the drink like she's describing the moon landing for the first time, and I have to admit, her enthusiasm is a nice distraction despite not having the energy to return it.

I glimpse Declan disappearing behind a door to the break room and feel a pang in my chest. And then I feel another one out of shame for feeling the first one. I shouldn't be concerned with his whereabouts. I shift my eyes back to Harper and her amazing teeth and red bow.

"Oh," she interrupts herself. "By the way, I'm supposed to let you know that you were put on the schedule for overtime hours?"

"Yes, that's right. When is closing again? Do I just stay late and lock up?"

"They're actually separate from being a barista, technically. The coffee shop is undergoing renovations. So, overtime hours would start at seven tonight. And you'll be working with raw wood and paint and stuff. Is that okay with you?" She looks up at me from under furrowed brows.

"Oh, yeah. That's totally fine. I can't promise I'll be good at it, but I think I can definitely handle paint and some tools if I'm given instructions," I say. "I will be given instructions, right?"

"Yes." Her eyes dart away from me and ping-pong around the coffee shop.

I raise my eyebrows.

"You will be given instructions . . . from Declan." She spits out the last part so fast I second-guess if I've heard her right.

"From Declan?"

"From Declan." She nods like someone is standing behind me watching her deliver the line.

"Is there an overtime team or . . ." I ask, hoping against all odds that other people on staff will be there.

"Nope!" she says and then starts backing away. "Alright, well, now that that's all settled, let me know if you need any help on drinks. I'll be one holler away at the cash register."

I'm left blinking at her retreating frame.

Awesome.

Overtime hours are with Declan.

Just Declan.

Alone with the one person who couldn't want to be with me less.

I look up at the order screen and begin preparing my first latte on the job, mind reeling in the process.

But honestly, the information pales in comparison to how strange I feel in the aftermath of losing Lottie. I'm twitchy, out of body, but I try to force myself to feel the cool metal of the espresso machine's wand as I sift coffee grounds. To actually see what my eyes are looking at as I pull shots of golden espresso. I move in slow motion in a weird hypnotic state, like I'm trying not to startle myself.

Working with Declan tonight feels like it might break me. But not because it's him. Well, that's not entirely true. But it mostly has to do with the fact that I haven't cried since Lottie passed. Didn't cry at the funeral. Walked around and waited for it to feel real.

I keep narrating to myself what happened, waiting to see if I'll finally have the appropriate reaction. Lottie died. Lottie is dead. My favorite person doesn't exist on this planet anymore. Every few seconds I recite it like a chant. One I keep hearing but still don't understand. She's gone.

It was strange. The most important person in your world could die, and then you slipped on your shoes and went to work the next day. Life moves on as usual. You stand there and ask customers what milk they want in their coffee, and they just tell you. They don't pause and say, "Oh, wow. Are you doing alright? Can you believe what just happened?"

Because they don't know. They can't see it on you. Can't tell by the look on your face. What feels obvious to you is invisible to them. I don't know the story behind anyone coming in here either, I realize. If it's the coffee they'll drink before they propose to the love of their life, or if it's the first latte they've bought since their loved one died. The world has carried on as if the axis of my life wasn't bent and thrown away.

But the one person who might be able to read through me is Declan. And I didn't know what I feared more: that he would take one look at me and know what I was feeling, or that he wouldn't.

Chapter 10

When I come home between my shift and overtime hours, I walk through the front door of Lottie's house to find my mom sitting on the floor in a pile of photos and journals, clear boxes scattered all around her. I forgot that we'd be the ones responsible for cleaning out the house in her wake.

When someone dies, you don't just get to mourn them. You're inundated with a list of tasks to complete after their death. When will we move out? I think for the first time, and then am shocked by the fact that it's the first time I've thought about it. How could I not have thought about that? My thought spiral is interrupted by my mom's voice.

"Look at what I found!" she exclaims, holding up a pink journal.

"Oh gosh," I sigh. "Put that thing away."

"Why? Isn't this where you wrote all your cute little stories?"

Cute little stories. That's precisely why I never shared them with anyone. Anyone other than Declan. The thought makes my stomach clench. I'm so glad I got over that childish fantasy. The stories in there are emo enough to bring a 2010 Tumblr fanatic to their knees.

"I don't want to look at it," I say, irritation lacing my voice.

She ignores me and opens it to a random page.

"Look, baby! You wrote about Declan in this one." She giggles at the open page in typical motherly fashion. "Oh, it's too cute!"

Why is she laughing right now? She's cleaning out Lottie's house because she died and she's laughing.

I drop my bag by the door and stalk over to her, snatching the crumbling pink journal from her hands.

"I don't want—" The words die in my throat as my eyes snag on the gel pen scrawlings from my youth.

(Rewrite this part. It's getting slightly too obvious that this is about Declan.)

"Oh, gosh." A strangled cry erupts from me. Rewrite this part? I didn't even have the decency to attempt fictionalizing my obsession with Declan. And to think if he'd ever accidentally read it. A literal shiver runs through me.

"Come on. It's sweeeeeet!" my mom singsongs.

"It's not so cute anymore now, Mom. I have to see the man tonight."

"Oh?" She suddenly looks intrigued. "Tonight?"

"For overtime hours," I supply. "EY was able to move my

start date to September, so I will be here to help you get everything settled." I gesture to the boxes of Lottie's belongings. "But I still want to go to New York and . . . well, you know." I wave my hand as if it fills in where my words left off.

Support you, is what I don't say, but I'm sure she knows from our previous conversations. She pauses riffling through the photos and looks up at me. Something is going through her mind, I'm just not sure what.

"So, you're moving away in September?" she asks.

Ahh. There it is. She's sad that I'm leaving.

"Yeah," I say, guilt lacing the word. "But I'm only going because—"

"Yes," she interrupts. "I know, baby."

Silence stretches between us. The weight of our new situation settles into our bodies. She'll be here all alone now. Who knows where she'll live. *Don't worry, Mom. I'll support you*, I think to myself as I observe her worried expression. My phone begins trilling, "Hopelessly devoted to youuuuu"—gosh, I really need to change my ringtone—and a photo of Faye's perfect smile fills my screen.

"Faye's calling," I say. "I'll be right back."

I make my way to the guesthouse as I press the green circle to answer her call, pink journal in hand.

"Hey, Faye! How's my married woman doing?" The gravel crunches beneath my feet as I take the path to my current bedroom.

"UGH!" she groan-yells into the speaker. "My mom is the absolute worst!"

"Woah there, feisty one. What is going on?"

"She's just ridiculous. She finds a way to do this every time. Stephen's family always hosts a huge party for his birthday in July, and suddenly my mom is demanding we come home the exact same weekend. She has way too much time on her hands with not working," Faye says.

Her voice seems to be put on pause as I contemplate this. "The older you get, the more you realize you become mini-me of your parents. Good and bad. It won't matter how much you fight it, con." It was a sentiment Lottie always spoke about, and it never made sense at the time. I figured it was because I didn't have memories of my father, so how would I know if I was becoming a mini me of my dad?

Faye complaining about her mother's abundance of time from not working is starting to sound pretty similar to how her life has panned out.

"Like, you had zero interest in throwing me a birthday party, and suddenly because Stephen's mom is notorious for her 'amazing parties' you want to throw one? He's not even your son!" Faye's voice cuts back through my thoughts. "It's just ridiculous."

"Yeah, that is so strange," I say, trying to muster up the energy to empathize with her. The funeral was one week ago. I haven't felt much empathy for anyone but myself lately.

"If it's only three months of marriage and she's already getting this weirdly territorial, she shouldn't be surprised if we never move back home." She scoffs. "She should consider herself lucky if we even come home for Christmas at this rate."

She continues ranting as I punctuate here and there with an "oh my gosh," or "you're kidding" at the right moments, but when I look at the clock, I see that she's been talking for over thirty minutes.

Usually I'd never notice. I always loved when Faye came back to the apartment with a hilarious story to tell or something to rant about, but today I just don't have it in me. I was proud of myself for not caring at first, but as the minutes tick by, it starts to bother me more and more that this is the first time she's called me since Lottie passed, and it's to rant about her mother.

At least you still have her, I think cynically, and then immediately feel bad for having the thought. Everyone's suffering is subjective. And yet, my body wilts the longer she speaks.

"Anyways, that was dumb. I just had to call you and get it off my chest," Faye finishes.

"Haha. Yeah, no worries. That is so dumb. Sorry you have to deal with that," I respond, meaning it.

"How are things with Declan?" she asks.

I feel stupid for the way my chest deflates. I was expecting the next question to be "How are you?" because of the obvious elephant in the room.

"Oh, fine . . ." I trail off, too distracted by the thoughts I can't say in my head.

I'm not thinking about Declan much because Lottie just died. She died and I'm sitting in the house that was hers. I'm thinking about how much longer we have until my mom and I have to find somewhere to stay with the finances we don't have.

But instead, I say, "Speaking of, I gotta go. I'm doing overtime hours at the coffee shop."

"Ooo! I hope he'll be there!" she coos.

As the silence rings out in the wake of our call, I picture myself floating out at sea, the tide taking me farther and farther from shore. I begin to struggle, but no one on land seems to notice. I can keep wading for a while, I think to myself, and kick my feet harder.

Five Years Ago

Declan picks me up at the house at seven p.m. just like he said he would.

I expected him to be waiting in his car as per usual, but when I throw open the front door, he's standing stock-still beneath the soft glow of the porch light with a bouquet of flowers in his hands. He looks like a modern-day James Dean.

I actually mentally whistle.

Declan tightens his grip on the bouquet, crinkling the brown paper.

"If the look on your face means you're reeling a bit, then you're not the only one," he says with a sweet lilt in his voice.

JUST FRIENDS

He knows exactly what to say to disarm his chronic charm and put me at ease.

He extends his arm, holding the bundle of cotton-candy-pink and blue hydrangeas out to me. I take in a sharp breath at the sight. My favorite flowers, because I've always loved how they look like colorful cotton balls from far away.

"Wow," I exhale. "These are beautiful. How did you even get them?" We don't have many hydrangeas in Seabrook.

"I'm glad you like them." He leans in and gives me a quick peck on the cheek, the brief encounter with his warm sandalwood scent doing my heart rate zero favors. "Shipping is a crazy invention." He winks.

I stare down at the fluffy flowers in a stupefied state. Pretending not to like someone for over a decade starts to become second nature. And my body hasn't caught up with the fact that I don't need to anymore.

"These are gorgeous!" Aunt Lottie says, pushing past me to say hi to Declan.

"Hi, con," Lottie says, patting him on the cheek. She has to reach her arm up to do so, his height towering over her by an entire foot. "Take care of my baby, okay?" she chides, pointing the infamous finger at him. But coming from her, it's more endearing than fear-inducing.

"Yes, ma'am. I will." Declan beams down at her, dimples flashing from his cheek and chin.

She pats him on the cheek twice before turning around and shoving me out the door. "Okay, con! Have fun!" She shoos me toward Declan and then slams the door shut.

"Woah! Well then!" I say, giggling as I fall into Declan's arms.

"I guess that's our cue," he says.

"I guess so."

"Alrighty, Little Bird. Right this way." He steers me from behind as I keep my hands firmly over my eyes. We stomped through a grove of trees until we reached the edge.

"Okay, you can open your eyes now."

I blink a few times, adjusting to see that we're in the center of a semi-circle created by massive cliffs hemming us in. Beneath my feet is a small patch of sand that gives way to clear turquoise water.

"Uh-huh." I scoff-laugh, momentarily dazed by the sight. "How did you find this place?"

"Google Maps is crazy useful, it turns out," he remarks.

I drop the awe from my expression and pin him with a glare. "First 'shipping is a crazy invention,' and now Google Maps. Excuse me for being curious."

"I'm kidding!" He laughs. "I found this place when I was on a run. I thought the trail was just a random dirt path, but it spit me out onto sand. And I knew instantly I wanted to take you here on our first date. Your curiosity is removing the smoke screen from all the romantic tricks I have up my sleeve."

I snort a laugh. We gravitate to the center of the sand and choose a spot with a view of the ocean, moss-covered rocks towering behind us. It feels like we've been dropped into the soft cradle of the earth's hands. A secret place, just for us.

"This is unbelievable. It looks like the magical cave from that Australian mermaid show," I say, settling next to him. The sun has already set beneath the horizon. Faint silver streaks are cast over the moonlit water in its stead.

"I call it 'secret beach.'" His eyes twinkle with the childlike joy at having shared the nickname with me. It's horrendously cute.

"How long have you wanted to take me on a date?" I ask. "Or like . . . when did this stop being platonic for you?" I point between us.

He picks up sand and lets it fall through the cracks between his fingers. A slight smile tugs at the side of his mouth.

"Now *that* is a loaded question." He looks over at me, arms wrapped around my knees like his.

"Why is it loaded?" I poke, hoping against all hope that his crush has existed for even a fraction as long as mine has.

"I think," he starts, looking out at the waves. "It was less of a single moment, rather a string of repeated instances that snowballed until it was this huge thing that smacked me in the side of the head. And I knew I couldn't resist it anymore."

I've never felt blood pump through my veins so viscerally.

"Wow," I say, becoming monosyllabic. "Yeah, that's . . ." I nod my head into oblivion.

Declan peeks at me from the corner of his eye and then breaks, descending into abrupt laughter. The warm rasp of it is boyish in a way that makes my cheeks heat.

I am so far gone, I think helplessly.

"Okay, well!" he protests, still laughing. "I can't be the only one who admits something. What was the moment for you?"

Oh gosh. I contemplate diminishing the truthful answer. It would be easy to. I've been lying to myself for so long about my feelings for him that it is kind of hazy, but I decide starting our relationship with half-truths would be a bad idea and risk it.

"I think the real answer might freak you out, but for the longest time, I didn't believe you'd ever see me in that way, and I also didn't want to risk ruining the friendship." I sneak a glance at him to weigh his reaction. It's unbearably kind. His eyes squint in concentration, and his body language is perfectly at ease, unhurried.

"Mm-hmm. I didn't want to ruin it either," he says. "But come on, that wasn't an answer. You're acting like a politician right now."

"Well, if you want me to be completely honest with you—"

"Which I do."

"Then . . . I honestly can't remember a time when I wasn't a little bit obsessed with you."

The sound of a wave breaking is the only thing that dares make noise in the wake of my confession, and I think I might fall forever through the empty space, until finally, Declan breaks into a grin and catches me.

"You're joking," he teases.

"I'm not."

"No, be serious with me right now. You're telling me that when I was five years old and had thick black-framed glasses attached to me via necklace and my two front teeth weren't close enough to be considered neighbors, you were 'a little bit obsessed' with me?" he challenges, eyebrows raised.

"Yes! Dead serious!"

"And this is our first date, why?" he shouts at the sky.

"Because! You know why!" I say instead of the actual answer.

"Because . . . ?" he challenges again with a teasing smile, refusing to let it go.

"Because so many girls threw themselves at you and they were all so impossibly pretty, and you still didn't want them. So, I took it as evidence that if you didn't want them, you definitely didn't want me. Actually, no. You know what it was?" I say, more to myself than him. "I thought you enjoyed my friendship because it was a nice escape from all the unwanted attention you got. So, I wasn't going to be the idiot who added to your list of people you needed to avoid." I laugh to ease the honesty of my admission.

I look down, focusing on drawing circles in the sand.

Without speaking, he takes my chin in his hand and turns my face to him.

"Blair," he pleads. "*You* are impossibly pretty. And I know I never acted on it, but trust that I always wanted to. You are the only girl whose attention I wanted, before I even knew other girls existed. And even after discovering other girls did, and do in fact, exist, the same is true. It's always been you for me." His green eyes don't so much as waver. It's like he refuses to blink until I believe him.

I try my best to soak it in. To stare back into his eyes and accept that what I wanted my entire life was happening. But I rasp out a breathless laugh, shaking my head out of his grasp.

"Now that we're . . . dating, I don't think you're supposed to know that other girls exist."

He pins me with a glare, playfully shoves my shoulder.

"You are impossible to compliment," he says, exasperated.

"No, no. I'm sorry. You're right. I am impossibly pretty," I say.

He throws his head back with laughter. "Okay, but I'm serious," he says, voice level. "You've seen me through every stage of life, and you never preferred me more or less based on how football was going. It sounds so stereotypical, but you saw the way people at school went from not paying attention to me at all, to gawking at me in the hallways after winning championships. If they said my name, it was because the word football was attached to it. I never liked that. I still found myself only caring about what you thought of me. And it was never the football you cared about. The way you spoke to me never changed."

"Of course not, Declan. That stuff is awesome but it's kind of irrelevant in the grand scheme of things. At least, inasmuch as it relates to my obsession with you," I say not so ironically. "I'm proud of your accomplishments, don't get me wrong. But you could do anything and I would find it impressive. You know that."

He smiles like the sentiment is still novel to him. Special and new.

And then without speaking, he starts to move toward me. I relax onto my back in the sand, and he crawls over me, boxing me in with his hands on either side of my face, his lean body hovering above mine, muscles in his shoulders straining with the effort. And then his face slowly morphs into a smile of pure wonder, lighting up his eyes. "I enjoy that answer very much."

"Of course you would." I heckle.

His shoulders bounce as he laughs above me. The moonlight illuminates his messy tousle of hair from behind and I take a turn giggling in disbelief as the improbability of this new reality settles between us. He goes quiet at the sound, like he needs to be still to marvel at me. And when I realize, I go still too. But then his face parts in a grin again and his head drops. It's like playing a game of hot potato, lobbing the imaginary force of it back and forth. Laughter begetting laughter begetting laughter.

Finally, the last of our laughter fizzles out like finishing the last sip of bubbly, and we allow the silence. I think he's a second away from bending his elbows and lowering his mouth onto mine when he says, "Wanna play the question game?"

"Sure," I exhale, a mixture of shock and unmet want.

He quickly bends his elbows and tucks his hands into his

chest, unfolding next to me onto his back. The crash of waves fills the pause as he situates himself.

"Okay. First question," Declan says. "If a crystal ball could tell you anything about your future, what would you want to know?"

I catch him looking at something in his left hand.

"Are you reading from a list?" I demand.

"Maybe," he says, faux shyness creeping into his voice.

I shake my head, but then the answer hits me. I contemplate choosing a lighter one, but I can't think of a decoy in time. So out it comes. "I'd probably ask if I'll ever see my dad again."

The darkness has gone from navy blue to nearly black except for the subtle glow of the moonlight. If the world didn't feel so still, I don't think I'd have offered this level of candor.

Declan rolls onto his side in the sand, facing me with his head on his bicep.

"You know," his voice is soft, like an outstretched hand inviting me in. "It's on your dad for never coming back. Not you."

I stare at a specific star in the sky, scared of how my face will betray me if I look at him.

"Yeah, I know," I choke out. "I just think—" I press my lips together.

"You just think what?"

"I know my dad is the only one to blame for his actions. But knowing something and believing it are two different things."

I feel Declan's meaningful stare on the side of my face, but I don't turn. If I meet his eyes and see sadness in them, I'll stop saying how I really feel. And it feels good to say it out loud for once.

"You blame yourself?" Declan says it like a fact. "For how

he left you and your mom. You've somehow deduced that it was your fault?"

"Well," I huff, turning to meet his eyes finally. "It sounds so wrong when you put it like that. But when you're five and no one is telling you what's going on, it's only natural to make up your own conclusion. Even if the information you've gathered with your tiny mind is incorrect."

"Hey," Declan protests. "My five-year-old brain loved your tiny mind. As unformed as it was, it was responsible for all your cute little expressions."

My mouth splits into a smile.

"But in all seriousness, I know what you mean. About knowing something is true but not believing it. You came to the false conclusion that there was something about you that caused your dad to leave, and you started believing that so long ago, it's hard to spontaneously not believe it anymore. Even with your grown-up brain." He taps the side of my temple playfully. I laugh and then his expression becomes grave again. "But, Blair, someone who chose to leave you must be the stupidest man in the entire world. There's just no other explanation."

The corners of my lips wobble and I have to smash them together to prevent my chin from trembling too. "That's what you said our freshman year too."

"Hah," he laughs. "I must still be bad at comforting you then."

"No," I say quietly as I relax my head into the sand and stare at the sky again. "You're very good at it."

He must know I've laid down to avoid being looked at while I fight grateful tears, so he joins me in looking at the sky.

"I don't know if your dad is in your future, but I know I will be," he says, voice husky like it's been forced from his throat. "If you let me be."

"Of course I will." There's nothing I want more, I don't add.

We let the tender hope of it lay between us. The twinkling stars and whispering ocean are our only witnesses.

"I would like to know what I'm doing for work at the age of forty," he says abruptly.

I chuckle, his sudden way of talking has always been my favorite. "Why forty? And why work?" I ask.

"Because," he says. "If I do end up making it to the NFL, it's not a career that lasts your entire life. Unless you're Tom Brady and you play football until you're, like, eighty. But sometimes, I get scared that I don't have my finger on the pulse of anything other than football. I don't know what I'd find myself doing once I didn't have to think about it twenty-four seven. Which is kind of destabilizing, you know?" he finishes with effort, punctuating each word.

"Hmm," I muse, craving a deflection from the rising panic of where we'll be in that many years. We don't even know where we're going to college. "First of all, you will make it to the NFL, and second, anyone who uses the word 'destabilizing' in a casual sentence is smart enough to figure out what to do with their time."

His eyes dart down to my mouth, half-smirking as I wait for his chuckle. After it arrives, I take a more sincere approach. "You're too creative to stay bored for long. You like engineering, right? You could build stuff."

"That's not a bad idea," he says, more so to himself like he's rolling the thought over in his mind. "Not a bad idea at all."

The seed of doubt worms its way back to the forefront of my mind. I don't want to put a damper on our first date by thinking so far into the future, but we've already applied to colleges. Don't we need to put some forethought into how we'll last past high school?

"Declan," I start, unable to push off the racing thoughts. "How is this going to work if we go to different colleges?"

"We applied to a lot of the same ones, right?" he replies, not missing a beat.

"It's just that . . ." I peter off, realizing I'm in danger of souring the mood.

My hand subconsciously lifts to my mouth to chew on a hangnail.

"Hey." Declan shifts himself up onto his elbow and gently grabs my wrist, pulling my hand away from my mouth. "I know it's scary to think about where we'll end up in a few months, but let's talk about it. Walk me through what you're thinking about."

"Well," I falter.

Apparently converting my feelings into words is a pathway my neurons are unfamiliar with. "It's just that . . . okay, let me start here."

I push up on my elbows in the cool sand. "The other day I was talking to my mom about all the colleges we applied to, and she made an offhand comment about how I'd need full-ride scholarships to attend any of them. And when I pushed and asked if she was being dramatic, she laughed in my face. I legitimately can't go to a single school I spent all this time applying to unless I get a full ride. Full. Not half. Not a quarter. Full."

Declan nods silently, allowing me to go on.

"And I know this is going to sound terribly cliché, but it feels like that saying that goes 'Walk like a duck. Talk like a duck. Hang out with other ducks. You start to think you are a duck.' But I'm not a duck, Declan." My voice rises.

"Woah, woah, woah," Declan says, catching my gesticulating arms. "I was following so well until this duck comparison."

"What I mean is, I grew up in this town because my great-aunt could afford it. So, I hung out with kids whose parents could afford it. And I started to forget that I wasn't like them. Everyone rattled off the list of Ivy Leagues they were applying to and I somehow followed suit without much thought. So much so that I forgot to ask my mom if we could afford it. I just assumed we could because everyone else can. But if I want to go to college, I have to pay for it!" I say, driving my pointer finger into my chest. "And also, I can't be going to college for *creative writing*. What was I thinking?" I spit the words out like they're obscene. "I need to be strategic. I need to put myself in a position to get a high-paying job. One high enough to support me and my mom."

Declan is nodding with force now, eyes skimming the sand as a hand scrapes his chin, deep in thought.

"So, your mom didn't tell you that you'd be the one paying for college on your own?" he asks.

"Well . . . yeah, I guess she just assumed I knew that," I concede, not liking how it sounds. "But she didn't want to deter me from trying to apply to any big schools because she has some weird blind faith that I'll be able to get full scholarships and . . . I don't know, Declan, you know how she is. She's not one for many words and I guess this is one of those things that slipped through the cracks."

"Slipped through the cracks? Isn't that a pretty big thing to let 'slip through the cracks'?" he says, stress peaking his voice.

"Hey, calm down," I try to say soothingly. "I'm stressed about it too. That's why I'm bringing it up."

"Sorry, it's just hard to stay calm when I just got you and now I have to worry about losing you soon."

"You're not going to lose me, Declan," I say, touching his arm. "I mean, we'll figure it out, right?"

He doesn't move away from my touch, but he looks down, jaw grinding.

He shakes his head, hand coming up to rub his chin again and the sight makes my stomach drop. "I'm sorry, it's just—you know how much pressure I've been under since I was a kid, Blair. My dad has made it his chief goal for me to play D1 at an Ivy League and then straight to the NFL. It's already so much to think about."

My stomach aches and I feel the need to run and hide. I never want to add to the pressure he feels, but I don't want to compete against his dad and football.

At my silence, Declan looks over at me. "Are you okay? I don't mean to scare you, I just want to let you know where my head is at."

"Yeah," I mutter. "No, that makes sense. It's just . . ." I shake my head. "I don't want to be second fiddle to football, you know?"

I feel like I walked off a cliff saying that out loud. But then, Declan exhales, looking sorry. "Hey, come here."

I obey immediately, climbing on top of him. He chuckles at my sudden conviction, and I watch his Adam's apple bob with the movement. His hands drift to my waist, supporting my weight as I hover above him.

"You won't ever come second to anything. Okay?" he says from under me.

I nod, a small smile tugging at the corner of my mouth. He reaches up to palm my cheek and I lean into it.

"You'll always come first," he breathes. "Nothing tops you."

My cheeks heat and I hope the darkness hides it. The only natural response I feel is to say the forbidden L word, but I know it's too early, so I fold over him to stop myself. Our chests meld and warmth spreads through me. Sometimes the weight of love is more frustrating than pleasurable.

I turn my head in the sand by his ear and only manage to mouth the words *thank you*.

"One day, when I'm playing football, you'll be an author. I'll be reading your books every second I'm not on the field," he says softly, wrapping his arms around my back and holding me against him.

I'm robbed of speech. There's frustration in not being able to communicate how much his words mean to me. I'm grateful words aren't the only way to communicate.

I kiss his temple, softly at first, and then move to his cheek. After that, I kiss his forehead and slowly drift down to his nose.

"Please, Blair," he grinds out.

"Please, what?" I ask, feigning innocence.

"*Please*," he begs. "Kiss me now." Yearning coats his expression so intensely that it looks like he might die.

I let out a full-bodied belly laugh. His unhidden longing is disarming in a way I can't resist.

I still, elbows bending beneath me, causing my full weight to lower on top of him. I prop up my upper half, shuffling my forearms in the sand beside his face. In the time it's taken me to readjust, Declan's face is filled with even more anguish.

"End me now," he says, as if to himself before impatiently curling his fingers around the nape of my neck and pulling me down to meet his lips.

The kiss is hungry and searching, and I feel everything with a new level of intensity. I become aware that this is the point of no return. The one that starts and ends my ability to enjoy anyone or anything else with this much fervor.

This moment, with the waves lapping gently to shore, and the deep darkness, is too perfect. Completely on our own, the stars as our only witnesses to the moment I've dreamt of for years.

Declan, who I never imagined reciprocating my feelings, is beneath me. Opening himself up to me in rare and precious ways, finally letting the mysterious curtain drop between us.

It fills me up so quickly that, for a moment, I feel weary. Unsure that I can trust something so perfect to stay.

"You'll always come first." I repeat the sentiment he offered me earlier, holding on to the promise with a grip that hurts.

The truth is, I have more faith in the probability of his leaving than this moment being the catalyst of his staying.

Chapter 11

"**Y**ou still use those?" I hear myself ask.

The tiny bell above the doors chimes as I walk into the coffee shop at seven p.m. Declan is bent over the counter, pencil behind his ear. I follow his gaze to see a small notebook open before him.

He doesn't look up; the pause of his foot tapping is the only clue that he's heard me. It's so dark in here, I think to myself. The glow of a floor lamp is just enough light to see his shadowy figure. He's lurking in here like a vampire who doesn't want to be seen.

"What, pens?" he says finally, without looking up from his notebook.

"No. The journals."

"Oh. Yeah, of course," he replies like it's obvious.

Okay. That's all I'll be getting from that then.

He used to carry a leather pocket journal that would fit in the back of his jeans, so at odds with the football equipment spilling out of his bag. I'd always assumed that he was planning certain routes or plays, but I'd poke at him, joking that he looked like a tortured poet from decades past, always ready for inspiration to strike. He'd just laugh one of those evasive laughs and change the subject. I never did find out what he was writing in them. He's certainly not plotting football routes anymore.

"If you want to get started, the ceiling needs a top coat. You'll have to use the ladder to reach it, if that's okay?" he asks, gaze staying pointedly down.

"Yeah. Sounds good. I put 'pretty good at using a ladder' in my application so," I reply, deadpan.

He doesn't offer so much as a polite chuckle.

Ouch

I drop my bag and walk to the center of the coffee shop where the ladder stands at attention, bucket of clear varnish ready beside it. Balancing the bucket in one hand, I lift my foot to the first rung and breathe out, trying to silently encourage myself.

If I take any longer to climb this thing he might notice, so I push off and climb the rest of the steps with as little thought as possible, ignoring the way my heart rate speeds up. I make the mistake of looking down, and the tiniest squeal escapes my throat.

"You good?" he calls from below.

"Yup! All good!" I call back, but my voice wavers slightly, giving me away.

"I would uh— I would take that job but I can't . . ." He trails off, gesturing at his leg.

The one that has a limp.

"Oh! Oh, no worries at all. I love ladders. Love it up here." I look around, trying to hide the lie with my acting skills.

I finish my climb up the ladder and look down again, noticing that I can see his notebook from this height. It's not fully in focus, but I make out a sketch of . . . a birdhouse? I look around and realize the floor is covered with a litany of them, taken down for painting the ceiling I suppose. They were the ones hanging from nearly invisible string from the ceiling earlier today, exactly like the blueprint in his sketch.

Reds, yellows, greens, and blues. Every single one is painted in a color-blocked fashion. Whimsical really. Some small and some large, all with silver clockwork-looking wheels placed on the sides.

"Did you make those?" I call from above, completely in awe. I've forgotten my fear of heights at the sight of them.

He looks up at me for the first time, eyes following my finger to the various wooden creations.

"Oh. Yes." He clears his throat, returning to his drawing. "I did."

"Wow," I mumble. The answer shouldn't surprise me, and yet it does.

Every piece of new information is a jagged reminder of the life he's forged beyond my scope. Evidence of the distance between us.

The muscles in his back sway as he removes the pencil from behind his ear and presses it into the paper.

"When did you learn to build things like that?" I ask, curiosity spurring me on.

There's a sizable pause.

"After the accident," he says finally. "When I was on bed rest."

My heart rate kicks up as I try to figure out an appropriate response. We've never discussed the accident, never had the chance to, but he continues for me.

"Do you remember when I got a few scholarships for engineering?" he asks, gaze unmoving from his notebook.

"Yeah. Of course," I say, voice losing bravado.

"I still had some interest in building, so I did some studying at home. Tinkering with my hands helped distract me from the fact that . . ." He pauses and starts again. "From not being able to run anymore. Train. Play football and all that."

It's the first time either of us has ever acknowledged the suddenness with which his life was changed that night. I'm shocked at his willingness to discuss it, with me of all people, but he relays the information coolly, unbothered by both the events he's discussing and the person he's discussing them with. His unshakable calm has remained intact, it seems.

"That makes sense," I reply, eyes staying trained on the birdhouses. "Well, they are very impressive. I could look at them all day."

"Thanks," he replies, voice strained.

The brief discussion of his past is more disorienting than the small height I'm balancing from, so I lift the paintbrush to the ceiling.

"Do you mind turning on a light?"

JUST FRIENDS

Declan looks up. "Yeah, of course. Sorry about that." He flips the overhead lights on and then strides back to his notebook.

"So, why are . . ." He stops mid-sentence and starts again. I'm surprised you're back in town."

My paintbrush pauses mid-stroke.

"Yeah," I huff. "That would make two of us."

I return to glossing the ceiling, mulling over his forwardness. His sudden interest in speaking to me. But then I recall that he's always carried on conversations in this way. Not wasting time with filler, always cutting through the fat and going straight for the meat of a conversation. It's just been a while since I've been a part of it.

"It was a surprise for you, too?"

Is he fishing for the reason I came home? I thought he knew.

"Umm, yes. Definitely a shock."

"And why's that?"

"Lottie's illness ramped up out of nowhere. We thought she had stage two lung cancer. They were treating her accordingly, and then when she wasn't responding to treatment, they took another scan and realized it was stage four." I feel the familiar ball of tension form in my throat. The memory of the phone call that changed my life. "My mom told me two weeks before graduating Pepperdine. I got here as fast as I could. And I'm glad. I got to spend some good quality time with her. Collected as many stories from her life as possible."

I keep my eyes trained on the ceiling, not risking a glance down to see his reaction.

"I'm so sorry, Blair," he replies, voice softening. "I'm sure she appreciated that more than you can imagine."

I nod. "Thanks for saying so."

A beat passes.

Oh gosh. Please don't let him be one of those people who gets awkward talking about difficult—

"And you're working here because . . ." He trails off, waiting for me to fill in.

"I had to defer my job."

"Your job in New York City, working as an author?"

Oh. He remembered.

It takes me a second to realize he assumed New York City from my rambling about it in high school. Not from any concrete knowledge of my life now.

His words feel like a punch to the gut. But also, much too intimate. He's the only one I trusted to tell. It feels like he's brandishing a weapon by reminding me.

No one else in my life, not even my mom, knew that being an author had been my biggest dream. The one that was so true to my soul that it felt like treason to say it out loud. It was vulnerable to admit your dreams. It gave people a detailed map of how and where to hit you to make it hurt the most—painting the red X on your back for them.

But what bothered me most about the whole thing was the fact that I hadn't written a single line of prose in years, until after the funeral a week ago. Lottie's death had me scrambling for purchase, and writing felt like getting traction under my feet.

"Hah," I chuckle weakly. "New York City, yes, but . . ." I trail off, voice hardening. "Writing isn't—" I stop and try again. "That's not my dream anymore."

My gaze falls from the ceiling, settling on one of the metal ridges on the ladder. I hear Declan's work boots echo off the wooden floor. He stands below me, crosses his arms, and looks up.

"What do you mean it's not your dream anymore?" he asks, eyes locked on mine.

"Because," I continue. "That was a child's dream."

"Yes. It was."

I stare down at him. He stares back; a challenge held in his hard eyes. "It was a child's dream because you were a child when you dreamt it. Doesn't mean it was an invalid one."

My eyelids flutter wildly in rapid succession. An expression I'd only ever seen on TV and didn't think existed in real life. A glop of clear goo threatens to drip from my paintbrush, giving me an excuse to tear my gaze from his and back to the ceiling.

"Sure . . . but, it was childish," I rebut. "I mean, just completely outlandish. Thinking I could make enough from the stories I wrote, let alone be able to support my mom while doing so." I scoff, a self-conscious, evasive sound. "It was much too risky of a bet."

"Sure. But a lot of good things are a risk," he replies, voice firm but low, like he's disappointed by my conclusion.

"Well," I sigh. "I guess it just wasn't a risk I was willing to take. A lot of people take risks and fail, you know. We just don't hear those stories as much. Clearly. Because they're not big enough to tell the tale. They're holed up behind a cash register like my mom." The words tumble out before I have the chance to vet them.

He doesn't respond, so I look down at him. His sage-green eyes are soft but pained. They glow slightly in the lamplight, and I have to tear my eyes away, unable to bear the feeling growing in my stomach. His eyes. That look. It brings back memories at a dizzying speed. Me yelling "Do you not understand anything about me?" and storming out. Never to see him up close again. Until now.

"Sorry, that was . . ." I mumble. "Uncalled for. I'm just anxious to get to the job I have waiting for me."

He nods, shoulders dropping marginally.

"It's a consulting position. In New York City. Consulting analyst, technically," I tack on, hoping my openness will make up for the outburst.

"Oh. That's awesome. You're only here for the summer then?"

"Yep! Just for the summer. Gotta save up for the move, and then I'm out of here," I say with faux enthusiasm, waving the paintbrush in the air.

"Just a few more overtime shifts and you should be good to go then," he says up at me, and then strides back over to his notebook.

"Can you help me with something, actually?" he asks.

"Sure," I say, holding the paintbrush out to him like a question mark.

"You can put that down for now. Hold on a sec." He walks to the corner of the room and grabs the raw slabs of wood leaning against the wall. "I'm building out a bar for customers to sit at, where they can watch the baristas make their drinks or just get their work done without taking up a table with multiple spots." He gestures toward the half-finished bar area, tracing the invisible vision in the air with his hands. "I've got the wood measured out here. Could you help me hold it steady while I drill it into the ground?"

"Of course," I say, grateful for the distraction.

He stands in the center of the shop holding a slab of wood upright as he waits for me to replace his hands, so I climb down the ladder and meet him there, taking the slab from him and keeping it steady in the exact position he demonstrated.

He takes the pencil from behind his ear and marks something on the wood, then puts it back, making the soft bristles of his hair move slightly. From this close, I can smell the faint woodsy aftershave scent of him. I can see the new crinkle lines by his eyes as he squints in concentration. The color of his mouth is just as vibrant as it was when we were kids. He flicks his eyes to me, and I flinch slightly, having forgotten I wasn't observing him in isolation.

"Hold steady," he says softly.

And then he bends down to drill the wood into the floorboards. We haven't stood this close to each other in years, and I try to distract myself from marveling at his quick, efficient movements, but I have nowhere to look as I keep both hands on the slab, so I keep staring. It's a bit awe-inducing to watch him work. I missed the part of his life when he learned how to do all this, and seeing it up close feels disorienting.

In between drills, I ask, "Did you end up going to college?"

He stills, one knee bent as he rummages around for another nail.

"For engineering," I add, hoping I didn't cross an unspoken boundary.

He steadies a nail in place. "No. I didn't." He continues drilling. "Self-taught."

"What was that?" I ask, the sound of his voice starting and the drill stopping too close together to make out.

He stands to full height, taller than when he was seventeen. The single slab of wood is the only thing between us, and for a moment I tense, not knowing if he's about to speak or expects me to.

"I taught myself," he clarifies, and then walks over to a pile of wood in the corner.

"You taught yourself how to build?"

"Mm-hmm," he hums. The sound is bright, open, despite his lack of eye contact.

He takes a measuring tape out of his back pocket and lays it on a slab of wood, then picks it up and brings it over to me.

"For this one, I need you to hold it horizontally, like this." It balances on top of the one he just drilled.

"Got it."

I stand in the middle of the slab, making sure to keep it flat, while Declan walks over to my side to drill it down.

"I watched a lot of YouTube videos of random dudes building decks for their wives or doghouses for their dogs, and then eventually started with trying to build small things when I wasn't mobile yet. And then about eight months into that I tried building bigger projects with my uncle who's in construction," he says, eyes trained on the wood as he makes a notation with his pencil again.

I wasn't expecting him to offer up that much detail, and with this tiny peek behind the curtain that closed shut between us, I become aware of how hungry I am to learn more about what he was doing during all that time.

What he was doing during his first week without me. His second month. The third year. There was so much unknown, stretching between us like an ocean. It felt like he'd just handed me the oar to a row boat. I wanted to keep paddling until I got to his shore.

"That's so cool," I start, mind racing in a million different directions of ways to encourage him to continue opening up. "So, you did that while you were recovering and then you what? Got this job and moved up the ranks? Or did the owner contract you to do renovations?"

"I guess you could say that," he says, and then the deafening buzz of the drill drowns out all other sound.

I'm expecting him to continue when he finishes drilling, but he doesn't. Just moves back to the pile of wood and measures a new one before bringing it over.

"So," he starts, eyes focused on his measuring tape and pencil marks. "You went to Pepperdine for writing?"

"Hah-gah." A strangled laugh forces its way out of me. "Not quite. Pepperdine, yes. But not for writing. I majored in economics with a minor in psychology."

Declan pauses, returning the pencil to behind his ear. "You majored in economics?"

"Yes . . ." I say. "Is that difficult to believe?"

"No, it's just . . ." He returns to lining up the wood and finding a nail. "I guess it's just surprising for someone who loves words so much."

I'm momentarily stunned. From a man who wanted nothing to do with the details of my life, to assuming he knows how they panned out.

"I can love both," I rebut.

"Both what?"

"Words and . . . economic theory."

He chuckles slightly at that and I feel a flush of satisfaction.

"Yeah. I guess." He steadies a nail over pencil markings, preparing to drill it in. "I just figured for someone so enraptured by words her whole life, they'd still somehow worm their way into your adult life. Even if not professionally."

"Enraptured. Good word."

"My point—"

"Taken," I finish for him. "We already went through this," I say, annoyance and perhaps a tiny bit of defensiveness bubbling out. "Besides, isn't this pretty far from what you wanted to do?" I gesture to the pile of wood and the coffee shop surrounding us.

"Yeah, I guess it is . . . but not because I didn't try my best at my first choice," he says, and then begins drilling again.

"Excuse me? What are you trying to imply?" I spit over the sound of the drill.

He stops drilling and looks at me. "I stopped playing football because I didn't have a choice. You had a choice."

My neck physically cranes backward. "I had a choice? Where exactly was my choice, Declan?" He starts walking back to continue rifling through the slabs of wood, so I talk to his back. "I only went to Pepperdine because they gave me a full ride. I wasn't going to waste that on a creative writing degree only to be humbled the moment I was spit out into the real world. Not all of us have rich parents to fall back on if our unrealistic pipe dream doesn't pan out. Who was I supposed to fall back on? Lottie?" I emphasize her name like a curse, knowing it will land with the intended shock value.

Declan stops, turns around, and looks at me. All challenge leaves his eyes. A sympathetic, pity-filled look replaces it. Like he knows my outburst is really misplaced grief taking itself out on him. Which isn't an excuse, and I realize it immediately.

"Oh, no," I say, shaking my head, shifting my weight from leg to leg, and placing my hands on the slabs of wood in front of me for lack of a better idea. "You don't have to look at me like that. I shouldn't have said that."

"I'm sorry," he says anyways. The two words are filled with so much care, delivered with an intimacy that shouldn't be there. I feel the urge to flee.

He stops and crosses the room, places a hand on my shoulder, and dips his head to meet my eyes. "You're right. I shouldn't have—" I rip my shoulder away from his touch.

"No, you really shouldn't have said anything, but I shouldn't have either. And you don't need to comfort me. I'm fine," I protest, but he holds my eyes and I feel a whimper forming, threatening to come out. He stares at me, like he knows it's a lie before I do. I press my lips into a thin line, the force with which I'm trying not to cry becoming a painful, expanding orb in my throat. I slide my fingers back and forth on the wood mindlessly to distract myself, but then something sharp catches, and I pull my hand back with a cry.

"Ah!" I grunt an embarrassing sound, the pain of it shocking me. "Ow. Ow. Ow." I keep my tone dry despite the sharp stinging sensation spreading through my palm. I bring it to my lips to soothe it.

"Woah." Declan grabs my wrist. "Don't put it in your mouth. There could be splinters." His voice is calm but insistent.

"Come here." He beckons me to the section where drinks are prepared. He pats the countertop, and I hop onto it. He disappears, retreating to the back room briefly before returning with a first-aid kit under his bicep, brow furrowed in consternation.

I look at the ceiling to avoid the tears forming. The cut doesn't even hurt beyond the initial slight sting, but the grief I felt before is threatening its way up my throat again.

"Let me see it," Declan demands.

I give him the hand that's been cut. It looks worse than I originally thought. Not just a splinter. I must have grazed it over a nail or thin piece of wood sticking up. Declan touches my wrist so tenderly that I almost pull back. His touch is so light it tickles. I use the opportunity to stare at him, watching him assess my hand like it has the secret to his life's problems written within it.

"It doesn't look like it will need stitches. Do you have your updated tetanus shot?" He begins taking the antiseptic solution out of the first-aid kit with force.

"Um." I bite down on my lip to stop my voice from quivering. "I think so?"

His brow furrows again, this time it looks more like frustration. Is he upset with me?

"This might sting," he warns, before pouring the antiseptic onto my thumb.

"Agh!" I grab his shoulder with my free hand. My thumb digs in, and the new muscles I feel hold up beneath my grip. He feels familiar and entirely new. When did he get shoulders like . . . like *that*?

Declan's mouth pulls up on one side, gathering into a grimace.

"Sorry," I whisper, and retract my claw from his shoulder.

"Don't be sorry," he says. His voice dips so low it comes out raspy. He looks up at my face. Our eyes latch onto each other like a familiar, forgotten thing being recognized again. Like all the history we've been pretending to forget comes racing back to us, too ingrained in the fabric of who we are to ignore. My heart judders in my chest. After lingering for a moment too long, Declan averts his gaze back to my hand and finishes wrapping it in a bandage.

A tear falls onto my hand. Declan sees it and looks back up at me, confused.

"Are you okay?" he asks.

JUST FRIENDS

The tear is just as shocking to me. I made no conscious decision to cry, but it was undeniably the truth: a single tear was sliding down my hand. More tears begin to fall.

The grief I've been trying to outrun has finally caught up to me, and it's mixing with the grief of Declan and me. Looking at me with recognition in his eyes ripped the safety pin out of my carefully contained emotional grenades. I hate this, I think with sudden force. I hate how much time I've dedicated to trying to get over him, as if it were my life's work, only to stand next to him and feel a similar rush of emotions coming back after a few conversations and tender looks.

"I'm fine!" I say finally, wiping the tears off my face in a hurry. "It just stung a bit more than I was expecting." I force out a laugh, but it comes out damp and unconvincing.

I jump off the countertop, ready to return to the wood and get busy again, entirely shocked by my own reaction. Crying in front of him was as unexpected and impossible as Lottie walking through the doors right now. I'm almost past Declan when he grabs my wrist, my back still facing him.

"Blair," he breathes, sounding disappointed.

"I'm fine, really." I yank my hand back like his touch stung, causing me to stumble a step. I straighten and stalk off, trying to move past this embarrassing moment. It's the worst, trying to move past your awkward behavior with more awkward behavior. I feel his gaze on my back, unmoving from where he stands.

"Blair, hold on a sec—" he tries again.

"No, I'm fine. I just—" I wave my hand as I walk out the front door. "I just need a moment."

Had Declan been less persistent, perhaps I could've gone back to helping in silence, but now, the stream of tears returns, and I break out into a run without thinking. Well, there was some thinking. The only motivation being to get away from the possibility of Declan seeing me like this. I rarely see myself like this.

The cool ocean breeze hits my face as I race through the back alley. The sun is setting, and most of the town's tourists are tucked away into dimly lit restaurants or cozy inns. Luckily, not many people witness me fleeing the coffee shop in my half-crazed panic. I cannot cry in front of him. Not in front of anyone, but especially not him.

So, I keep running, not sure where I'm headed. At the bottom of a hill, the street becomes sand, spitting me onto the beach. This is perfect, I think. I just need a moment to cry here, and then I can go back inside, chalk it up to the cut on my hand.

I've run as close to the shoreline as possible without getting splashed. The roar of waves crashing onto sand sounds like the earth's mutual lament. I sit down, wrapping my arms around my knees, and continue sobbing.

The waves continue to crash over themselves, rolling right up to my toes before pulling away. I'm grateful to have grown up by the water. The waves have witnessed my tears countless times, coddled me as I envied doting fathers teaching their daughters how to swim, and now, as I shed my first tears for the woman who helped raise me, body taken by the unforgiving wrath of cancer.

No one told me grief would feel so physical. It was the heaviness that sat at the top of my thighs, a bone-deep fatigue settling into my extremities like wet cement being poured down my limbs. My thoughts don't race, but they don't settle either. They're unclear. A wild mixture of disbelief and hopelessness, fighting for purchase over one another.

It's the feeling of a magnet being attached to the right side of my head and the tops of my knees, dragging my body into the fetal position. I give in to it, letting my cheek settle into the frigid sand.

This, I think, finally, feels good.

I must have been lulled to sleep by the white noise of the waves, because the next thing I see is Declan's large, attractive mouth, sideways in my vision.

"Blair?" it says, taunting me with that pillowy bottom lip. "Blair."

"Huh?" I mumble, the confusion of the first few seconds of consciousness fogging my thoughts. "Where am I?"

"You fell asleep," he says. "On the beach."

"Oh," I whisper. Well, that's embarrassing.

Crying is a tiring business it seems.

"Let's get you up. It's almost midnight."

"WHAT?" I say, startled, disorientation increasing my panic.

"It's okay, Blair. I checked on you two hours ago, went back inside to clean up a little, and then came back out here. Wouldn't want you getting swept out to sea," he remarks.

Right, I think. Wouldn't want that.

He hung out with me while I slept on the sand? I'm too tired and confused to parcel out how that makes me feel. More confused, most likely. He gestures to me with his forearm, offering for me to take it. I do, using it to sit up. I feel like I've been hit by a bus.

I stand and we shuffle through the sand together. The night sky surrounds us, the twinkle of starlight visible in the lack of city lights. Something, I realize, I would lose when I move to New York City.

We've almost made it to the street when I stumble, a wave of dizziness hitting me. Declan's hand shoots out, wrapping around the right side of my rib cage to steady me.

"I'm driving you home," he says, voice suddenly hard.

"What? I'm fine. Just a little dizzy from standing up too fast," I protest. "And the . . ." I look at the bandage on my hand. ". . . blood from earlier."

"You stood up five minutes ago. And the cut was hours ago." He walks in front of me, not stopping to check if I'm following until we make it to the street.

"I'm parked right around the corner," he says. "It's like a two-minute drive—"

"Gosh, can you just stop? I told you I was fine."

What am I doing? I don't even recognize the sound of my own voice right now. It must have been embarrassment disguising itself as anger.

He pauses and looks at me, eyes unreadable in the darkness.

"Sorry." I rub my eyes with my palms, wishing I could bury my face in the sand again. "I'm just gonna—" I gesture weakly behind me and then start walking backward up the street. "I'm gonna go."

I spin around and start speed walking, my cheeks heating up like a match has been struck beneath them. The sound of his car door slamming shut echoes behind me and I breathe out finally.

Embarrassment fuels my steps all the way until I make it to the guesthouse and close the door behind me.

I thought I successfully mourned Declan. I thought the wound had closed. But now I suspect it was more of a mal-union. When a bone breaks, if you keep it in the wrong position, it will heal, but incorrectly. It feels like I'd been walking around for years, feeling fine enough, only for one night to make me realize I'd been walking with my leg bent at a ninety-degree angle.

Four and a Half Years Ago: Senior Year

Declan and I had transitioned from being friends to dating with the ease of switching trains. They were quite close and perfectly adjacent, but the destinations were very different. We'd fast-tracked our senior year in a daze. College applications and football practice took up most of our energy. And every time the stress of where we'd go after high school came up, he kissed me until my shoulders dropped, and thoughts became unviable.

My head is bent over Declan's dining room table, where we spend our evenings doing homework. A crick in my neck forces me to look up from my notebook. It's been two hours, and despite Declan's relentless patience, I still have a baffling inability to understand the mean value theorem and how to apply it to the calculus equations before me.

"How about we take a break with an episode of *Upper Leagues*?" Declan suggests to my crooked frame.

Upper Leagues is a reality show that follows college football athletes training to be scouted by the NFL. It's good insight into what Declan might experience soon.

"Yeah. How 'bout we do that," I mumble, embarrassed by my lack of calculus comprehension.

I typically read a book while he watches the show, falling into companionable silence like a well-rehearsed dance. We shuffle our sock-clad feet up the carpeted stairs and enter his bedroom.

"What's this?" I ask, motioning toward the letter with a huge college emblem stamped on it sitting on his desk.

"Oh," Declan says, seeming just as surprised as I am. "Must be some mail my mom brought in."

He walks over to the unopened letter and rips into it. Boys, I think, shaking my head. Clawing their mail open like a bear instead of neatly tearing open the top. I watch in anticipation as I see the landscape of his face change. The crease between his eyebrows deepens, his eyes scanning the letter faster and faster.

"What is it?" I ask.

"It's—" he starts and stops, continuing to read.

"You're killing me here. What is it!" I say in an attempt to lighten the dread gathering in my stomach.

"No, it's just . . ." He trails off again, eyes moving down the paper. "Notre Dame University."

His dream school.

Oh gosh. Did he not get in?

The look on his face isn't a good one.

"Oh no. I'm so sorry, Declan." I breathe, reaching for his forearm.

"No, no, it's not that." He shakes off my touch. "I got accepted."

I swallow the lump in my throat.

"Oh! That's . . ."

. . . 2,217 miles away from my dream school, I think to myself.

"That's awesome!" I try to smile up at him.

He shakes his head. "Blair, it's not awesome. It's a million miles away from where you'll be."

My final college letters had come in last week. I'd made it into three of the five I applied to, but only received a full ride to Pepperdine. Meaning I couldn't go anywhere other than Pepperdine. Which would've been the happiest day of my life, had it not been the only school without a football team.

"Yes, but . . . but we both got into our dream schools. That's amazing!" I force out.

He scoffs. I've never heard him make such a cold sound. "There's nothing amazing about killing our relationship."

I rear back in shock.

"It wouldn't kill our relationship," I say in a weak voice. "People do long distance all the time. We can make it work, we can—"

"But what about our plan? How are we going to have time for long distance when I'm training? If you thought high school football took up a lot of my time, you have no idea what's in store. Multiply it all by a thousand and then add the time change, homework, and FaceTime or texting to the equation. It seems plausible at first but then try to keep it up for four whole years. It's insanity."

"So, you'd rather just end this? You don't even want to try?" I say, voice wavering.

"Of course not, Blair." He takes a step toward me, laying his hand on my shoulder, and I feel the ball of dread loosen for the first time. "You can just come with me. Right?"

"What?" Now I'm the one to flinch from under his touch.

"Come with me," he repeats, green eyes boring into mine.

"What do you mean 'come with you'? I didn't get into Notre Dame."

"I know, but . . ." he starts, ruffling his hair, his hand drifting down to rub his neck.

"Oh my gosh," I breathe. "You have got to be kidding me."

An unexpected burst of anger rises in me at the realization of what he's offering. A second ago I felt tiny. Now, I feel the astonishment expanding beyond my body in heat waves. He wants me to drop my dreams of going to Pepperdine to follow him, where I'll be without a degree, without a path to getting a career, and without anyone I know other than him.

"I know it sounds crazy but trust me." He grabs both my shoulders, passion raising his voice. "I've already had coaches tell me they see more potential in me than most of the guys playing on their college teams right now. I can do this for us, Blair. I can support us."

I shake my head. "That's not the point, Declan. It's not just about me. What about my mom? Do you even remember the reason I wanted to go to Pepperdine in the first place?"

He looks down, shaking his head like I didn't understand him.

"It's not just about my life. It's about my mom's too," I spit. "And look at us! If step one of our 'plan' could go so awry then what makes you think steps two, three, and four will go smoothly? We don't even know if you'll make it to the NFL!

I'm not going to follow you around like a puppy and cross my fingers, hoping you'll make it in four years and still manage to love me in all that time too," I seethe, hating myself as I hear the desperation in my voice. Whether it's desperation to prove him wrong or to be understood, I don't know.

Most of the kids at our school had the privilege of taking gap years to "find themselves," to study abroad in London or Barcelona to experience a different culture for the fun of it. I didn't have that privilege. Suggesting I did and could waltz over to whatever state Declan lived in to . . . what? Date him? How would I even afford to live there? The fact that he thought it possible at all showed how different our circumstances were.

I knew I couldn't make anyone else care like I did. They didn't see what I saw. My mother had been working on her feet at the convenience store since I was five. She was always complaining about her back. Always had sweat above her brow. She never brought a single friend or man over to the house, because it wasn't hers. None of it was. It was all Lottie's. I wanted to buy her freedom from that.

"I could support her too," he adds.

It feels like the walls start closing in at the sound of his words.

"Declan," I start, shaking my head again. Trying desperately to clear it. "Do you not understand anything about me?"

"What are you talking about, Blair?" he says, exasperated. "If I make it to the NFL, and I will make it, those contracts would be able to support this entire town. You wouldn't have to think about working at all. Your mom could retire. Isn't that your dream?"

The words he's saying are nothing but nectar, and yet, my vision is blackening at the periphery.

"You don't get it, do you?" I plead.

He shakes his head infinitesimally, and the tiny movement breaks my heart.

"That's what my mom did," I say in a tiny, ragged voice, feeling a thousand miles away.

"What?" Declan says, voice softening. "I didn't hear you."

"That's what my mom did." I repeat, louder this time. "She followed her husband who promised her a good life." I laugh. The sound is ugly. "And look where she ended up."

Declan looks fearful for the first time.

"It's not about what you could provide me, Declan. It's about not putting my life in the hands of other people. What you'll accomplish will be great, but I need to do the same for myself. I won't let anyone else be responsible for that." I shake my head through the tears blurring my vision. "Plus, you wouldn't want that. All the pressure of supporting me and my mom? I thought you hated pressure." I spit his earlier words back at him. "You don't need to feel any pressure juggling me and football anymore. I want to do this for myself anyways."

"Blair, I understand that but—come on. It's us we're talking about. I love you. We were going to build our lives together. College is just the one step in the way. You can trust me on this," he tries, voice taking on a new kind of urgency.

"Hah." The sound gurgles out of me without warning. "That's what my dad said too. Oh, and let's see," I fake confusion, looking around. "Hmm, where is he? Anywhere around here?"

"Blair—"

"Oop! That's what I thought. Nowhere to be found." My laugh comes out sadistic, I hardly recognize the sound. I feel like I floating outside my body. "Right. My mom believed him when he promised that, unlike me right now, and where did she end up?"

I shake my head, voice finally losing its snide lilt. "I'm all she has, Declan. I'm sorry but I can't rely on you. That's what she did. I won't be making the same mistake."

I walk away before he can stop me. I hold the image of my mother's face in my head as I rush down the staircase, out the front door, and into my car. I didn't realize Gwen was standing in the garden until I shoved my keys in the ignition. I look down sheepishly at the sight of her and put the car in drive. I let the inability to conjure my father's face fuel me all the way home.

Chapter 12

The second my eyes open to the bright sunlight peering through the guesthouse, the memory of crying in front of Declan last night bombards me. I have to shove my face deeper into the bedsheets to endure the physical cringe cascading down my body.

This, I realize, must be what people refer to as a vulnerability hangover. Obsessively, I replay the moment my eyes welled with tears, and I feel the persistent, nagging shame of . . . of what? Why did it have to be so embarrassing? Lottie died days ago. But it wasn't my deep-seated hatred of displaying emotions that was the problem. It was the fact that Declan could see through my attempt at being okay. It was the fact that being in his presence again made me not okay.

On instinct, I grab my phone from the nightstand and swipe open my messages.

APARTMENT 302

Roshi

> This girl in our incoming class is trying to get us to sign up for some janky app her brother made to connect us before the semester starts. Has she not heard of Facebook??

Faye

> LMAO. Isn't that like the exact origin story of Facebook 😭

Roshi

> Okay housewife! Didn't know you knew so much about Zuckerburg's origin story

Faye

> Ever heard of Netflix? 🙄

Our group chat has been dying. The time between responses has slowly grown longer since we parted ways on that gloomy May evening in our apartment building's parking lot. From text messages ping-ponging back and forth like a pickleball match to a few hours between stilted jokes and updates to a day or two before a single reply comes through.

We've never ventured through the murky waters of long-distance friendship, so a period of adjustment is to be expected, but I feel the bitter twinge of resentment flitter through me.

Roshi hasn't called since Lottie's death. I understand she's busy, but the semester hasn't even started yet. What will our friendship be like when law school does start? And Faye *has* called me, but she complained about *her* mother the entire time.

I can't find it in me to reply to their messages. And as juvenile as it is, I can't help but wonder how long it'll take for them to notice my absence.

That's not healthy communication, my brain lectures. *Yes, I know that*, I reply to myself. *But not asking how your friend is doing after their second mother dies is pretty crap communication too, in my humble opinion.* That does the trick to silence the nobler voice in my head.

A loud knock at my door startles me. The door handle wiggles and my mom scoots herself inside, holding the bright green mug I made in second grade and shutting the door behind her. Despite the distracted look on her face a second ago, I catch the moment of effort as she puts on her happy, everything-is-alright face. "Good morning, honey! How was work last night?"

"Ughhhh." I force my head under a pillow dramatically.

"My goodness! That bad?" she says, crossing the small room to sit at the foot of my bed.

"No, it was fine," I lie. "It's just . . . not New York."

"Oh, sweetheart. You don't need to be in such a rush to leave." She pats my ankle through the sheets adoringly.

I'm about to argue with her that, yes, I do, when she says, "Hey, sit up and drink this. I need to update you on Lottie's will."

"Her will?" I ask, removing the pillow from my head and sitting up to take the mug of steaming coffee from her outstretched hand. "Oh, you're the best."

I take it and pull a long swill of the warm latte. The espresso is smooth and rich, the milk perfectly foamed.

"Did you make this?" I ask, shocked.

"You're not the only barista in this house," she jokes, deep smile lines cresting her eyes. "Speaking of houses . . . I finished wrapping up the details of Lottie's will with her lawyer yesterday. And it turns out she left you something. Well, left us both a lot of something."

My mind begins racing with all the possibilities of what that could mean. She continues before I can open my mouth to speak.

"I don't know if you know this since you were pretty young when she bought it, but she owned a small house closer to downtown Seabrook. She rented it out for passive income, but she left it to you, in her will." She's looking at me like a little kid who's being told bad news.

"Oh my gosh." My voice comes out as small as if I were the kid she's imagining me to be. "That's . . . that's great news, right?"

"Well." My mom tilts her head to the side as if weighing the pros and cons. "It is amazing news in my opinion."

"But . . . what? What are you not saying?" I urge, sensing she has cards she doesn't want to reveal.

"But I know you don't want to stay here." She looks around at the guesthouse, in almost the same condition as it was when I arrived a few weeks ago. "You're practically still packed and ready to fly away at the drop of a hat." She chuckles but it lacks heart.

It's the most my mom has ever let on that me leaving would be difficult for her. She's always said my eventual moving away is just part of life. And if her stoicism is for show, I've believed her act.

"I thought you were excited for me to go? I was only going because—"

"Yes, I know, honey." She cuts me off.

I furrow my brow. She never lets me talk about working to support her. To eventually retire her. Isn't that what she wants?

Just tell me what you want, and I'll do it, my mind urges.

"Anyways," she pushes on, talking fast enough to pummel past the split second of rising emotion. "The other thing I wanted to tell you was that . . ."

I've never heard her speak so timidly. It has me leaning toward her in anticipation.

"Well, Lottie also left me the house."

"This house?" I screech, pointing down. "This whole house?"

She nods.

"Oh my gosh," I say, so breathless it barely forms the syllables required to make the words. "That's . . ." I shake my head, tears forming in my eyes. "Incredible."

I try to blink the tears away, not wanting to scare my mom off, but the news lands with a surprising force. It's so final—Lottie is really gone. The fact that we were discussing her things because she wasn't here to have them anymore made my chest feel like collapsing, but at the same time, the crushing weight of gratefulness was there too.

This was everything I ever wanted. To give my mom a place of her own. A place where she felt free to make decisions purely because she wanted to. Not because she was sacrificing her wants for mine. And here it was, at the cost of Lottie's life, something I never would have been willing to give had I been given the choice.

"Wow," I say.

My mom's eyes glisten, so subtle that I'm unsure if it's just the trick of the light, before she continues. "And she left me her convenience stores."

My eyes widen.

"All seven of them," she adds.

My mouth hangs open, but I can't choose the first words to leave it. At my inability to respond, my mom forges on.

"But hey, one thing at a time, right? Let's go visit the cottage she left you first. I'll be out front while you get ready, okay?" She pats my ankle through the fluffy comforter again like she just told me what was for dinner, not like she just delivered news that would change our lives in ways I couldn't even process right now. She stands to leave and disappears as quickly as she appeared. That woman. The ever-elusive nymph. Even-keel to the point of being unsettling. But maybe that's what you learn to do when you become a single mother overnight. Despite being so much like her, there are so many things I don't understand about her.

After yesterday's meltdown, it feels like the dam inside me has been opened and closing it might be impossible. But as I'm left sitting on my bed, ten pounds heavier with this new information, I allow myself two seconds of bafflement before shuffling out of bed and continuing in the only way I know how. The only way I've *seen* how. I throw on clothes without looking at them and meet my mom at the car downstairs.

If there's a piece of Lottie left in the world, I want to see it immediately.

Chapter 13

"This is it?" I ask, eyes bulging out of my skull.

"Mh-hmm." My mom nods.

It's gorgeous. The cottage is a single-story home tucked between cypress trees, lavender bushes, and grass that looks as fluffy as a baby lamb. You wouldn't notice the quaint house if you weren't paying attention. It seemed like an afterthought in comparison to the whimsical landscaping. I wouldn't be shocked if fairies flew out and started tending to the land.

My mom ambles up the gravel path that leads to the house.

"The real estate agent is busy hosting an open house today, so she left us the keys," she says.

"Why does it need a real estate agent?" I ask, realizing how out of my depth I am being given an entire house at the age of twenty-two.

"Well." She sticks the key into the rounded door and wiggles it back and forth. "You're about to have a lot of options, and since I know you don't want to stay here, I figured we should have a real estate agent help you with all of them." Her voice sounds brittle, like she doesn't enjoy saying it.

All of my options.

A few months ago, I wouldn't have been able to conjure up a single reason why I'd want to stay in Seabrook, California. I hadn't been expecting to come home at all, and now I was entering my dream home, the property in my name.

My breath hitches as I walk inside. The ceilings are sloped and low. The wooden floors creak, and the floor plan hints at the age of the home, having a random two-step staircase down into the living room, which is merely a hop away from the kitchen.

"Watch your step. This is called a sunken living room. My grandparents had something like this," my mom says as she walks ahead of me.

The space is so small it feels like you're standing in the kitchen and the living room at the same time. Just enough space for some books, a desk to write my romance novels, and the husband and kids I hoped to have but could never fully picture.

My mom watches me take it in, face blank.

"I want to ask you what you think, but I don't at the same time," she says in a small voice, walking toward the bedroom without meeting my eyes.

"What do you mean? It's . . . perfect." At her silence I continue, "Right?"

She points at something behind me. "Look."

I follow her finger to see the bedroom. But what she's referencing must be the sliding glass doors leading into a garden. No, not just a garden. A lavender farm.

"Is that—" I rush over, slide the glass door open, and pad outside. "Oh my gosh," I say, breathless. "Are you kidding me?"

Fluffy lavender heads float wistfully in the wind, huddled together like they'd die if they were pulled apart. There's a rough path through the center of the yard made up of random stones and the occasional red brick. It's barely visible through the forest of flowers growing discordantly on both sides.

"Lottie had a green thumb," my mom says, coming up behind me. I can hear the smile in her voice. "She wasn't the one maintaining this one, but she is the one who had the vision for the whole thing."

"Why didn't she ever show me this?" I ask.

"She bought it long before we ever moved in with her. Had been renting it out to family friends for years. And then in more recent years, she hired someone to manage it and started doing short-term rentals, so." She shrugs. "She just . . . never got around to it, I guess."

And now she never will.

It's the closest we've gotten to acknowledging Lottie's absence.

"But hey!" She reverts to the fake peppy voice I've learned to shrink away from. "She was clearly still thinking about you since she gave it to you."

I nod. Lips pressing into a thin line.

"Yeah," I say.

"But no pressure, sweetie. I know how much you wanted to go to New York, and this will still be yours even if you don't decide to live in it," she says with a forced lightness.

She's trying to act like there's no pressure to go one way or another, but her tone is off. Her body language is icy. Sometimes I wish there was pressure from her to stay. At least it would be a pure, unhidden desire. Expressed because it was true. Not a placation to prevent me from feeling guilty when I already do. Because this thing she does, skirting around topics, hiding emotions, putting on a fake happy voice when she's clearly not feeling happy, makes me feel unsettled. Sometimes I just want to shake her shoulders and scream, "TELL ME HOW YOU REALLY FEEL, MOM!"

"Mom," I start. "This whole like, 'I know how excited you are to go to New York' thing, you do realize why I want to go there, right?"

"Oh, yes, yes, yes, sweetie, I know! I know," she says the words so fast, already waving her hands and shaking her head like she wants the conversation to stop. She turns around and enters the bedroom.

"No, stop for a second," I say, voice stern.

All of this is already too overwhelming for me to handle without her skirting around her true feelings. I'm feeling smaller and smaller beneath the reality of Lottie's death and this huge new responsibility by the second. I need her to be honest with me, to guide me in this.

"I don't talk about New York all the time because I'm enamored by the city and crawling out of my skin to sit in an office building all day. I do kind of romanticize that, sure. The independence of moving and proving that I can make something of myself, but—" The words get lodged in my throat. I don't actually know how to admit this to her. "I don't—I just—I want to do that for you." I gesture my open hands toward her. "You gave me everything my entire life. You were always working so that I could have everything, and I am so grateful for

JUST FRIENDS

that. But, now I want to be able to give you that. To give you rest. To see you finally relax and . . ." I shrug, trying to emphasize how okay I would be with the idea of ". . . maybe you could even date someone. I don't know. Whatever you want to do with your independence I would be fine with. I just want you to feel freed up enough to do things because you want to. Not because you have to for me."

I'm out of air now that it's out. If I thought I had a vulnerability hangover this morning, I can't imagine what I'll feel like tomorrow.

My mom doesn't say anything for a beat. I'm about to start talking again to fix what I've done when she says, "Oh, Blair." She shakes her head. "You've always been the sweetest girl."

I nod furiously, anticipation and the intensity of my emotions swelling inside me like the tide.

"But you don't have to do that for me."

"What?" I ask, stunned. "Why? You don't have to feel guilty about it if that's what it is. I want to do that for you, Mom. It would be my joy. And I'm not just saying that." I gesture wildly with my hands, pleading, urging her to understand. To give me something in return.

"Oh honey," she scoff-laughs, in a motherly "that's so cute and naive" way. "I don't need you to take care of me, baby."

My eyebrows furrow.

"Do you think Lottie made me work at the cash register all those years?"

"Yes?" I say, honestly. "I mean, not like, forced you, but like gave you a job, yeah."

"No!" she exclaims, scaring me slightly. "I begged Lottie to let me do that. She would've just let me live in her house with you. She probably would've paid for everything for both of us! She love, love, loooooved you so much. Oh my goodness.

You have no idea how much she loved you. You were like the daughter she always wanted, truly."

Tears sting my eyes. Not again, I think. I keep my lips pressed tight, urging my tear ducts to dry up. I tense every cell in my body, willing myself to listen to her words without crumbling.

"But I was excited to work." She sighs and rolls her eyes in an expression of relief. "Oh my goodness, I was so excited to work. To make something of myself like you said. I relied on your father for everything. I let myself get so—" She shakes her head and moves on. This is the most I've ever heard her open up, but she'll probably never tell me what she endured under my father's hands in detail. "I didn't want to go from relying on your father to relying on Lottie."

"So, did we only live with Lottie because . . . you wanted to?" I ask.

She smiles softly, seeming to ponder her answer before speaking. "In Vietnam, living with your grandparents is very common. We probably would have done that, but since they had already passed away, and I couldn't provide you with a father figure, I thought living with Lottie would be a close second. Don't get me wrong, if she hadn't let us live with her, it would have been much harder." She blows out air, eyes wide. "Much, much harder. But you know we always make things work. And above all, I just wanted you to grow up in a house full of love."

I smile back, a small, broken thing.

"Wow," I don't manage to say more as I try to process everything she's revealed. To learn that it was love fueling her actions instead of stress had my world tilting on its unreliable axis. "You definitely gave me that. And so much more."

Her eyes soften with affection as she studies me. "You

know, con." She inhales. "Something I learned after leaving your father is that creativity is not just in how a painter paints or how I sew my own clothes, or writing stories like I know you like to do."

Blood races to my cheeks. How do mothers always know more than they let on?

She continues, "I learned that creativity was also in how I could construct a beautiful world for you. Especially because the one I thought we'd have came crashing down. Of course, you don't picture your daughter growing up without a father. But I also never could have foreseen my relationship with Lottie. I had so many aunts growing up, her and I were never that close. But then look how that turned out. She became our rock." Her voice warbles, but she blinks and somehow it steadies out again. "Working at the convenience store was not easy but I loved doing it. That money was mine because I earned it. And what I earned all went to you. That's how I wanted it to be. You are mine, baby. If I did it for you, I was doing it for myself."

Her words land like a miniature, life-altering earthquake in my body. I can feel pieces of land I once believed to be concrete shifting. It was disorienting to learn that the way I perceived certain childhood events didn't portray them with complete accuracy. Or at least, they weren't the full picture. It was like at Lottie's funeral when her friends told stories that didn't sound anything like her.

The adults in my life were more three dimensional than I'd been capable of seeing. To me, Lottie was my calm, comforting second mother. She wasn't a rambunctious teenager who once drank and dated a litany of boys. But the two didn't contradict each other. Had I perceived my mom as this powerless being who needed my help, when in reality she had been living her dream this whole time? It was so similar to my own dream, and the very reason I stormed out on Declan, offering to support me. It wasn't about the support; it was about the gratification of doing it yourself.

"I know my childhood wasn't conventional, but because of you, it really felt like a fairy tale of an upbringing. I loved every second of it."

"Ohhhh, Sweetpea," my mom coos, head dipping as she smiles with warmth in her eyes.

"I mean that. You're a creative genius in my eyes."

"Well, I'm glad you think so because you're just like me." She winks, defusing the intensity of the conversation in a second and moving on. "Now, you've got to see this. Come here." She walks through the bedroom and back into the living room, pointing at something on the wall.

I follow her to see a small, wooden bookshelf, only a few books wide. It's attached to a desk, sitting right next to the TV. I recognize so many of the books as the ones I read as a child. Perhaps she had bought the same ones I read to stock the shelves. My eyes catch on Divergent. One of my favorite YA dystopian series in sixth grade. I take it off the shelf and flip through the pages. I see the beginnings of pen scratchings and I smack the page to keep my place, half in disbelief as I bring the book closer to my face.

$$D + B = <3$$

The tiny letters are scrawled in black ink at the top of the page. I slam the book closed. This was my copy of Divergent. I remember sharing my love for this series with Declan, teasing him about his similarities to Theo James when the movie adaptation came out. I frantically put it back in its rightful place on the shelf.

"What?" my mom asks.

"Oh, nothing. I think it's my old copy from when I was a kid," I mutter.

"Aww. No kidding!" She takes it back off the shelf and flips through it.

I cringe, waiting to see if she notices the pen scrawls. She does.

"D and B?" She squints, saying the letters in a painfully slow drawl. "Oh! Is that about Declan? That's too cute!" she squeals, back to her normal self.

"Haha." I take the book from her and put it back on the shelf.

"You know." She shakes her finger. "You could ask Declan for help checking this place out. I don't know anything about houses, obviously, and this one is pretty old. You could get some good advice from him."

"Oh, no. I wouldn't want to bother him with that." I brush past her, moving into the kitchen, which is two wooden steps up and out of the sunken living room.

"I know you think that boy hates you, but I'm telling you, con. Ask that boy to jump for you and he'd ask how far."

"The saying is '*how high*,' Mom."

"Whatever. You know what I mean."

"Yeah, yeah."

I fiddle with the sink, turning on the tap just to do something with my hands.

"Oh my gosh?" I turn around at the sound of my mom's surprise. "Is that . . . ?" She's pointing through the front window.

My heart drops into my stomach. It's like my Declan radar never learned to turn off.

"Con, oh my goodness, it is! It's like God heard us!"

I run through the living room to peer over my mother's

shoulder, and look through the window. Sure enough, Declan is walking down the driveway of the house directly across the street. Retrieving an empty trash can from the curb in low-waist jeans and a fitted black tee.

"He doesn't live there, does he?" I ask, voice betraying how much weight I'm putting in the answer. For some reason I pictured him still living with his parents, in the house I basically grew up in.

"Uhhh," she starts, a knowing smirk on her face. "Unless he's dog-sitting, I think that boy lives there."

I sigh.

"September can't come fast enough," I mumble.

My mom gives me a scathing side-eye, but I don't miss the corner of her mouth pulling up as she looks at Declan, walking back inside his house.

Allegedly, his house.

Chapter 14

Many things had come as a surprise in the past month. But enjoying the quiet mundanity of making lattes was a welcome one. It forced me to take each day five minutes at a time: looking the customer in the eyes as I took their order, the crush of the coffee beans, whisking them into obedience, and the iridescent stream of espresso collecting into a shot glass. And when that five minutes was up, it was on to the next. It felt meditative, necessary for the fragile state I was in.

Processing Lottie's death felt like an impossible task, but the cottage she left me felt like a tangible way to *work* through my grief. I saw the two paths as vividly as I could see the milk diluting the espresso in front of me.

On the one hand, my dream house had been dropped into my lap, but it was in a town littered with emotional land mines. I still held on to New York City, because even if it wasn't to support my mom any longer, I was *sure* Lottie's death would become easier to digest. Or, if I was being honest with myself, easier to ignore. Easier to drown myself beneath the crushing weight of work in a city where I'd never made memories with her.

And the other land mine, the one who had hired me, the one with kind eyes and a low voice, the one who literally lived across the street, was the other, more active threat.

Because the thing was, when I *wasn't* in Declan's orbit, the thought of opening myself up to another human being enough to constitute a relationship sounded less appealing than eating an entire pack of Sour Skittles and then swishing peppermint mouthwash around my mouth—which I knew from experience. Filling the hundreds of micro-tears in my gums with stringent mouthwash was such an intense burn; all my thoughts went white.

And wasn't that a microcosm of relationships? All the tiny ways you offer up your soul are left as smoking craters when all is said and done. And regardless, I felt plenty fulfilled working toward retiring my mom and spending time with Roshi and Faye in between. But now that I *was* in Declan's vicinity again, I was acting touch starved—a version of myself so distilled to the point of becoming an unrecognizable, craven being. I felt embarrassed for myself being this affected by him.

But it was an inevitability when it came to Declan. He reminded me of all the ways I had forfeited believing I could meet someone who made me feel seen the way he did. Talking to other people felt like going to turn on a lamp only to realize

JUST FRIENDS

it wasn't plugged in. You expect light, but you're met with awkward clicking sounds instead. For Declan, that light switch was connected to his emotions for me. And they were pointedly off. So, living in the cottage across from him was not an option. Not a healthy one, at least.

The other road was the one I would take, surely. The one that led to New York City in September. The only one I could emotionally handle. Surviving July and August in Seabrook already felt like an impossible feat.

"Hey." The sound of a mousy voice squeaks from behind me. "Blair?"

I turn around, latte in hand, to find Harper. Her white apron is tied around her waist, blond braids resting on each shoulder, and spider lashes opened wide with anticipation.

"Yes?" I say, and regret how suspicious I sound.

"Me and some coworkers are going bowling tonight, and I was wondering if you'd want to join?" She twists her hands in front of her, nervous.

I felt like I'd be crushing a six-year-old's pleas for ice cream if I said no, but I also had zero interest in deepening my ties to anyone here when I'd be gone in two months.

"Uhhh." I scratch the back of my neck. "Which bowling place?"

"Jonny's Pints and Pins on Forth Road," she replies.

"I might need to help my mom tonight, so I'll let you know," I say, hoping I can drift away unnoticed after my shift and then apologize tomorrow when I realized I didn't have her number to tell her I couldn't make it.

Harper seems unsatisfied with my answer, but a man with jet-black hair walks in, and I excuse myself to take his order. I reach the cash register and look up, but my eyes meet his chest. I have to crank my neck back to meet his eyes, and I mentally hear a creaky cartoon sound effect to match the movement. *Is there an NBA team passing through Seabrook?*

The man who wants coffee is wearing a navy button-down, sleeves rolled halfway up his forearms, and tan Carhartt pants. His style is reminiscent of . . . Declan. Gosh, I can't even look at another man without being reminded of him. *Craven, fallen being*, I think to myself.

"Hi, good morning," he says, gaze pinned on me for a second longer than I'm used to. Like he's taking in the totality of my face.

"Good morning," I reply, and pray that my cheeks aren't visibly red from someone so attractive perceiving my existence. "What can I get started for you?"

"I'll do an Americano if it's not too much of a hassle." He smiles, and it causes his scruffy cheek to gather into a dimple.

I *giggle*. The response is so knee-jerk that I feel betrayed by my own body.

"That is no problem at all, sir. Can I have a name?"

"You sure can. It's Calvin," he says like I wanted to know his name for more than a coffee cup.

"Perfect. I'll have that right out." I turn the payment screen toward him and hurry to the bar to make his order, willing the warmth to drain from my face.

Harper sidles up beside me as I start pulling the espresso.

"I see you've met Calvin," she whispers not so subtly beside me.

I shoot her my best side-eye, but she laughs in response.

"And he seems to have taken notice of you too."

"I don't know what you're talking about. I'm a professional. I do not fraternize with the customers," I retort mock sternly.

She leans in further to my side and says, "Well, it looks like he's working up the courage to ask you something when you turn around."

My heart jackhammers.

"Yeah, he probably looks like he's frothing at the mouth because I'm holding the drink he's addicted to."

"Mm-hmm. But he wants to get addicted to youuuu," Harper singsongs as she prances away from my ear.

I shake my head.

It seems Harper has found her in with me: gossiping about boys. Before this, she's been as antsy as a chihuahua around me. I shoot her my deadliest glare, and she smiles with both rows of teeth.

When I turn around, Americano in hand, Calvin is waiting at the bar, eyes already set on me.

It doesn't mean anything. He's just really excited for his Americano, and he doesn't have a scrolling addiction. Which is rare, and that is why his eye contact is startling.

"Calvin," I call as I slide the paper cup across the bar. "One Americano."

"Thank you," he says, swiping the cup. "Oh, it looks like you forgot something."

"Uh-oh! I'm so sorry. What did I—"

"Your number. It seems to be missing." He pretends to inspect the cup, looking under it and spinning it a full revolution in his hands with a look of utter confusion.

Despite myself, I exhale a breathy laugh. I respect his commitment to the bit.

"Wow," I say, fumbling for what to say next.

But a loud thud startles me out of the moment. I turn around to find Declan surrounded by three massive cardboard boxes strewn around the floor.

"Oop," Calvin exclaims, setting his drink down. "Let me help with that."

He lifts the part of the counter that separates me from him and passes through like he's done this before, then crouches down to start gathering the boxes.

"Hey, Calvin," Declan says with a bored look on his face.

"Hey, buddy. Tough day?" Calvin asks.

"Yeah, you could say that."

Calvin stacks the final cardboard box into Declan's arms, making sure they're balanced before taking a step back.

"Alright. You got it, pal?" Calvin says.

"Yup. Got it," Declan replies and continues his journey to wherever he's headed.

Calvin turns around to face me, but he's closer than expected now that he's behind the counter.

I look up at him and gulp.

"I guess I should probably get out of here," he says, shyer than I'd expect him to be capable of.

"I guess so," I reply as I watch him lift the countertop and pass through. "Oh! My number! One second, let me look for a pen."

He exhales and puts a sarcastic hand on his chest. "Thank goodness. I thought I was going to have to ask *again*."

I chuckle and frantically search for something to write with, but I can't find anything. Declan strides past me, hands empty this time.

"Hey," I whisper to him. "Do you have a pen?"

He looks stunned that I'm talking to him for a moment and then says, "Yeah. One sec."

He disappears to the back room and I tap my foot while I wait for him to reappear.

JUST FRIENDS

Sorry, I mouth to Calvin across the bar, and mime waiting for a pen as best as I can.

No worries, he mouths back with a grin.

Declan pummels through the double doors. "Here," he says, handing me a black pen. He starts walking away the second it meets my hands.

"Thanks," I say to his back. He doesn't acknowledge it.

I scribble my number onto Calvin's cup with a smiley face and my name and then slide it over the bar to him. "Here ya go."

He studies it. "Blair. That's a beautiful name." He looks up with a smile and nods. "I'll be in contact."

"Oh, thanks. I will respond to your contact!" I shout as he walks out the front door. "Oh my gosh," I slap both hands over my mouth, wanting to crawl out of my skin.

Harper looks at me from the cash register, a poorly hidden smile blooming on her face.

"I can't believe I just said that," I say to her.

"Honestly, I can't either," she giggles, incapable of sounding mean.

"'I will respond to your contact'? Who says that?"

"You, apparently." Harper looks amused to be in on something with me.

Declan shuffles past me *again*. This man never stops moving.

"Oh, Declan," I call.

He motions with his eyebrows for me to go on.

"Hey, uhm," I start, not quite sure what I was planning to say. *How do you know the man who asked for my number?* didn't really flow off the tongue. "Who's Calvin?" I ask instead.

"Calvin?" he repeats, scratching his eyebrow with a slight head tilt.

"Yeah."

"He owns the auto shop down the road. Comes in pretty often at lunchtime," he says, looking away.

I nod. "You guys pretty close?" I continue, trying to justify my reason for stopping him.

He shrugs.

I nod, slower this time.

He grabs a rag and starts wiping down the countertop, coffee grounds falling off the side.

"Oh, don't worry. I can get that," I say, putting my hand on his arm.

He stiffens slightly and I yank my hand back, embarrassed by my reflex to touch him.

"No. It's fine," he says, returning to wiping, the muscles in his forearm flexing and relaxing with the effort.

"Are overtime hours available for tonight?" I ask. Switching topics seems like a good idea.

"Oh. I can't actually. Everyone's going to Jonny's Pints and Pins after work." He returns to scrubbing the already clean countertop.

I nod again, beginning to turn since I can't think of anything else to say.

"You should come," he adds abruptly, as if the guilt of not inviting me weighed on him in the silence of my turn.

I didn't want a pity invite from Declan. Me being there was probably the last thing he wanted.

"That's okay. I have"—I wave my hand in the air—"stuff to do."

Gosh. That's the best I could come up with? What about 'I have to finish the novel I decided to write' or 'Ernst & Young wanted to do another interview with me for fun because they can't wait for my arrival in September'?

"Stuff?" he repeats, mouth pulling up into a sly grin.

Was he . . . *teasing* me?

"Yep! Tons of *stuff* to attend to," I reply, mouth flattening into a straight line.

"Like what?" he challenges.

"Like . . ." I chew my lip, trying to conjure up a believable response. "You know. I just have some loose strings to tie up while I'm here."

"Right," he allows, eyes looking everywhere but mine, probably searching for a new section of the countertop to clean. "Well, you should really come tonight. As manager I'm supposed to encourage team building and all that," he says in a rush, and then disappears behind the swinging double doors again.

When my shift ends, I find myself searching the back room for Declan as I hang my apron on its designated hook. Cardboard boxes and metal shelving units cover the concrete floors, similar to the back of the convenience store. He's nowhere to be seen.

"So are you coming?" Harper asks as she hangs her apron on the hook next to mine. "To bowling," she clarifies.

"Oh, uhhhh," I stall. Turning her down for a second time seems cruel, and now that the sun was threatening to set, the thought of going home to the house without Lottie in it made my stomach flutter. Grief really did feel so much like fear.

"Yes, actually. I am," I respond.

"No way! Okay, awesome! I'll see you there."

She smiles excitedly and trots away, and I'm left to wonder what I've just agreed to.

Chapter 15

Jonny's Pints and Pins must be new because I never saw it in my eighteen years growing up in Seabrook.

The busy tourist season over the summers has done good things for the town, I suppose, if it means having this bowling alley with an adjoining brewery. And it's strangely leprechaun-themed, which I guess is *good*?

A small group of coworkers from the coffeehouse is huddled together, calling out what size they require for bowling shoes. I don't notice Harper beside me until I feel a tap on my shoulder, and she says, "I'm gonna grab a pint. Want anything?"

JUST FRIENDS

I'm shocked that she's over twenty-one.

"I'm okay," I respond. She nods before scurrying toward the bar.

The lighting is dim. There are radio hits a decade too young to be considered vintage blaring through a tinny speaker. I follow my unlikely group of coworkers to our bowling lane.

"Anyone need bumpers?" a girl named Sonia asks, dark hair sashaying as she looks back and forth at everyone.

I shake my head no. Everyone else does too.

"Just me?" she laughs self-effacingly. "Alrighty, then! Let's bowl!"

I sit on one of the two benches facing each other, politely watching Sonia toss the bowling ball down the lane like a terrified cat, yanking her hands back and squealing when it escapes her fingers. It zigzags dejectedly down the lane, hitting the bumpers a record amount before finally making it to the end. One pin hit.

"Aw, man! How is that even possible? The whole point of bumpers is that you *hit* the pins," she pouts, making eyes at a scrawny kid everyone calls "Grom" sitting across from me. I sense a budding romance forming between them. He's the first person her eyes flicker to every time she makes a joke.

Someone gets up to bowl next, and I look around at the leprechaun-themed scene. Declan said he would be attending, and yet, I don't see a hint of him. I watch Grom pick up a marble-green bowling ball and throw a perfect strike, followed by a girl named Luna, who is so quiet I've never heard her voice, even while taking orders.

When it's my turn, I choose a medium-sized ball and aim for the leprechaun's hat behind the bowling pins, but my body does not follow suit and the ball rolls down the gutter. I make eye contact with Luna as I walk back and we both titter silently.

Harper waltzes back and sets a clear mug filled with an amber liquid onto the table as I resume my spot.

"Oh, hey!" I say, relieved to see her. "Is the bar backed up? What took you so long?"

"How's the bowling going, Blair?" she asks, ignoring my question as she plops down beside me. Her thigh touches mine even though there's enough space to avoid it.

"Pretty good, I think." I point at the TV screen hovering from the ceiling. My name is dead last.

She punches me in the shoulder playfully, eyes a little glossy. "What the heck? Are you some sort of secret phenom or something?"

"Yeah," I say, deadpan. "Professional bowler was the job I was supposed to have instead of this one."

"Really?" she asks, suddenly not understanding the bit. I can smell the alcohol wafting off her breath.

"No." I don't elaborate and lean away, but not enough to where she'd notice, I hope.

I feel more than see Declan's arrival as he ambles over to our lane. His face is serious, the freckle on his lip and neck visible even in the dark bowling alley. I can't choose which one to pay attention to more.

Lip freckle. Neck freckle. Lip freckle.

"Oh *shiiiii*–" Harper sputters, swiping the clear jug off the table and knocking the rest of the liquid back before Declan comes to a stop beside us.

"Harper," he says, voice even like a father who was kind but meant business. "Can we have a word, please?"

Harper only nods, getting up and wiping her mouth with the back of her hand.

She walks in front of him, head hung low as he saunters behind her. His limp is in clear view as he walks away.

JUST FRIENDS

Are you not allowed to drink outside of work? Or is this considered a work event? Maybe she used a fake ID.

I mull over the strange interaction between Declan and Harper, trying to understand what I've just witnessed. Their relationship seemed to go beyond manager and employee. It didn't seem romantic, more sibling equivalent if anything, but that, too, didn't make sense. I'd never seen Harper in all my years growing up here, so where did she come from?

I take my turn to bowl, distracted by my thoughts, and offer a cheer and a whoop to meet the minimum social requirements for my coworkers on their turns. I order a strawberry lemonade from the QR code on our table, and then swipe over to the Apartment 302 group chat.

Roshi

How's being a barista treating you, Blink?

It's the closest thing to "How are you?" I've received from either of them. I spin my thumbs, considering how to respond to the text and the stirring sensation I feel in my chest every time I think about Roshi and Faye. I miss and resent them at the same time.

The ripped leather of the bench sags to the left as someone sits beside me—moss-green carpenter pants and loafers, his fancy shoes. I can tell who it is without lifting my gaze. Isn't it funny to have the ability to recognize someone by the precise position of their legs, the degree each foot faces, the exact angle at which they relax when they sit?

"Where's Harper?" I ask, setting my phone beside my thigh.

"I got her a ride," Declan says, looking at the scoreboard on the screen above us.

"A ride where?" I push.

"Home."

"Why—"

"I think I saw your mom's car parked in my neighborhood yesterday," Declan cuts me off.

I would've kept pushing about Harper had he not taken me so off guard.

"Oh?" I feign shock, considering how I should play this. "What neighborhood do you live in?"

"A little further downtown from the coffee shop. Off Maple and Brickstone." He motions the directions with his hands like an eighty-year-old man.

The sight makes me want to smile before I think better of it and suppress it. Declan always gave the vibe that he was a grandpa inside a young man's body. It was wholesome in a way I could never credit other men being.

"Oh!" I pretend for recognition to hit me in this moment. "Near the beach, right?"

He nods in confirmation.

"Yeah, she was there. I was too, actually."

He looks at me, waiting for me to elaborate. I allow myself one second to stare at the hair falling over his brow in perfect disarray before obliging him. His hair had never decided whether it was blond or brown, so it settled on being both. *And the glasses haven't made an appearance in a while*, I think.

"Lottie, uhm." I clear my throat and feel self-conscious that he'll think I'm incapable of keeping it together at the mention of her. He wouldn't be wrong, and yet. "She left me a house."

He furrows his brow thoughtfully. "The one across the street?"

"Across the street from what?" I ask dumbly, wanting him to spell it out for me.

JUST FRIENDS

"Oh, across the street from mine, I mean." He's the one who looks self-conscious now. "That's where I saw your mom's car parked, at least."

Did you also scan every parking lot for my car, for my mom's car, after we became strangers?

"I didn't know you lived there. When did you move in?" I resist the urge to bite my nails as I wait for his response, wondering if the desperation to know him is emanating off me in cartoon heat waves.

"About two and a half years ago," he says, staring at Grom as he gets up to bowl and then cheering for him as he gets another strike.

Two and a half years ago? He would've been barely twenty, moving into a nice house in downtown Seabrook.

"Did you . . ." I start, trying to figure out a way to ask without prying. "Did your parents sell the other house?"

"No." He runs his hand up his shoulder, messing with his shirtsleeve. I notice the muscles in his shoulder as he presses his arm into the leather between us. "They still live there."

I nod, but I've only become more confused. *Did he buy the house? Did his parents buy it for him? Or is he renting with roommates?*

"How many roommates do you have?" I ask, taking a sip of my lemonade.

"None." He looks at me.

I stare at the hue of his mauve lips. I wish mine were that color naturally. I rub my lips together self-consciously. I see him notice.

"Oh. Cool," I manage. "That's nice, then. Living alone. Having your own space."

Am I usually this bad at conversation?

"Yeah." He shrugs. "It's okay."

I nod to show I've heard him, then swivel my head to Sonia, who needs something more sophisticated than bumpers if she wants to hit more than a single pin. The people around us "ooo" and "aww" in sympathy as the ball discards itself into the gutter yet again.

"Will you live in it?" he pipes up, now looking at me like he's desperate for me to share something. Or maybe I'm imagining that he is.

"The cottage?" I repeat as I figure out how much to share with him.

"Mm-hmm," he confirms.

"No," I snap. "No, I'm leaving in September."

He looks at the scoreboard again and I wonder if he heard me.

"Why?" He returns his ivy-speckled eyes to me.

"Consulting job got deferred, remember?" I did tell him this, right?

"Yeah, but . . ." He pauses, seeming to think for a second. "Now you have the cottage. Why not stay?"

Why would he want me to stay? Especially when it's directly across the street from him? The depraved part of me starts reading into his words like they'll provide what I so desperately want.

"There's not much left for me in Seabrook," I reply.

He stares at me.

A beat.

Two.

So long that I map every section of his irises where it looks like bombs of bluish iridescent shimmer have exploded between pools of sage green. I stare at how the two colors swirl together until I've forgotten what we were talking about.

A waitress comes to offer refills. I hand her my empty

cup. I don't remember tasting a single drop of the strawberry lemonade.

"Would you like anything to drink?" the waitress asks him, blinking a couple times when he turns around to look at her.

"A water would be great, please," he says, voice kind. I get a glimpse of his dimple as he turns back to face me, smile washing from his face like the last suds from a car wash being rinsed away.

"Will you excuse me for a moment?" he says.

"Oh, yeah. Of course."

He stands to greet everyone, and it's in this moment that I realize he hasn't spoken to anyone else here. Even though he's our manager. And this is his event. He sat next to me immediately and showed no interest in joining a different conversation.

I watch with interest as he greets Grom, dapping him up and smacking him on the back like guys do. Sonia and Luna smile at him excitedly, and they all usher him over to grab a ball as they enter his name on the screen beneath mine.

He walks up to the lane with his long legs, rears the ball back, and releases it. It flies down the middle in a perfect line. *Strike*. They all cheer for him, and he spins around, smiling sheepishly. My lungs constrict at the sight of his dimple. He was great at football; I guess I shouldn't be surprised that he is still athletic.

To my shock, he walks back over to me, resuming his spot on the torn leather seat. "So, that Calvin guy from earlier . . ." he starts, brushing his chin in thought. "You guys going on a date while you're here?"

"Hah." I snort. "He's the one with my number, so we'll see."

The question was interesting though. Would I go on a date with him if he asked? In college I would've turned him away without a second thought. No matter how attractive. I was dead set on chasing my independence, not stopping for a moment to hand my heart over to a boy just for him to drop it when he got bored.

But now? The independence I chased wouldn't arrive until September, no matter how fast I ran. Lottie was gone. My friends were across the country. Nothing looked like I thought it would. So, why not do something else out of the ordinary? At this point, I didn't think anything could be as scary as my actual life. The one that existed without Lottie in it. I felt like I was in a horror movie. A boy taking me out and then dropping me would be an interesting side plot at best.

"But, yeah. I think I will if he asks." I reach for my cup, forgetting that I handed it to the waitress for a refill, and put my hand under my thigh instead.

He's silent for a second, looking up at the scoreboard. "He's not worth your time," he says, leaning forward with his elbows on his knees.

I become aware of my heart beating as I try to decode what he's implying. Especially coming from him. Someone who didn't think I was worth his time after an entire lifetime spent together.

"You would know about that, wouldn't you." It flies out before my mouth has a chance to meet with my brain. I watch it land, shoulders flinching as if I've physically thrown something at him. I dig my fingers into the underside of my thigh where he can't see my hands.

"Someone not being worth my time, or me not being worth yours?" he asks, staring at me like my answer will provide his next breath.

His energy is so concentrated on me, I forget there are people surrounding us, drinking, eating, having fun to the beat of pop music. My ears pick up the thud of dropping bowling balls and muffled cheering as if from a hundred miles away. My eyes only see Declan, like the light stops illuminating all else once it reaches the periphery of his solemn face.

"The former," I breathe.

Why did I just admit that? I berate myself internally. But then I picture him sitting on the curb outside Lottie's funeral, face blushing as he referenced the friends he shouldn't have known about. The ones he only knew because he'd checked on me.

I watch his eyes dart from my left eye to my right. Then down to my lips and back up again.

"You've always been worth my time, Blair."

His words feel like a vacuum, sucking up my ability to hear anything else as they reverberate through my ears.

But before I can respond, his phone rings. He stands up sharply and crosses the bowling alley and bar as he takes the call.

I replay his words, but I can't make sense of them.

Why wasn't I worth his time for the past four years?

I glance at the scoreboard, my name still last, and stand up to leave without saying goodbye to anyone. I throw a ten down for my strawberry lemonade.

Chapter 16

"You've always been worth my time, Blair."

I spent the weekend practicing imaginary retorts like, "Really? Is that so? Then explain how I was so worth your time that I didn't hear a thing from you for the past four years."

But he walks in midway through my shift, and what I actually say is, "Hey, um, do you think we could move my overtime hours to tomorrow, by chance?" He looks up, green eyes finding mine, and I feel a click. I have to look back down at the cappuccino I'm preparing to neutralize how aggressively I flinch.

JUST FRIENDS

"If the reason is good enough, I think the boss can make that work," he replies in a dry voice. Was he really being sarcastic right now?

"Right. Well, the reason is tonight is the only time the real estate agent can look at Lottie's cottage with me."

He sidles up next to me behind the bar as I finish pouring the cappuccino into a mug, relaxing against the counter in a way that makes it hard for me to focus. I call out over his shoulder, "One cappuccino for—" I look down at the receipt but there's no name, so I leave it on the bar.

A man with the curliest mop of blond hair I've ever seen comes bouncing up to the counter and takes it with a warm smile. Declan nods in recognition at the man and then crosses his arms, clearing his throat while pinning his focus back on me. "And you have to look at it with a real estate agent why?"

I check the screen for the next order and start pouring beans into a grinder while I say, "Because I'm leaving soon, and I need to figure out what to do with an entire house that was left in my name," I explain. Albeit a bit defensively.

He just nods like he's deep in thought.

The silence stretches as I prepare the next latte. Declan stays perched against the countertop, arms crossed, eyes down, lips pursed, like he's solving a difficult equation.

I glance at him. "Are you trying to figure out your new plans for tonight or what?"

Declan releases a breathy chuckle, dropping his folded arms and then turning to rest his forearms on the bar. "Yeah, something like that. Can't leave this area taped off forever." He motions to the section of unstained wood surrounded by blue painter's tape.

My eyes follow and, in that moment, a thought prickles the back of my mind. It bubbles to the surface like it had been boiling ever since my mom said, *"You could ask Declan for help checking this place out. You could get some good advice from him."*

I could sit here and pretend it was his impressive woodworking skills that made me crave his advice, but I wasn't gullible to my own lies anymore. I wanted to be near him ever since his mysterious comment at Jonny's. His words made me feel seventeen again, wondering why he made his mom turn me away on his doorstep when he got home from the hospital.

"Speaking of . . . building," I start, as unsmooth as a pothole-ridden road. "Would you . . . maybe . . . like, want to stop by and help me figure out if the house is in terrible condition?"

He stares at me from under raised eyebrows. Either he couldn't decipher the words through my choppy way of delivering them, or maybe he was trying to figure out how to let me down gently.

"I mean," I start babbling again. "Because you live across the street and I figured maybe you could pop in, but if you had other plans then just forget—"

"Blair," he interrupts. "What time?"

"Um." I pour milk over the side of the ocean-themed cup at his question. "Like five thirty?"

"I'll see you there." He nods, throws me a rag to clean up the spilled milk, and then moves past me, disappearing into the back room.

The dash of my car reads 5:10. I'm about to back out of the parking lot when my passenger door opens.

"Oh my gosh!" I squeal, my heart rate skyrocketing as I slam on the brakes.

Declan's tall frame bends into view, an unreadable expression on his face. "Sorry."

"I could have run you over," I yell, exasperated.

He presses his lips together like he's holding back a laugh. "Just thought we'd ride together since I walked to work today."

He makes it sound like obvious logic, so I don't bother resisting. "Oh, sure. That's fine, get in."

My eyes don't see the road the entire sixteen-minute drive to the cottage. Every part of my body is buzzing with the awareness of Declan being in my car for the first time since high school. I still find everything with him novel. He could cough, and my brain would inform me it was the first time I'd heard him cough in four years.

Finally, we pull up to the cottage, and I park in front of the sprawling lavender sprinkling the grass like a watercolor painting. "You walked to the coffee shop from here?" I ask, glancing at his house across the street.

"Mm-hmm," he replies, stretching his arms behind him like my car cramped each of his long limbs. "Had a lot on my mind," I hear him mumble.

"The real estate agent should be here any second," I inform him.

He's standing in front of the gravel path like a statue. The sun is hitting him like a spotlight, his hair and dimple gleaming like a cartoon sparkle.

I motion for him to follow but he keeps staring at the house like it's the Mona Lisa. "What are you looking at?" I ask.

He shakes his head like my voice popped his reverie. "Nothing. It's just—it's funny."

I stare at him, urging him to go on in my silence.

"I just—" He waves a hand, looking sheepish all of a sudden.

"I've looked at this house a thousand times through my window. Never thought I'd be walking through it with you."

My eyelids flutter, like blinking will fix my hearing. "Oh."

Moving past him as quickly as possible, I walk up the gravel path. I already have a key, so I open the door, gesturing for Declan to enter. "Well, here it is. We can take a look around while we wait."

Declan bows his head before ducking inside, his work boots causing the wood flooring to creak as he moves through the living room.

He walks the space as if he were at an art museum, looking around with a gleam of grandeur and reverence in his eyes. It's like he's living in equal parts awe and disbelief. "Wow." He exhales. "This design style is one of my favorites. Very 1920s."

"Yeah. That's the first thing I said when I saw it too," I deadpan.

Declan offers me a smirk. He keeps peering around, brushing his finger along cracks in the wall. "I imagine it must be difficult to take it all in."

"What is?"

"This house? The arched doorways." He gestures at them. "That tile in the kitchen? A desk with a bookshelf? It's just like you always wanted. And now it's just . . . yours."

He moves into the bedroom, tracing every square inch with his eyes.

I swallow, but it goes down slowly, the familiar lump of grief forming in my throat.

Yours. I don't want to let that word sink in. To let it make Lottie's death feel permanent, let it settle into my bones.

"Yep," I confirm, following him. "It is kind of freaky."

He pauses his inspection of the bedroom to look at me. "How so?"

JUST FRIENDS

"Just, you know, I don't know. How accurate it is to what I dreamt of having one day as a kid," I confess.

I keep my eyes trained on the sliding doors from the bedroom, scanning the garden through them. Declan follows my line of sight.

He looks back at me with wide eyes and the ghost of a smile blooming on his lips. "Like that?"

I smile before I can hide it and nod.

He opens the sliding glass doors, stepping into the garden and gesturing at the bed of lavender. "A garden right outside your bedroom? Are you kidding me right now?" He makes an exaggerated "can you believe it" face and the sight of his boyish excitement feels like someone shivved me between the ribs.

It was as if he'd kept my dreams safely tucked away next to his all this time. Like whether or not I achieved them was just as precious to him as it was to me.

"Man," he says, gaping, brushing the lavender with his fingertips, the sunlight painting his wavy hair gold. "This is ridiculously beautiful."

I know he's talking about the garden, but he keeps his eyes trained on me when he says it. A warm swath of awareness tingles the back of my neck.

What do you see when you look at me?

He waltzes back into the bedroom, his eyes scanning every inch of the floor, walls, and ceiling once more. The scruff on his jaw, the muscles in his back, and the way he surveys the space make it seem as though he could have built this house with his own hands. *He's so grown up*, I think as I watch him.

"So," he starts. "You want to sell this place? Rent it?"

"Yeah, something like that. I didn't expect to be responsible for a home until I was close to thirty, so I don't really know my options, honestly."

"But you know you don't want to stay?"

"What's here for me?" I laugh without mirth. "My great-aunt surely isn't."

He's silent, hand falling away from the wall.

"She's still here though, in a way," he offers tentatively, like I'm a cat who's easily spooked. "Even in this house."

"Believe in ghosts now, Declan?" I try at humor, but he doesn't allow it.

"No, that's not what I meant." He saunters closer to me. So close that I can see the blue flecks in his irises. "Her memory. Her love. Her charm. It still exists here. You can tell by the way this house is decorated, even. I see so much of you in it."

I clamp my lips together until they're white, emotions getting lodged in my throat. It's the first time I've heard someone other than my mom talk about her since she's passed.

"That's why I have to leave," I choke out. "She's everywhere." *You're everywhere*, I don't say out loud.

He takes another step toward me. Instinctively, I take a step back, but my back meets the bedroom wall. "You don't have to leave," he says, but it's too soft. It comes out more like a plea.

He scans every inch of my face. Eye to eye and down to my lips. I can hear my shaky breath as it escapes.

But I do have to leave, and I can't tell him why. Declan, to me, became like a blade buried deep in my side. Over the years, we fused so completely that removing him from my life seemed life-threatening. And then he was ripped away from me overnight, and I'd been trying to clot the bleeding ever since. How would I survive being near him again when the original wound never healed?

JUST FRIENDS

I dip out of the bedroom and escape to the living room. He follows, returning to inspecting the house without missing a beat.

He saunters up to the bookshelf like he was in the middle of a long walk. "No way," he huffs. "A copy of Divergent? It really is like this house is yours," he says, reaching for it.

"It's a popular book," I deflect, hoping he doesn't find the page I scribbled our initials on.

"What was it you said when the movie came out?" he asks like a dare, flipping through the pages.

I already know what he's referring to by the teasing lilt in his voice.

"You don't look anything like Theo James now," I say.

"Right, yeah. Of course not." He feigns innocence, shaking his head with an ironic, puckered expression. I chuckle. I'm grateful he's distracted enough to put the book back on the shelf. "So, what I'm hearing is that I did look like him, though? At one point in time."

"That one point being as a kid, perhaps. Just a little bit," I allow.

"Hey, I'll take it. To have looked like him at all is an honor."

He squats down, inspecting the cracks snaking along the wall before pacing the living room floor. At the sound of a deep creak, he retraces his steps, bending to press his fingers against the spot. Without warning, he begins jumping up and down, his work boots echoing off the floorboards. I laugh from the shock of it.

"Pier and beam. That's great," he mumbles to himself.

I shouldn't find it intoxicating to watch his face harden in concentration as he inspects the wood floor, as he flicks light switches on and off, as he strides into the kitchen to test the water and stove. The look on his face is so boyish, focused. I remember being obsessed with figuring out how to become the object of that focus. And I had always been a high achiever.

"Still gas powered. That's nice. I don't like all the electric stoves they put in homes these days," he comments.

"How do you know so much"—I gesture at the oven he just tried—"about all this? Houses? Building?"

"What? Turning a stove on and off?"

"No," I spit indignantly. "That's not what I meant."

I can feel him grin. He turns around, hands resting behind his back as he leans on the kitchen sink. This man looks like he was born to lean on things.

"I learned a lot. From the coffee shop," he says, eyes holding mine.

"The coffee shop," I repeat, feeling left out of something obvious.

"Mm-hmm," he hums. "This house is amazing, Blair. Lottie left you quite the gem." He moves on swiftly, exiting the kitchen. There's one small bathroom and a laundry machine closet on the other side of the house.

"Yeah, I agree. She's very quaint, but . . . very nice," I call to his back as I sink into the living room couch. "So, you don't see any glaring problems with it?"

"Eh," he says, voice calm. "Minor touch-ups are probably the only thing you'd need, but they seem mostly cosmetic, which is awesome. The foundation seems sturdy, and I don't feel any uneven spots. All the doors are opening and closing smoothly. That's just my opinion from the naked eye, though. You'll know for sure after getting the inspection done."

That eases the pressure in my chest a little.

"Right. The inspection," I repeat, my obvious lack of knowledge revealing itself.

"Oh, that stuff is easy. I can help you out." He slides the doors to the laundry unit closed and joins me on the living room couch, weight shifting the cushions as he plops down beside me. He throws his arms out, draping the back of the couch, careful not to graze my shoulders. "So, where's your head at?"

I stare at the TV in front of me, trying to ignore the way it feels like an invisible wall of heat is lighting up the skin on my back where his arm hovers, just a slight lean away.

"My head is all over the place if you want me to be honest," I say, dread lacing my voice.

"And I do."

I glare at him facetiously and then look back at the coffee table in front of me, wondering if Lottie's hands touched every item decorating it.

"I mean, this place is beautiful, obviously. Seabrook is beautiful. And now I have a house here that is truly unbelievable. Like in the literal sense. I-do-not-believe-this-is-real-yet, unbelievable. But I'm not taking it for granted. At least, I think I'm not taking it for granted." I exhale. "It just wasn't what I planned. Throwing away everything I've worked for the past four years feels reckless to me. I'm trying to figure out if I can feel what I thought I'd feel there, here."

Declan is silent, and the moment I decide to look at him, I know it's a mistake.

His eyes are deep pools, and I've jumped in. I feel the panic of my feet not reaching the ground.

"I get that."

His words land in my chest with a satisfying click like clock hands overlapping at midnight. He practically spent his entire life working for a career he never got to achieve. He never planned on staying in Seabrook, and yet, here he was.

He probably understood what I was feeling in this moment better than I understood how I was feeling. Our eyes hold for another beat, and I can see him contemplating something. I see the moment something shifts, and he decides to speak.

"Is it okay for me to admit that I'm really glad you're back?" he says in a voice so low it rumbles.

My body buzzes, taking note of his shoulder an inch from mine. My eyes frantically search his face, looking desperately for a clue as to why he would say that. But all they find is anguish, written in the lines by his eyes as they search mine pleadingly, waiting for my response. My mouth goes dry.

"Can I admit something, too?" I say so quietly he has to lean in.

He nods infinitesimally for me to go on, but I bite my lip, not ready for how the air would change if I said what I wanted to.

"You can say it, Blair. I probably deserve it," he urges. The last part is so soft, I think I've imagined it.

"I—" I exhale, frustrated before I've even begun. "I think part of me wants to stay. Just not if—"

"Hi! Hi!" A shrill, high-pitched voice calls as the front door swings open.

Declan stands up slowly, putting room between our bodies on the couch like we weren't just veering toward territory we've avoided for years.

"Oopsies! Already unlocked," she says with a laugh, wiggling the key out of the door. Her blond hair reaches the top of her skirt as she walks through the living room, one stiletto-heeled foot at a time.

At once, I am very grateful that I asked Declan to be here. My mind can't think clearly through the fog of ancient desire and grief coursing through my body.

JUST FRIENDS

She struts up to us at the couch, hair swishing back and forth, texting furiously with long, neon yellow manicured fingers.

"I'm Emily!" she says, mouth parting into a grin as she shakes Declan's hand.

"Declan. Nice to meet you." He gives her a closed-mouth smile. It accentuates his dimple. "And this is Blair. The one this home actually belongs to."

I give her a distracted nod.

"Oh! Perfect. Well, nice to meet you guys. Since I can see that you've already taken a look around, I'm assuming this meeting is because you're ready to put it on the market?"

Put it on the market? The words were a concept I'd heard before, but I couldn't process that the question was being directed at me. My mind was still muddied by the shock of her death and the existence of this house. How was I supposed to decide like it was a game of rock, paper, scissors? Wasn't there a rule about not making big decisions for six months after a life change?

Declan takes notice of the panic on my face and jumps in to respond.

"Actually, Blair is interested in exploring her options before making a decision." His tone is kind but firm. It's the same tone he uses when he's delegating tasks to the employees at the coffee shop. And even through my panic, I find watching him take the reins of the situation without being domineering attractive. Definitely not what I'm supposed to be contemplating right now, I chastise myself.

"Oh, okay!" She stops texting. "Well, for a property like this, you could have a nice nest egg for yourself." She looks me up and down. "Especially for someone so young."

Funny. She didn't look at Declan like he was so young.

"We're looking at about six hundred seventy-eight square feet. Tiny, but walking distance to the ocean in this part of town . . ." She flips through something on her phone. "You're probably looking at about one point two," she finishes, looking up at Declan.

One point two? As in a hundred twenty thousand dollars? That would be *more* than a nice nest egg, that could be enough to—

"Million," Declan clarifies, looking at me.

"MILLION?" I blurt, forgetting myself and the fact that Emily is staring at us.

"I'll give you two some privacy." She manages to look like someone rolling their eyes without actually doing the motion before walking to the kitchen to continue texting.

"M-million? Are you messing with me?" I clamp my hand over my mouth to stop the onslaught of nervous rambling I feel making its way up my chest.

Declan seems to be fighting a smile.

"Why are you laughing? Are you being serious?" I plead.

"I'm sorry. I'm not laughing." He's literally laughing. "It's just, I thought you knew that."

I stare at him, stupefied.

It feels like I'm living in one of those fantasy books where a sixteen-year-old girl is told she just became queen of an entire kingdom because her father died.

"Obviously I didn't know that, Declan! I just graduated college, and my mother and I lived rent-free in Lottie's house our entire lives. How was I supposed to know this tiny cottage was worth over a million dollars!?" I'm trying to whisper-yell so as to not further reveal how ignorant I am to Emily, who is hitting her phone screen so vehemently, I'm shocked her nails aren't chipped.

My head spins with the possibilities of how that much money could change my life—not only mine but my mom's, too. We could be taken care of for . . . life? How fast can two people go through a million dollars? Would I have to pay taxes on that? Also, why is Declan not shocked? Why does he know so much about real estate?

"Was your house a million dollars?" I step toward him conspiratorially, voice hushed so that Emily doesn't overhear.

The question seemed too ludicrous to be answered seriously, but when Declan's face doesn't change, I realize that it's not too ludicrous.

At his silence, it dawns on me. "Oh my gosh. It was."

"We have a lot of catching up to do," he says near my ear, looking over my shoulder to make sure Emily is still busy texting.

"Yeah!" I hiss. "Ya think?"

I could say yes to selling the house right now and move to New York City within the month. This would change everything. But at the same time, if I had that much money, why would I move to New York City? I look at Declan, notice the glisten on his bottom lip, and then remember. Oh yeah. That's why.

But if Declan wasn't in the picture, I had still spent the past four years ignoring myself in order to achieve what I believed would bring me and my mom independence.

Could I still attain that autonomy here? In a house I didn't earn, across the street from a boy I spent my whole life loving, in a city where Lottie's absence was apparent on every street corner? It seemed so . . . painful. But it was painful either way.

Grief swirled in my stomach. I didn't want to flippantly rush my way through this, but the decision felt like a confrontation. One that confirmed Lottie was really gone. I couldn't just leave Seabrook knowing this house was here.

"How much do you think she could charge a month for rent here?" Declan asks Emily.

Without looking up from her phone, she says, "Oh, at least thirty-five hundred. And that's on the low end."

Declan looks at me to gauge my reaction. There's concern pinching his eyebrows, and his bottom lip juts out slightly from the tension.

"And if she wanted to live here? Is it paid off? Property taxes?" He gestures with his hand like, "insert etcetera details."

"The house is fully paid off. You'll still be responsible for property taxes, but luckily for you, California is below the national rate." She says it like I'm not that lucky.

Fully. Paid. Off.

I feel like I'm living in a multiverse. I imagine parts of my body getting stuck; my heart and lungs staying in this house, writing novels by the beach, while my brain and hands go to New York. I mentally glitch back to the present.

"Why don't we discuss this over a meal. You're gonna need some time to process all of this," he says in a low voice by my ear. I feel the heat of his breath brush the sensitive spot on my neck, a strand of hair bristles slightly. In any other scenario, I'd find it suggestive, but I know he's only doing it so Emily won't hear.

I manage a nod.

"Thank you so much for your help, Emily. Blair's going to take some time to weigh her options, but we'll notify you as soon as we decide. Lovely meeting you." He gives her one last dimpled smile. I look at her and nod like, "Yeah, what he said."

"Oh! Okay," Emily stutters. "I'll lock up then. Good luck thinking."

And with that, Declan throws his arm over my shoulder and ushers me out the door. I'm too dazed to notice that his arm is over my shoulders until much, much later.

He walks me through the front yard, which I would usually take a moment to marvel at, but I follow his lead all the way to my car, eyes unseeing.

"Actually"—he gestures for me to switch spots with him—"I'll drive."

"Huh?" I mumble, feeling far away from reality.

"I'll drive. You need to think."

I nod numbly and choose to crawl over the center console rather than get out like a normal person to reach the passenger seat.

I hear Declan's deep, gravelly chuckle from behind me before he sinks into the driver's seat and closes the door.

"Jeez," he says, moving the seat back. "It can't be safe to sit this close to the wheel."

Despite the mix of panic and confusion swirling through me, I laugh. I laugh so hard that I have to place a hand over my stomach to recenter myself. He starts to drive, I'm not sure where, and I keep laughing. I can't stop.

"Blair," Declan says, starting to realize I'm no longer laughing at his comment.

I keep laughing. Tears form in the corners of my eyes.

"Blair," he repeats in a stern voice, but nothing can stop the spiral of emotions I'm descending into.

"Whoo! I'm sorry," I say, wiping the tears that threaten to fall. "This is just too good, isn't it?"

"What's too good?"

"All of this!" I gesture wildly to the houses we're passing. "Look at that house."

He looks to the right.

"One million dollars. Look at that house." I point to the left. "Probably, hmm, let me guess: one million dollars. And guess what else? One of them is mine!" I throw my head back and cackle, the part of my brain that cares about social cues completely short-circuiting.

Declan is silent, his jaw muscles clenching as he lets me experience this weird stress response. First, laughing at the funeral, and now this? I was learning new things about myself.

"Oh, and even better. You own one of them too." My voice takes on a quality I've never heard before. It's biting, the way I knowingly remark on something unspoken between us, traces of anger peeking through.

"Blair." He places a hand on my shoulder. "I know this is all really overwhelming."

"Yeah!" I cut him off. "And you know what else is really overwhelming about the whole thing?" I don't wait for him to respond. "The fact that you were my best friend my entire life and now I don't even know how you ended up in the house across from mine. It's actually kind of funny if you think about it. I mean, what are the odds I don't see you for four years and then suddenly my aunt dies and I live across the street from you? It's like the world's practical joke on us. You just can't escape me even after stonewalling me out of your life like I was a disease you needed to avoid. But you know what's even worse? What's worse is the fact that I still feel our . . ." I can't conjure words for the first time during my outburst. "I still feel our . . . our bond." I wave my hands ironically like I'm describing something make-believe. "I don't know, Declan. I just want to know how we ended up like this."

I say it all. Everything I've been holding back since seeing him again for the first time. I say it to the side of his frustratingly perfect profile in one broken, garbled mess as he stares at the road.

Silence stretches on, the sound of tires bumping down the road our only song.

I'm so occupied with the tension that I don't realize he's slowed down until we're pulling off the road and into a neon-lit drive-thru.

I recognize it as Murphy's Drive-Thru. A local favorite. *Our* local favorite. At least, it used to be. We'd come here twice a week sometimes, ordering greasy burgers and thin fries, sharing a milk shake over the middle console, talking about our futures or making fun of the town's famous hippies walking by.

"And that's why we," he says, pointing between him and me, "are going to talk." He pulls into the line of cars waiting to place their order. "But not before getting some food in us."

"I don't need food right now."

"Mm-hmm," he hums drily.

I scoff.

"Hey, Jesse," he says to the six-foot-three teenager dressed in a red apron and hat, black iPad in hand. "Can I get two cheeseburgers Murphy's way with two sides of fries? And then one Oreo milk shake, please."

When he finishes paying and pulls up to the next window I say, "How do you know my order is still the same?"

"Is it not?" he asks, looking at me sideways through thick lashes.

I look away. "No, it is," I admit in defeat.

I swear I can feel him smile.

He collects our order and pulls into a parking spot. He unwraps our burgers and balances the fries on the dash, fitting two red straws into the Oreo milk shake.

He hands me my burger. "Here you go. Just like you like it."

My angry confusion melts at the sight of the greasy burger, soft sesame bun enclosing a perfectly cooked patty and gooey cheese. Murphy's way is their secret sauce (which is likely just a variation of Thousand Island) and french fries stuffed between the patty and cheese.

"Thank you," I mumble before snatching the red-paper-wrapped burger from his hands like a grumpy tween. Turns out, you can't snatch a burger from someone's hand without looking dumb.

We eat in silence. The sun droops lower and lower in the sky, turning the dusty fence in front of us a thousand shades of brown. When the sun makes its final performance before slipping beneath the sea, it casts its warm yellow rays over the entire town, enveloping the cozy cottages and sea-worn buildings in its golden embrace like a massive hug.

"Okay, Blair," Declan starts, wiping his hands with a napkin and crinkling the wrapper. "Let's talk."

Chapter 17

I blink at him through the harsh car light. The sun has retired, leaving us in the dark.

"Do you want me to explain how I ended up in that house or—"

"I want you to start at the beginning," I cut him off.

He studies me like he's unsure if he should.

"Okay." He looks like he's calculating something. "The beginning meaning the accident, I assume?"

I nod.

He brushes a hand down his face, eyes going distant like he was returning to that brisk December evening. "Well, you know how it starts. I'd just won state championships for the third year in a row, and everything just goes chaotic after a win like that. The band was playing. Confetti was popping. My teammates were screaming, slapping me on the back, picking me up. I mean, you know. You've been there. It was the typical stuff, and that part is all a blur now."

I was there, I think, but don't say. I watched that part. It's the stuff after that I've tried to picture for years—made a disjointed, stitchwork Frankenstein of the memory that felt like mine by envisioning it a million times over. My breathing becomes labored in anticipation of hearing the words from Declan himself.

"My teammates urged me to get to my car quickly to be the first at High Tide Diner. You know how everyone went there to celebrate?" He raises his eyebrows.

I nod mechanically.

"If we didn't get there first, we'd be blocked out of our own celebration from the crowd. So, I started beelining it across the parking lot."

I've dug my nails into the center console without realizing it, but Declan continues like it's a funny story.

"I ran into Cole on my way to my car. He was shouting, 'Congratulations, Dec! I'll see you in the NFL,' then I put my helmet on to make some joke, but his face went pale like he'd seen a ghost behind me. I was confused because my peripheral vision was gone after putting the helmet on, and when I turned around, I saw a car speeding around the corner. It was already so close. I've tried replaying this part in my head so many times, tried to slow it down and remember what I saw in those last few moments. It happened so fast, but in the few seconds I had before the car hit me, everything slowed down. It was like in the movies when something explodes and your hearing goes out; time itself seems to stand still. I thought that was, you know, for cinematic effect, but apparently, it's pretty accurate." He *chuckles*. "The car itself looked like a red blob, but the top was down, and I could see the kids inside. And that's pretty much the one thing that's still so vivid, after all these years—the way their faces dropped when they realized they were going to hit me. They were laughing so hard until they weren't. And then I woke up in the hospital."

He pauses to look at my face as a tear escapes and I have to cover my mouth. I wasn't expecting to react so viscerally. I'd spent over four years with the outline of this story. And I'd imagined it so many times it started imitating memory. But it paled in comparison to the vivid colors Declan was using to fill it in.

"Are you okay?" he asks, going to touch my shoulder.

"Yes, I'm fine," I say, steeling myself. "Please, continue."

"Okay," he says, offering a small smile.

I'm aware that he shouldn't need to comfort me during the retelling of his getting hit by a car, so I clamp my lips together and will my tear ducts to dry.

"Well, when I woke up in the hospital, I remember slowly blinking awake to a weird white room with beeping monitors. And then a nurse started firing off questions, asking me how I felt and what I remembered. I basically told her what I just told you." He subconsciously rubs his jaw.

"Then, the doctor came in. He told me my left hip shattered upon impact. My left femur was broken, along with a dislocated shoulder. Oh, and I had a concussion," he adds.

"The doctor smiled as he said this next part. He said I was 'extremely lucky,'" he says with quotation marks. "As there was no internal bleeding and seemingly no damage at all to my brain or spinal cord. Which, I agree, of course. The odds of me putting my helmet on seconds before getting hit are unbelievable. I'm grateful for that. And I still can't remember why I did it. Can't remember what the joke was going to be. But . . ." His face falls.

"My entire life, as I knew it, was over in a single moment. They said I'd be bedridden for at least six months, with physical therapy after that. A hip break as severe as mine took at least a year to recover. And I'd probably still have a limp when I did recover." He pauses. "But the first thing I asked after all that was if I could still play football. *I need football to keep my dad happy*, I remember thinking. And you." He looks at me, and my heart protests in my chest. "I thought about you, about our fight. The way I—" He shakes his head, collects himself, and then backtracks.

"Anyways. The doctor . . . he just gave me this, like, sad little half smile. That's when I knew. Football wasn't in the cards for me anymore. Everything I worked for my entire life . . . *poof*. Just like that. I didn't believe him at first. I was winning my third state championship just a few hours ago.

I was going down the path to play professionally and have multimillion-dollar contracts thrown at me, and then the next moment, everything went black, and I woke up with none of that? The thing I built my entire identity on was just gone in an instant. And yet, I was still here. Still had to go on without the thing that made me who I was."

Everything he's said before this sounded rehearsed. Probably from having to tell it so many times. But this last part seems to rip new emotions to the surface. I can see him tensing his jaw, trying to stay composed. He stares at the steering wheel like he's waiting for his body to stop betraying him. Seeing his face like this, the agony as he relives it, I can't sit and watch any longer. I hurl myself over the center, gather him into a hug, and sob into his neck, unable to stop the tears at this point. Maybe sometimes it was okay to let people see you cry on their behalf. It was a small way to show you glimpsed the pain they'd experienced.

"I kept staring at the door—the hospital room door and then my bedroom door—hoping you would walk in any second, and terrified that you would." His words are muffled by my neck.

"Why—what do you mean by 'terrified that I would'?" I ask, pulling back and settling into the passenger seat.

He rolls his bottom lip into his mouth like he's tasting the response. "Because—" He stops, shakes his head, and starts again. "Because I was angry at you for how you left us. But also, because I was angry at myself for telling you to trust me. To rely on me because of my future in football. And then there I was, lying in a hospital bed, never going to play football again. I couldn't picture looking you in the eyes after that."

I stare at his pained expression, trying to make sense of my warring emotions.

"I'm so sorry for walking out on you during that fight, Declan. I didn't think that was the end. I thought we would just take a few days to cool down and then work it out like we always did." I wipe tears from my eyes. "I've thought about it almost every day since. I never would have done that if—" I shake my head. "There was no way for me to have known that was the last time I'd see you. You have no idea how sorry I am for that. I've spent every *second* of the past four years feeling sorry about that. I wish I would have done a million things differently. But I'm not the only one to blame."

His jaw muscle ticks. "*You just left.* You walked out. And it was from me telling you to follow me to college, which I regret now, *of course*. But I don't think you understood that I chased my football career because I loved it, yes, but when it came to you, I only loved so much because it could provide for us. That was my way of loving you; being able to provide for you. But you took it like a slap to the face."

"I didn't take it like a slap to the face," I retort.

He presses his lips together. "You practically accused me of being your father."

I flinch at his words. "I know that sounds harsh, Blair, and I'm sorry but—"

"No," I interrupt. "I did do that. But I think we both know by now it was more about me not becoming my mother than you being anything like my father."

Declan blinks at me, unsure if my words are an olive branch. They were intended to be.

"But regardless, I wanted to save us. I was willing to do long distance. I was willing to make it work. But you didn't even want to *try*. It seemed like the requirement to be with you was giving up my dreams to follow yours or nothing at all," I say, voice surprisingly calm despite the emotion rising in me.

"That's not true, Blair. Not at all." He straightens in the driver's seat, leaning over the center console. "I believed I was supporting your dreams by chasing mine. You were going to give up being an author because of the money. I was trying to solve that by going and making the money! And look, you went your way and . . ." He trails off, but the unspoken words have already left their mark.

"And what? Here I am in Seabrook working for you?"

"No, that's not what I meant," he says, regret weighing heavy on his face. "I wanted to make your dreams come true. And then I lost mine overnight and I couldn't imagine facing you. It felt like the ultimate confirmation of my failure, so I

JUST FRIENDS

just—I couldn't. But I get it. Those were horrible reasons to block you out and I understand why you couldn't forgive me—"

"Who said anything about not forgiving you?" I ask, rearing back. "I don't blame you for a second for feeling like that, Declan. Even if I completely disagree with your logic. I just wanted you to let me in when I was at your door and ready to sit at your bedside. I would have done anything you needed if you would have opened that door." I scoff. "Or at the very least, I'd have liked to . . . I don't know. Get a text back?"

"What do you mean?" he says, eyebrows furrowing.

"What do you mean, 'what do you mean'?" I counter. "I would have forgiven you for anything Declan. It's *you*."

His eyes home in on me like he's trying to read the subtitles of a foreign film.

I look around inside the car with a quickening heartbeat, trying to understand why he looks so confused, but nothing has changed. We're still cloaked in darkness and the flickering neon glow of Murphy's Drive-Thru. "What . . . what's wrong—"

"Then why didn't you ever write me back?" he asks, eyes widening.

"What do you mean, write you back?" I ask slowly, a pit opening in my stomach.

He sighs, throws a hand over his face, and drags it down. "My letter?"

My eyes bulge. "Your letter? What letter? What are you talking about?"

"You never got it," he states, face turning grave.

"Got what, Declan? You're freaking me out."

"I sent you a letter. Apologizing. Asking you if—" He stops as if cut off.

"Asking me what?" I plead, getting exasperated.

"Asking you if you wanted to . . . see me. To talk things out? I don't know, it was a long time ago at this point," he says quickly, looking defeated. Or maybe he was embarrassed?

I stare at him, half in horror and half in hopeful disbelief as the gears of my heart start squeaking back to life. His eyes stay trained on the steering wheel.

"Wh—" My voice wavers, but I manage to ask, "What were you apologizing for in the letter?"

He looks up at me, like I've just altered his entire reality. I hold my breath with the hope that he's about to change mine. "I was apologizing for being angry at you," he says in a measured voice. "I was apologizing for not being able to see things from your perspective. I was apologizing because you were right. You couldn't rely on me, and I was sorry that I ever asked you to. And I was apologizing because I let my pride keep you from seeing me in that state. And I lost you because of it."

He lets the words tumble out like they were waiting behind his teeth, glad to be let free. His eyes are sad, pulled down at the corners with regret. My heart keens painfully in my chest as I withhold myself from reaching over the console to brush his cheek with my thumb.

"What? Why didn't—" I shake my head, cutting myself off in confusion. "If I had gotten that letter, I would have forgiven you, Declan."

He looks up at that, and his face slowly lights up with fragile hope. Tentative, like it might not be solid enough to put his weight on. I feel the same fragile hope blooming in me, but then, his face dims like an intruder broke into his mind and turned off the lights.

"That's nice to know." He releases a disbelieving laugh, looking down at his lap. "Nice to know that you *would* have forgiven me. *If* you had gotten my letter. But you just . . . didn't?"

I'm breathless as I situate myself into a straighter position. "Do you not believe me?"

"You just, what? Didn't get it? Do you not check your mail, or did you move dorms or did—"

"No!" I insist. "I didn't! And I did check my mail. I *do* check my mail. Letters get lost all the time, Declan. I think *I* should be the one wary that this letter even exists."

He laughs while looking down, the waves in his hair bouncing a bit. I'm not in on the joke. "It exists, Blair. I can assure you. I wouldn't forget writing a letter like that."

"Okay. Well, why didn't you ever . . . I don't know. Like, call me? Perhaps *a text message* would have sufficed?"

"Because I thought you—" He presses his lips together. "You would understand this if you read the letter, but I thought your lack of response *was a response*. I thought I was carrying out your wishes by letting you move on without me."

Maybe it was sweet, and I should have felt relieved, but four and a half years of pacing around, glancing at my dark phone screen, hoping against all hope that he was going to walk through my dorm room's door bubbles to the surface.

"I've spent the last four and a half years believing you wanted *nothing to do with me*." I cry, my dignity deciding it has no use in comparison to the truth I've been hiding for years. "Do you know what that feels like, Declan? To have your entire existence intertwined with someone for twelve whole years, and then get it ripped away from you overnight? To think that after everything we shared, I was easy to block out and move on from like some . . . distant, inconvenient, forgettable memory?"

My voice echoes through the small car and I'm left heaving

like I've just run a mile. He doesn't look up at me, and the carriage of his body goes stiff. It's like he's using every ounce of willpower not to leave the car.

And then, finally, his face softens, and when he looks at me, I notice a slight glisten in his eyes. "Yes, Blair. I do. I know exactly what that feels like."

His words clang against me like waves slamming a cliff.

Could it have been true, that through all these years, he was feeling exactly what I had been feeling? All those nights I spent in a heap of tears, picturing him living blissfully without me, had he been doing the same? Because of a letter I never responded to that I never received?

"I'm sorry I didn't get your letter. If you felt anything close to what I felt, then . . . that *sucks*. That really, really sucks." I heave a laugh in place of tears. "Truthfully, I should have reached out again but I—I was being . . . passive. I waited on you to come to me like I was waiting for my dad to show up all over again. I was, I don't know, testing you, I guess." The admission barely makes its way out. "But I hope you realize, Declan, I never held anything against you. I thought you were holding something against me."

He looks down, shakes his head. "I don't know if I should laugh or cry right now." A laugh so weak it could pass as a cough escapes him, and then he looks back at me. "I wasn't holding anything against you either, Blair. Not at all. *Man*—" He grips the back of his neck, pressing his lips together. "I'm so sorry for all the time we lost." His voice is filled with regret so deep it sounds like anger. Both of his eyes fill as they look at me, and mine follow. I wonder if I've become a blurry mess in his vision, too.

We both let quiet tears stream down our faces in the weak neon glow. Declan reaches his hand through the space between us and wipes my jaw free of a tear. The dimple in my chin presses in to prevent more from spilling.

"So, what do we do?" I ask, helpless.

I want everything from him and don't have the slightest clue how to begin getting it. Every year. Every lost year. I want it back. I want us to spend every foreseeable second together until the memory foam of our bodies returns to their forgotten positions. I want to come *home*.

"Let's try to be friends again," he offers gently.

The corner of his mouth flickers into the suggestion of a smile before faltering, waiting for my reaction.

Friends. Right.

The thickness in my throat turns to cement, but I try to swallow past it and smile.

"Yeah," I sniffle. "Friends. Let's . . ." I nod and I don't stop.

He dips his head to try and catch my darting eyes. I still. I try to offer him my best smile. He laughs a little, and I pocket the sound to unfold tonight. He turns his head sharply to look at the dash. I follow his eyes: 9:59 p.m.

In the cold silence, I can hear "Drive" by the Cars playing faintly through the speakers.

"I didn't hear the music this whole time," I say quietly, almost to myself.

His eyes flit up to the dash. "Me neither," he replies.

Declan looks at me again, and this time, it's different from how he looked at me when we first got in the car. It's unhurried, lingering.

"I'm going to drive you home now, Blair," he says softly before putting his seat belt on and putting my car in reverse. "You've had a long day."

My mind berates itself as I buckle myself in and face forward.

Friends. That horrible feeling of free-falling in my stomach was precisely why hope was so dangerous. You couldn't allow it in. Not even a little bit. Because I'd spent four and a half years getting rid of hope, trying to make the reality of his rejection sting less, only for one conversation to let hope seep in through the cracks and tear everything wide open again.

Chapter 18

My fictional characters are seconds away from leaning in for their first kiss when my mom comes scurrying into the back room of the convenience store. I'm sitting on an upside-down crate, laptop open to the manuscript I've been writing since the funeral, with zero sense of how long I've been lost in my fictional world. Long enough to feel my butt bones tingle with numbness from digging into the plastic-waffle gridding of the crate.

"Honey." She shuffles toward me with a smile on her face, and I slam my laptop shut. "Look what I just found." She stretches out her hand, revealing a film photo small enough to fit in your back pocket.

I hold it up for inspection. It's a grainy image of Lottie, twenty years younger, and a small girl standing by her side in front of a house. My mom circles behind me, peeking over my shoulder at the photo.

"Recognize anything?" she questions, with the obvious implication that I should.

"Is it . . ." I bring the photo up for closer investigation. "Oh, that's me! And . . . is that the cottage?" I point to the terra-cotta pot that's taller than I am in the photo.

"Yep! You have been to the house. Even if you don't remember it," my mom practically squeals.

The cream-colored arched doorway was difficult to recognize in its pristine condition. Now, it was almost completely overtaken by the lavender bushes that seemed larger than the house itself.

It didn't seem possible, but perhaps the wave of déjà vu I felt entering the house for what I thought was the first time, was my body's memory of it.

"Well, anyways," my mom sings, "just thought you'd like to have that. What a full-circle moment now that it's yours, huh?"

"Yeah, no, definitely, that's . . . that's wild." I try to sound cheerful despite the agonizing swirl of "should I live there, should I not" stirring in my stomach. "So full circle."

A phone starts ringing on the desk that used to be Lottie's. She scurries over to it, platform sandals squeaking as she goes. I notice the way her face shrinks in consternation the way it always has.

"Hello," she says, voice wary.

She listens to the person on the other end, eyebrows crunching and lips thinning into a hard line. I could cross-stitch that expression on her face from memory.

"Yes, I hear you. Okay, yes, um," she says, fumbling to put the phone between her ear and shoulder while she searches for her pocketbook calendar. "I'm so sorry. It looks like I got one of the locations mixed up and . . ." She pauses to listen. "Yes, once again, I am so sorry. It won't happen again. Okay, bye."

She sets the phone down slowly, like she's in a daze, and starts picking at her hair. It's a stress response I've watched her resort to my entire life. As if her thoughts were connected to the strands of her hair, tugging at them like the movement might bypass her skull and untangle her thoughts.

"Mom?" I call. "Everything alright?"

"Yes! Oh, yes, all good!" she says in her fake peppy voice, turning her back to me to avoid meeting my eyes.

Okay, so . . . definitely not "all good."

"Do you need help with anything? I don't have overtime hours tonight."

She pauses for a long moment with her hands on the desk. I expect my efforts to offer help to be brushed past like they have been my entire life, but all of a sudden, her silence is interrupted by a stiff gasp for air. Like she can't breathe. Oh, gosh. Something is happening to her. My first instinct is to wonder how she's choking when she wasn't eating anything. But then her shoulders erupt into tiny spasms as she covers her mouth, and I realize she's crying. And trying with all her power not to. It was such an unprecedented event, I thought choking more probable than tears.

"Mom?" I ask, rushing to her side.

"Sorry," she mumbles through a sob, keeping her head bowed.

"Are you okay?"

She manages a nod, but her eyebrows crumple beneath another wave of tears.

"Mom, come here."

Her head is buried in her hands, but I pull her tiny frame to my body regardless.

My mom is crying, my brain narrates to itself, unable to believe it. I've never seen my mother cry. And I discover that she does so very silently, other than the jolt of an inhale punctuating the space every now and then.

"Don't resist the tears, Mom. It'll be worse if you're all tense. Just let it out."

Her body relaxes in my arms slightly. Which from her, feels like progress.

"I'm sorry, con." She wipes at her eyes and pulls away from me. "It's just been a lot with the convenience stores now that Lottie is . . ." She trails off.

"Gone?" I offer.

She nods quickly.

"I've overlapped or forgotten to schedule multiple employees for their usual hours and every time it feels like I've just messed up their entire livelihoods, and I feel so bad. I didn't think managing seven locations would be easy, but this is—"

She shakes her head. In the silence, I'm aware that this is where I'm at risk of losing her. What she's admitted in the past two minutes surpasses anything she's ever communicated in the past twenty-two years.

"Mom, let me help you," I blurt, before evaluating the logistics of that offer. Especially after last night, I'm even more confused about the house and where I stand with Declan. But my mom was priority above all those feelings. Making myself uncomfortable so that she wouldn't have to be was easy after a lifetime of seeing her give up everything for my happiness.

"No, no, no, no. I'm sorry for burdening you with this, con. I should have never done that in the first place." She waves at the space she was crying in as if it'll push the memory away like a cloud of smoke. "I'll figure it out, it's okay."

All her effort trying not to burden me worked when I was a child and didn't have the full context to understand. But now, I saw everything, and I felt burdened by her inability to accept help.

She starts to head back to the front of the convenience store, and I realize if I want her to accept my help, I can't just offer it.

"Hey, Mom?" I call to her retreating form.

She pauses. "Yes, sweetie?"

"Email me the log-in for the master schedule. I'll be in charge of it from now on."

"Sweetie—"

"Nope," I interject, walking up to her and grabbing her shoulders. "Don't you dare bother with trying to convince me otherwise. I want to do this. So, please. Do me a favor and let me."

She gives me a soft smile, and the way her shoulders melt under my hands bolsters my decision even further. This time, she's the one to pull me in for a hug, and it feels like the sun warming my skin on a chilly day.

I lose track of time holding her, bodies intertwined in the back room of a convenience store that once belonged to Lottie, surrounded by cardboard boxes of candy and soda. Without her saying it, I know that my mother feels like she's failed me. Believes it was weak to let her daughter catch her in a moment of pain. But she doesn't know how relieved I feel seeing her cry.

She was the only other person who'd felt the cataclysmic shift of life before and after Lottie. I felt isolated in those memories, and it was eating me from the inside out. But seeing that I wasn't alone after all made it seem bearable.

We were both carrying the same weight up the same mountain. Both refusing to share the burden, thinking that shouldering it alone would spare the other. And yet, it only made it heavier for both of us.

I look at the photo over her shoulder, staring at Lottie's smiling face and the tiny version of me clinging to her leg, and let it cement the decision churning inside me. New York City was about helping my mom, but staying in Seabrook could be too.

"Blair?" My mom swings open the door to the back room of the convenience store two hours later. I'm still on the same red crate, in the flow of writing my romance novel, with a new tab open to the convenience stores' master schedule sheet.

"Yeah?" I shout.

"Someone is here for you." She nods toward the front of the store.

My eyebrows furrow in suspicion, and I awkwardly stand to follow her.

A few customers are milling about the small store. The cash register is left useless without my mom running it. My eyes scan the aisles, but I don't see anyone.

"Who is it—" I start to ask, but my mom raises her eyebrows and flicks her eyes behind me. I spin around.

Declan is standing by the ice cream freezer, wearing a tan Carhartt jacket and a small smile.

"Hey, Blair," he says gently.

In a panic, I look back at my mom, only to find a poorly

hidden grin on her face. She drops it in an instant and scurries back to the cash register.

"I'll leave you two to it. And don't worry. My ears are closed!" she shouts with her hands over her ears like a child.

"Oh my gosh." I drag a hand over my face, feeling like a teenager again. "You don't need to close your ears, Mom. We're . . . we're just friends." The words feel like sandpaper coming out of my mouth. But I do my best to neutralize my expression and turn back around to face Declan. "Do you want to . . ." I jerk my head indiscreetly at the front door.

He nods with his lips pressed together like he's holding back laughter and follows me to the metal bench in front of the store. I situate myself on the cold metal and try not to let the confusion show on my face.

He relaxes beside me like he's been lounging for hours and digs into his jacket pocket.

"I know this is abrupt, but . . ." He reveals a folded piece of paper and stretches it toward me. Gingerly, I take it, conscious not to let our hands brush. "Last night I was sketching renovations for the coffee shop, and then I got to thinking about the layout of the house Lottie left you. And—I can only imagine how difficult it's been to process her death and the fact that she left you a house here, especially when you thought you'd be in New York City right now, so I thought sketching some of the potential improvements you could make to the cottage might"—he shrugs his shoulders—"might help bring the vision to life, let you picture yourself in there more. But no pressure either way. I just like sketching stuff in my free time, so don't feel like you have to—"

I laugh. I interrupt the sweetest thing I've ever heard with a laugh because I've never seen Declan so flustered before.

"I'm gonna shut up now." He looks down with a grin on his face.

I've never seen him even slightly self-conscious, and the sight makes me flustered. "Sh—should I open it now?"

He nods generously. "Yeah. Oh, yeah."

Peeks of sketches flash until the paper is fully unfolded to reveal a perfect, hand-drawn blueprint of the cottage. My eyes dart around the sketch. He's drawn the layout of the house in pencil, and his ideas for what could be changed or added are written in pen. Little arrows jut out to the text, and for some reason, it's picturing him drawing those little arrows that sends me over the edge.

"Declan, this is—" A lump forms in my throat. "This is gorgeous. And so thoughtful. I don't know what to say. Thank you doesn't even begin to cut it."

"Nothing to cut," he replies in a delicate voice. And then, in a surlier tone: "Except, maybe some walls in that tiny house. Cut those doors off the laundry section there and free up some space. Sounds difficult, but it's all easier than it looks."

I chuckle at his insouciance, and we let our eyes meet. They hold for a beat. Two. My smile fades, but our eyes remain locked, and the tingle that shoots down my spine feels much too intimate for the moment. I rip my eyes away.

"Okay, well." He pushes off his thighs to stand up. "I'll let you get back to . . ." He waves his hand at the convenience store.

"Writing," I blurt for a reason unbeknownst to me.

He falters in his retreat, eyes lighting up with surprise. "Writing?"

I nod, sheepish.

"You're writing again?" His entire face brightens. "What are you writing about?"

JUST FRIENDS

You, my mind screams like a juvenile.

But out loud, I shrug and say, "I'm trying to write a romance novel. And I'm forcing myself to finish it this time."

I'm shocked at the confession. I haven't told anyone else yet. Lately, I've been having more conversations with Declan than my actual friends.

His smile fades, and I stare at his lips, the ones that always look like they've just eaten fresh cherries. I think about the way I've kissed him a thousand times through the pages of my book. His eyes press into mine so hard I'm surprised they don't pin me to the convenience store wall. "That's good, Blair," he says, voice suddenly strained. "That's really good."

I'd never heard a statement sound so much like "I'm proud of you" without saying the words.

I offer him a grateful smile. He nods repeatedly and walks backward, raising his hand to say a wordless goodbye.

And then I'm left in front of the convenience store I was raised in, with a blueprint of Lottie's cottage in my hands, the matured form of my first love walking away.

Chapter 19

There are aspects of myself that are unrecognizable since Lottie's passing. Things I would have considered "out of character" two months ago are now my natural dispositions.

For example, calculating how long I have before seeing another human being to make sure I have enough time to cry without my face looking blotchy. Or constantly thinking about what Roshi and Faye are up to. Or most notably, my inability to spend an entire day alone. Like right now. I took the day off work to figure out what I'm doing with the cottage, but I find myself searching for something to procrastinate with instead of facing the life-altering decisions I have before me. My mom has zipped off to one of the convenience stores to start some litany of never-ending tasks, so she's not around for me to bother, and I've already opened my manuscript and stared into the void of the blank white page and blinking cursor for long enough to count as "writing."

Usually, I'd go on a run or journal or do any other number of things I used to find bearable before this gnawing sensation of anxiety opened in my stomach at the thought of Lottie not being around. At the thought of my world being irreversibly changed.

So, that's how I ended up on the cottage's doorstep. Alone. I've visited with both my mom and Declan. But perhaps taking it in by myself will help move the decision-making process along. Especially after seeing my mom cry for the first time yesterday, leaving Seabrook was starting to sound like a lofty concept from my previous life. The one that had Lottie in it.

As I'm unlocking the door and stepping inside, an incoming call from Roshi lights up my phone.

Huh. It is her first time calling me since Lottie died, the part of my brain teeming with resentment remarks. But what was I expecting? Was I going to continue measuring her by some impossible measuring stick? You didn't call me then, so if you call me now, I won't pick up.

I hit answer.

"Hey, Rosh," I say as the door swings open.

"Blink!" she trills. "Ugh, I've missed you! Sorry I haven't called. Prep for law school has felt precariously close to actual law school. But how is everything? Fill me in!"

Her voice is so excited, but my updates for her aren't. How do I begin to tell her that every section of my life feels shrouded in hurt and indecision? In the four years we've been friends, I'd never been the type to be emotional. How would I start now?

As I'm mulling it over, I've already allowed too long a pause to stretch on as I step into the quiet living room.

"Blink?" Roshi says wearily. "You alright?"

And those two words are all it takes for everything to come gushing out.

I stare at the bookshelf attached to the small desk, lined with books Lottie bought for me as a child, and in a tiny, breaking voice, I say: "No." A sniffly inhale punctuates the word. "I'm not alright."

"Oh, Blink," she coos in sympathy. "No, don't cry. Or do cry but tell me everything."

And so I do. Falling onto the cream-colored couch I was on a mere eighteen hours ago with Declan, I tell her everything about the cottage, the convenience stores, and the letter I never received. And for the first time, I let Roshi listen. And she does. It shouldn't have shocked me, but I had excluded the possibility before giving her the chance.

"He made you a blueprint?" Roshi shouts.

For some reason, my first instinct is to duck, as if Declan can hear her from across the street.

"Yes, Rosh. And it's probably twenty times cooler than you're picturing it to be. It's beautiful." I stare at the unfolded drawing on my bent knees.

"And you're not asking this man to pull out his tool kit and come over right this second . . . why?" She adds an ironic lilt to her voice, and I picture her right eyebrow rising like it always does when she thinks I'm being an idiot.

"Because!" I cry, indignant. "The conversation ended with us agreeing to be friends again. Just friends, Roshi!"

"Okay? And do friends not help each other renovate houses after literally sketching the blueprint?"

"Well, maybe they do. But . . ." I exhale, frustrated and

unpracticed at forming the words. "Apparently, this letter that he tried sending me was, like, an apology? He was asking to meet up and work things out, I'm assuming, based on the way he was describing it. But the vibe was very 'that was four years ago' and 'what's in the past is in the past.' He clearly doesn't want anything he wanted in that letter to happen now. Which was obviously awkward for me because . . . well, because I wanted him to still want whatever he wrote in that letter to happen. Which is dumb. We're adults now. It's not like that anymore."

"That's not dumb, Blair. You guys have a lifetime of history together, and he's literally hand-drawing blueprints of the house you own across the street from him. I'd be in love, too."

"I'm not in love."

"Right. And by not in love, you mean your souls are intrinsically, infinitely, irreparably intertwined because practically all your earliest memories have been made with him and even as an adult you've been incapable of going one day without thinking about how he's the only person on planet Earth who will understand you in the way that he does."

"Ugh, Roshi." I groan, elongating her name like a curse. "What are they teaching you at *lawyer* school these days. You don't need more training on how to soliloquy my ears off."

"Okay, okay! I'm sorry, I'm done. But listen, if this man sent you a pen-and-paper, delivered-by-owl letter to confess his feelings to you, I don't think you should be expecting him to admit if he still feels something for you after just finding out you never read it," she grinds out dramatically. "The man is probably reeling! So, be friends with him. Friends friends." Her tone is suddenly nefarious. "And see where it goes from there."

Hmm. Her words are shockingly comforting. In our time

at Pepperdine, Faye was always a serial monogamist, while Roshi was dropping her current fling and searching for the next. If anyone knew how to navigate confusing dynamics, it was her. If anything, she was the arbiter of them.

"So . . . keep your enemies close is what you're saying," I deadpan.

"No, Blink. No enemies. Just act like a friend would act. Ask him for help. Open up a bit. We all know that's a foreign language to you, but this is Declan we're talking about. You've been his friend before."

Yeah. I have been. And it was the source of pain and longing for years. Both while we were friends and then in the aftermath of not being friends. The few months we actually dated was the only time he wanted me in the way I wanted him to.

I don't know if I have the emotional bandwidth to be his friend again when I always end up wanting more. But as I hit end call on Roshi, I feel the invisible tug between Declan's and my houses. Unfortunately, he was looking like the only buoy in the middle of this vast, friendless ocean right now. Being his friend might just have to cut it.

The house is silent and I'm trying to envision what my life would look like here, in Seabrook. I'd be a short drive from my mom. I could help her manage the stores. I could keep writing my romance novel. Maybe I'd actually finish it this time, especially if I wasn't a consultant. It all seems good.

But then my mind starts picturing Lottie waltzing around the tiny kitchen island in a long dress. I don't even have memories of her in this yellow-tiled kitchen. But she was here once. And I picture her hands placing every piece of decor on the coffee table. On the shelves. Did she place my favorite books above the desk to remind me of my love for words? To push me to write below the authors that inspired me in the first place? Or is that wishful thinking?

Locking the door behind me, I hop back into my car with my journal and laptop in a striped tote bag and head to the beach. Cypress trees fly past my rolled-down windows in a hazy blur, and the breeze feels saltier by the second. I park in the secret spot I've had since the day I got my driver's permit and trek down two wooden steps onto the soft white sand.

Surfers dot the waves in the distance, and the locals whose mansions are practically built on the sand are throwing huge pieces of bark to their dogs. I take my spot under my favorite tree. The roots are thick enough to sit on, and the fluffy, Lorax-looking branches make a flat canopy above my head. I've always loved how the tree hems you in from above like the palm of an outstretched hand.

Taking my journal out and balancing it on one of the roots, I unfold Declan's blueprint and stick it between journal pages to study. On the front, he's suggested adding wood to support the windows and replacing potentially rotting sections in the doorway. On the back, arrows point to his neat handwriting, explaining his ideas.

"Tear down laundry room wall and extend kitchen. Connect the tiny island to a wraparound bar to give it a coffee shop feel but keep the space open to the living room." And by the bedroom: "Build a mini deck out to the garden. Lay new stones to build a path. You can use while watering plants."

For some reason, "you can use while watering plants," scribbled in black ink, brings tears to my eyes. Lottie used to wear aged yellow gloves to carry her huge watering can to her garden, where she would water each plant with meticulous care. In my memory, the sun shines behind her smile lines, and butterflies dance around her brightly colored dress, mistaking her for a flower. Watching her take care of her plants felt like watching someone fall in love. She looked at them adoringly, like they were whispering compliments only she could hear.

For the first time, I could picture myself living in the cottage. Waking up from the spill of light through the sliding doors. Making myself a latte and enjoying it on the small wooden deck. Purchasing gloves of my own to water the garden I would make in her memory. And then settling down at the desk to write or help my mom with managing the stores. For once, the thought of living here didn't feel like a prison built by grief, it felt like the key to unlocking the prison doors.

It would still be painful, but it wouldn't be as painful as being alone in a tiny New York City apartment, thousands of miles from the beautiful town that reminded me of her. If I missed her, I wanted to come to this tree, by this ocean.

Tears are falling from my eyes when I hear shuffling in the sand in front of me.

"Blair?" the voice says.

I wipe my tears before looking up to find Declan in a wet suit, with wet hair and tanned skin, staring down at me.

"Declan?" I reply in shock. "You . . . surf?"

He laughs softly as he shakes his head, and the movement makes tiny droplets of water spray from his hair. "I'm not sure you could call it surfing quite yet. I started last year and I'm still not very good, considering the . . ." He gestures to his left leg. The one that has a limp.

"Oh, right," I say in a small voice. "That's awesome, though. You look . . . awesome."

I clamp my lips shut the second the words are done flying out. He chokes a laugh at my regretful expression. "Not like that. You know what I meant. Like, oh it's you in surf attire, that's awesome. Like in the way that surfers look cool, but I wasn't saying that you—"

"Thank you, Blair. I'll make sure not to let it go to my head." He offers me the slightest curl of his mouth in that familiar, knowing way. It takes this from embarrassing to intimate.

I let my head drop, unable to withstand the way I feel with him looking at me while looking like that. Dripping wet, ocean-water-drenched hair and dark wet suit towering over me. Give a girl a break. My eyes land back on his blueprint, now with two teardrops wetting the page. He must follow my eyeline because he says "Whatcha got there?" like he knows exactly what I've got here.

"Oh, uh." I dab the teardrops with my cardigan. "I was just looking over your blueprint sketch again. It's . . ." I nod awkwardly. "It's really beautiful."

He sits beside me in the sand and despite the freezing-cold ocean water soaking his wet suit, I feel a wall of heat. He doesn't say anything in response, just stares at my profile for a beat.

"Is there something wrong, Blair?" he says tenderly.

Just the fact that he knows there's something wrong makes my throat squeeze. I thought I'd successfully hidden all clues of my tears, but I guess he was just being polite. I have to keep my eyes on the sand to maintain any sense of composure.

"Lottie," I start, voice cracking. I clear my throat and try again. "Lottie loves gardening." I use the present tense out of habit, but he doesn't correct me. "And your idea for a pebble path through the garden just—I don't know. It was the first time I could really picture myself living there. Making a garden. Taking care of plants just like she used to."

Declan nods. "That's awesome," he says in the most heartfelt, genuine voice. But his use of my previous, awkward word choice makes a wet chortle fly out of me.

"No, I'm being serious!" he insists.

"Oh, I know!" I say through laughter. "I know, it's just funny. And awesome."

"It is huge though, really. I know it's just an idea, but even the thought is progress." He runs his hand through his wet hair and then shakes his head like a dog after taking a bath. "It took me months to picture anything close to normal life after the accident. Even going to the grocery store with my mom for the first time felt like an impossible task." He looks away for a moment. "Just getting through the parking lot without flinching was hard."

"Oh—wow," I sputter, start again. "I'm so sorry. Gosh, that must have been so hard. I didn't even think about that," I admit, head shaking while I stare at his cheekbone. He's looking out at the shore, eyes squinting in concentration.

"No, that's alright." He brushes it off. The hurriedness of his voice when things turn earnest reminds me of . . . me.

"You know," I start, voice sputtering like a car engine on the first day of winter. "I pictured what it must have been like for you so many times. The hit, and the hospital, and the recovery. But I never pictured you sad. Or scared."

He turns to me and traces the outlines of my face with his eyes like he's committing it to memory. His green eyes soften into emerald pools, and I feel slightly off balance staring into them.

"Really?" The side of his mouth pitches up like I've just told him he's handsome.

"Yeah, really," I say, nodding. "Sounds kind of stupid now that I say it out loud, though. You were hit by a bloody car."

He laughs, and the dimple under his lip deepens. "Turns out, the car ended up being not that bloody."

"Oh my gosh." My stomach flips. "You can't just say things

like that, Declan. I'm not used to it yet," I yell, indignant. "Man, that's grim."

My reaction causes him to laugh harder. The sound of it is warm and full. I wish I could bottle it and take a bath in it.

And that's not what friends picture when their friends laugh, I remind myself.

"That's alright. I've acclimated enough for the both of us."

"Yeah, well, I haven't," I protest, voice losing humor. "It was one thing to picture it. It's another to hear it from your perspective."

His face melts into a look of thoughtful consideration, head tilted at me like he's seeing something new.

"I guess I know what you mean. I never pictured you sad at Pepperdine. You were always free and happy and . . . laughing, actually, in my imagination."

Now, that causes a dry laugh to splinter out of me. "I wish that were the truth, but no. I was like a sad little puppy. Lost from home." I confess it to the waves because if I look at him, I won't be able to speak.

But Declan doesn't laugh, so I risk a look over at him. Our eyes latch, and then his gaze trails down my face and lingers on my mouth. "I was the same way," he admits quietly.

I let his eyes rove over me like hands, pretending our admissions aren't the closest we've gotten to "I miss you."

Waves crash as we let the silence stay taut between us. I concentrate on a drop of water dripping from a tendril of his salty hair. My breathing stops being a subconscious function.

"Come to my house," Declan says, breaking us out of our reverie.

"What?" I blurt.

"I'll show you how I renovated it. And you can ask me anything you want."

"Anything?"

"Anything." His voice is gravelly and sure.

Butterflies start a war in my stomach, and I try to call a ceasefire.

"Meet you there?" I ask.

"Meet you there." He nods, and I catch a grin blooming on his face as he stands.

Chapter 20

Watching Declan thread his wet suit through a rung on the roof of his car makes me feel like a voyeur, spectating the routine he's clearly gone through hundreds of times. His hair is mussed from half-dry salt water and his face looks refreshed. When he's done, he motions for me to follow him to his front door, and I stare at his relaxed posture as he ambles up the driveway.

He fits the lock in the door and swings it open. "And here it is!" he says in a dry, theatrical voice with the flourish of his hand.

I gasp. If Declan was a house, this is exactly what he would look like. Smooth, cherry wood. Low, angular ceiling. Exposed beams. A living room filled with chairs made to lounge in. Not sit. Lounge. I can picture him sprawled out in the leather recliner with his head balanced in his hand, pencil behind his ear as he stared at a blueprint. "This is—" I shake my head. "Gorgeous."

"Oh, thank you," he chuckles warmly. "Please, come on in. Make yourself at home."

Taking my shoes off at the door, my eyes scan the small dining room that leads to the living room to the left. There's a deep, wine-colored couch and leather recliner bracketing a cobblestone fireplace. A woodsy scent envelops my senses. It smells like him. Everywhere.

"So." Declan strides to the mantel above the fireplace and takes down a framed photo. "This is what the inside looked like originally if you want to give that a look."

I follow him into the living room and take the photo from his hands.

"As you can see, I didn't change too much. The house had these great mid-century modern bones with this spunky-looking roof. They call it a butterfly roof." He leans in to tell me that fun fact like he's letting me in on a secret, and I feel heat creep into my face. "So, I just added the wood paneling to the living room and kitchen walls, stained the floors darker, added some new cobblestones to this fireplace. I did some touch-ups in the bathrooms, but other than that, it's the same."

"Wow," I breathe. "And you did that all by yourself?"

"Yeah, pretty much. It was a fun way to stay occupied," he replies, voice low and resonate. "Maybe this will give you some inspiration for what you could do to your house. It's a different style, obviously, but it could use about the same amount of work. Or not. You could move in and fix it up as you go. And I would help you out. Either way."

Your house.

He sounds eager for me to move in. The amount of hope that gives me causes a swift dose of panic to follow. Why did I feel so affected by him wanting me to stay in Seabrook? But maybe the answer was simple. He was my best friend, then. He could be my best friend now. And I was craving that sense of being known so often lately. Perhaps I was just feeling the comfort of having someone who knew me so intimately back in my life.

"And you said you moved in two years ago, right?"

"Yup. Just about." He sticks his hands in his pockets, smiling at me to encourage my eager question-asking. He did say I could ask anything.

"And how . . ." I trail off, ping-ponging my eyes through the space again. Without being so forthright, I want to ask him how he afforded it. It was easy to forget my lack of access to him now.

"And how did I swing it?" he guesses, reading me like a book.

I press my lips together, looking caught, and nod.

He exhales while grabbing hold of the doorway, and the way he leans with his arms stretched above him causes a patch of skin between his shirt and jeans to flash. I grit my teeth, looking away.

He smiles. "Are you hungry, by chance? After surfing, I'm gonna require a meal before rehashing that whole story."

I shrug my shoulders. "Yeah, I could eat."

"Okay, cool. I'm gonna take a quick shower. Do you want anything to drink? Water? Lemonade? Coffee?" he asks, body halfway behind the doorway.

Settling onto the couch, I reply, "No, I'm okay. Thank you, though."

He slaps the wall and points. "Be right out."

The sound of water gushing through pipes starts, and I sit on my hands, peering around the space that Declan has called home for two years. From the living room window, I can see the cottage across the street. It is a strange feeling seeing it from this perspective.

The garden is unwieldy and wraps around the small square of a house, whereas this home is a rectangular single-story with a funky roof. Declan's house is cherry-stained wood and vaulted ceilings, whereas mine is creamy neutrals and arched doorways.

Mine. It was the first time my mind referred to the cottage that way. The feeling settled into my stomach. Not unpleasant. Just new.

A few moments later, Declan claps from the doorway. "Alright, what're you feeling? Tacos? Ramen? Breakfast for dinner?"

He reads the way my lips flicker.

"Breakfast for dinner it is," he says for me, smiling with a knowing look in his eyes.

His hair is wet, again, but this time from the shower instead of the ocean, and I have to manually stop my face from showing signs of longing. I was going to need a break from his incessant, easy smiles and laid-back demeanor if I wanted to be his friend. He hadn't looked this comfortable all summer, and it was doing things to me that I didn't want to name.

Settling into a torn-leather booth at the back of the Snug Spoon, our waitress rushes out balancing steaming plates of pancakes in both hands. "I have a three-stack of maple sugar pancakes and a triple chocolate chip buttermilk stack. Everything looking good?" she singsongs.

"Yes! Looks great. Thank you so much," Declan replies with a dimpled smile.

"Okay," I say, cutting into the maple sugar pancakes. "Tell me how you ended up in that house, finally."

Declan grins at my lack of patience and picks up his fork and knife. "Oh, that little tale. It's a fun one."

I can tell by his tone that it's probably going to be a tragic one.

After swallowing a bite, he says, "The short story is that my dad sued the owner of the car that hit me."

My fork falters on its way to my mouth.

He smiles. "Told you it was a fun one."

"Declan," I sigh, upset at his deflection mechanisms. "You are ridiculous," I huff. "But please, continue."

He laughs, humored by my reaction to his macabre attitude, but after a moment, he grows serious. "The kid in the driver's seat took the brand-new convertible from his uncle's house. He already had a record for speeding in school zones and driving with too many passengers. So, they considered it something they call 'negligent entrustment' because the uncle practically handed over the keys, even knowing all this about him. And then, that night, he and his friends had been drinking. So, it was a pretty cut-and-dry case."

I try to remain as neutral as possible, but internally, my eyes are bulging out of their sockets. At both the way Declan maintains perfect composure while retelling the story and the ludicrousness of the situation. Just hearing about it fills me with rage. How he was able to sound calm was bizarre to me.

"In classic Randall fashion, he took it upon himself to sue

for the cost of surgeries plus the value of scholarships I would no longer be able to use. Which, in case you forgot, I got scholarships to six different schools. Most of them full rides." He smirks at me with sarcastic conceit. I cough a surprised laugh. "And on top of that, because Randall never lets anyone get off easy, he sued for the 'lost ability to earn a living.'"

"Mm-hmm. Sounds like him. Well, the suing part, not the Matthew McConaughey impression you just slipped in there."

Declan lifts his eyebrows like they're shoulders he's shrugging. His actual shoulders shake with laughter as he shovels another forkful of pancake into his mouth. Only Declan could laugh while retelling the aftermath of getting hit by a car.

Randall, Declan's father, was a stern man who'd been head of a philanthropic committee called the Cypress Grove Community Fund for decades. It was responsible for distributing money to maintain Seabrook, providing scholarships, and hosting charity galas. His role in the small community made the Renshaws a well-known and well-loved family in this tiny, beachside town, which was why he cared about Declan's accomplishments so much. It was also why winning a lawsuit was relatively easy based on their good rapport.

He swallows his bite. "By the time we won the case, I was finally walking on my own and actively figuring out what I wanted to do with my life. So, I figured buying the house on Brickstone was a good first step. It was a smart place to hold the money, plus, I could finally get out of my childhood home and get some separation from Randall and Gwen's good ole expectations." He says his parents' names dully. "Being in the house you grew up in always feels like regression for some reason."

"Heard that." I raise my water. Those words rang truer than the sky being blue. "And did it work?" I ask, wondering about the house across from his under my name.

"It did, actually. And, you know, I'm grateful for my parents . . ." He nods as he chooses his next words. "But I didn't realize how much stress I was under the whole time I lived with them. You'd think being hit by a car would cause some sympathy, but my dad seemed more concerned with how it killed my future career instead of being grateful that I was still alive. The sympathy he was earning from his son getting hit by a car had run its course, and it was time for me to impress him again," Declan says with a sarcastic lilt. It was the closest he veered toward anger, which was something he didn't even show when relaying how he got hit by a car.

"Man." I shake my head, pushing my empty plate forward. "Randall sounds like a piece of work." I wanted to say more, but I was aware that it was still his father, and a son would always care about his father's approval, no matter how broken the relationship. "Has he backed off a little more since then?"

"He has." Declan wipes a hand over his mouth in thought. "Although, I feel like it's less a result of any character growth, considering my work on the coffee shop giving him a new reason to brag."

"At least he's proud of you becoming manager?" I offer, shrugging.

Declan laughs with a jolt of his chin. "Right. Manager."

"Why is that funny?" The words trickle out like a broken faucet.

"Oh." He jerks his eyes up to mine. "I thought you knew."

"Knew what?"

"That I was the owner?"

"Of the coffee shop?"

"Yes, Blair." He chuckles. The sound is light and sweet. "You didn't know?"

I shake my head, feeling bamboozled. Which, at this point, was difficult to achieve.

"Wait, but . . ." I lean back. "Everyone refers to you as the manager?"

"Because I am. But I am also the proud owner." He grins ironically, straightening up and smoothing out his shirt like that should make it more obvious.

I laugh from shock, propping my elbows onto the table between us.

"Okay, wait." I wave my hands. "So, now you have to tell me how that happened."

He laughs so hard that the space between his temple and cheek pinch together, and the sight makes me bite the inside of my cheek. He mirrors me and puts his elbows on the table, leaning in.

"Well, after moving into the house and starting renovations, I still had some cash from the lawsuit to start something with." He motions with his hands like he's outlining a blueprint on the table. "And going to college felt too painful if I couldn't play football. So, I mapped out some of my interests and figured: 'Okay, I really enjoy building things, but I also want to work on a team.'" He relays it like he's narrating his inner monologue. It's so cute and boyish that I grin. "And then, one evening, I was strolling through downtown when I saw a for-sale sign on a run-down property. I pictured myself opening a coffee shop the second I stepped inside. So, I put an offer in, got it, and then just dove in full force and figured it out as I went. And here we are." He smiles a soft smile that makes me go warm inside.

I sit back in the booth, convinced only Declan would be capable of being so successful without hinting at it, even the tiniest bit. I've been working under him all summer and he never walked around the place like the owner.

JUST FRIENDS

"And you love it?" I ask.

"Oh yeah. So much. I get to lead a team. I'm familiar with all the regulars now. And anytime I get some whacky idea, I can build it and add whatever I want to the shop."

"Like the birdhouses," I marvel.

"Exactly. Like the weird birdhouses." He beams with pride.

"What are the metal wheels on the side of them?" I ask. I've been wondering since the first day I walked into Seabrook Coffee House.

His mouth quirks to the side. "I'm shocked you noticed that. They're pieces of a disassembled clock."

I shake my head in reverent disbelief. "You are the world's most unassuming nerd, Declan. And you're just hiding in plain sight."

He morphs into a look of fake outrage, dropping his mouth. "Oh please. Sounds like a classic case of the kettle calling the pot black here."

"It's the pot calling the kettle black," I correct.

"My point exactly. You're a little nerd too. I've never seen a person more enthused by a dictionary before." His elbows already on the table, he leans in closer to me. I don't think he even knows he's doing it.

"Okay? Says the guy who just used the word 'enthused' to insult a girl who likes looking up synonyms," I counter in a dry tone. "It's a writer thing."

"Oh." He raises his eyebrows. "Look who's admitting she wants to be a writer now."

I roll my eyes and look away.

"Okay, well, that leads to my next question," I deflect.

"Shoot."

"Does that mean you were the one to hire me after my awful interview?"

He looks thoughtful while he rubs the back of his neck. "Yes. That is correct. Which, by the way, wasn't the worst interview I've ever done."

"Really? I fudged every question on purpose, and you knew that."

"Well, yeah. But I thought it was because you hated my guts."

"Then why would you hire me?"

Declan's expression turns solemn.

"If I'm honest, I thought it would be a good way to earn your forgiveness."

"You always had my forgiveness," I insist.

"But did I?"

"Yes!" I explode, and his eyes burn into mine, begging for more of an explanation. "The only thing I hadn't forgiven you for was not saying goodbye to me. For dropping me with no explanation. Sitting around waiting for you to show up made me feel five years old again."

He flinches.

"But now that I know that wasn't true, of course I forgive you, Declan. And I never hated you. Ever."

He takes a moment to process my words, and then his shoulders soften, and he looks relieved. "I'm glad." His voice is too soft, and I feel warmth spread through my cheeks. "I guess I can admit I'm pretty stoked to find out you weren't trying to live the rest of your life without ever seeing me again too." Declan smiles, but there's a tinge of sadness behind it.

"Did you really believe that? That I was fine without ever seeing you again?"

"Oh, of course," he says quickly.

I wince.

JUST FRIENDS

"You were so eager to pursue your dreams, I thought you were excited to not have me holding you back anymore."

"You never held me back," I say, shaking my head. "You and I both wanted to pursue our dreams. That's one of the things that bonded us, but your dreams seemed so much bigger, and I was scared of relying on you," I confess. "But that was dumb. Considering I spent the next four years just wishing I could rely on you anyway."

He nods, but his eyes are narrowed like he's unconvinced.

"It's not dumb. I wasn't someone you could've relied on anyway."

"What are you talking about?" I protest, but my voice comes out small.

His eyes flit to the door behind me like he's ready to leave. "I was—" He shakes his head instead of finishing the sentence. "Down and out, let's just say."

I nod slowly. I think I'm gathering his meaning. "But you're not anymore?"

"No," he says without missing a beat. "No, thank God. The way I felt after the accident feels a million miles away now. I was absent in my own body, it felt like. And I shut everyone out because of it. But not anymore, obviously." He looks at me.

How much longing must be written across my face right now?

"I understand that. Not in the exact way, but, you know."

"No, you do," he reassures me. "Grief is very similar in my opinion. The world keeps hurtling on, but you feel stuck in the moment where everything changed."

"Yes. And things that felt easy to you before feel impossible to accomplish now. Like texting my friends back. They're not doing anything wrong, but I feel this endless well of resentment toward them. I just don't have it in me to joke around and—" I shake my head.

Declan's eyes go sad, and it takes me a second to realize why. The place I'm in now is a glimpse into why I couldn't get a hold of him after the accident. Except, my external world is different now, yes. But for him, his internal world was too. His own body was broken and with it his life. How much must he have been trying to process as a seventeen-year-old boy, laying in his childhood bed?

He looks at the exit again and I know he doesn't want to rehash the past right now.

"So, the cottage," I blurt. "You think the renovations would be easy?"

Declan nods. "I think so."

"And you could, possibly, maybe help with some of them?"

His face hardens. My stomach free falls.

"Aren't you moving soon?" For the first time during this conversation, he removes his elbows from the table and leans back in the booth, arms crossed.

Swiping my water off the table, I take a long gulp to hide my flaming cheeks. Why are my cheeks flaming?

"That's the current plan," I say, setting my water down and tracing the rim. "But my plan is looking a little flimsy now with the house situation." I release a wry laugh.

He rolls his lips inward. He's gone quiet like he used to when he was trying to solve a difficult problem. But those green eyes are simmering with something. Whatever the emotion is, he fights it.

"Blair, you know I'd love to help you. With anything. But, with the house, if you're leaving soon anyways, I don't like starting things I can't finish."

JUST FRIENDS

His eyes burn into mine and I physically resist squirming in the booth. What am I supposed to say to that? I have the urge to insist that I'm staying, but I can't be making promises I don't know if I can keep.

The waitress comes back with the check, saving us from the stunted silence. I reach for my wallet.

"Don't. I got it," Declan says, voice low.

We return to his car, and I can't breathe without feeling self-conscious about the sound. The song he was showing me on the drive over is still playing and he turns it off quickly, leaving us drenched in silence. Pinks and purples swirl in the distance as the sun is pulled under the sea, and by the time he pulls into his driveway, the moon fashions the sky instead.

"Well, I'll see you tomorrow." He breaks the silence with a flat voice and steps out of the car without looking at me.

That's my cue to leave, I guess.

"Alrighty," I say, awkwardly, opening my door. "See you tomorrow."

I shut the car door and strut across the street to my car, hurrying to get inside and on the road.

What just happened?

Was he upset that I was leaving? Or that I would potentially stay?

I don't like starting things I can't finish.

I mull over the meaning of his words until I'm drifting off to sleep. I've let the statement simmer at the edge of my mind for so long that it starts fermenting into a different substance altogether. Because the conclusion I kept coming back to, the one thing that couldn't possibly be true, was that he was talking about us.

Chapter 21

Harper sashays up to me behind the bar, and at her exuberant smile, I realize I haven't seen her since her abrupt departure from Jonny's Pints and Pins.

"Harper!" I exclaim. "Where have you been?"

And then, in a moment that shocks even me, I pull her in for a hug.

"Why, hello! I missed you too," she teases, squeezing me back.

We're both scheduled to make drinks while Sonia works the register, so in between calling out names, Harper fills me in on her weekend.

JUST FRIENDS

"So yeah, Chicken is all better now, and I just have to start putting my hairbrush in a drawer." Chicken is Harper's cat, who repeatedly has trips to the vet after coughing up fist-sized hairballs. Literal, Harper-colored hairballs. "But anyways, sorry about my behavior at Jonny's. I haven't had a slip-up like that in over a year and—" She shakes her head with widened eyes, looking down at the milk she's foaming.

"Slip-up? What do you mean by . . ." I trail off.

"Oh." She shoots her eyebrows up at me. "Oh wow, sorry. I thought it was obvious. The drinking?" She searches my eyes for the meaning to land.

"Ah . . . yes, yes." I overcompensate for my shock by being overly solemn, voice going low and eyebrows furrowing. She snorts a laugh.

"No, no. Don't worry. It's not like a serious alcohol problem. Well, maybe that's what everyone with alcohol problems says, but I have this agreement with Declan that I can't drink if I want to work here. Plus, the whole fake ID thing is pretty frowned upon, I guess."

She continues pouring the cappuccino into a mug and then calls out "Ryan!" at the counter, like she didn't just drop a ginormous piece of personal lore.

Her blithe demeanor gives me the confidence to ask: "And how did you and Declan come to that agreement?"

"Well, I was only drinking because it was an excuse to get out of the house. I grew up in foster homes, for context. But then, you know the Richardsons?" I nod. She nods back and continues, "Yeah, so they adopted me when I was seventeen, and I still had the little drinking habit. And no one would hire me because of it. But Declan was opening this shop and told me he would give me a chance if I gave up the drinking. So, I agreed, and we shook hands."

"And you're how old now?"

"Almost nineteen," she says, flashing me a grin.

"Wow." I blow out a breath. "I did not know any of that."

"I thought Declan would have told you."

I blink too quickly and whip my head toward her.

"And why would you think that?"

"Because . . . he's always yapping about you?"

"He's always what?" I cry.

"Yapping," she replies. "You know, like, 'Blair this and Blair that' nonstop." She moves her hand like she's controlling a puppet and tucks her chin to imitate his voice.

Her words feel like dry ice spreading through my chest, resistant hope warring with reason inside me. "I'm sure that's not—"

"Oh my gosh." She rolls her eyes. "You two are so annoying." She throws a rag on the counter dramatically and turns to face me, hand on her hip. "You know, on the day you came in for an interview, I recognized you from a photo that fell out of his wallet one time. It was you two on the football field back in the day, and he was wearing the whole shebang: big ole helmet and shoulder pads and he had his arm around you and it's all cute and whatever. Never had a clue that you were the girl he'd been yapping about to me all this time. But when I saw his face after he interviewed you?" She whistles. "Dead giveaway."

Blood drains from my face.

"Oh no." She snaps her fingers. "Hello? Blair? Blink for me. Come on, girl."

"Hey, Blink is my nickname," I say, hurtling back to the present.

"Yeah, well, I can definitely see why!"

"Sorry, I just—your words are very kind, but it's not like

that anymore between Declan and me. We're cordial now, but . . ." I cut myself off, not wanting to expose the way yesterday ended between us.

"Cordial?" she tuts. "Is that what we're calling infatuation these days?"

"Harper!" I chide, ducking at the rising sound of her voice.

"Listen," she says, dipping her voice to a near whisper and sidling up beside me. "I don't know what makes you think he feels that way about you, but I know people who knew him from before the accident. And they said it changed him. Overnight, all his hopes and dreams went poof." She snaps her fingers again. "And ever since, that boy has been so scared of letting himself want anything. Or anyone, I should add."

She walks away and I'm left with vertigo trying to process her words.

I didn't need to be fed more hope that Declan still felt the invisible string between us—that he was just too afraid to show it. I was feeding myself that particular brand of false hope by the boatload. I was choking on it.

It's evening now, and Declan should walk through the doors at any second for overtime hours. Settling onto a stool at the half-finished bar, I open my laptop to the convenience stores' master scheduling portal and double check that everyone has the correct shifts while I wait.

But even as I drag names across the screen, Harper's earlier words press at my mind like a persistent migraine. I still can't reckon with how her words line up with his actions. He wanted to try being friends. And I thought we were doing that pretty well, until we weren't. He invited me to his house, took me out for a meal, and then he closed off like we were coworkers having a strictly professional meeting.

The tiny golden bell above the door chimes as he steps inside, and he wastes no time ripping the crewneck he's wearing over his head. It ruffles his hair, and he brushes a hand over it sloppily with a distracted look on his face.

"Hey, uh, I gotta get some stuff from the hardware store down the road really quick. I'll be right back," he says, hardly making eye contact with me.

"I'll come with!" I say, not giving him a chance to respond as I shut my laptop and hop off the stool.

"Oh, it's just some random nails and stuff, I don't need—"

"It's okay. I wanna learn."

"About . . . building?"

"Yeah. I might need it. For the cottage," I say in three staccato sentences.

He rolls his lips inward and stares at me like he's waiting for me to break character. But I don't, so he nods and then turns to head to his car. I silently follow him and climb in.

We don't talk, but he turns up the song that was already playing—"How Deep Is Your Love" by the Bee Gees. I try to convince myself that it means something. And then I try to convince myself that it means nothing.

I sit on my hands and look out the window, avoiding the invisible wall of frisson I feel every time I sit this close to him.

"Alrighty," he says, putting the car in park. "This will be a quick trip."

He exits the car and power walks up to the tiny store named Bolts and Builds. I have to add a shuffle-hop to my stride to keep up with him.

We amble together in silence through a foray of buckets

filled with screws and bolts. My eyes see but don't process any of the information written on the tiny labels.

"We're looking for screws an inch and a quarter long," he says.

"Got it. Screws. Inch and a quarter." I nod like I'm taking orders. "Oh! Found it!" I pick up a silver screw from a bucket.

He narrows his eyes and takes it from me to inspect. "This is a conical screw. We want flat heads."

"Oh," I say in vocal italics, drooping my head as I pluck it from his fingers and drop it back into the bucket. "Sorry. I thought the comical screw *was* flat."

He doesn't turn around, but I catch the tiny bounce in his shoulders, presumably from a silent chuckle. A zing of satisfaction shoots through me, quick and hot.

"Okay." Declan slides a plastic package off a display. "These are the ones we want for the bar we're building. See how the top is flat?"

I nod.

"It will sit flush with the wood. Which will make it look better. If I were to build the deck for your cottage's backyard however, I would use these screws." He takes another package off the shelf and holds it up to me.

"Oh," I say in a small voice. "That's very cool."

It was, actually, very cool. But the casualness with which he referred to building me a deck for "my cottage" was making me dizzy. I couldn't remember the last time I envisioned New York City. Or consulting. Or staying up late in a corporate office by myself. I stopped having those fascinations ever since my mom broke down in the back of the convenience store.

Declan and I mosey up to the cash register, and as he pulls out his wallet to pay, I see the edge of a photo peeking up behind some cash. My breathing catches as I try to study it without him noticing my bug-eyed stare at his wallet. But he slides his credit card out and pays with a quick tap before returning the wallet to his back pocket. Evidence of the maybe-photo disappearing with it. Was that it? Was that the photo Harper claimed Declan had of us in his wallet?

I trail behind him to the car in a daze, replaying what Harper said about Declan's reaction to seeing me again for the first time. I try my best to reconcile that image with the silent man now driving beside me. If cognitive dissonance was a movie, this would win most accurate depiction.

We get back to the coffee shop and I still haven't settled from the jolt of hope that shot through me at the sight of the tiny picture's edge, but I don't need to, because Declan wants me to stain a table he built. Our comfortable silence is easy to fall into again once the sound of his drill whirring starts and I have the paintbrush in my hand to distract me.

We continue until the sun has gone down, leaving one floor lamp illuminating the space. I remember the beginning of the summer when I came in to help him. I thought the lights were off because he didn't want them on—like some reclusive vampire character. But now I realize it was because he got so enraptured with what he was working on that he didn't notice until it was completely dark.

When the sun has finished setting, Declan's voice sounds from behind me, tentative and grave. "Can I ask you something?"

"Of course," I reply without turning around, brushing a section of wood with stain.

A few seconds pass without a sound, and then slowly, he says, "What were your last few moments with Lottie like? If you don't mind me asking."

My hand pauses its pass on the wood like I've hit an invisible wall. A well of emotion rises in my chest, and not because the question is too emotional to answer, but because he was the first one to ask it at all.

"Oh," I say, voice already shaking. "Yeah, no, I don't mind you asking." I rearrange my legs beneath me in a criss-cross position and dip my brush into the stain again. "You know, I was writing about this the other day, actually." I glance at him, and he nods for me to go on, like he can sense my trepidation.

"It really struck me how mundane our last handful of conversations were. Because, at first, there's all this pressure to ask all the right questions. You're so aware that it's your last chance to learn anything and everything from them. So, I spent a lot of time asking her to go over every decade of her life. I asked her about times that were most significant or transformative, and I was so meticulous about writing every answer down. But then the last time I spoke to her, we talked about stupid things. Like, the dress I was obsessed with wearing in middle school, and if I was going to eat the leftovers in the fridge or get takeout that night. We small-talked. And it really stressed me out, thinking that I was wasting her last moments talking about these random, inconsequential details. But now, I think she was happy to be talking about those things with me, because that's what loving someone is. It's sharing the tiny, stupid, mundane things about your life, because they're everything to the people you love."

A warm tear slides down my cheek as I hold the image of Lottie's wan face on the mechanical bed. I look down to collect myself and swipe it away, and don't notice that Declan has moved from his spot to sit next to me.

"Sorry," I mumble, wiping the tear with the back of my hand. "It's just, I don't know how to explain the feeling. But the whole thing—her getting sick, her dying, felt like this unexpected, violent shift in my life that turned everything upside down. And yet, somehow, it was all so infuriatingly routine. It just felt so cruel that it was so life-changing to me, but not for anyone else. Everyone was acting so normal. The hospice care nurses. The lady in the purple pantsuit they sent to tell me she was dying. The people at the funeral home who held the door open for me. Even my best friends. Everyone was acting so painstakingly casual. And it made me want to throw something at the wall to shake them all up in the way I felt shaken up. The way I feel shaken up." The words tumble out with the force of my emotion behind them, and I feel self-conscious now that they're laying between us. "I'm sorry. That probably sounds selfish. Obviously, everyone else was acting normal because people die. That's just a fact of life. And I was somehow expecting everyone to feel the desperation I felt, but that's not possible because—"

Declan places his hand on my wrist. "I know exactly what you mean."

I look down at his hand. Up into his eyes. They're open to me, like he's offering a bridge he wants me to walk over.

"I felt exactly the same way after the accident. The anger. The frustration. The confusion. No one responds in the way you want them to. And you can't blame them, because they don't know what you want. But, at the same time, it's infuriating because everyone's just thinking about how awkward they feel about it, instead of caring about how much you need them to be brave for you. None of my teammates reached out for the first three weeks. Three weeks. And when they did? It was some fake bull crap about how I was gonna get back on the field soon."

"You're kidding me," I scoff.

"Unfortunately not." He laughs, shakes his head.

The sentiment rings true. Platitudes were somehow the go-to encouragement in light of tragedy, yet all they did was remind me how far my experience was from the person saying them. Because if they were any closer, if they had ever felt something remotely similar, they'd never say something as useless as that.

"Did they even ask what bones you broke? How long you'd be out?"

He shakes his head no.

"Why does it seem so obvious and yet, no one just asks how you're feeling about the whole thing?" I plead.

"They think it's rude. They think they'll be reminding you of it like it's something you can forget about. Or they just assume everyone else is checking on you. Which ends up leaving you with no one checking on you."

That lands like a blow to my chest. I blink a few times.

"Is that what's happening to you right now, Blair?" he asks in a softer voice.

I press my lips together as hard as possible, but the corner of my lip wobbles and everything unravels. A choke of a sob breaks free from my throat.

I would feel more embarrassed if Declan didn't look so unsurprised.

"Come here," he whispers and pulls me into his chest. I grasp his middle from the side. Our bodies press together in our seated positions on the wood floor, and it feels like the past four and a half years never happened. He places his chin on my head, and I breathe in the comforting scent of him between disjointed breaths. "It's okay," he says gently, rubbing my back and placing his other hand on my head. "It's okay, Blair. I'm here."

His gentle words cause me to cry harder. Because against everything I'd expected from coming home, he was here, with me. Not an ounce of him seemed uncomfortable or panicked. He was patient and understanding and calm when I was anything but. When it felt like everyone else had disappeared into their busy lives, he was here, catching me.

"It will take time," he coaxes, petting my hair with a soothing pressure. "I know it seems unbearable now, but in time, it won't feel so impossible."

Time.

It was the inevitable chasm I needed to cross in order to heal from this pain. But it also dawned on me that time was the one chasm between Declan and me, and in this moment, I knew it had done nothing to erase what I once felt for him.

The realization dries up my tears, and my breathing eases into a steadier rhythm. I wipe the hair from my face and look up at him. He looks down at me, gentle eyes searching mine, only a slight lean away. They flit down to my lips once, and they part by reflex.

"Blair," he murmurs, voice breaking. "I can't do this."

"Do what?" I rear back, but his strong arm is still holding me.

"Be your friend." It comes out fast, like he's scared for me to hear the words.

My eyes frantically search his face for a sign, but his eyes are full of dreadful longing, and he makes no move to lean away from me.

"I don't want to be your friend either, Declan," I whisper.

Something flashes in his eyes, like he's passing through the realm of disbelief to awe and wonder, and then his mouth crashes into mine.

His lips taste the same. It's the first conscious thought I

have when our lips meet. But then, his hand drifts from my hair, around to cup my jaw like he needs to feel all of me to make sure I'm real, and I don't think anymore.

His hand on my lower back presses into me like a plea. "Come here," he whispers into my mouth, and I laugh by his ear as he helps me climb on top of him, paintbrush tossed to the side.

When I settle on top of him, he doesn't rush in for more like I expect him to. Instead, he brushes front pieces of hair behind my ears, letting his eyes study me like he's been waiting for the chance.

"I miss you, Blair," he says gently, brushing his thumb over my cheekbone.

"Don't miss me anymore. I'm right here," I whisper, voice cracking.

I bend down to reach his lips and the kiss is less hungry this time. The first kiss felt like grasping hold of a fleeting moment. This one feels like coming home.

Our bodies meld like the memory foam of our skin, and blood, and muscle is made up of the outline of each other, and after a few minutes, I pull back to look at him, our noses still brushing. "I've missed you too, Declan. But what is this? What are we doing?"

"What we should have been doing four years ago," he replies without missing a beat.

Our voices are hushed tones in the lamp's glow. Like if we talk any louder, we'll realize what we're saying and revert to not saying anything at all.

"And why weren't we?" I plead, not letting myself trust this yet.

"You know why," he says, his voice softening, eyes melting into mine. I take advantage of the opportunity to stare at him.

His swollen lips and searching green eyes, and something new above his left eyebrow, so small I never noticed it until now—a tiny scar. I brush my finger over the raised skin, swallowing the regret of our past.

What I would give to have been there for him in recovery.

His eyes dart between mine, reading the fear in them.

"I was friends with you for twelve years, Blair. And then I had none of you at all. But I can't do it again. I can't be your friend and pretend like I'm not picturing my life with you."

My face tingles in disbelief. All I ever wanted was to be wanted by him. Even when I hated myself for it.

"Then don't pretend anymore," I beg in a broken, barely audible voice. "Why would you pretend?"

"Because I thought you were leaving for New York soon. And I want you to stay, but I thought it would be like the college fight all over again. You wanting to pursue your dreams. Me standing in the way. Asking you to stay for me. I didn't want to lose you again."

I sigh, searching his entire face in disbelief. "Did you ever consider that I wanted to leave because I couldn't bear the thought of living here if I could only be your friend?"

His brows furrow.

A shocked chuckle escapes me.

"You didn't see how much of my indecision with the cottage came from it being across the street from you?"

Declan's mouth parts to speak but nothing comes out, like he's so stunned by the realization that a cough of a laugh escapes instead. "I must be daft, I guess."

"Yeah," I chortle. "And British."

The corner of his mouth curls.

"Declan, why would I not be thrilled to be given a beachside cottage?"

"Because it wasn't what you planned. Because you've been dreaming of this job and moving to New York for years. You can see my confusion, right?"

"Yes. Totally, I do. Because all of those things are true. But the truer thing, the little detail I had to leave out when talking to you, was that I couldn't stand living in Seabrook if it wasn't going to be *with* you." The words are irreversibly out, and I am weightless, untethered from anything solid as I wait for his response.

"Then let's stop pretending." He brushes his thumb under my eye, wiping away a tear I didn't feel. Then he presses a kiss to the soft skin of my cheek. The right and then, slowly, the left. The grazing warmth of his lips sends tiny fizzes exploding through my nerves, and I shiver.

"Come to my dad's charity gala with me," he whispers.

"What?"

"It's soon, and we can dress up, eat a meal, dance together. Consider it our second first date."

"Wait, wait." I shake my head, pushing myself off his lap and settling beside him. "Everything I said was true, but I still don't know if I'm leaving at the end of summer yet."

He pauses, passes a hand fleetingly over his mouth in consideration. "That's fine. Honestly, I'm willing to do this with you if you want to, Blair. I've let enough come between us to know none of it was worth not having you. Distance or not, you can take all the time you need to figure it out, but if I'm that big a part of your consideration, we might as well start now."

My brain can hardly process the words coming out of his mouth being reality. And perhaps it is my inability to process this being real that makes me so bold. I grab the hand fiddling over his jaw.

"I've done enough friendshiping with you for a lifetime,

Declan. And enough living without you, too. If I haven't made my intentions clear, I'd like to never do either of those things ever again. *Please*." I try for ironic, gripping his wrist dramatically, but the words are true. He barks a laugh at my delivery, and I feel an electric bolt of satisfaction.

"And now that I know that"—he kisses me between the words, cradling my head with the hand I was holding—"I want to make my intentions very clear." His eyes bore into mine like he's been set free from invisible shackles. "I want you. And I will do whatever it takes to make you remember why you wanted me."

My heart takes off without permission from my brain and I let it. There's no running after it now. "I can get on board with that," I whisper, and picture myself accepting the award for biggest understatement of the century. A satisfied smile blooms across his face, and I press my lips to his to taste it.

Little does he know, remembering why I want him isn't the hard part. It's trusting that I should.

Chapter 22

The next day, I follow my mom around to the convenience stores to help her make a list of things she needs to get done or hire someone else to do. We're driving home when we pass the turn that leads to the house Lottie left me.

"Can we stop at the cottage? I forgot something there when I stopped by Tuesday," I tell my mom.

"Of course, honey," she replies eagerly. A beat passes and I can somehow hear the cogs in my mom's brain turning over before she says, "You went to the cottage by yourself?"

"Mm-hmm," I hum. "Is that surprising?"

"No!" she says, overly cheery like her real answer is yes.

"I thought you were feeling some mixed emotions toward it. That's all."

"I was. Am, I mean. But Declan looked at it with me, like you suggested, and he even sketched this little blueprint with ideas to spruce it up."

My mom gasps, delighted. "He did not."

"He did. Did you know he renovated his own house?"

"No, I did not. But it doesn't surprise me. That boy is very determined." She shakes her head in awe.

"Don't I know it," I mutter, and smile to myself.

After a few pacing steps to search for the crewneck I could have sworn I left here, I give up and look for where my mom has wandered off to. Through the bedroom's clear doors, I find her standing in the garden. She's brushing her fingers over the lavender heads in the sun's gentle glow, just like Declan did when I brought him here. They're so fluffy, you can't help but touch them.

There's a faint smile on her lips. She takes a deep breath, and as she exhales, the lines in her forehead fade. I can't remember the last time I saw her this at ease. I step through the sliding doors and join her, dancing my fingers lazily over the silky lavender tops.

"Isn't this gorgeous?" my mom says, closing her eyes to bask in the sun.

"It is," I reply in a weak voice.

We stand in the garden, letting the warmth drench us for minutes on end without saying a word. And in those few minutes, flashes of what could have been and what is flip through my mind like a roll of film.

Me—what could have been: moving into a tiny New York City apartment. Lottie alive, Declan estranged. Work and work and more work on the horizon.

JUST FRIENDS

The film skips.

Me—what could be: moving into a cottage by the sea. The chasm between Declan and me closed. The bridge: the street between our houses. Lottie gone, but my mom still here. An old, forgotten dream unearthed and sprouting to life—a book I thought I might never write, about a boy I thought I might never see again.

And somehow, perhaps miraculously, the fragility of my new decision becomes unbreakable inside me.

"Mom?" I interrupt the blissful silence.

"Yes, hon?" She paces through the garden, inspecting each flower and leaf.

"I'm going to tell Ernst and Young to give away my spot. I want to stay here and help you run the convenience stores," I say in one hurried breath.

She stops mid-step, then looks at me with wide, disbelieving eyes.

"I'll live in this cottage and work on my romance novel in my free time. And plus, Declan and I might be something again and I want to see that through," I add. If there's anything I know about my mom, it's that she doesn't want people to make a big fuss over her. I need to make her think this is about more than just her. And maybe it really is.

"Huh," is all she says at first, and my heart starts pounding. But after a few seconds of contemplation, she walks up to me. "Con, I want you to answer me as honestly as possible, and I know your tells so don't even try to lie." She points a not-so-intimidating finger in my face. "Are you sure you want to do this? I need to know you're not making a rash decision because you're worried about me. You know I'm always going to be okay."

I exhale a ragged breath, laughing a little. "Yes, Mom."

I grab her shoulders and look her in the eye. "Promise. Most of this decision is entirely selfish. I want to write my book more than I want to breathe air sometimes. And I didn't think it'd be possible," I say, my voice cracking. "But Lottie made it possible."

I blink back full-on tears, and my mom's eyes well up too.

"She gave us everything. And even in her absence, she's giving us everything again," I barely get out.

My mom nods and wipes at her tears, then reaches her hand out to wipe mine.

"I knew I raised you right, con," she says with a broken smile. She throws her arms around my middle. Her gardenia scent fills me with warmth. But after a second of thinking in her embrace, I laugh into her hair and pull back.

"Hey, wait! What is that supposed to mean? What would you have thought of me if I went to New York?"

She shakes her head with a sweet smile. "I mean, I raised you right because you know what's important. And sometimes"—she looks back at the cottage Lottie gave me—"circumstances can shift what's most important."

A swell of emotion tightens my throat, and I throw my arms back around her. Lottie's unexpected passing changed things for us. And it felt validating to realize that was okay. Maybe I would have pursued a prestigious job in New York City and lived a more "glamorous life" if she hadn't passed this year. But then I wouldn't have reconciled with Declan, and I wouldn't have spent all this time with my mom, and the mere thought of completing my first novel never would have crossed my mind.

So much had changed this summer. But as I hugged my mother's tiny frame, I finally felt the first nudge toward accepting that change. How was it possible that so much good had been born from something so bad? It didn't feel plausible. Or even acceptable. But maybe it was the truth.

Chapter 23

Can I pick you up from your place @6?

Nope! Pick me up from the cottage. 😉

Getting a head start on renovations?

Something like that.

Yesterday, after calling Ernst & Young to tell them I wouldn't be taking my position, my mom helped me move my things into the cottage. It was disconcerting: the fact that I was capable of demolishing everything I spent the past four years working toward in a five-minute phone call. But I felt nothing but relief when I hung up. I typed four thousand words of my romance novel with a comical amount of fervor and then passed out in my new bed.

Today, I took over some administrative tasks for my mom, typed another two thousand words into my Word document, and got ready for tonight's gala.

I've been spending the past ten minutes peeking out the living room window, waiting for Declan to cross the street to my door. It feels like a lifetime has passed when he finally exits his house.

He's in a dapper, midnight blue suit, hair the closest to tamed I've ever seen it. Something about the rare put-togetherness of his appearance makes me feel overly aware of my existence. He put in effort for *me*.

My heart starts drumming in my chest, and I stand from the couch to smooth out my wine-red floor-length dress. Lottie gifted it to me two summers ago, and I picture how she would smile if she saw me in it now.

A knock at my door startles me out of the thought. I exhale fast. Why do I feel like a middle schooler who's about to go on her first date? I swing the door open. Declan and my eyes meet, and it feels more invasive than the Spanx digging into my thighs. His mouth parts like he's about to speak, but he closes it as his eyes skim my body.

"Blair, you look"—he raises a hand to the back of his neck—"jaw-dropping."

"Thank you," I say. He studies me for another moment,

and the blatant indulgence in his eyes causes me to speak again, like a knee-jerk-need to kill earnest moments. "Mm-hmm. That's weird."

"What?"

"Your jaw is still firmly in place." I furrow my brow, searching the bottom half of his face.

A boyish laugh rushes out of him, so fast it changes the landscape of his entire face in an instant. And I think, those tiny lines that crinkle by his eyes when he smiles will never not make my heart clench with painful adoration.

Declan helps me into his car and then drives us to the banquet hall. The stunning venue sits at the top of a cliff, with a breathtaking ocean view, black rocks jutting out melodramatically. The type of place that costs thirty thousand dollars to rent for a single night.

Older couples are stepping out of luxurious cars, brands I have never heard of, in opulent ball gowns and accompanying men in suits. My breath becomes uneven as I recognize the parents of my old peers. It will be my first time seeing Declan's parents since the accident.

"Come on," he says softly, holding his elbow aloft so that I can loop my arm through his. My breath stutters as I remember that he brought me here as his date.

"Yes, monsieur," I tease.

Declan exhales sharply through his nose in response.

My hand tremors slightly on his arm, and my eyes can't focus on a single target, darting around anxiously at the patrons entering around us.

"Okay, so here's what's going to happen. There will be a five-course dinner comprised of tiny geometric shapes that barely look like food, a few thank-you speeches, and some dancing. We'll dance like we're in one of your favorite fantasy books, and we can play that game where we guess who the highest donor will be." He speaks soothingly in a low voice near my ear as we approach the entrance.

I nod and blow out a breath. Declan going over the order of events eases my nerves. The nerves I hadn't said a word about. Registering that fact sends a familiar zing down my spine.

We pass a sign that reads: **TIDES OF CHANGE**

And then in a smaller font below that: **Preserving Seabrook's historic charm, marine life, and wildlife habitat**

We find our seats near the front of the ballroom, at a round table covered in a white cloth, delicate china placed in perfect formation. Declan pulls my chair for me, tucking it in as I sit down.

"Thanks," I murmur.

He takes the seat to my right. The rest of the seats are occupied by faces I don't recognize, but there are two empty spots across from me. A glass is clinked into the microphone, quieting everyone and signaling the official start of the event. I look up to find Declan's mom, Gwen, behind the microphone, and my body unexpectedly tenses. My vision goes fuzzy at the edges, and I have to remind myself not to stare at her with wide eyes. The last time I saw her face, I was on her front doorstep, begging for the opportunity to see her son.

"Good evening, everybody!" she purrs, hair balanced in an impressive updo. "Welcome to the Cypress Grove Community's annual charity gala." She pauses to allow the audience's applause. "We know you've all been hard at work, and we are grateful for your generous contributions to the Tides of Change fundraiser this year. And of course, none of this would have been possible without my husband, Randall. Randall, please come up, honey."

At an intimidating six foot three and a stern set to his jaw, he strides from the side of the ballroom as the crowd erupts in applause again. He smiles and waves with the perfect amount of bashfulness to pass beneath the bar of conceit. Randall checks every box when it comes to being a charismatic man. Everyone in Seabrook loves him. But I've always found him unnerving. Perhaps it was from seeing the amount of pressure he put on Declan behind the scenes. The pressure of keeping up the appearance of a perfect family, garnering accomplishments that deserve their peer's veneration.

But it seems like Declan has grown up to crave the opposite. He could have led with the fact that he owned the coffee shop, but I had no idea until this week. It was like he'd rather people underestimate him so that he knew your affection was coming from a trustworthy place.

My train of thought is broken when I hear Gwen's voice go soft. "Randall, my beautiful husband, thank you for all that you do, not only for this community but for how you take care of us at home, first and foremost. As you all know, our family has been through some unexpected trials in the past few years." She glances at Declan, and when she catches sight of me, her eyes flicker with something. Her expression falters for a split second, but she recovers so quickly I think I've exaggerated it. "But your steadfastness and strength has been the grounding pillar that guided us through the toughest of days. And despite it all, somehow, you still managed to support the health of this thriving community." Gwen gestures to the audience with a dramatic flourish, eyes shining beneath the spotlight, and everyone breaks into applause again. The speech feels forced to me, but something about the way Gwen and Randall are locking eyes right now feels real. Weighted in a way I can't pinpoint. I glance over my shoulder at Declan, who is clapping along with the crowd with an easy smile on his face.

They invite the guest speakers and auctioneers to the stage and then take their seats at our table. But a new speaker begins talking so I don't have the opportunity to acknowledge them yet. I feel Gwen's presence across from me like a wall of heat as I try to appear focused. We're brought the geometric food that Declan promised, and everyone eats in tiny, polite bites while the auctioneers present the bidding opportunities. The sound of cutlery clinking against fine porcelain and small talk fills the ballroom like an orchestrated symphony. I pretend to be a seasoned guest.

When the presentations end, I turn to face Declan, eyes wide with the subtle panic of saying hello to his parents. He dips his head with a discreet nod. He places a hand on my back and says, "Mom, Dad, I believe I mentioned Blair has been back in town for the summer, and I, uh, I've brought her here as my date."

Randall breaks into a warm smile. "Hi, Blair. It's nice to see you again. And my, my, you look well!"

"Thank you. It's good to see you too." I smile, feeling like a child again beneath his gaze. Then my eyes flicker to Gwen, and I catch the way her mouth tenses with some unnamed emotion before schooling back into a polite grin.

"It's nice to see you, sweetie," she says, offering an awkward wave from across the table. Her stack of gold bracelets tinkles with the movement.

We small talk about my time at Pepperdine and I start to panic when it veers toward what I'll be doing now, since I've yet to inform Declan that I've given up my spot at Ernst & Young.

But Declan relieves me of having to say anything else by offering me his hand and asking "May I have this dance?" with a hopeful expression.

"Do your worst, Declan Renshaw."

His lips curl with a coy smile as he takes me by the hand. Declan was always an unexpectedly suave dancer. Although it shouldn't have come as a surprise, considering he was one of those people who was infuriatingly good at everything they tried.

"Don't worry. I'm not so coordinated anymore," he says like he heard my thoughts.

My heart fractures. I've been failing to remember how many areas of his life have been affected by the accident. I've been slow to remember that I was experiencing the Declan after the accident, not the one before it. It wasn't lost on me how easy I found it to harbor resentment toward people not remembering my current affliction, and yet, I was forgetting Declan's regularly.

It was a pointed reminder that the experiences people didn't witness would never resonate as deeply with them as they did with you. If you wanted them to be appreciated, it was your responsibility to share them—it wasn't on others to understand something they had never seen. I mentally chip away at the wall I've been secretly constructing against Roshi and Faye.

Other couples fill the dance floor. The ones who have been married for decades are easy to see. Twirling and spinning each other around without any effort of thought displayed on their faces.

Declan leads the way, tugging me forward by the hand, and when he finds a clearing, spins me around, bringing his other hand to my waist in one fluid motion. A surprised laugh leaps out of me without my permission. I can't help it. He is charming. It was objectively true. And fine, I could admit, I felt charmed.

We gently sway back and forth. The Righteous Brothers croon, "And time can do so much. Are you still mine?" And I swear Declan's grip tightens around my waist at the lyric.

My stomach takes flight.

He seems to be enjoying this dance with me in the simplicity of our silence, but I am stewing with the secret of my decision to stay in Seabrook. I want to dive headfirst into whatever is happening between us, but I don't want to scare him off by announcing I'll be living in the cottage across the street on our first date.

But what was I going to do? Not tell him I was already living there? I wouldn't be able to keep up the charade for more than a week.

"Declan," I say in a rushed voice. "Can I tell you something?"

"Of course," he breathes, looking down at me like I'm precious to him. "You can tell me anything."

I nod and catch myself grazing my teeth over my bottom lip.

"I called Ernst and Young." Declan stiffens for a moment and takes us offbeat with the song. "To tell them I don't want the job anymore."

At first, his eyes widen like he's not sure he heard me correctly. But then he exhales in a rush and smiles, shaking his head like he's scared to feel hopeful.

"Because . . ." He quirks an eyebrow up in question, elongating the word while he waits for me to fill in.

"Because my mom needs me here. And . . . I want to be here. I know it sounds crazy, and way too fast, and you and I just started talking again, but you're right. We should see where this will go because we've wasted so much time—"

The sound of my voice disappears as Declan cranes his

JUST FRIENDS

head down to kiss me. The kiss is urgent, like he can't go on living another second without pressing his lips to mine. I arch back with the force of it, and it makes me giggle like a lovesick girl, vibrating our lips. I feel his smile as it blooms.

He pulls back slowly.

"Woah, there." I chuckle. "I didn't know how you'd react, but I definitely forgot to consider whatever *that* was as an option."

"Sorry." His mouth quirks on one side. "Like you said, we've already wasted so much time."

I tip my head back and laugh. All the built-up nervous energy escaping in a moment.

"You were scaring me, talking all slow like that. I thought I was already getting dumped not even halfway through our first dance. But no, this is the best news I've heard in a long time."

"Really?" I ask in disbelief.

"Yes. Are you kidding me? Are you shocked by that?"

"Well . . . this is technically our first date—"

"Second first date."

I laugh. "Right. Our second first date after four whole years, and I'm telling you I'm moving into the house across from yours. That doesn't freak you out at all?"

"Why would the girl I've waited for my entire life moving in across the street freak me out?" He says it like it's the truest thing about him. Like it's obvious and he is unafraid.

"You're not scared that we're moving too fast? That whatever broke us apart back then won't crop up and choke us out again?" I ask.

He stares down at me and presses his lips together in thought. His eyes sparkle in consideration in that way they always do when I've asked him something serious.

"No, Blair." He shakes his head emphatically like he's found his conclusion. Like I am his conclusion. "I think 'moving too fast' is the last thing someone would use to describe us." He chuckles. "I've wanted you longer than I can remember wanting anything else. And there have always been things in the way. I'll never forget always calculating how long we would have been dating by the time I got to propose to you. I thought sixteen years was a pretty huge bet, so might as well wait as long as possible to start dating you." He smiles ironically, and I cough a laugh.

"There's no way you were calculating marriage with me at, what? Eight?"

"Eh, I think seven."

I swat his shoulder and gape up at him. "You're lying."

"I'm not!" he retorts. "I'm dead serious. It was torture. But now? There's nothing in the way of us anymore, Blair. Nothing about being with you scares me at all. It's being without you again that terrifies me."

I let myself melt into his words for three full seconds before my body's hardwiring kicks back in.

"Are you sure that's the *only* thing that terrifies you about being with me? I can name a few more if you need help." My attempt at veering the conversation out of serious territory fails before it's even done leaving my mouth. Declan tilts his head at me with a knowing look and I know I can't avoid the mixture of hope and panic growing in my chest. He knows all my tricks. And he doesn't want to play when it comes to this.

"Sorry. It's just a lot to take in. Yesterday morning I still thought I was leaving at the end of summer, and now . . ." I widen my eyes.

"I get it." Declan squeezes my hand. "But promise me one thing."

I nod up at him.

"Promise me you won't run away again without an explanation."

"Promise," I say in a shallow breath.

The tension by his eyes seems to fade, and he looks at me like I'm a figment of his imagination.

And that makes things click. I ran away after our conversation about college; the prospect of both of us pursuing our goals seeming to tear us apart. And four and a half years later, he was still scared I would run away to chase those same ambitions. But circumstances changed, and so did my dreams. I wasn't scaring him off by moving across the street from him, I was easing his biggest fears.

"Now, tell me, what was Pepperdine like for you?"

I laugh. Declan's abrupt conversational habits were still so refreshing after all this time.

We spend the next four songs ignoring the beat as I tell him story after story about Roshi picking up guys at parties. About Faye being a fashion major who set up strange mannequins in random parts of Apartment 302. I would almost have a heart attack every time I went to the restroom in the middle of the night.

An older man shimmies up behind Declan and slaps him on the back. "It's good to see you on the dance floor, buddy!" he says.

"No way! Mr. Lawson, it's so good to see you." Declan interrupts his own excitement to introduce me. "Mr. Lawson, this is Blair," he says to the man. "Blair, meet the man who helped me walk again."

My heart shudders. Both with heartbreak and relief. I've never been more grateful to someone I've never met before. I shake his hand and then watch as Declan talks with the most animated look on his face. I feel rightfully back in the place I always longed to be.

During a natural lull in conversation, I excuse myself and make my way back to find the dessert table. There are so many people who want to talk to him, being the son of the person hosting this event, and I've stolen him away for as much time as possible.

As I'm pushing through the crowd of swarming bodies, a hand grips my upper arm from behind.

"Blair," a woman's voice demands, and a cold sweat breaks out on my neck. I'd recognize that voice anywhere.

I spin around to find Gwen's gorgeous face and tower of blond hair staring back at me with a grim expression.

"Mrs. Renshaw," I say, practically bowing.

She smiles but it looks forced. "Can I offer you a drink? I want to talk somewhere a little quieter."

"Oh," I say in surprise. "No, that's okay. I'm good with water."

She presses her lips together and floats over to a sparser area. I follow her. Blood starts pounding in my ears. Seeing her up close makes me feel like the seventeen-year-old girl sitting on her porch again. I spent hours staring at the front door, patiently waiting for the chance to see her son. But instead, she swung the door open and told me Declan didn't want to see me. That if I wanted what was best for him and his recovery, I would leave him alone. And I obeyed. A little too well.

"So, are you and Declan on again?"

The ball in my throat constricts. "On again?" I choke out.

"Sorry, is that not something the kids say these days?" she chortles. "On again? You know, like dating."

"Oh!" My heart lurches. Gwen was always kind to me as a kid, but something about her aura right now feels threatening.

JUST FRIENDS

Like I need to choose my words carefully. "Technically, I think Declan and I are on our first date for the first time in . . ." My voice goes quiet. "In four years. But I think the intention is to date again, yes."

I hold my breath, not sure what I'm hoping for. Her approval, I suppose.

"Wow. You guys are brave." She mumbles the last part as her eyes focus on something behind me, so as much as I want to clarify what that means, I don't have the chance to.

She grabs a flute of champagne off a server's tray and then looks back at me with a raise of her brows before taking a sip.

"Now, I hate to bring this up here, but I heard someone very close to you passed away recently? Your . . ." She tilts her head for me to fill in.

"My great-aunt," I supply.

"Ah, yes. Your great-aunt, my apologies. I am very sorry for your loss."

"Thank you." I nod quickly. "It was sudden, but I had time to say my goodbyes and—" My voice breaks so I press my lips together and nod some more instead of finishing my sentence.

Gwen smiles at me in sympathy and places a hand on my shoulder.

"You know, my mother passed away when I was around your age," she says.

I inhale. "I'm so sorry. I didn't know that."

She removes her hand and takes another sip of champagne. "Yes, and you know, those things are very hard. Grief is a very overpowering emotion. You can be as strong as ever and then whew! It's just a different beast, and it shows no partiality." She shakes her head, and her eyes go distant like she's going back to that place. "I made some decisions during that time that can only be explained by not being in my right mind, if you know what I mean." She squints at me like we're in on the same joke, but I feel like I'm very obviously on the outside.

"There are boys I dated and people I hung out with that I *never* would have if my mother hadn't passed." An abrupt laugh bubbles out of her. "But who can blame me? I was in a world of hurt. I was just seeking comfort. And you can't make good decisions when you're in that much pain." She looks to the left and I follow her gaze to see Declan talking to an older man in the distance. We both seem to watch him for a second, and then I rake my eyes back to Gwen's perfect profile. She takes a slow inhale like she's lost in old, forgotten memories. "My only regret is hurting people along the way. I thought they were what I needed at the time, but once the fog cleared, I was able to see what a terrible fit we were. And besides, it wasn't fair of me to rely on them when I wasn't emotionally stable enough to give them anything in return." She tilts her head as she looks at me, narrowing her eyes like she's assessing if I've caught the real meaning of her words.

And I have.

The words she didn't say are louder than the ambient chatter of the ballroom, which seems to whoosh around me like my head's being dunked underwater.

I would have rather she scream in my face.

I become aware of my heart beating in my chest. My mouth goes dry.

"Hi, Mom," Declan says, appearing beside Gwen. "I see you've done some catching up with Blair." He hasn't looked at me yet and he's smiling with so much joy that I feel my stomach turn.

Am I in too much pain to make decisions clearly? Am I going to end up hurting Declan again?

JUST FRIENDS

When Declan's eyes catch mine, his face falls. All the happiness slides away at the sight of my panicked, far-off stare, and it feels like a microcosm of what's to come.

"Blair," he starts. "Are you okay? You look pale."

I stare back at him, unable to move as the fear of what his mother implied races through my brain. I can feel her stare burning the side of my face as she awaits my response. I can feel her waiting for me to make her words come true. The thought of interacting with him while she watches makes me feel nauseous.

What if I really was doing this because I just wanted an escape from grief? Lottie only died two months ago. How could I be capable of making such a big commitment right now?

"Um, yeah," I hear myself mumble. "I'm fine. Everything is good. Just a little crowded in here. I think I— I think I just need to make a phone call really quick."

Declan's brows furrow as I back away. He glances at Gwen and when I notice the satisfied look on her face, I spin on my heel and speed walk across the ballroom. I don't breathe or think until I've made it to the double doors.

Immediately I push through them.

The cool night breeze hits my senses, and breathing feels easier for a moment.

I fish my phone from my purse and dial my mom. It doesn't feel like a conscious choice, rather muscle memory taking over. But I feel panicked and now that it's started, I don't know how to tamp it down. I just need to get away from Gwen's assessing glare and Declan's hope-filled expression. I need space to think.

"Blair?" She answers on the first ring.

"Hey, Mom. Can you come pick me up?"

"Uh." I hear her standing up and rustling around. "Yes, sweetie. Hold on."

I text her the address and she confirms that she can. We hang up and I cross my arms. I squeeze my eyes shut and try to focus on the ocean's frigid breeze hitting my cheek.

"Blair?" Declan says, footsteps sounding from behind me. "Hey, are you alright? What just happened in there?"

Tears start streaming down my face at the sound of his voice. I hate how quickly his mom's words got in my head. But they're in there now, and I need space to untangle the yarn-sized knot forming in my thoughts.

"I'm so sorry, Declan," I whisper, hardly meeting his eyes as he steps around me.

"Blair, look at me." He places the nail of his thumb under my chin and lifts. "What's going on? You can tell me anything. No more running away, remember?"

I'm doing it again, my mind taunts. *You ran out the first time, and you'll keep doing it because you don't know how to let him love you. So, don't let him love you.* Another tear streams down my face and over his hand.

"I can't do this right now." I ping-pong my finger between us. "I'm such an emotional wreck, I don't even recognize what's happening to me most days. I can't drag you through that, too." The words scrape out of my throat like a jagged thing trying to break free.

"What?" Declan shakes his head like a physical attempt to reject the words. "You don't believe that, do you?"

"Of course I do. I'm proving that with how I'm acting right now," I cry. "I feel fine one second, and then the next it feels like my world is tilting, and I can't breathe anymore. I can't prepare for it. I can hardly name it while it's happening. It's like this foreign object has taken residence in my body, and I don't know what it is, and I want it out, and I just can't—" I take a gasping breath.

"Breathe, Blair." He steps toward me and takes my writhing face in his hands. "I need you to breathe."

"I—" I hiccup painfully. *"Can't."*

I try to force air in, but it feels like I'm sucking through a tiny straw. The right side of my face starts tingling. I try to suck in air again, and it comes in two staccato bursts. The first, shallow and abrupt, and then another quick, jagged gasp.

"Come here," he whispers and uses his palm to cradle my head as he pulls me into his chest.

His body is warm, and I concentrate on the pressure of his palm on the back of my head. It feels like he's protecting me from the entire world with that one hand. I quiet enough to hear his heart beating. And finally, I exhale. My next breath in is steady, uninterrupted by involuntary gasps. He caresses my back with his other hand, slow and firm.

"You're okay, Blair," he says softly into my hair. "You're okay."

"But I'm not," I whimper. "That's the problem, Declan. I'm *not.*"

He goes silent and my face crumples into his chest one last time before I do what I need to do.

I push away from him and look up into his eyes, hardening mine. "Thank you for tonight. It was perfect. You are perfect. But I can't do this right now. I need space from us because I can't—" He looks like he's about to interject, and my voice rises on instinct. "I just can't choose this right now. I don't know if I'm thinking clearly, and I don't want to hurt you again."

"Blair, what—what are you doing? What is this? Did my mom say something to you?"

I press my lips together and shake my head.

He takes a step toward me.

"Don't do this," he pleads, reaching for my hands.

I take a step back and wrap my arms around my chest. "I just— I need a few days to think. I feel like—" It feels like my head is about to combust, so I blurt exactly what I'm thinking. "How am I supposed to know I'm thinking clearly if I'm not thinking clearly?" My voice breaks, desperate with longing to finally, for once, do the right thing. To not hurt him again.

His eyes soften like he sees the war going on in my mind. And it's not one waged against him. Or even us. It's against myself.

Declan looks like he's about to say something, but my mom's car pulls up to the curb and I run to it like it's a red buoy in an endless sea.

"I'm so, so sorry, Declan. I just need some space to think. That's all. I'm so sorry." I repeat it pathetically as I open the passenger door and step in. I'm still repeating it in my head when I arrive home.

I'm sorry, Declan. I'm so, so sorry.

Chapter 24

APARTMENT 302

Yesterday 11:39 p.m.

> I know this is a lot to ask . . . but let's say hypothetically I'm in a crisis. How quickly could you guys get to Seabrook?

Today 10:28 a.m.

Roshi

> It might be a lot to ask, but you never ask for anything, Blink.

Roshi

And it just so happens to be my one free weekend before school starts. I can be there by tomorrow! 😊

Faye

I'm sure Stephen can survive one weekend without me. 😊

In the cottage's bedroom, filled with the scent of lavender and sunlight, I'm sitting with my laptop over my covers, oscillating between my manuscript, budget spreadsheets, and the master scheduling portal for the convenience stores. I breath out a relieved sigh at the thought of Roshi and Faye being here tomorrow afternoon and shoot my mom a text to let her know the plan.

I didn't leave bed other than to make coffee, and pee out said coffee, for a full twenty-four hours. The last time I did this it was because of the flu. Now, it was the disease of distrust festering inside me. I was well acquainted with the feeling of distrusting other people. But not being able to trust myself was entirely new.

Hopelessly, helplessly, the longer I thought about the past two months, the more Gwen's words rang true. I'd been making life-altering decisions like choosing between a burger or chicken nuggets off a drive-thru menu. If she was right about that, how could I be sure the rest of her words wouldn't come true? That when the fog cleared, I would see the ways in which Declan and I didn't fit with startling clarity. That the first time we broke apart was proof of our incompatibility, and diving in headfirst while grief's claws still held me by the throat was a purely selfish decision. One made for my comfort alone.

I silenced the notifications on my phone, but Declan's texts were making it through to my computer anyway.

Declan

> Blair, I know you asked for space, but I just wanted to let you know I had a wonderful night with you. Tears and all. Please, take all the time in the world you need to think. Grief isn't something you can run away from. And if you try, it will tackle you from the back. And no one likes a surprise tackle.

I hate myself for the way my heart flutters at the sight of his name alone, and the stupid smile that creeps onto my face at the football reference. But his words make my chest ache for him. In my own grief, I kept forgetting he was no stranger to pain. The grief of losing your life as you knew it came with its own set of complicated emotions. Everything was uncharted territory for me, but maybe, for him, it wasn't. Maybe my grief wouldn't create a ravine between us.

I start to type out an over-explanation of where my head is at and then delete it. Wasn't it manipulative to drag someone through your contemplations about them while saying you needed space? And it wasn't even contemplation about *him*. He was everything I wanted and more. It was about my inability to understand if I was thinking clearly during such an emotional time, and if I was using him as a safety blanket against the harsh reality of my new world—and here I was, doing it again.

I slam my computer shut and drop my head into my hands.

Hot, frustrated tears spill from my eyes from confusion so thick it feels like my thoughts are trudging through mud. Emotionally, I felt like an empty well when it came to other people. There was only enough energy for my own pain and no one else's. Grief, at this stage, felt inherently selfish. So, how would I be capable of giving Declan the love he deserved? I could hardly listen to Faye complain about her mother-in-law for thirty minutes.

And besides, Lottie hid her suffering from her closest friends. She even hid it from me and my mom to the best of her ability. All the way to the painstaking end until she lost control of it.

And my mom protected me from the details of my father's torment my whole life. No matter how much I pried, she never unearthed the specifics. And to think, she was in the middle of losing the man she loved, swallowing the dream life he promised her, and figuring out how to be a single mother, and yet, she never relied on me to shoulder the weight.

She went to great lengths to prevent her emotional distress from affecting my childhood, and although I still wanted to hear the story, I'm grateful she shielded me from things I was too young to bear at the time. So, wasn't love hiding the pain you were in for the sake of others? Or was it letting them in?

The next morning, a knock at my door startles me while brushing my hair. I tiptoe to the door, hoping against all odds that it's not Declan coming over to check on me. And to my utter shock, I see Faye and Roshi's fish-eyed bobbleheads in the peephole.

JUST FRIENDS

"Ahhhh!" I scream, whipping the door open. "How did you guys get here? I thought you would call when you landed?"

Faye flashes her beauty pageant smile. "Your mom sent us a sneaky text telling us to call her when we landed. She picked us up from the airport this morning and was so excited to show us around your hometown!"

Roshi sheds her coat. "Yeah, Blair! How long were you going to keep this gem of a town hidden from us? This place is like the perfect set for a Nicholas Sparks book."

I cackle my disbelief as I pull each of them in for a hug.

"Aw, I can't believe you guys are here." I jut my bottom lip out. "Thank you so much for dropping everything and coming out so last minute."

"Oh, hush! You deserve the world. Now let us in. We have way too many bags for a two-night stay." Roshi boogies past me through the doorway with her suitcase like an auntie in a movie. Overly comfortable and unwilling to accept your sappiness.

Faye follows her in, and I watch as their jaws drop. "Shut up," they say in unison.

"This is all yours?" Roshi shouts.

"I mean, what you're looking at now is pretty much the whole house. But yeah, isn't it cute?"

"Um yeah! You think? I'm trying to furnish my house, and let me tell you, I don't have the eye for interior decorating like I thought I would. And Stephen is no help in that department."

Her words make me grateful in an instant. A house, fully furnished by Lottie herself, was a blessing I would never get over. I give them the short tour, and then set up Faye's things in my bedroom, and unbox the blow-up mattress I had shipped overnight for Roshi in the living room.

There was an ease with which they slipped into my home,

as if no time had passed. It made me wonder what I was so upset with them about. Perhaps it was easier to convince myself they "weren't there for me," when what I was really mourning was our distance.

After getting them settled in, we walked the short couple blocks to a cliffside view of Seabrook. The town seemed to be showing off. The sunbeams danced on the waves, which glittered as they splashed against the rocky cliffs. The ancient trees stretched their spindly branches as if guarding the landscape.

"Wow, Blair," Faye said, awestruck by the view. "Why have I never even heard of this place before meeting you? It's absolutely breathtaking!" She clutched a hand to her chest like a rich, elderly woman.

I chuckled. "Yeah, not many people have. Everyone seems to be pretty secretive about it."

"I would be too if this is where I grew up," Roshi added.

I've stared at the beauty of this place for so long, it's become my normal. But seeing it through their perspective gives me fresh eyes. Just two months ago, I might have been embarrassed—embarrassed that I had given up a prestigious job to stay in my hometown and write a book with no prospects of publishing. But I'd never felt freer, in one sense at least. In the other, the cloying agony of wanting Declan but not wanting to hurt him nipped at me.

That night, after eating dinner, we settle into my little seaside cottage, or what Roshi and Faye are referring to as my "Nicolas Sparks movie-set-house." It feels like I've lived here forever with them making themselves cozy in the living room. And with our pajamas on, candles lit, and soft jazz playing on the television, Roshi finally breaks open the conversation I've been steadily avoiding.

JUST FRIENDS

"Okay, Blink," she starts, getting settled beneath a fuzzy cream blanket on the couch. "I've never heard you refer to yourself as 'in crisis.' So, let's hear it. What's going on?"

I blow out a big breath, eyes going wide.

"Oh boy," Faye quips.

"Yeah. Oh boy, indeed," I reply, and then, in a surprising turn of events that shocks everyone, including me, I tell them everything. Every painstaking detail. So much so that the earth must have made its full rotation by the time I'm done speaking. Not actually, but it feels like a lifetime has passed when Roshi finally pipes in to say: "And why do you think you'll hurt him?"

"Because I did the first time. And that was before any of this grief stuff hit. If we do this again, I don't want it to end. Ever. And I definitely don't want to be the one responsible for hurting him a second time. But how am I supposed to know I'm in a healthy enough mindset to be making a commitment that big? What if I'm too emotionally weak and he ends up having to support me all the time, and then he feels tired of having to take care of me? I cry every single day now, and I never know when it's coming, and when it does, he'll feel like he needs to drop everything to be there for me. Isn't it selfish to enter a relationship like that?" I plead.

"Okay, yes. I hear you, one hundred percent. But first off, grieving doesn't make you 'emotionally weak.' I can understand not wanting to start a relationship like this, but you can't spend the rest of your life waiting for a time when both of you are in perfect headspaces for a relationship. You will inevitably be supporting each other through something or another in this lifetime. It's not always going to be a perfect fifty-fifty split. And secondly, from what you've said, it doesn't sound like Declan is scared off by your tears in the least. And actually, a third point I'm just now thinking of, and not to diminish your grief at all, but this sounds a little bit like a case of CMIL," Faye says tentatively.

"What's that?" I ask.

"Crazy Mother-In-Law."

"He's not even my boyfriend, let alone my husband, Faye."

"Yes, I know that, obviously. But doesn't what Gwen said feel a little manipulative? You weren't doubting yourself at all until she planted those things in your head. And now you don't even know if you can trust your own judgment to have good judgment. It's like this weird circular argument."

"Yeah," Roshi chimes in. "I will say, Blair, you've never been one to doubt your choices. Faye and I have to talk twenty people's ears off before we make a decision, but you've always just kept it all in here, no problem." She taps her temple.

"That's true," I mutter, going inward.

"And didn't you mention that Gwen was the one who wouldn't let you through the door when you were trying to visit Declan all those years ago?" Roshi adds.

"Well, technically Declan told her he didn't want to see me."

"And why didn't he want to see you?" Faye asks.

"He said it was because he didn't want me to see him . . . in that state." My voice peters off.

"Like, injured, and bedridden, and weak?" Roshi supplies for me.

I nod. "I wouldn't care what state he was in. I just wanted to see him. Be there with him."

They nod in unison and something stirs in my chest.

I just wanted to be there with him.

Through every emotion he was having. Anger and shame and heartbreak, complete despair. And that's what he wanted with me, now.

JUST FRIENDS

It was like Declan and I were reliving our past—but in reverse this time. He hadn't wanted me to see him weak, and now I shuddered at the thought of him being with me at my lowest. Both of us believing we were protecting the other from pain by hiding our suffering.

But hadn't the past two months taught me how much I disagreed with that? I had to force Lottie to let me stay by her bedside as she was dying, and I watched my mom refuse to ask for help even as she drowned before my eyes. In the end, they caused the very pain they were trying to protect me from. And though their intentions were good, I couldn't keep doing the same—to Faye and Roshi, and most of all, to Declan.

And besides, *there is little I wouldn't be willing to do for Declan.* The thought clangs through me as if dropped into my mind from above. Swiftly, the flutter of fear follows it. I want Declan, and not just in the emotional-safety-blanket way.

Not because he dampens the stomach-churning effects of grief. Not because he's a distraction. If anything, he was the exact opposite. He was the one who led me through my tears. Led me to face the life-altering reality when I wanted to pretend it wasn't real. And even at the bottom of my grief, I knew, deep in my gut, I would still have it in me to be there for him. It would be my joy to pull myself out of my world to be a part of his. The realization is startling. I couldn't picture wanting anything close to the depth with which I wanted Declan. So, why did I feel so terror-stricken?

"Oh my gosh," I breathe. "The thing Lottie always used to say—it's happening to me."

Faye and Roshi were still, waiting for me to snap out of my strange inwardness and explain.

"Lottie used to always say this phrase." The familiar, painful knot forms in my throat and I berate myself to keep it together.

I take a moment, try to breathe, and continue. "She would say, 'the fear part only comes when it's love.' But you know, she would say it more in her accent that I never heard until other people told me she had one."

Roshi laughs. "Relatable."

"And I never understood what that meant, but she said I would know it was real love if it felt so big, it became scary to admit. If I felt transformed by it, felt like I'd be losing a part of myself if I lost it. And I do feel that fear now, but not because I don't think it will work between us, but because I think it really will. Except, on the horrifying condition that I have to let him in on my grief as it happens. Which you guys know I'm terrible at. I've never even cried in front of you guys until now. But these days I really have no control over it." In perfect irony, my voice crumples like a soda can being crushed and I bow my head to hide my contorting face.

Faye and Roshi scootch from their sections of the couch to reach me in an instant. I feel both sets of arms wrap around my shoulders and I finally allow myself to let go in front of them for the first time. My tears are for Lottie, because I did feel like I lost a tiny part of myself when I lost her. But they were also for the fear I felt, because I couldn't escape the way I loved Declan.

The surge of emotions pours out now that I've let myself admit them. I did feel entirely transformed since seeing Declan again. Staying in Seabrook despite the grief that awaited me at every corner felt possible because of him. He was the insistent voice that reminded me of my love for writing. So much so, I was angry at him at first for reminding me of the dream I tried so hard to forget. But he pushed back on my self-doubt. Believed in me when I didn't believe in myself. And now, I had a nearly completed manuscript on my computer. In so many ways, being near him brought me closer to myself. And that was what scared me most. I had already been in love with him. I had never fallen out of love with him.

"What are you feeling right now?" Faye asks gently once my breathing calms.

"I'm thinking about how—"

"I asked you what you're feeling, not what you're thinking," she protests, but her delivery makes me laugh. "You are such a thinker. Think, think, think! I'm convinced all your problems would be solved if you just let yourself *feel* your emotions."

"I don't know how to do that," I burst out. But after a moment of silence, I let my head fall into my hands as I release another wave of sobs.

"There you go!" Faye points at me. "Would you look at that. You are a very fast learner indeed. You're getting the hang of it right there."

I look up and pin her with a glare through teary eyes.

Roshi claps as she honks with laughter.

"You guys are ridiculous," I say with affection.

"And you're in love. Our blinky Blairy is in love. Finally," Faye singsongs, kneeling on the couch and clutching her hands to her chest.

"Not finally. Just again," I say.

Roshi and Faye look at each other with wide eyes like they don't recognize this version of me sitting on the couch.

"Oh my gosh." I cover my face with my hands. "Do you guys want to know a secret? Since we're already exposing everything about me right now?"

"Spill," Faye demands.

"Declan may or may not live right across the street."

Roshi and Faye freeze like they're being pranked. They look at each other again, then slowly turn back to me. And then they scream.

"Oh my gosh! Blair, you self-effacing freak. I forgot about that. Why didn't you remind us the second we came in?" Roshi yells, picking up a couch cushion to fling at me.

"Hey, you didn't tell me that!" Faye whines.

I shrug and cover my face in self-defense.

"Well, now that I know that, you think I'm just gonna let you sit there? Get up! Get up!" Faye squeals.

They both fly up from the couch. Roshi, to throw soft things at me, and Faye, to physically pick me up from the corner I've been occupying.

"You are literally ridiculous. I can't believe you're a real human being who has avoided being in love with their best friend for this long. Get up, right now, we're going to the bathroom to do your hair," Faye rants as she sticks her pokey fingernails into my armpits to lift me up, and then pushes me to the bathroom, whipping out my hairbrush.

"You guys, it must be midnight at this point. I can't just barge over there in my pajamas and bang on his door," I argue.

Roshi checks her phone. "It's only eleven twenty-three. You're going over there. And you're right. You can't wear pajamas. Put this on." She rips the first black dress she sees from my closet and hands it to me.

"You're kidding me. I am not wearing a dress to walk across the street."

"Oh, but you are," Faye says matter-of-factly. "Arms up."

And that's how I end up in a little black dress at eleven thirty-five, crossing the street with Roshi and Faye peeking through my living room blinds. The second I step outside, the ridiculousness of the dress hits me. I try to turn around and run back inside, but Roshi and Faye barricade the door. I roll my eyes, secretly grateful for the excuse not to chicken out. Faye gathered the top section of my hair into a half-up hairdo and curled my curtain bangs to frame "the petite features of my face."

Crossing the street and onto Declan's lawn takes no time at all, and it feels like I blinked and appeared at his doorstep. The memory of me waiting on his childhood home's doorstep reverberates through me like a dissonant note and internally, I cringe. But I forgave that. Now, I had to hope he would forgive me for running away. I raise my hand and knock.

Silence.

I turn around and squint my eyes at Faye and Roshi's not-so-subtle window peeking and throw my arms up. They wave frantically as if to say, Just try again! So, I lift my hand once more and knock. Still, nothing. No footsteps. No television sounds in the background. Not a sound.

Disappointment ricochets through me, and I suddenly feel naive for thinking Faye and Roshi's plan would work. This isn't some grand romance book ending. He's probably entering REM sleep at this very moment like a normal person at eleven thirty-eight.

The bitter sting of rejection spreads through my limbs as I cross the street, but the moment I walk through the cottage's front door, they smother my encroaching shame with emphatic coos, shoulder pats, and assurances.

Padding into the bathroom, I lock myself inside to peel off my black dress and hop into bunny-printed pajamas. Even with the door closed, Faye and Roshi are shouting encouragements. I laugh them off like they're a nuisance but secretly they are helping.

On Sunday morning, Faye and Roshi are leaving, but they

would leave me with more confidence than I felt all summer. I hadn't witnessed myself being open with people often, but I discovered they were a soft landing. It was confirmation that the people in your life could only be as close to you as you let them. Which I hoped to apply to Declan, in ways that were closer than friendship allowed.

Loving Declan came naturally to me. It was, potentially, the one thing in my life I never had to try at. The one place where feeling came more naturally than thinking.

"Promise us you won't chicken out once we're gone." Faye blocks me from retreating to the bedroom the second I unlock the bathroom door.

"You can trust me on this. I'll sit on his doorstep all week if that's what it takes for him to let me in," I promise, and the proclamation takes root inside me.

We decide to call it a night, but before the hands of sleep claim me, I think about the nearly finished manuscript on my laptop, my best friends beside me, and the cottage that holds them all. I fall into the deepest sleep I've slept all summer.

For the first time, I could sense that I hadn't just returned to my home again, but I had returned to myself, too.

Chapter 25

Car rides after dropping off loved ones at the airport have always struck me as particularly eerie. From loud, trilling goodbyes and tight hugs to abrupt silence. Alone in the car with my thoughts as their journey began and mine with them ended.

As Roshi and Faye gathered their luggage from my trunk, we promised to start doing weekly calls to keep up. Long distance would become our new normal, and our commitment to staying close would be the testimony to what we still had despite the miles between us.

I drive back to the cottage in a contemplative daze. Would

Declan be home at this hour? And if he was home, what would I say?

The hilly road spits me onto my new street before I've decided the answers to any of these questions. I park at the curb and walk through my overgrown front yard. There's a letter laying on my doorstep. That's odd, I think to myself. I have a mailbox at the front. But when I bend down to reach it, I notice my name written on the front in small, black letters.

I feel the thud of my heart in my chest.

When I pick it up, I notice how soft it feels in my hands. Wrinkles run through the envelope like it's been crumpled and flattened out multiple times.

I check over my shoulder like someone is watching me, fish my keys out of my purse, and stuff myself inside as quickly as humanly possible. I plop down onto the cream couch and begin tearing into the letter. Like a bear, I think to myself. Like a boy. Like I watched Declan do with his college acceptance letter.

I reach inside and pull out a piece of composition notebook paper. Its edges are frayed like it was torn out of a journal. Inhaling a shaky breath, I read:

Dear Blair,

Let me start this letter by saying I am sorrier than words can describe. I haven't seen you or spoken to you in 250 days, and I can't stand to go one more. The last time I looked at you, you were in the stands at the championship game. You didn't see me, or maybe you pretended not to, but you looked beautiful. Slightly aloof, as always, with a weary look on your face. And in that moment, I promised myself I would apologize to you after the game, to beg for you to come back. I swear it. If you had caught my eyes

JUST FRIENDS

maybe you would have understood. But I never got the chance to because, well, we both know what happened.

I heard you tried to see me at the hospital, but they were only letting family in. And when I was out of surgery and back at the house, I heard you waited on my porch for hours. I was probably in one of the medication-induced sleeps I was in almost every day, but when I woke up, my mom told me you were at the door. I told her to turn you away. I told her I didn't want to see you. I know she told you to leave. I know you did. And I didn't text. And I didn't call. And for that, I will never forgive myself. But I beg you to read the entirety of this letter so that I can explain. I don't expect your forgiveness, but I will never be able to live with myself if I don't try. So here it goes.

The way we ended was my fault, Blair. I regret asking you to give up your dreams to be with me and rely on mine. I thought I was being the person you wanted me to be, providing for you and your mom, but it was arrogance disguising itself as nobility. Truly, there is nothing I look back on and shudder to think about more. I regretted my words before the accident, but after, the shame multiplied to a suffocating degree. You were right. And I knew you were right before I woke up in the hospital.

But afterward, when standing up to use the restroom required two nurses and ended with me screaming in pain, I couldn't imagine letting you see me like that. Like I still am. You were right not to rely on my future career when it still had a good chance of existing, but now, it is completely gone, for good. I felt embarrassed. I felt pathetic. I felt worthless. And above all, I felt ashamed of myself for ever suggesting you trust me with your future in the first place.

But I've been sitting in my childhood bedroom for

eight months straight, recovering, thinking. I have so much time to think in this stupid bed. Some days are okay. Some are boring. Every day I try to walk and get angry all over again. But one thing is always the same.

I think about you. How much I miss you. How dumb I was for turning you away when you wanted to see me. I would give anything now to let you see me. Crutches, and pain medication, and hopelessness, and screaming in pain while trying to walk, and all. I don't care if I look pathetic. This is me right now, and I've always known you loved me for more than football. For more than just what I could give you. I don't know where along the way I started believing you saw me like my dad does. Like I'm worthless if I'm not bringing home achievements. Like I'm unlovable if I'm not giving you something to show off.

You were always the opposite. So much so, that the one time I did try to offer you my accomplishments, we ended up here. So, why, in my right mind, would I ever block you out? I don't know, Blair. That's the horrible thing. I don't know what I was thinking.

I didn't want you to see me out of control, and in wanting that, I took away all your control. I stripped you of any say in us having a relationship.

And that's not what love does. Love doesn't choose itself. It doesn't only consider one side of the story. And love doesn't shrink back from pain either. Which definitely isn't something I need to be explaining to you. You have such a big heart, I actually get concerned sometimes. It must be bursting at the seams of your chest, Blair. I don't know how it stays in there. Seriously, see a doctor.

But anyways.

I assumed bad character of you by thinking you

wouldn't be here for me since I have nothing to give you in return. But there's practically a photo of you in the dictionary next to the word selfless. Gosh, that was cheesy. I'm cringing reading it back already. But it's true. You've centered your entire life around giving back to your mom. What teenage girl thinks about those things?

All of this to say, I know you're doing just that right now: going to Pepperdine to study hard and get a good job to help retire your mom one day. And I won't ever find myself in the way of that dream ever again.

But if I could ask you to believe one thing, believe this: There is nothing about you that caused my idiotic actions. You are perfect, Blair. You are everything I could ever want. It's actually difficult to think about for too long. It makes me so scared to think I've lost you forever. And I genuinely don't think I'll ever find anyone who understands me like you do ever again. That's the truth.

I know that must be hard to believe. I know that I messed up in a way too big to just ask forgiveness for. But if you would give me the chance, I'd love to tell you how sorry I am in person. Face to face. I just want to see you. Even if it's for you to yell at me. Or slap me. You can. As hard as you want. I deserve it. It would be an honor, honestly.

But if you never respond to this letter, I will respect it as your choice to move on with your life. You deserve to be with someone who loves you in a way that makes you feel like the funniest girl in the world. The prettiest. The sweetest. The smartest. And if that's not with me, I'll wish you true happiness, with whoever that may be.

But you best believe, if it doesn't end up being me, I'll still read every single book you write. I'll go to the bookstore every day until I see your name on the shelves.

You're gonna go far. I hope he holds your hand all the way there. I hope it's me.

I miss you, Little Bird. If you can find it in your heart to forgive me, fly back to me.

-Declan

Loud, primal sobs rack my body. I have to cover my mouth to muffle the sounds. If there were ever a time not to think, just to feel, this would be the moment I'd trace back to. The outside world seems to completely fade away. It's just me, and the tears racing down my face, and the letter on my lap.

I fumble for the discarded envelope on the floor and flip it over to read the address on the back. It's addressed to the dorm I lived in my freshman year at Pepperdine. Everything is correct. The room number. The street. The zip code. How did I not get this? How has it finally found me now? I collapse over my lap and mourn the years we could have saved if I'd read these words.

This was so much more than Declan made it out to be. It wasn't just an apology. It was confirmation of everything I've ever wanted from him. And beyond that, it was the answer to the question I had been debilitated by since the charity gala.

Back then, I wanted nothing more than to see Declan. If he wasn't able to speak, if he wasn't able to move, if he was simply asleep, I just wanted to be by his side. Because it was him. It's how I felt with Lottie, too. And now, the pain I felt in her absence? He wasn't scared of it. If anything, he knew what I was in for more than I did. And he was running my way. My body feels weak as I stand up, open the front door, and run across the street to Declan's house. The fog of morning fading curls around me as I make my way to his front porch, trying to catch my breath as anticipation vibrates through me. My hand lifts, but before I can knock, his door swings open. His blondish-brown hair is mussed, and his shirt is crumpled like he's been bent over building the bar at the coffee shop.

"Declan," I say, breathless.

His eyebrows crumple, eyes wary beneath them. "Did you read it?"

My lips flatten in an attempt not to cry, but when he sees my reaction, his bottom lip goes unsteady too, and I throw myself into his arms.

"I'm so sorry," I cry. The words are muffled by his shirt. "I'm so, so, so sorry, Declan. How did I not get the letter? How did you find it?" I rear back, looking up at him.

He looks down at me, tension creasing the space between his eyebrows, and his mouth twitches to speak but makes no sound.

"Can we sit?" he says.

I nod and he steps aside. I make my way to his living room couch, wiping my face.

He takes a seat next to me, head hung low while his eyes blaze holes into the floorboards. After a moment of silence, he breaks his staring contest with the floor and dips his hands under my legs, scooping me from my spot on the couch and into his lap. I release a tiny, startled sound at his forwardness. When I settle, he brushes a piece of hair behind my ear.

"That's better." He exhales. "Well, there's not going to be an easy way to explain this, but, after the event, when you said you spoke to my mom . . . I know you said she didn't say anything to you, but I had an odd feeling about the whole situation. So, the next night, I went to my parents' house to talk to her." His eyes flit away and the muscle in his jaw ticks like he's nervous to go on. "Finally, after hours of back and forth, I got her to admit that she took the letter out of our mailbox. The letter I thought had successfully made its way to you."

My hand drifts toward my mouth, jaw unhinging in disbelief.

"I wasn't leaving my bedroom, let alone the house, much at the time, so even getting downstairs to put the letter *in* the mailbox was a feat. She told me the mail was picked up, and obviously I believed her. Had no reason not to." He stops and shakes his head like he needs to stop himself from getting too worked up. He sighs, continues. "She tried to justify her actions by saying she was just 'carrying out my original wishes.' You know, my wishes not to see you," he adds sheepishly. "And obviously this doesn't justify anything, but that day I got the acceptance letter to Notre Dame, and we fought about our futures, she was in the front yard when you stormed out. So, from her perspective, you left, and I was completely lethargic in your absence. I don't think she would have meddled in our relationship at that point, but then the accident happened, and almost losing me switched something inside her. Like the sudden loss of control made her go into overdrive trying to protect me from ever getting hurt again. Even emotionally. And I guess in this scenario she deemed you as the threat she needed to protect me from." My face must fall because he rushes in to add, "But I really don't think she's going to be a problem anymore."

"What? What does that mean? How can you know that?"

Declan's eyes dart between mine, searching. "Do you remember what she was like when we *were* dating?"

I rack my memory but come up short when it comes to Gwen during our short, blissful stint of a relationship senior year. At my blank expression, Declan says, "Exactly. She stayed out of our way. After talking to her last night, I'm almost one hundred percent certain she's realized that if her goal is to keep me safe, then keeping me away from you is the exact opposite way to accomplish that goal. She was embarrassed, which is rare, said that her mental state and actions during that time are unrecognizable to her now. And then she tore up the house looking for the letter. Told me to tell you she hopes returning it can be the start of her apology, and that she'd love to apologize in person but she also wants to give you space." Declan looks like he's in physical pain delivering the words.

Perhaps it's the shock of all these new revelations, but my mind is still fixated on him. On the words he wrote when I thought he wanted nothing to do with me.

"Declan," I start in a cautious voice. "The stuff with your mom we can deal with later. As pissed as I may be that I never got this letter, I can't imagine what almost losing your son would do to you. But the words you wrote." I hold up the crinkled letter, shaking my head. "I need to tell you how sorry I am."

"Blair, no. It's okay."

"Declan. Let me apologize to you," I demand, wrapping my hands around his neck. "I am so sorry for walking out on you at the gala. I completely freaked out about where this was going. You know how fresh into grief I am, and I started wondering if it was selfish of me to start a relationship with you when I am practically, like, I don't know—this human cocoon. Just, you know, I'm very inward right now. And I don't want to drain you with how much comfort I might need. I don't want to hurt you again. But then, I probably did in the process because I said I'd stop doing the running away thing, and then I did the running away thing."

"It's okay, Blair. My mom got in your head. Grief is complicated and—"

"No," I interrupt. "Okay, well, yes. She did. And grief is complicated. But it's not so complicated that I can just run away from you when it feels hard. Especially because, then I started thinking about how much I wanted to be there for you after the accident. I wouldn't have cared if you cried for sixteen hours a day, or didn't make eye contact with me, or didn't have the energy to say anything. I literally just wanted to sit by your bedside. That's it. And I know we can't change the choices we made in the past, but we can control the choices we're making right now. And I want a future with you. I want this." My interlaced hands tighten around his neck, and I dip my eyes down before looking up at him again. "I want you, Declan. And we can't keep letting difficult things be excuses to block each other out anymore. We keep trying to be perfect for each other and it's so—" I shake my head. "It's so dumb. Hard things will keep happening in life, but I want to go through them with you. I am so confused at my own emotions these days and I'm the one they're inside of, so it is terrifying to imagine letting someone into that, but I will let you in, if you want to be let in. And I really hope you do because one of those emotions is how much I love you and I honestly couldn't ever and still can't picture my life with anyone but you."

He stares at me like my words change something vital about him and he's reconciling all the ways it might reorient his being. His eyes dilate, this time I'm sure, and he wraps his hands around my waist to pull me in. "I'm glad you finally agree," he says before his lips crush mine. *Home,* my brain screams, like a knee-jerk reaction. I pull back.

"That's it?" I cry. "It's just that easy for you?"

"It wasn't." He shakes his head, releases a weary laugh. "But it's been four years and now it is. Back then, I didn't have the words to articulate what I was feeling. I was resentful. So,

JUST FRIENDS

so resentful, and it had zero direction. Instead, it just exploded on everything in my vicinity. And worst of all, it landed on you. You can't know how much I regret that. So, yes. 'That's it.' I've lost way too much time with you already. I don't want to lose a second more."

"Me neither." A tear slides down my cheek as I smile.

"And Blair?"

"Mh-hmm?"

"I love you too." He swoops me into another kiss and it feels like everything I've ever worked toward was a lousy distraction from what I really wanted. Like everything I've ever worked toward was a lousy distraction from what I really wanted. Every moment spent fearing this conclusion was a pathetic denial of what I already knew to be true. He was my first love, and he is my last.

Declan pauses to look at me with an expression so precious I think I might explode. He's still holding my jaw in his hands, and I laugh with disbelief as I stare into the same eyes I fell in love with when I was five years old. I weave my fingers into his disheveled hair and pull him down to kiss me again. He complies. Greatly.

At first, the kiss feels like an apology. Then it morphs into a promise. Some are languid, mourning for lost time. Some are impatient for the future we've pictured since we were kids. We pause, laugh a little, with relief and realization that this is not our last kiss. But the first of the rest of our lifetime.

"Wait," he says, threading his arm under my legs to return me to my spot on the couch before standing. "I have something for you."

I chuckle. "What? How did you have time to—"

"Just wait here." He stalks past the kitchen and then I hear a door opening and closing.

He comes back hiding something with both hands behind his back.

"Okay, ready? I made you something," he clarifies.

"What! How did you have time to make me something?"

"Well," he says ironically, raising his eyebrows and tilting his head to imply the days we spent apart gave him ample time.

I grimace, shrugging my shoulders.

"I was shocked at how much you noticed the birdhouses, so, I thought you might like one of your own." He spins the object out from behind his back, revealing a small birdhouse, like the ones hanging from the coffee shop ceiling, except this one is color-blocked in pastel pinks, yellows, oranges, and greens. The disassembled clock parts still adorn the sides. "All of the birdhouses I've ever built remind me of you. I thought it was time the Little Bird herself had one of her own."

"Are you kidding me?" I howl, standing up like the couch is on fire. "Oh my gosh."

He hands it to me, and I hold it in my hands like it's made of glass. I admire the delicacy of the detailed door, rounded at the top like my cottage's front door, with my mouth slightly agape.

"This is beautiful, Declan." I try to elongate the word to emphasize my weight of feeling, but there aren't enough words in all of language to describe how special, how seen I feel in this moment.

"And check this out." He reaches for the birdhouse's tiny door and opens it. "There's an actual room inside, and I placed an even smaller room inside it. I have another present for you in there. But you're not allowed to open it yet."

"You're joking." I squeal, peering inside at the dollhouse-like interior. "When can I open it?"

JUST FRIENDS

"I don't know," he says with a sardonic grin. "You can't ever open it technically. You have to break into it with a hammer. But don't worry. One day, I'll let you see what's inside."

My jaw drops. "How am I supposed to be that patient?" I protest.

He points at me. "That response is exactly why I made it entry by blunt force only."

I roll my eyes at him playfully and then set the birdhouse down to thank him. I thank him thoroughly. And when the thanking moves to his couch, I pause, remembering something. "Declan, I have a question."

"Yeah. Anything," he replies in a husky voice.

"Do you . . . I don't know, maybe have a photo of us in your wallet?"

He stills for a second before realization dawns on him. He smirks like he's been caught. "How'd you know?"

"A little bird at the coffee shop might have told me."

"That's strange. I only know one Little Bird at the coffee shop."

I jolt.

"Oh, I almost forgot. I need you to fire me."

"Excuse me?" He rears his chin back from beneath me.

"Yeah. I can't work for you anymore. You've been a terrible boss."

"Fine." He furrows his brows. "You're fired."

"Thank you," I say, pleased. "Wait, who's going to help you with renovations now? Should I help you find some—"

"Oh, no. You're good. I don't need any help."

"What do you mean? There was no one doing overtime hours before me?"

"Nope. I made that job up." He smiles. "For you."

My head tilts. "Excuse me?"

"Yeah." He chuckles like it's obvious. "I was doing the renovations just fine on my own. But you said you needed a job with overtime hours, so I just figured . . ."

My heart protests in my chest once again. This man.

"Well, thank you, first of all. That was extremely charitable especially considering how unskilled I am with power tools. But also . . ." I swat his shoulder.

"Ow! What was that for?"

"For being a sneaky, sneaky boss," I jibe. "But you are a *generous* sneaky boss. I'll give you that."

"I *was* a sneaky, sneaky boss," he corrects.

"Right. Well, on the upside, now that I'm not your barista, I can finally finish this romance book."

"Slacker. You haven't finished it yet?"

"I've been a little busy slinging lattes for you, sir. But I'm nearing the end."

"Okay. Well, let me help you out. Let's think of a good ending."

"What, like, help me think of a line?" I ask.

"Yeah. Every book needs a great last line."

"Okay, then. Give it to me. What d'you got?" I am fully expecting a horrible idea.

He looks up like he's pondering. "Oh, okay. What about this. The last line isn't actually dialogue because they're too busy snogging. So, there'd be the start of dialogue but then it's cut off by—"

I tip my head back and cackle. "First, 'daft' and now 'snogging'? Do you have a confession to make about reading strictly British romance books?"

He just grins at me in answer, and I laugh a disbelieving laugh.

"Kissing instead of talking is probably more realistic in real life," I say, side-eyeing him.

"Trust me. I know," he replies, with a blinding, heart-clenching, freckle-emphasizing smile.

"But in romance novels it's nice when they tie everything together."

"Okay, then. You're the writer. Show me how it's done."

I bite the inside of my cheek in thought. "Oh. Here's a good example. Like in your letter to me, there was a line you wrote at the end. Do you remember it?"

His mouth parts, closes. "Say it for me."

I puff out a breathless chuckle. "It was something like, I miss you, Little Bird. If you can find it within yourself to forgive me, fly back to me."

"And you did." His eyes soften.

"And I did."

I see relief flood Declan's face and my heart keens. We both forget to think about my romance book's ending because ours is just beginning. And I'm here to stay, I will my face to say. But I think he knows. He pulls me down and wraps his arms around me, tight like he's imagining when he didn't have me. And to think, grief and pride almost kept us apart. The pride of having to grieve especially. He moves the hair that's fallen over my forehead and places a gentle kiss there. And finally, I don't think. I just feel the steady beating of his heart beneath his chest.

Being his feels like coming home.

Six Months Later

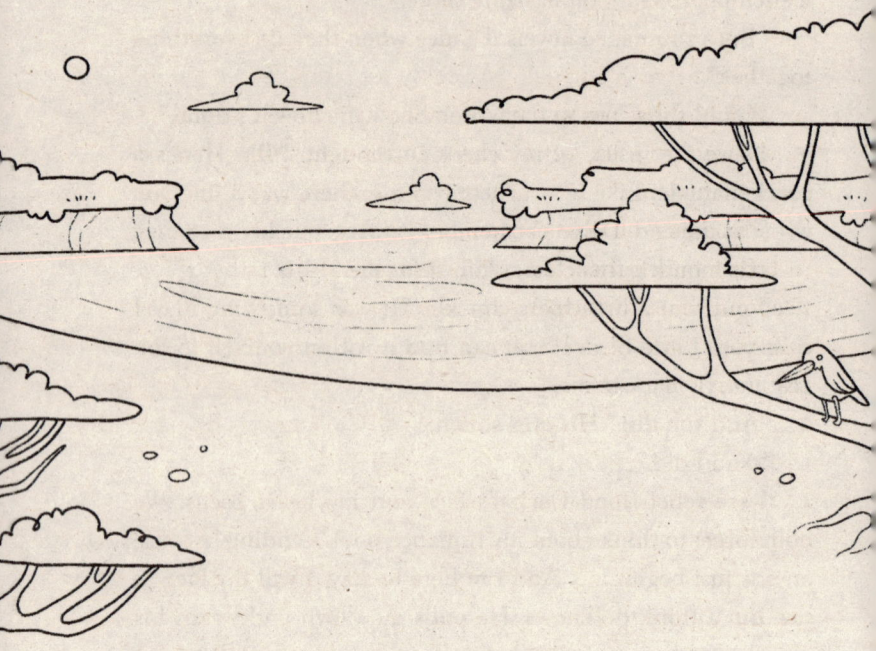

"Declan!" I shout from my cottage's living room. He comes sprinting in from the garden, face sweaty and gloves dirty from building the deck out there. "Look at this." I point at my mom's first Facebook post in thirteen years. It's a photo of her in a red minidress holding a bright orange drink on a white sand beach. Sunset colors paint the sky behind the massive smile parting her face.

It reads:

> You are looking at a retired woman! Woohoo!
> And look at my baby! She wrote her first book!
> That's right! My baby wrote a book!

JUST FRIENDS

<u>LINK TO BUY MY BABY'S BOOK!</u>

GO BUY THAT SUCKER SO I CAN
KEEP BEING RETIRED!
Text or call me, because like I said,
I'M A RETIRED WOMAN! WOOHOO!

"Oh my gosh," he laughs while absentmindedly rubbing my shoulders. "Does that link even work?"

"I have no idea, but I am not gonna check. It's the sentiment that counts."

Managing all the convenience stores quickly switched to trying to sell them. So, with Declan and his father's connections, we sold them to a sweet Korean family from San Francisco who moved down to Seabrook to run them. I still maintain a part-time consulting position, and in my free time, I shop my currently self-published book around to literary agents.

"Are you ready for our date tonight?" Declan asks from above me.

"Six thirty. Secret Beach. Wear a dress. I know!" I say, repeating his instructions back to him.

He nods and then gives me a quick kiss on the cheek before putting his protective gloves back on.

"Okay, you can open your eyes now!" Declan unclasps his hands from my face.

We're standing in the middle of Secret Beach, our favorite spot: feet in the sand with a perfect view of the horizon, the ginormous rocky cliff hugging us from behind. Everything about our secret place is the same, except this time, there's a path lined by massive candles. It leads to a wreath of blue and white hydrangeas, with one red rose at the top. Lottie's favorite flower.

"Declan," I gasp, grabbing his shoulder. "What is this?"

He finally looks me in the eye, a hesitant smile tugging his lips. The freckle on his bottom lip spurs into action at the movement.

"Come on," he breathes, voice so low I can barely hear it over the crash of the waves.

He leads me by the hand through the narrow, candle-lit path to the head of the flower display and turns to face me.

"Oh my goodness," I cry. "What is happening!"

Declan smiles. Okay, I think I know what's happening.

"Blair," Declan says, reaching for my hands. "I've known since the day I met you that my greatest joy in life would be asking you to spend the rest of our days together. That was seventeen years ago, and I still feel just as excited to bend down on one knee today as I imagined I would then. Loving you has been the easiest thing I've ever done. It's so easy that everything else feels arduous in comparison. Yes, arduous. I had to throw a big word in because I know you love those. And I'll keep learning big words to impress you for the rest of our lives."

I hear myself release a tearful laugh. As Declan's determined eyes bore into mine, the wind and waves dim to a distant whirr. There is nothing else in the world but him right now.

"You have changed my life in too many ways to count. Even when I wasn't physically near you all those years, every day, your presence was like a visceral grip around my heart, refusing to let go. And I won't ever let it." His hair whips across his forehead from the wind as he crouches down and reaches for something behind the wreath of flowers. I'm expecting to see a small box, but the pastel birdhouse he made me comes into view instead. I gasp, clutching my mouth. And then he procures a small mallet.

"What is going on?" I murmur.

"When I gave you this birdhouse, I told you there was something inside," Declan says, opening the pastel wooden door. "I hid something in here that I knew would come in handy for this very day."

He reaches the mallet into the birdhouse and gently taps the front panel of the tiny box inside. It falls open, revealing a crumpled piece of paper and . . . a pebble?

"Years ago, on the high school football field, I jokingly called you a blue-footed booby. Do you remember that?" He raises his eyebrows in anticipation.

A shocked laugh escapes me. "Yes? Those birds with insanely blue feet?"

"Mm-hmm." He nods with a look of satisfaction. "And I showed you the video of them offering a pebble to the bird they wanted to be their mate." He reaches into the tiny inner room of the birdhouse and offers the pebble in his outstretched hand. "So, this is for you, my Little Bird."

I throw my head back, laughing as the wind whips my hair into my mouth. I accept the smooth gray pebble from his hand.

"And this is too," he says, removing the crumpled scrap of paper.

I take it from him with a shaking hand and unfurl it. Declan's delicate handwriting comes into view:

"Will you marry me?"

It is scrawled in black ink, indented by the paper's folds. By the depths of the creases, it looks like it's been folded for years.

A tear falls from my face onto my shaking hands.

And when I look up, Declan is down on one knee, holding a diamond ring inside a velvet box.

"Here is the actual rock I would like to offer you," he jokes with a sideways smile, freckle stretching with the movement. "Blair Lang, will you marry me?"

"Yes," I cry, shaking my head. "Yes, Declan. Yes, yes, a million times yes."

I could write novels about the smile that explodes across Declan's face. And I probably will. Declan slides the ring onto my finger, exhaling a breath when it fits perfectly. He gathers me into his arms and lifts me off the sand. In my peripheral vision I see my mom, Roshi, Faye, Harper, and . . . Gwen, running toward us. Distant whoops and hollers echo off the rocky cliff from our tiny audience.

"Oh my gosh," I cry at the sight of them. Declan sets me down for a moment, adjusts his grip on my waist, and then picks me up again and starts whipping me around in a circle like I'm as light as a rag doll. "Declan!" I screech. "You never would have known you were hit by a car with the way you throw me around," I scream as the sand and sea swirl in my vision.

He lowers me until my feet hit the sand, and when I'm done steadying myself I look up to find a challenge written in his expression.

"I'll show you how well my legs still work." He charges toward me.

A scream flies out of me as I try to run away, but he's too fast, and I'm too dizzy. He wraps his arms around me from behind and squeezes and we descend into hysterical laughter, the happiness of this moment bubbling out of us. Our audience runs up to us, popping bottles of champagne and snapping flash photos of our sweaty faces.

JUST FRIENDS

This moment is perfect. I'm filled with a gratitude so deep it feels heavy as I look at my friends' jubilant, laughing faces and even Gwen's awkward attempt at celebration. Getting to this moment required things I found terrifying: forgiveness and trust and grief. Even falling in love with Declan was scary. But being in love with him? Being loved by him? It was more natural to me than breathing.

The tiniest tug of grief threatens to pull me out of this moment as I remember Lottie's absence, but when I look at Declan's beaming face, I know that even having lost someone I loved, I have gained another someone back. And I will never lose him again.

Turn the page for an exclusive, behind the scenes annotated chapter by Haley Pham.

Five Years Ago

ANNOTATED BY HALEY PHAM ♥

Keeps his word even on the small stuff >>>

Declan picks me up at the house at seven p.m. just like he said he would.

I expected him to be waiting in his car as per usual, but when I throw open the front door, he's standing stock-still beneath the soft glow of the porch light with a bouquet of flowers in his hands. He looks like a modern-day James Dean.

I actually mentally whistle.

Declan tightens his grip on the bouquet, crinkling the brown paper.

"If the look on your face means you're reeling a bit, then you're not the only one," he says with a sweet lilt in his voice.

Waiting in the car = platonic
Knocking on the door = dating!!!

Can you imagine being JUST FRIENDS for over a decade, and then suddenly, FINALLY, transitioning to dating?

[margin note top-left: My real-life favorite flower because there aren't many in Texas!]

JUST FRIENDS

He knows exactly what to say to disarm his <u>chronic charm</u> and put me at ease.

He extends his arm, holding the bundle of <u>cotton-candy-pink and blue hydrangeas</u> out to me. I take in a sharp breath at the sight. My favorite flowers, because I've always loved how they look like colorful cotton balls from far away.

"Wow," I exhale. "These are beautiful. How did you even get them?" We don't have many hydrangeas in Seabrook.

"I'm glad you like them." He leans in and gives me a quick peck on the cheek, the brief encounter with his warm sandalwood scent doing my heart rate zero favors. "Shipping is a crazy invention." He winks.

I stare down at the fluffy flowers in a stupefied state. <u>Pretending not to like someone for over a decade starts to become second nature. And my body hasn't caught up with the fact that I don't need to anymore.</u>

"These are gorgeous!" Aunt Lottie says, (pushing past me) to say hi to Declan.

"Hi, <u>con</u>," Lottie says, patting him on the cheek. She has to reach her arm up to do so, his height towering over her by an entire foot. "Take care of my baby, okay?" she chides, <u>pointing the infamous finger at him</u>. But coming from her, it's more endearing than fear-inducing.

"Yes, ma'am. I will." Declan beams down at her, dimples flashing from his cheek and chin.

She pats him on the cheek twice before turning around and shoving me out the door. "Okay, <u>con</u>! Have fun!" She shoos me toward Declan and then slams the door shut.

"Woah! Well then!" I say, giggling as I fall into Declan's arms.

"I guess that's our cue," he says.

"I guess so."

[margin note left: Blair's mom will point a similar finger in her face in the future. Some habits continue on.]

[margin note right top: Lottie has no problem appreciating them! LOL]

[margin note right bottom: I have such fond memories being called "con" by my mom and aunts :)]

HALEY PHAM

[handwritten note at top:] I love how he calls her "Little Bird" their 1st time at Secret Beach because a few years later... He'll BE PROPOSING ON THE SAME BEACH!

"Alrighty, Little Bird. Right this way." He steers me from behind as I keep my hands firmly over my eyes. We stomped through a grove of trees until we reached the edge.

"Okay, you can open your eyes now."

I blink a few times, adjusting to see that we're in the center of a semi-circle created by massive cliffs hemming us in. Beneath my feet is a small patch of sand that gives way to clear turquoise water.

"Uh-huh." I scoff-laugh, momentarily dazed by the sight. "How did you find this place?"

"Google Maps is crazy useful, it turns out," he remarks.

I drop the awe from my expression and pin him with a glare. "First 'shipping is a crazy invention,' and now Google Maps. Excuse me for being curious."

"I'm kidding!" He laughs. "I found this place when I was on a run. I thought the trail was just a random dirt path, but it spit me out onto sand. And I knew instantly I wanted to take you here on our first date. Your curiosity is removing the smoke screen from all the romantic tricks I have up my sleeve."

[handwritten margin note:] when he finds a cool spot and instantly pictures taking Blair >>>

I snort a laugh. We gravitate to the center of the sand and choose a spot with a view of the ocean, moss-covered rocks towering behind us. It feels like we've been dropped into the soft cradle of the earth's hands. A secret place, just for us. *H2O!!*

"This is unbelievable. It looks like the magical cave from that Australian mermaid show," I say, settling next to him. The sun has already set beneath the horizon. Faint silver streaks are cast over the moonlit water in its stead.

"I call it 'secret beach.'" His eyes twinkle with the childlike

JUST FRIENDS

joy at having shared the nickname with me. It's <u>horrendously cute.</u> I love when an aggressive word is next to a sweet one.

"How long have you wanted to take me on a date?" I ask. "Or like... when did this stop being platonic for you?" I point between us.

He picks up sand and lets it fall through the cracks between his fingers. A slight smile tugs at the side of his mouth.

"Now *that* is a loaded question." He looks over at me, <u>arms wrapped around my knees like his.</u> He mirrors her body language.

"Why is it loaded?" I poke, hoping against all hope that his crush has existed for even a fraction as long as mine has. !

"I think," he starts, looking out at the waves. "It was less of a single moment, rather a string of repeated instances that snowballed until it was this huge thing that smacked me in the side of the head. And I knew I couldn't resist it anymore." ☆

I've never felt blood pump through my veins so viscerally.

"Wow," I say, becoming monosyllabic. "Yeah, that's..." I nod my head into oblivion.

Declan peeks at me from the corner of his eye and then breaks, descending into abrupt laughter. The warm rasp of it is boyish in a way that makes my cheeks heat.

<u>I am so far gone, I think helplessly.</u> YEAH. YA THINK?

"Okay, well!" he protests, still laughing. "I can't be the only one who admits something. What was the moment for you?"

Oh gosh. I contemplate diminishing the truthful answer. It would be easy to. <u>I've been lying to myself for so long about my feelings for him that it is kind of hazy,</u> but I decide starting our relationship with half-truths would be a bad idea and risk it.

Blair is very talented at lying to herself. :)

"I think the real answer might freak you out, but for the longest time, I didn't believe you'd ever see me in that way, and I also didn't want to risk ruining the friendship." I sneak *when someone doesn't make you feel rushed or judged while talking >>>*

a glance at him to weigh his reaction. It's unbearably kind. His eyes squint in concentration, and his body language is perfectly at ease, unhurried.

"Mm-hmm. I didn't want to ruin it either," he says. "But come on, that wasn't an answer. You're acting like a politician right now."

"Well, if you want me to be completely honest with you—"

"Which I do." ← *Still a foreign concept for Blair to say*

"Then . . . I honestly can't remember a time when I wasn't a little bit obsessed with you." *how she FEELS!*

The sound of a wave breaking is the only thing that dares make noise in the wake of my confession, and I think I might fall forever through the empty space, until finally, Declan breaks into a grin and catches me.

"You're joking," he teases.

"I'm not."

"No, be serious with me right now. You're telling me that when I was five years old and had thick black-framed glasses attached to me via necklace and my two front teeth weren't close enough to be considered neighbors, you were 'a little bit obsessed' with me?" he challenges, eyebrows raised.

"Yes! Dead serious!"

"And this is our first date, why?" he shouts at the sky.

"Because! You know why!" I say instead of the actual answer.

"Because . . . ?" he challenges again with a teasing smile, refusing to let it go.

"Because so many girls threw themselves at you and they were all so impossibly pretty, and you still didn't want them. So, I took it as evidence that if you didn't want them, you definitely didn't want me. Actually, no. You know what it was?" I say, more to myself than him. "I thought you enjoyed my friendship because it was a nice escape from all the unwanted

She finally catches Stefani saying how she feels here.

JUST FRIENDS

attention you got. So, I wasn't going to be the idiot who added to your list of people you needed to avoid." I laugh to ease the honesty of my admission. ← Struggles to say things earnestly.

I look down, focusing on drawing circles in the sand. I definitely
Without speaking, he takes my chin in his hand and turns have this in
my face to him. common
with Blair!

"Blair," he pleads. "*You* are impossibly pretty. And I know I never acted on it, but trust that I always wanted to. You are the only girl whose attention I wanted, before I even knew other girls existed. And even after discovering other girls did, and do in fact, exist, the same is true. It's always been you for me." His green eyes don't so much as waver. It's like he refuses to blink until I believe him.

I try my best to soak it in. To stare back into his eyes and accept that what I wanted my entire life was happening. But I rasp out a breathless laugh, shaking my head out of his grasp.

"Now that we're ... dating, I don't think you're supposed to know that other girls exist." ← DEFLECTION TIME!!

He pins me with a glare, playfully shoves my shoulder.

"You are impossible to compliment," he says, exasperated.

"No, no. I'm sorry. You're right. I am impossibly pretty," I say.

Declan carries being serious/sincere for them, too.

He throws his head back with laughter. "Okay, but I'm serious," he says, voice level. "You've seen me through every stage of life, and you never preferred me more or less based on how football was going. It sounds so stereotypical, but you saw the way people at school went from not paying attention to me at all, to gawking at me in the hallways after winning championships. If they said my name, it was because the word football was attached to it. I never liked that. I still found myself only caring about what you thought of me. And it was

It's destabilizing when your identity is wrapped up in something that can change. And for Declan it did. But Blair won't!

never the football you cared about. The way you spoke to me never changed."

"Of course not, Declan. That stuff is awesome but it's kind of irrelevant in the grand scheme of things. At least, inasmuch as it relates to my obsession with you," I say not so ironically. "I'm proud of your accomplishments, don't get me wrong. But you could do anything and I would find it impressive. You know that." → Even under-water basket weaving!

He smiles like the sentiment is still novel to him. Special and new.

And then without speaking, he starts to move toward me. I *Oh, shoot!* relax onto my back in the sand, and he crawls over me, boxing me in with his hands on either side of my face, his lean body hovering above mine, muscles in his shoulders straining with the effort. And then his face slowly morphs into a smile of pure wonder, lighting up his eyes. "I enjoy that answer very much."

"Of course you would." I heckle.

His shoulders bounce as he laughs above me. The moonlight illuminates his messy tousle of hair from behind and I take a turn giggling in disbelief as the improbability of this new reality settles between us. He goes quiet at the sound, like he needs to be still to marvel at me. And when I realize, I go still too. But then his face parts in a grin again and his head drops. It's like playing a game of hot potato, lobbing the imaginary force of it back and forth. Laughter begetting laughter begetting laughter.

[margin note left: They're laughing because they can't believe that they're finally on a date!]

Finally, the last of our laughter fizzles out like finishing the last sip of bubbly, and we allow the silence. I think he's a second away from bending his elbows and lowering his mouth onto mine when he says, "Wanna play the question game?"

"Sure," I exhale, a mixture of shock and unmet want.

He quickly bends his elbows and tucks his hands into his

[margin note right: I wanted to subtly reference my favorite books and this line is a spin on a line in the Red Rising series by Pierce Brown. His sent is: "Deal begets deal, begets de so... min is a worthy s...]

JUST FRIENDS

chest, unfolding next to me onto his back. The crash of waves fills the pause as he situates himself.

"Okay. First question," Declan says. "If a crystal ball could tell you anything about your future, what would you want to know?"

I catch him looking at something in his left hand.

"Are you reading from a list?" I demand.

"Maybe," he says, faux shyness creeping into his voice.

I shake my head, but then the answer hits me. I contemplate choosing a lighter one, but I can't think of a decoy in time. So out it comes. "I'd probably ask if I'll ever see my dad again."

The darkness has gone from navy blue to nearly black except for the subtle glow of the moonlight. If the world didn't feel so still, I don't think I'd have offered this level of candor.

Declan rolls onto his side in the sand, facing me with his head on his bicep.

"You know," his voice is soft, like an outstretched hand inviting me in. "It's on your dad for never coming back. Not you."

I stare at a specific star in the sky, scared of how my face will betray me if I look at him.

"Yeah, I know," I choke out. "I just think—" I press my lips together.

"You just think what?"

"I know my dad is the only one to blame for his actions. But knowing something and believing it are two different things."

I feel Declan's meaningful stare on the side of my face, but I don't turn. If I meet his eyes and see sadness in them, I'll stop saying how I really feel. And it feels good to say it out loud for once.

"You blame yourself?" Declan says it like a fact. "For how

[margin notes: Night time + no eye contact = rare moment of Blair opening up / This question is from the "36 questions to fall in love" list. / Blair is only 17 years old here, but I feel like this has applied to my early 20s!]

he left you and your mom. You've somehow deduced that it was your fault?"

"Well," I huff, turning to meet his eyes finally. "It sounds so wrong when you put it like that. But when you're five and no one is telling you what's going on, it's only natural to make up your own conclusion. Even if the information you've gathered with your tiny mind is incorrect."

"Hey," Declan protests. "My five-year-old brain loved your tiny mind. As unformed as it was, it was responsible for all your cute little expressions."

My mouth splits into a smile.

"But in all seriousness, I know what you mean. About knowing something is true but not believing it. You came to the false conclusion that there was something about you that caused your dad to leave, and you started believing that so long ago, it's hard to spontaneously not believe it anymore. Even with your grown-up brain." He taps the side of my temple playfully. I laugh and then his expression becomes grave again. "But, Blair, someone who chose to leave you must be the stupidest man in the entire world. There's just no other explanation."

The corners of my lips wobble and I have to smash them together to prevent my chin from trembling too. "That's what you said our freshman year too."

"Hah," he laughs. "I must still be bad at comforting you then."

"No," I say quietly as I relax my head into the sand and stare at the sky again. "You're very good at it."

He must know I've laid down to avoid being looked at while I fight grateful tears, so he joins me in looking at the sky. "I don't know if your dad is in your future, but I know I will be," he says, voice husky like it's been forced from his throat. "If you let me be."

JUST FRIENDS

"Of course I will." There's nothing I want more, I don't add. We let the tender hope of it lay between us. The twinkling stars and whispering ocean are our only witnesses.

"I would like to know what I'm doing for work at the age of forty," he says abruptly.

I chuckle, his sudden way of talking has always been my favorite. "Why forty? And why work?" I ask.

"Because," he says. "If I do end up making it to the NFL, it's not a career that lasts your entire life. Unless you're Tom Brady and you play football until you're, like, eighty. But sometimes, I get scared that I don't have my finger on the pulse of anything other than football. I don't know what I'd find myself doing once I didn't have to think about it twenty-four seven. Which is kind of destabilizing, you know?" he finishes with effort, punctuating each word.

"Hmm," I muse, craving a deflection from the rising panic of where we'll be in that many years. We don't even know where we're going to college. "First of all, you will make it to the NFL, and second, anyone who uses the word 'destabilizing' in a casual sentence is smart enough to figure out what to do with their time."

His eyes dart down to my mouth, half-smirking as I wait for his chuckle. After it arrives, I take a more sincere approach. "You're too creative to stay bored for long. You like engineering, right? You could build stuff."

"That's not a bad idea," he says, more so to himself like he's rolling the thought over in his mind. "Not a bad idea at all."

The seed of doubt worms its way back to the forefront of my mind. I don't want to put a damper on our first date by thinking so far into the future, but we've already applied to colleges. Don't we need to put some forethought into how we'll last past high school?

"Declan," I start, unable to push off the racing thoughts. "How is this going to work if we go to different colleges?"

"We applied to a lot of the same ones, right?" he replies, not missing a beat.

"It's just that . . ." I peter off, realizing I'm in danger of souring the mood.

My hand subconsciously lifts to my mouth to chew on a hangnail.

"Hey." Declan shifts himself up onto his elbow and gently grabs my wrist, pulling my hand away from my mouth. "I know it's scary to think about where we'll end up in a few months, but let's talk about it. <u>Walk me through what you're thinking about.</u>" *A foreign concept to Blair*

"Well," I falter.

Apparently converting my feelings into words is a pathway my neurons are unfamiliar with. "It's just that . . . okay, let me start here."

I push up on my elbows in the cool sand. "The other day I was talking to my mom about all the colleges we applied to, and she made an offhand comment about how I'd need full-ride scholarships to attend any of them. And when I pushed and asked if she was being dramatic, she laughed in my face. I legitimately can't go to a single school I spent all this time applying to unless I get a full ride. Full. Not half. Not a quarter. Full."

Declan nods silently, allowing me to go on.

"And I know this is going to sound terribly cliché, but it feels like that saying that goes 'Walk like a duck. Talk like a duck. Hang out with other ducks. You start to think you are a duck.' But I'm not a duck, Declan." My voice rises.

"Woah, woah, woah," Declan says, catching my gesticulating arms. "I was following so well until this duck comparison."

"<u>What I mean is, I grew up in this town because my great-</u>

[left margin, top to bottom:] When I wanted to go to college for dance. And realizing this to be true. And realizing that at 17 is pretty scary!

JUST FRIENDS

aunt could afford it. So, I hung out with kids whose parents could afford it. And I started to forget that I wasn't like them. Everyone rattled off the list of Ivy Leagues they were applying to and I somehow followed suit without much thought. So much so that I forgot to ask my mom if we could afford it. I just assumed we could because everyone else can. But if I want to go to college, I have to pay for it!" I say, driving my pointer finger into my chest. "And also, I can't be going to college for *creative writing*. What was I thinking?" I spit the words out like they're obscene. "I need to be strategic. I need to put myself in a position to get a high-paying job. One high enough to support me and my mom."

Declan is nodding with force now, eyes skimming the sand as a hand scrapes his chin, deep in thought.

"So, your mom didn't tell you that you'd be the one paying for college on your own?" he asks.

"Well . . . yeah, I guess she just assumed I knew that," I concede, not liking how it sounds. "But she didn't want to deter me from trying to apply to any big schools because she has some weird blind faith that I'll be able to get full scholarships and . . . I don't know, Declan, you know how she is. She's not one for many words and I guess this is one of those things that slipped through the cracks."

"Slipped through the cracks? Isn't that a pretty big thing to let 'slip through the cracks'?" he says, stress peaking his voice.

"Hey, calm down," I try to say soothingly. "I'm stressed about it too. That's why I'm bringing it up."

"Sorry, it's just hard to stay calm when I just got you and now I have to worry about losing you soon."

"You're not going to lose me, Declan," I say, touching his arm. "I mean, we'll figure it out, right?"

He doesn't move away from my touch, but he looks down, jaw grinding.

327

HALEY PHAM

He shakes his head, hand coming up to rub his chin again and the sight makes my stomach drop. "I'm sorry, it's just—you know how much pressure I've been under since I was a kid, Blair. My dad has made it his chief goal for me to play D1 at an Ivy League and then straight to the NFL. It's already so much to think about."

My stomach aches and I feel the need to run and hide. I never want to add to the pressure he feels, but I don't want to compete against his dad and football.

At my silence, Declan looks over at me. "Are you okay? I don't mean to scare you, I just want to let you know where my head is at."

"Yeah," I mutter. "No, that makes sense. It's just . . ." I shake my head. "I don't want to be second fiddle to football, you know?"

I feel like I walked off a cliff saying that out loud. But then, Declan exhales, looking sorry. "Hey, come here."

I obey immediately, climbing on top of him. He chuckles at my sudden conviction, and I watch his Adam's apple bob with the movement. His hands drift to my waist, supporting my weight as I hover above him.

"You won't ever come second to anything. Okay?" he says from under me.

I nod, a small smile tugging at the corner of my mouth. He reaches up to palm my cheek and I lean into it.

"You'll always come first," he breathes. "Nothing tops you."

My cheeks heat and I hope the darkness hides it. The only natural response I feel is to say the forbidden L word, but I know it's too early, so I fold over him to stop myself. Our chests meld and warmth spreads through me. Sometimes the weight of love is more frustrating than pleasurable.

JUST FRIENDS

I turn my head in the sand by his ear and only manage to mouth the words *thank you*.

"One day, when I'm playing football, you'll be an author. I'll be reading your books every second I'm not on the field," he says softly, wrapping his arms around my back and holding me against him.

I'm robbed of speech. There's frustration in not being able to communicate how much his words mean to me. I'm grateful words aren't the only way to communicate.

I kiss his temple, softly at first, and then move to his cheek. After that, I kiss his forehead and slowly drift down to his nose.

"Please, Blair," he grinds out.

"Please, what?" I ask, feigning innocence.

"*Please*," he begs. "Kiss me now." Yearning coats his expression so intensely that it looks like he might die.

I let out a full-bodied belly laugh. His unhidden longing is disarming in a way I can't resist.

I still, elbows bending beneath me, causing my full weight to lower on top of him. I prop up my upper half, shuffling my forearms in the sand beside his face. In the time it's taken me to readjust, Declan's face is filled with even more anguish.

"*End me now*," he says, as if to himself before impatiently curling his fingers around the nape of my neck and pulling me down to meet his lips.

The kiss is hungry and searching, and I feel everything with a new level of intensity. I become aware that this is the point of no return. The one that starts and ends my ability to enjoy anyone or anything else with this much fervor.

This moment, with the waves lapping gently to shore, and the deep darkness, is too perfect. Completely on our own, the

329

stars as our only witnesses to the moment I've dreamt of for years.

Declan, who I never imagined reciprocating my feelings, is beneath me. Opening himself up to me in rare and precious ways, finally letting the mysterious curtain drop between us.

It fills me up so quickly that, for a moment, I feel weary. Unsure that I can trust something so perfect to stay.

"You'll always come first." I repeat the sentiment he offered me earlier, holding on to the promise with a grip that hurts.

The truth is, I have more faith in the probability of his leaving than this moment being the catalyst of his staying.

> Cynical little Blair. But can you blame her line of thinking given her past?

Acknowledgements

The first and greatest thank-you I would like to offer requires a bit of context first, because I wouldn't be writing these acknowledgments without him. In April of 2023, I was reading Stephen King's *On Writing* on a long flight to Japan. The tiny seed I'd been trying to ignore for years was slowly sprouting. I wanted to write a book. It was a fearful thing, because it meant so much. I didn't want to screw it up. So, I put *On Writing* down, closed my eyes, and prayed. I asked God something to the effect of: "Please, show me if I'm supposed to write a book. Because I really want to, but not if I don't have your blessing. This is too big a thing to do on my own." About thirty minutes later, my phone lit up with a text from a girl I rarely spoke to. It was a video of her scrolling through the first draft of her completed manuscript. The text read: "Just thought you'd find this fun." My heart almost stopped. I rarely ask Jesus for signs; he has already done so much, but I took that moment and let it bolster my courage to pursue the dream I tried to ignore for so long. And luckily, God also gives us people.

Thank you to my manager, Brooklyn Gordon, whose work aso lucky to have met you and even luckier to work with you. Thank you to my editor, Emilia Rhodes. I am convinced you are a superhero. You are patient and gentle, and I am forever grateful to you for believing in me. Thank you to the other

ACKNOWLEDGEMENTS

hard-working members of the Atria team: Dominick Montalto, Elizabeth Hitti, Michaela MacPherson, Shelby Pumphrey, Sofia Echeverry, Paige Lytle, Dayna Johnson, Kathleen Rizzo, Vanessa Silverio, Megan Rudloff, Nicole Bond, Sara Bowne, Rebecca Justiniano, and Davina Mock-Maniscalco.

Thank you to Lynn Painter for reading the first chapters I had ever written of this story and encouraging me to keep going. You probably had no idea you were the first person to ever lay eyes on my words, and your generosity did more for me than you'll ever know. Thank you to Lauren Roberts for replying to every single niche question I had about the writing process with in-depth voice memos. Thank you to Bryana Kay, Nick Iby, and Isaac Carlton for responding to every desperate text asking if a line was "weird," and for celebrating me on this crazy journey. Shout-out to my tiny terrier Chihuahua, Spock, who was never farther than five feet from me during the writing of this book. My deepest and warmest and truest thank-you to my husband, Ryan. You listened to my crazy plot ideas and helped me work out every flaw. You are a natural storyteller, and although you don't write books, you tell stories in every medium you touch. You believed in my ability to write this book more than I did most days. I am honored and privileged to be married to someone so outrageously joyful, kind, talented, and generous. Thank you to my parents. To my mom, who checked out the maximum number of books we were allotted from the library beginning when I was four and for reading every last one to me. To my dad, who made me confident in my voice by being confident in his. And last, the biggest thank-you to my audience, who championed this story before you even knew what it was about. That kind of optimism for a venture I never believed I could make meant more than you will ever know. On days

ACKNOWLEDGEMENTS

when I questioned why I ever thought I'd be capable of this, I remembered your enthusiasm and kept going. I hope to write you many more stories and continue recommending books I love to you, too. Alright, then. Bye! *tongue-taco-weird-slurp-into-the-camera-thing*

About the Author

Haley Pham is a content creator who has been building a dedicated online community for more than a decade. She has shared every phase of life with her audience and become a true tastemaker in the book world. Married to Ryan Trahan, another YouTube creator, they are a family of three with their Chihuahua terrier, Spock. *Just Friends* is Haley's debut novel.

Des mots en cafouille
III

Bertus van den Heuvel

Des mots en cafouille
III

Histoires courtes

Collection
VDH

Merci à Ötsie, notre chien
à Zapette, Tara, Chouquette, Yab-Yab
et Stroumpf, nos chats
pour leur « zen » attitude, fidelité et tendresse

Fontaine lès Luxeuil, le 31 août 2013.

Bortus

Ötsie

D'abord, sois le bienvenu, toi qui es en train de lire cet ouvrage. Aussi, permets-moi de me présenter :
Je m'appelle Ötsie. Ce nom m'est donné par Mary-Tine, ma maîtresse. À ma naissance ma naisseuse m'avait baptisé Aspi Brunswyk de Sauloises. C'est un peu long et un peu trop bourgeois. Mais que veux-tu, quand on est de race avec un pedigree certifié, on ne peut pas faire moins.
Il paraît que ma maîtresse avait été touchée par l'histoire de cet homme datant de plus de dix mille ans retrouvé avec ses vêtements, ses sacs de vivre, ses armes, ses cheveux. Trouvé dans les hauts sommets d'Autriche, les ethnologues l'avaient appelé Ötsie.

Moi, à quatre mois et demi

Je suis bien fier de porter son nom. Un trait d'union sacrément fort. Peut être que je suis comme elle, que j'aime ce genre d'histoires.
Pour la première période de ma vie, celle chez les naisseurs de ma race, je n'ai guerre de souvenirs, sauf que je suis le numéro six d'une portée de neuf. Ma pauvre maman en a souffert. Les numéros cinq et sept

n'ont pas survécu, le numéro trois est mort-né. Moi-même je n'ai pas une taille d'un mâle certifié. A distance, on me prend souvent pour une femelle.
Au bout de quatre mois, je fus vendu à Jeanne, une bipède humaine un peu hors du commun. Je ne connais rien en business et encore moins en argent, mais j'ai compris que ma naisseuse affirma à Jeanne que j'étais un bon coup pour un prix ridicule. Décidément, je ne valais pas grand chose. Tous mes frères et sœurs ont été adoptés par des humains pour un prix nettement supérieur au mien.
Jeanne m'avait mis dans un sac pour me transporter vers sa demeure.
Quelle catastrophe ! On m'a garé dans un enclos de cochon avec une gamelle de riz au bouillon et une vieille casserole d'eau. Je regrettais amèrement les boxes propres chez ma naisseuse.

Le lendemain, Jeanne m'envoya son compagnon pour venir me voir en me tâtant partout. IL constata que j'avais toujours toutes mes dents et mes quatre pattes. Il m'a fait tout un discours pour m'expliquer pourquoi Jeanne m'avait pris et qu'elle avait une grande confiance en moi pour ma carrière, une fois que j'aurais atteint l'âge d'un chien adulte.
Je n'ai pas tout compris, mais c'était une histoire de copines et de bébés-chiens.
Quelques temps après Jeanne m'amena vers le docteur des chiens. C'est que, malgré la quantité confortable de riz au bouillon de poulet je ne voulais pas grandir selon les normes de ma race. Jeanne n'était pas contente et voyait déjà que mes prestations

futures n'auraient pas l'écho espéré.
Le docteur me tâtait consciencieusement, se frottait la tête avec le dos de la main, fit trois fois hmmm, et diagnostiqua le verdict : j'étais mal nourri !
J'étais tout à fait d'accord avec lui, parce que tous les jours du riz pâteux au bouillon-cube de poulet n'était pas mon repas préféré. Surtout que j'avais encore de vagues souvenirs des biberons et autres petits plats de ma naisseuse.
Jeanne était vexée. Elle paya la consultation, me prit sous ses bras et partit sans dire un mot.

Le lendemain elle avait rédigé une annonce dans le journal du coin pour me donner à qui me voulait.
C'est comme ça que j'ai été adopté par Mary-Tine et Bertus.
C'était pour son anniversaire. Il avait lourdement insisté auprès de Mary-Tine, qui n'était pas tout à fait favorable à l'idée de chercher un chien, sauf de croire qu'il l'aiderait à marcher et marcher encore. Bertus avait besoin de faire des exercices pour le bien-être de son dos malade.
C'était très difficile, ils étaient même décidés à faire demi-tour. D'autant plus qu'ils n'avaient pas vu un colley. Seuls des caniches géants et noirs les regardèrent avec un regard absent. En effet, dans sa cuisine, qui servait également de bureau et chenil, il y avait cinq caniches géants avec une odeur plus que redoutable. Ils pataugeaient joyeusement dans leurs excréments. Une puanteur effroyable plombait l'atmosphère.
Elle fit comprendre que j'étais dehors dans un enclos

spécialement aménagé pour moi.
Jeanne expliquait qu'elle m'avait acheté il y a quelques mois dans un chenil spécialisé dans ma race. Le but étant, une fois adulte d'accepter une chienne pour que les choses se fassent pour avoir une rémunération ou un chiot de race et de pouvoir le vendre.
Le problème était que je n'avais pas la hauteur réglementaire pour être confirmé dans les annales de LOF.
D'autre part, aucun propriétaire n'a voulu laisser sa chienne dans cet environnement hautement insalubre.

Nous voyant assez intéressés elle s'adressa à Bertus et Mary-Tine:
- C'est une pure race !
- Ah bon ...
- Il est vacciné par son éleveur !
- Vraiment ?
- Il a ses papiers, regardez...
Bertus prit les papiers. Effectivement il y avait mon arbre généalogique mentionné dans le livret.
Mary-Tine m'avait pris pour aller sur l'herbe en dehors de la cabane. Elle était visiblement indécise. Je ne savais pas qu'elle était une farouche adepte du coup de foudre... l'homme, les chaussures, les fleurs, le coup de pouce au destin. C'est l'instinct aussi. Elle m'a appelé. J'ai décidé de mettre le paquet. Ce n'est pas tous les jours qu'il y du monde pour offrir un destin digne de mon état de chien. Aussi je suis venu sans discuter.
Elle m'a parlé doucement. Quelle différence avec ma patronne de ce temps là. Elle se tenait au niveau de

l'arrière de mon dos, j'ai levé ma tête comme en voulant mettre mon crâne sur ma colonne vertébrale... Un renversé de tête irréprochable ! Nos regards se sont croisés. Puis elle jubilait :
- Mais toi, tu es un amour de chien !
Et tu me crois ou tu me crois pas, elle avait les yeux mouillés, puis elle ajouta en me regardant :
- C'est bon, on t'emmène avec nous !
Elle était visiblement séduite par mon regard qui suppliait :
- Au secours, sortez-moi d'ici !
Et là, j'ai compris que rien ne serait comme avant.

Bertus s'adressait à Jeanne :
- C'est d'accord nous le prenons. Vous avez dit dans l'annonce que vous le donneriez ?
- Eh, oui, je le donne, mais j'aimerai que vous m'aidiez un peu à contribuer aux frais que j'ai eus à supporter.
- Et c'est combien notre contribution ?
- Je pense, qu'avec cent euros je ne vous volerai pas !
Mary-Tine et Bertus n'avaient plus envie de discuter. Ils lui donnèrent cent euros et à moi le bonheur de partir avec eux.

On m'avait placé sur la banquette derrière la voiture. Mary-Tine avait mis une vieille couverture.
Pendant le trajet, avec les fenêtres ouvertes, j'ai rapidement compris que je dégageais une forte odeur malfaisante, puisque mon nouveau maître avait fait la remarque très percutante :
- Punaise, quelle puanteur, ce chien !!
- Faut le laver sans attendre, ajouta Mary-Tine. Ça va

pas être facile de se débarrasser de l'odeur.
Quand nous arrivâmes à ma nouvelle demeure, Mary-Tine me déposa directement dans une sorte de bac à eau au fond du garage.
Au bout de quatre lavages mon odeur n'avait pas encore disparu.
Le lendemain Mary-Tine me transporta chez une coiffeuse pour chiens, ce que les bipèdes appellent une toiletteuse. Adriana, la fille de mes maîtres était en stage de toiletteuse, et se proposa de s'en occuper.
Démêlage, lavage, rinçage, répétés plusieurs fois, puis parfumage ont eu raison de mes odeurs. Quelques

Station de lavage

heures plus tard, je suis sorti de la boutique comme un chien beau et propre. Il y avait même des gens qui s'arrêtaient pour s'exclamer :
- Qu'est-ce qu'il est beau ce chien !!

En rentrant à la maison, j'avais le droit de rester dans la cuisine et même le salon.
En plus, avec plein de caresses et gentils mots.

Voilà, il fallait que je te raconte comment j'ai pris mes quartiers auprès de mes bipèdes dans leur maison.
Depuis ce temps, j'ai beaucoup réfléchi, observé, analysé, puis médité.
C'est ce qui m' amène à m'exprimer avec, ce que je

crois, une certaine dose de philosophie cynophile. Ceci en complément de la « philosophie » tout court, plus orientée vers les humains.

On dit souvent que le chien est l'ami d'un homme. Normalement l'homme doit être à l'inverse l'ami d'un chien.
Dans beaucoup de cas c'est vrai. Quoique l'homme se réserve aussi le titre de maître.
Voyons mon cas. Mes bipèdes ont une sonnette, une vraie sonnette. On appuie et on sonne.
Quand je me promène avec Mary-Tine je le vois bien, les autres canins attachés à quelques mètres de chaîne avec la seule occupation d'aboyer quand quelqu'un se présente ou passe devant la clôture.
En contre partie, ils perçoivent un bout de vieux pain, un peu de pâtes et un coup de pied s'ils mettent trop de zèle.
Moi, je passe la nuit au pied du lit de mes maîtres, quand il y a de l'orage, (j'ai peur quand ça tonne) je peux me garer en dessous du lit pour chercher la protection dont j'ai besoin.
Ma gamelle est toujours pleine avec d'excellentes croquettes et je bois de l'eau fraîche.
Je suis même en paix avec les cinq chats dans la maison. Mieux encore, j'ai lié une solide amitié avec Stroumpf, l'un des deux matous.
Quoi que, enfin-là, je trouve cinq chats c'est un peu exagéré, imagines-toi le contraire : cinq chiens et un chat ... Ce serait un vrai boxon. C'est moi qui te le dis.
J'aime beaucoup mes bipèdes. Souvent je leur fais une déclaration silencieuse. C'est-à-dire uniquement par le

regard. En plus ça me rapporte parfois un petit extra de la boîte spéciale de croques canins. En même temps je reçois une caresse, et on me dit que je suis beau.

Même si je sais que je suis beau, il est agréable d'écouter ce genre de déclaration.

Les humains sont pratiquement par tous les temps habillés avec des pelures qu'on apporte au corps. Nous les chiens, nous avons la fourrure naturelle. On est né avec. Les humains ont des poils sous le menton et parfois sur le torse pour les mâles, sur les pattes et l'entre-cuisse pour tout le monde.

Puis ils mettent des pelures qu'ils fabriquent dans les usines et ateliers. Les pelures dessous et dessus.

Nous les chiens, nous n'avons pas des dessous ajoutés.

En balade de santé avec Mary-Tine

Nos dessous sont des mystères que j'aimerai un jour percer pour avoir une sorte de vérité. Pas que cela soit nécessaire, mais à titre scientifique bonifié. Savoir où sont ses dessous peut être utile dans la vie.

Tu vois, quand il y a un événement, on se demande souvent ce qui peut être là-dessous. Rien n'est gratuit ou presque. C'est ce qui est dessous qui apporte la vérité. Des choses et incidents que nous ne voyons pas immédiatement. Et le dépouillement chez les chiens n'est pas possible. Rappelle-toi, nous n'avons

qu'une pelure, une fourrure et sans les dessus-dessous.
Notre dessous c'est le cœur, comme un écrin dans notre corps.
C'est que nous, les chiens, nous gardons une part de mystère de notre vivant. Ce qui nous donne le pouvoir de communiquer sans avoir appris à parler dans le vide comme des humains.
Normalement, je suis assez casanier, j'aime rester chez moi et observer le va et vient des chats, regarder mes maîtres et roupiller dans un coin tranquille.
J'accompagne Bertus quand il va chercher le courrier à la boîte aux lettres au coin de la rue, ou Mary-Tine en balade de santé.
Dans le jardin je réponds parfois aux âneries des petits chiens de notre voisine. De vraies pipelettes. Ça les excite. Faut bien exister quand on est de petite taille.

Il y a quelques temps la porte d'entrée est restée ouverte, et la tentation avec une dose de curiosité était si forte que je ne pouvais pas résister à l'appel d'aventure.
J'ai décidé de faire un tour en solo, ce qui m'est normalement interdit pour, ce qu'on m'a dit, ma propre sécurité.
Il paraît que je suis assez beau chien pour que je risque de me faire voler. En plus il paraît que c'est interdit par les lois humaines de permettre aux chiens de se promener sans accompagnement. Cela veut dire qu'on doit nous « tenir en laisse ».
Me voilà donc seul en vadrouille. Quelques rues plus

loin j'ai rencontré un collègue, lui aussi en vadrouille.
Après l'aboiement d'usage en guise de salutations sincères, il me raconta son histoire :
- Hier j'ai été obligé de monter mes dents au gamin de la maison, le fils de mes maîtres de huit ans qui a la fâcheuse habitude d'attacher ma queue à la poignée de la porte avec un lacet de ses baskets.
Il prétend que c'est pour m'apprendre à fermer la porte.
J'ai toutes les difficultés à défaire les lacets avec mes dents. C'est que hier, c'était trop, je lui ai grogné dessus et je lui ai montré mes crocs. A la suite de ça, ce petit con se mit à pleurer et raconta que je cherchais à le mordre. Ce qui est absolument faux, puisque j'ai seulement voulu lui faire peur.
- Et alors, les parents, qu'est ce qu'ils ont fait avec toi ?
- Ils ne m'ont rien dit directement ou peu, j'ai eu droit à un coup de pied magistral et ils m'ont envoyé dans mon coin avec un « pas bouger ».
C'est un peu plus tard que j'ai écouté la conversation de mes maîtres. Eux non plus ne savent pas que nous, les chiens, nous comprenons parfaitement ce que disent les humains, même si nous ne sommes pas capables de parler comme eux.
Le père déclara à sa femme qu' ils ne peuvent plus me garder dans leur famille, que je suis devenu trop dangereux avec leur fils, ce brave petit garçon qui ne cherche qu'à jouer sans méchanceté. Comme ils ne peuvent prendre la responsabilité de me donner à une autre famille, il ne restait qu'une seule solution : la mort par injection.

C'est pour ça que je me suis barré. C'était en chemin vers le vétérinaire pour me faire piquer.
Quand ils ont ouvert la porte de la voiture, je me suis sauvé en vitesse. Tu vois, j'ai toujours ma laisse autour du cou.

J'éprouvais de la peine pour mon nouveau copain. Pour l'aider à se remonter le moral, j'ai décidé de l'accompagner un bout de chemin et aussi de mâchouiller sa laisse en cuir pour qu'il reste juste son collier.
Quelques kilomètres plus loin, je lui ai souhaité bonne route avec un coup de langue et une révérence de queue, puis j'ai fait demi-tour pour retrouver mon nid à la maison. Inquiète, c'est d'ailleurs Mary-Tine en voiture qui m'a vu la première. J'ai eu la chance, moi, d'être caressé, tellement elle était contente de m'avoir retrouvé.

Cette histoire m'a fait beaucoup réfléchir. J'ai été obligé de me rendre compte que nous les chiens animaux « domestiques» dépendons uniquement des humains. Ils sont maîtres de notre vie et de notre mort. Ils peuvent nous juger, nous jeter, nous abandonner, ou nous faire exécuter. Pas de légitime défense sans pétitions.
L'abandon sauvage est certes interdit, mais pas « l'abandon » organisé et légalisé. L'exécution par injection est parfaitement légale. La peine de mort sans jugement équitable pour les chiens, chats et autres animaux domestiqués est toujours sans tabou, à condition de passer par des experts bourreaux en la

matière.
Malgré ma position très avantageuse, cette pensée me fait froid au dos et cauchemarder.
D'autant plus que dans ce monde actuel rien n'est à l'horizon qui fait espérer que cela change. Il paraît même que les humains entre eux ne font pas mieux dans certaines régions de ce monde. Et on ne parle même pas des relations de profit et de terreur mortelle envers certains animaux sauvages. La vie n'est pas facile dans ce monde des vivants.

Yaka I

L'amour ne s'arrête pas quand la vie se termine
*
Rien n'est perdu si tu sais profiter de ta journée
*
Quand on n'a pas la capacité de réfléchir, on prétend quand même d'avoir « son opinion »
*
L'espoir est le meilleur antidépresseur
*
Vous n'êtes pas dans la vie pour vous faire des amis, vous êtes dans la vie pour être un ami.
*
Le jour où il n'y aura qu'un seul Dieu sur terre, il sauvera huit milliards d'êtres humains.

Pierre Fasquelle

La note d'hôtel

Elsa et Olivier, un couple voyageant dans leur véhicule, décident de s'arrêter dans un hôtel indiqué par de grands panneaux au bord de la route.
Elsa est d'autant fatiguée, qu'elle a navigué dans les bouchons serrés des retours de vacances. Olivier n'ayant pas de permis (oui, oui !!) ne peut pas la remplacer.
La chambre est bien climatisée, aussi Elsa et son compagnon n'ont aucune difficulté à s'endormir paisiblement.
Environ quatre heures plus tard le couple se réveille, et décide de reprendre la route. Encore quatre cents kilomètres à faire pour arriver à domicile.
Passant devant la réception, ils réclament la facture ...de... 620 euros.
Étonnés du montant de la facture, ils refusent de payer sans une explication détaillée pour justifier ce montant excessif.
Le directeur est appelé en secours.
- Vous voyez, dit-il à Elsa et Olivier, notre hôtel fournit des prestations de midi à midi. Vous êtes arrivés vers onze heures le matin, et il est actuellement quinze heures trente. Je suis donc obligé de vous facturer deux jours.
Heureusement la nuitée d'hier midi jusqu'à aujourd'hui midi vous est facturée à cinquante pour cent du tarif

normal. C'était le jour de relâche de nos prestataires et artistes de spectacle que nous proposons à nos clients en forfait avec le tarif de l'hôtel.
En plus nous mettons à disposition un sauna spacieux avec massage personnalisé, une piscine avec jacuzzi et un buffet à volonté. Franchement Monsieur, Madame, 620 euros ce n'est pas cher !!

Olivier proteste vivement :
- Mais je n'ai pas utilisé vos prestations, nous ne sommes restés que quelques heures !
- Peut-être, répond le directeur, mais vous auriez pu en bénéficier en restant avec nous..

A contrecœur Olivier demande à sa compagne d'écrire un chèque de 120 euros.
- Mais, vous vous trompez monsieur, madame, c'est 620 euros et pas 120 euros.
- Je me suis permis de vous facturer 500 euros de frais pour baiser ma compagne, réplique Olivier.
- Mais, quand même, monsieur, je n'ai pas....s' indigne le directeur.
- Eh bien ! Elle était ici, vous auriez pu bénéficier de ses prestations !

Yaka II

Ne t'engage pas dans une vie commune pour *trouver* le bonheur, engage-toi pour *partager* le bonheur.

Le poids de la confiance

Antonin Bommelkerque, paysan éleveur de vaches produit lui-même du beurre. Vous connaissez peut-être, ce bon beurre de paysan.
André Fournil est boulanger. D'ailleurs avec un nom pareil, on ne demande pas plus...

André est indiscutablement le meilleur boulanger dans le canton et ses alentours. Aussi pour que sa brioche pur beurre soit à la hauteur de ses compétences, il achète son beurre chez Antonin le paysan qui baratte lui-même.
Après un certain temps de collaboration, André remarque que la motte de beurre diminue en volume.
Il s'adresse à Antonin pour lui faire part de ses observations.
Antonin proteste vivement et lui dit qu'il respecte toujours le poids demandé, soit trois kilos.
Le dispute allait bon train, André décida qu'il allait falloir trouver une solution. Il a besoin de ce beurre, parce que de très bonne qualité, et Antonin est le seul paysan dans le canton qui fabrique encore du beurre à la ferme.

Il décida de s'adresser au maire de leur commune pour qu'il se constitue en médiateur.
Antonin donna son accord. Tout ce beau monde se

retrouva chez Antonin pour faire la pesée de la motte de beurre.
Il plaça la motte sur la balance et sur l'autre plateau deux pains d'un kilo et demi, soit trois kilos de pain.

- Vous voyez, j'ai acheté deux pains ce matin chez André. Ce sont deux pains qui sont vendus pour trois kilos de pain. C'est comme ça que je pèse mon beurre, parce que moi, je fais confiance à mon boulanger.

Yaka III

Commencez avec le nécessaire. Ensuite, faites le possible. Et puis soudain, vous venez de faire l'impossible ...
*
Quand le cœur pleure pour ce qu'il a perdu, l'esprit rit de ce qu'il a gagné.
*
Un débutant voit de nombreuses possibilités. Un expert seulement quelques-unes.
*
La croissance spirituelle est la seule raison de notre existence sur la terre.
*
L'amour est toujours inquiet de l'autre.
*

Tu dis la politique ?

Un fils demande à son père :
- Papa, qu'est-ce que réellement la politique.
Mon garçon, c'est très simple. Regarde, j'apporte à la maison de l'argent, j'incarne le ***capitalisme***. Ta mère gère cet argent, c'est le ***gouvernement***. La bonne est la ***classe ouvrière***, tous nous avons un seul but, c'est ton bien-être. Par conséquent, tu es le ***peuple***. Ton petit frère qui est encore un bébé est le ***futur.***

Le fils réfléchit et propose de dormir une nuit.
La nuit, il se réveille en sursaut ; son petit frère pleure très fort parce qu'il vient de s'acquitter d'une forte commission dans sa couche-culotte. Ne sachant pas quoi faire il va dans la chambre de ses parents.
Il y a seulement sa mère dans le lit en si profond sommeil qu'il n'arrive pas à la réveiller.
Il décide d'aller à la chambre de la bonne où il voit son père au lit avec elle et ils font des choses très étranges. Ils sont tellement occupés que ni son père ni la bonne ne remarque qu'il est au pied du lit.
Aussi le garçon retourne dans sa chambre pour essayer de dormir quand même.
Le lendemain matin, le père demande à son fils s'il peut expliquer ce qu'est la politique avec ses propres mots

- Oui, dit le fils : Le **capitalisme** exploite la **classe ouvrière**, le **gouvernement** se met en sommeil. Le **peuple** est complètement ignoré et le **futur** est de la merde!

Yaka IV

Les attentes sont la semence de déceptions.

*

Quelques soient les difficultés que vous avez également eues dans le passé, vous pouvez aujourd'hui prendre un nouveau départ.

*

Soyez le changement que vous voulez voir dans le monde.

*

La vie dure toute une journée,
la mort dure plus que toute une nuit.

D'après Bouddha

*

Si mes opinions, mes pensées font de moi ton ennemi, c'est que tu ne peux plus nier mon existence.

*

Si tu dois combler un retard, tu risques de passer à coté de la vérité.

*

Vous avez plus de regrets dans votre vie de ce que vous n'avez pas fait que de ce que vous avez fait.

Excursion industrielle

J.P. Participe à une visite de l'usine de latex.

Il observe avec un certain intérêt la fabrication des trayons d'aspiration dans une production de biberons.
Il constate que la machine fait toujours les mêmes sons: blub, hop, hop, blub, ... puis le bruit « whoosh »
Le guide explique que son « blub » est causé lorsque le latex est versé dans la forme, le bruit de « whoosh » est le trou qu'on pique dans la tétine.

Arrivé à la machine des condoms, la machine rend les sons suivants: « blub blub, blub, blub, whoosh... »
J.P. écoute attentivement et dit au guide :
- Je reconnais le son" blub "du modelage, mais je crois que j'entends un « whoosh » comme on pique un trou ?
Le guide répond :
- Oui, c'est vrai, tous les quatre préservatifs on fait un trou.
- Pas possible s'effraie J.P., c'est catastrophique pour la vente des préservatifs !
- Mais non, rit le guide, c'est génial pour la vente des tétines de biberon! "

Invitation

Hier je t'ai tendu la main
T'as regardé l'autre côté
Je t'ai observé en vain
Avec ta sincérité rabiotée

Cloche pendue
La sonnerie en silence
Tirer la corde main nue
L'abreuvoir en potence

Je t'ai donné bien du fil à tendre
Des soucis que t'as inventés
Des promesses réduites en cendres
Tant de vérités tétanisées

Hier encore je t'ai donné à boire
Le pain à partager
T'invitant à t'asseoir
Et venir manger

À ce jour t'as voulu être l'incompris
Qu'on ne saisit plus en aise
Devant mon regard ébahi
D'un espoir trop obèse

Il me reste à croire
Que tu peux encore partager le pain
Que tu peux encore t'asseoir
Et voir que je te tends la main.

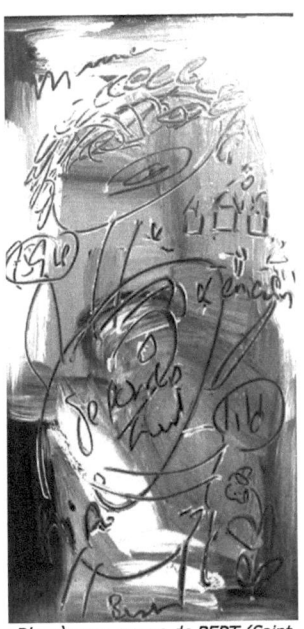

D'après une œuvre de BERT (Saint Marcel - 2004)

L'homme surmené

- Dites-moi ce qui ne va pas, il me semble que vous êtes un peu surmené, demande le psychiatre.
- C'est venu par mon mariage. J'ai épousé une veuve qui avait une grande fille.
Elle est maintenant ma belle-fille. Mon père est venu nous rendre visite, tombe en amour avec ma belle-fille et l'épouse.
Ainsi, ma belle-fille est aussi ma belle-mère ...
Entre-temps ma femme a eu un fils qui était automatiquement le beau-frère de mon père, parce qu'il est le demi-frère de ma belle-fille, qui est mariée à mon père.
Depuis que mon fils est le frère de ma belle-mère, c'est aussi mon oncle.
La femme de mon père accouchait aussi d'un fils.
C'est mon demi-frère, parce qu'il est le fils de mon père. Mais il est aussi un peu mon petit-fils, car il est le fils de ma belle-fille.
Depuis que je suis marié à la grand-mère de mon frère Je ne suis pas seulement le mari et le beau-fils de ma femme et je crois que je suis aussi mon propre grand-père !
C'est pourquoi je suis un peu surmené.

Conseils tarifés

Un avocat et un médecin se rencontrent lors d'une réception. Leur conversation, cependant, a été constamment interrompue par d' autres convives qui sollicitent le médecin pour obtenir quelques conseils.

Ennuyé, le médecin demande à l'avocat ce qu'il a fait pour éviter que les gens le dérangent quand il ne travaille pas.
- S'ils demandent des conseils, répond l'avocat, je les leur donne sans problème. Le lendemain je leur fais envoyer la facture.
Le médecin décide de suivre les conseils de l'avocat et le reste de la nuit, il note les noms et adresses de tous ceux qui viennent lui demander conseil.

Le lendemain matin, au moment où le médecin a voulu transférer la liste d'adresses pour la facturation à sa secrétaire, elle lui soumet la facture de l'avocat...

Yaka V

Ne t'engage pas dans une vie commune pour *trouver* le bonheur, engage-toi pour *partager* le bonheur.

La drague

Simon rencontre une femme plus âgée que lui dans un café. Elle avait toujours l'air très bien, même si elle avait déjà la cinquantaine bien sonnée.

Après avoir bu un verre ensemble tout en flirtant un peu, elle lui demande s'il n'a jamais fait un trio avec la mère et la fille.

- Euh, non ...» balbutie Simon complètement surpris.

La femme vide son verre et lui dit:
- Eh bien, ce soir, c'est votre jour de chance!

Elle l'invite à la suivre jusque chez elle. Arrivés, la femme allume la lumière dans le couloir et appelle en bas de l'escalier:
- Maman, t'es encore éveillée ?

Yaka VI

Les gens disent être à la recherche du sens de leur existence. En vérité le sens n'est pas quelque chose que vous trouverez mais c'est ce que vous créez.

Alpinisme

Kévin et Mathurin étaient les meilleurs amis et adeptes de l'alpinisme.

Lors d'une escapade Kévin glisse de 30 mètres dans une faille de roche.

Mathurin pleurait hystériquement :

- Kévin ! et déjà il pensait que c'était fini, mais quand il entendit un gémissement il souriait à nouveau. Tout espoir était permis.

- Kévin, cria Mathurin, je jette une corde, attaches- la autour de la taille et je te lève, mon ami.

Kévin répondit que ce n'était pas possible, parce qu'il avait les deux bras et les jambes cassés. A cause de la météo de l'automne, ce n'était pas possible de joindre les sauveteurs.

Finalement, ils décidaient que Kévin s'accrocherait avec les dents.

Aussi Kévin mordait aussi fort qu'il le pouvait dans la corde et Mathurin faisait tout son possible pour le hisser vers le haut.

Après quelques secondes il cria :

- Mathurin, mon ami, tu tiens bon ?

Puis il répondit :

- *OUI - OUIIIIIIIIII !!*

Coup de gueule d'Ötsie

La SPA dénombre 70 000 abandons en France rien qu'entre les mois de mai et de septembre, soit environ 80 % du total annuel.

Chiens attachés au mieux au portail d'une SPA, ou simplement à un arbre ou poteau dans la campagne ou simplement sur une aire d'autoroute.

Ou « mieux » encore simplement virés par la vitre du véhicule à une vitesse élevée.
Les chats ont le même sort que les chiens, s'ils ne sont pas carrément noyés dans une taie d'oreiller avec quelques cailloux.
Ou on laisse son animal en forêt pour lui donner « une chance ».

Je l'ai déjà dit, un animal fait partie des meubles selon quelques lois mal pensées. C'est dommage et vicieux, puisqu' un meuble peut être évacué dans une déchetterie. C'est malpropre d'abandonner ses gros déchets dans la rue...
Quand on est capable d'abandonner de façon criminelle un animal, on est assurément capable d'abandonner certains principes de la vie, même trahir le respect d'autrui.
Moi, comme chien j'ai la chance de vivre avec des

humains d'amour. Mais doit-on avoir de la chance uniquement, pour vivre sans soucis sa vie ?
J'ai vu à la télé que pas si loin d'ici les humains sont aussi abattus et « traités comme des chiens ».

Même, moins pénible à entendre, on dit aussi qu'il fait un « temps de chien ».
Pourquoi, vivre comme un chien c'est vivre de façon dégradante, sans respect ou sans considération ?
Est-ce que cela veut dire qu'un chien ne mérite pas le respect dû à toute nature confiante?
Nous les chiens, nous sommes aussi des être vivants.

Est-ce qu'on doit disputer l'incertitude que nous les chiens n'avons pas une âme, et de ce fait cela doit-il nous conduire à être « moins que rien » dans le langage courant humanoïste ?
Cette situation me reste en travers de la gueule, insoluble dans les espérances. N'empêche que nous les chiens, nous ne sommes pas rancuniers. Nous savons être fidèles dans le respect et l'amitié.
Nous sommes vraiment le meilleur ami de l'homme, espérons tous ensemble que les bipèdes du genre humain méritent un jour cette même distinction.

Gros coups de langue à toutes et tous,
Ötsie

La pilule

Un homme vient chez le dentiste et après un bref examen, le dentiste lui dit:
- Je dois vous extraire une dent. Je vais vous faire une petite piqûre pour que vous n'ayez pas de douleur.
Le patient attrape le bras du dentiste et dit:
- Non, s'il vous plaît, pas de piqûre, je n'aime pas et je ne le supporte pas.
- Pas de problème monsieur, dit le dentiste, vous n'êtes pas le seul. Nous utilisons un peu d'oxyde d'azote.
- Non, je vous en prie, pas ça non plus. Je vais être malade plusieurs jours. Je ne supporte pas l'oxyde d'azote.
Le dentiste disparaît et revient avec un verre d'eau et dit :
- Tenez, prenez cette pilule.
- Qu'est-ce que c'est ? demande le patient.
- Viagra, dit le dentiste.
L'homme regarde, étonné:
- On peut soulager la douleur avec ça ? demande-t-il
- Non, mais alors vous avez quelque chose à tenir pendant que je vous enlève la dent ...

Le courage

Un homme fraîchement décédé se présente à la porte du paradis.

Saint-Pierre assis devant son méga-computer fait défiler sa base de données pour voir si l'homme doit être autorisé à pénétrer dans le paradis.
Malgré la vitesse grâce à la nano-technique avancée, il fronce les sourcils et dit :
- Vous savez, ce n'est pas juste pour vous, mais je ne vois pas ce que vous avez fait de bon dans votre vie, ni de mauvais d'ailleurs. Si vous pouvez me raconter une bonne action dans votre vie, même une seule, alors vous pouvez immédiatement entrer à l'intérieur.
L'homme réfléchit un moment et dit :
- Oui, il y a eu cette fois où je roulais sur la route et j'ai vu un gang de motards qui harcelait une jeune fille.
J'ai ralenti pour voir ce qui se passait, j'ai vu, ils étaient au moins 20 types, en train de déchirer les vêtements de la jeune fille.
Furieux, je suis sorti de ma voiture, j'ai pris un démonte-pneu dans le coffre et je suis allé vers le chef de la bande, un géant énorme d'au moins deux mètres avec veste en cuir et une chaîne de son nez à son oreille.
Quand je me suis approché, les autres membres du

gang ont formé un cercle autour de moi.
J'ai tiré la chaîne du visage de cette brute et je l'ai frappé sur la tête avec mon démonte-roue.
Il lâcha la fille et tomba comme un roc à terre. La fille se mit à courir pour s'échapper.
Lorsque je me tournai vers le reste de la bande ,je leur dis:
- Que cela soit une leçon pour vous tous, de ne plus terroriser une jeune femme, ou je vais vous apprendre à tous de quel bois je me chauffe.

Saint-Pierre, totalement impressionné demande :
- Vraiment ? C'était quand ?
- Oh, dit l'homme, il y a environ deux minutes.

Yaka VII

Vivre c'est une faveur, le savoir c'est un art.

*

Chacun a la responsabilité de désobéir aux lois injustes

(Martin Luther KING)

*

Le silence est le sommeil qui nourrit la sagesse.

*

Sois toi-même, les autres se suffisent à eux-mêmes.

Le dîner

Un jeune homme va à la seule pharmacie de son village pour acheter des préservatifs. Le pharmacien propose différentes quantités, soit par 3, 6, 9 ou 12 ou bien en emballage individuel.

« Eh bien...», dit le jeune homme qui veut visiblement se la péter un peu, je connais cette fille déjà depuis un certain temps maintenant, ce soir nous dînons chez ses parents, puis nous sortons.
Ce soir, il va se passer ce qui va se passer ! Ça va être la première fois pour elle. Ça va être sa fête ! Il ne faut pas qu'elle soit déçue !
Alors comme je suis certain qu'elle va vouloir bien en profiter, je pense que j'aurais besoin au moins d'une boîte de 12 !

Plus tard dans la soirée, il est assis à la table avec sa petite amie et ses parents.
Les parents très chrétiens lui demandent s'il veut faire la prière de la bénédiction.
Il assemble les mains et commence à prier. Il demande de vive voix de bénir le repas et continue en silence de prier, et encore et encore... Il n'y a presque pas de fin.
Quand enfin il en termine, sa petite amie lui dit doucement:

« - Tu ne m'as jamais dit que tu étais si religieux? »
Il lui chuchote de retour:
« - Tu ne m'as jamais dit que ton père est pharmacien ».

La stagiaire

La stagiaire employée de bureau se tenait ébahie près de la déchiqueteuse.

- Petite, besoin d'aide?" demande un collègue.
- Oui, je veux bien, répondit-elle, comment ça marche ?
- Simple", dit le collègue, donne-moi tes documents.
- Je t'en prie, merci beaucoup. Les voici...
Le collègue introduit les documents, et dit à la stagiaire :
- Tu vois, c'est facile !
- Mais oui, je vois. Je vous remercie, mais d'où viennent ces copies maintenant?"

Yaka VIII

En amour,
il y en a toujours un qui souffre et l'autre qui s'ennuie
Honoré de Balzac

En panne

Anneke appelle l'électricien pour lui demander de venir parce que la sonnette de son appartement ne fonctionne plus.
L'électricien promet de venir l'après-midi même.
Le lendemain, elle rappelle et lui dit :
- J'ai attendu toute l'après-midi, pourquoi vous n'êtes pas venu ?
- Mais pour sûr que je suis venu. J'ai sonné au moins 20 fois. Personne ne m'a ouvert la porte !

Yaka IX

L'argent ne fait pas d' heureux,
surtout l'argent que tu n'as pas.
*
Tout a sa beauté, mais pas tout le monde la voit.
*
Tu seras riche, si tu possèdes quelque chose que
tu ne peux acheter.
*
Conseil d'économie en temps de crise :
Utiliser le papier hygiénique des deux côtés.

Orage

C'était une chaude journée d'été, et au moment où la mère d'un petit garçon s'apprête à le mettre au lit, un violent orage éclate.
Le petit garçon était terrifié et d'une voix tremblante, il demande :
- Maman, tu viens dormir avec moi ce soir ?
La mère câline son fils et dit:
- Désolé, mais je ne peux pas, je dois dormir avec papa.
Le garçon fit une pause puis dit :
- Il peut être grand et fort, mais c'est quand même un trouillard, hein ?

L'innocence

Deux petites filles en C.P. bavardent dans la cour de récréation. L'une d'elles informe sa copine :
- Hier, j'ai trouvé un préservatif sous la balustrade.
 L'autre répond :
- Qu'est-ce c'est une balustrade ?

Le bébé

Deux hommes gays décident d'avoir un bébé. Cependant, ils ne sont pas intéressés par l'adoption parce qu'ils veulent un bébé autant que possible de leur part.
Alors les deux hommes se masturbent en concert ensemble dans une fiole et portent leur sperme chez un médecin qui veut bien fertiliser la mère porteuse.

Neuf mois plus tard, le bébé est né. Tous deux cherchent leur bébé pris en charge dans la salle de la maternité.
Tous les autres bébés pleurent, sauf le leur.
- Mon Dieu, dit l'un l'un des gays avec une certaine fierté, notre bébé est le plus silencieux de tous ici !
L'infirmière ayant entendu, déclara :
- Oui, maintenant il est calme, mais attendez que j'enlève le thermomètre ... !

Yaka X

En cause, la crise. La lumière au fond du tunnel est provisoirement éteinte

La sagesse

Mahatma Gandhi s'apprête à embarquer dans un train en Inde.
Il a déjà un certain âge, aussi perd-il l'une de ses chaussures qui atterrit juste à côté des rails. Comme le train commence à bouger, Gandhi n'a pas pu reprendre sa chaussure. Alors avec calme , il se défait de son autre chaussure et la jette vers la chaussure perdue. Un passager perplexe demande à Gandhi pourquoi il fait ça. Gandhi en souriant lui explique :
- L'homme qui trouvera ma chaussure aura maintenant la deuxième pour faire la paire ...

Papotage

Deux chauves-souris, la tête en bas, côte à côte papotent :

- Tu sais de quoi j'ai peur maintenant que je vieillis ? -
- Non, de quoi ? demanda l'autre.
- De l'incontinence !

D'après une œuvre de Kényus van den Heuvel (Saint Marcel 2001)

Miraculé

D'après un tableau de BERT (2002)

Je suis un miraculé
l'incroyable chance
Je l'ai vu à la télé
On a parlé de la France.

Je suis un miraculé
J'ai le droit de discuter
Je l'ai vu à la télé
avec mon député.

Je suis un miraculé
Je mange à ma faim
Je l'ai vu à la télé
J'ai droit au pain.

Je suis un miraculé
Un jour je vais mourir
Je l'ai vu à la télé
Pas besoin de courir.

Je suis un miraculé
J'ai de la sagesse
Je l'ai vu à la télé
Que rien ne presse.

Je suis surtout un miraculé
Parce que je sais que tu m'aimes
Je ne l'ai pas vu à la télé
Quand-même !!

Yaka XI

Rien faire c'est compliqué,
tu ne sais jamais quand tu auras fini
*
Mon chef ne fait rien de sa journée.
Je suis son assistant.

La puissance

Il vécut une fois au fin fond de la Chine un tailleur de pierre qui était mécontent de son sort.
Il travaillait pour un homme extrêmement riche qui habitait dans une maison splendide.
- J'aimerais bien être à sa place, se dit le tailleur de pierre. Par miracle le tailleur de pierre était devenu un homme très riche en un temps éclair. Il possédait plus de richesses qu'il n'en a jamais rêvé.
Un jour, un haut fonctionnaire du gouvernement lui rendit visite. Tout le monde, riche ou pauvre, lui faisait une profonde révérence.
- Quelle puissance a cet homme puissant, pensa le tailleur de pierre devenu très riche. Moi aussi j'aimerais être puissant comme lui.
Aussitôt, il était transporté sur une chaise porteuse et tout le monde s'inclinait devant lui. Comme le haut fonctionnaire, il était aussi détesté par les gens qui ont dû s'incliner devant lui en enviant son pouvoir.
C'était une chaude journée d'été et le tailleur de pierre se sentait étouffé drapé sur sa chaise. Il leva les yeux vers le soleil de plomb et pensa :
- Le soleil est encore plus puissant que moi. Alors moi, je serais le soleil ! Le tailleur de pierre très riche et super puissant était désormais le soleil. Il brillait sans pitié sur la terre, brûla les champs, et affamait les

peuples par la sécheresse.

Un énorme nuage se figea entre le soleil et la terre. Le nuage donna la pluie. Toute la faune et la flore renaîtraient en force. Les lois de la nature s'établiraient à nouveau.

- Qu'est-ce que ce nuage de pluie est habile ! pensa le tailleur de pierre devenu très riche et puissant comme le soleil. Je voudrais être ce nuage. Ce qui fut.

Il était la nuage de pluie. Il a inondé les champs et les villages. Bientôt, cependant, il remarqua qu'il était poussé par le vent. Quel souffle ce vent, se disait-il. Et quelle force de pouvoir pousser les nuages !

- Je souhaite penser que je pourrais être le vent, se dit le tailleur de pierre devenu très riche et puissant comme le soleil, et frais comme un nuage. Et il était le vent. Il a déraciné des arbres et était craint par tous. Mais après un moment, il a trouvé quelque chose qu'il ne pouvait faire bouger. C'était une grosse pierre qui lui résistait.

- Cette fois-ci, c'est vraiment la puissance absolue pensait-il. Je voudrais être cette pierre. Et il était la pierre plus puissante que tout autre chose dans le monde.

Jusqu'à ce qu'il ait entendu le bruit d'un marteau et d'un ciseau en lui. Lui, la pierre la plus massive, a été abattu.

- Qu'est -ce que ce pouvait être ? Y-a-t-il encore plus puissant ? Se demandait-il.

Il baissa les yeux et vit un tailleur de pierre en œuvre.

Un peu d'histoire

Il s'appelait Fleming, un pauvre fermier écossais.
Un jour, il entend des cris venant du marais. Le fermier se dépêchait et courut dans la direction des cris. Et dans le marais il trouve un garçon terrifié, embourbé dans la boue jusqu'à la taille.

Le fermier lui jeta une corde qu'il avait toujours sur lui, et supplia de s'accrocher.

Sir Alexandre Fleming

Le lendemain, un homme de belle prestance se présenta à la ferme de Fleming. Il se présenta comme le père de l'enfant qu'il avait sauvé.
- Je tiens à vous remercier de tout mon cœur et vous donner une récompense, dit l'homme. Vous avez sauvé la vie de mon fils.
- Désolé, mais je ne veux pas d'argent, répondit le paysan. Je suis certain que vous auriez fait la même chose.
À ce moment, le fils Fleming entra dans la maison.
- Est-ce que c'est votre fils ?, demanda le visiteur.
- Oui, c'est mon fils Alexander, affirma le père avec fierté.

- Alors, acceptez que je finance les études de votre fils. Il recevra la même éducation que mon propre garçon. Ils vont grandir ensemble comme des frères et devenir des hommes dont nous pourrons être fiers.

Sir Winston Churchil

Le père Fleming accepta.
Son fils reçut la meilleure éducation dans les écoles et allait être diplômé de l'Hospital Medical School de St. Mary de Londres.

Plus tard, il sera mondialement connu comme Sir Alexander Fleming, ayant découvert la pénicilline.
Quelques années ont passé. Le fils de l'homme de belle prestance, Lord Randolph Churchil est touché par la pneumonie.
La pénicilline d'Alexandre Fleming sauva la vie de Sir Winston Churchil.
Concernant l'authenticité de cette belle histoire, il semblerait qu'il ne s'agisse que d'une légende urbaine.
Selon la biographie d'Alexandre Fleming écrite par Kévin Brown, Monsieur Fleming disait lui-même qu'il s'agissait « d'une bien belle fable ». Néanmoins, cette histoire fait du bien et la morale reste valable pour nous tous.

La précipitation

Un gendarme en poste au bord de la route à l'entrée d'un petit village arrête une voiture pour excès de vitesse.
- Gendarmerie Nationale, Papiers s'il vous plaît !
- Monsieur le gendarme, pitié, je suis déjà très en retard !
- Ça, je l'ai remarqué. C'est pour cette raison que je vous arrête. Vous dépassez de 30 kilomètre heure la vitesse autorisée. Merci de me présenter vos papiers et de souffler dans l'alcool -test que voici.
Le conducteur cherche encore à protester, mais en vain. D'ailleurs le gendarme ayant perdu sa patience appelle son collègue.
- Ce monsieur ne veut pas obtempérer à ma demande de présenter ses papiers et les papiers du véhicule. Il ne veut pas non plus souffler dans l' alcool-test.
Le collègue sort les menottes et explique :
- Soit vous sortez du véhicule et vous me suivez jusqu'au véhicule de la gendarmerie, soit je vous menotte de force.
Le conducteur suit le gendarme et s'assoit sur la banquette dans le van de la gendarmerie.
- Monsieur l'agent, laissez-moi vous expliquer...
- Il n'y a rien à expliquer, vous êtes en infraction ; en plus, il me semble que vous n'êtes pas en mesure de

reprendre la route. Aussi je vous emmène au poste.
Peut-être aurez-vous de la chance, le chef marie sa fille aujourd'hui, il va être de bonne humeur.
Ceci dit, je veux bien écouter votre explication, mais je crains de ne rien pouvoir faire dans l'immédiat.
Le jeune homme soupire et explique :
- Pour ma part, je crains le pire. C'est moi qui devrait se marier avec la fille de votre chef...

Yaka XII

Quand on se trompe 1 fois, c'est une erreur.
Quand on se trompe 2 fois pour la même chose, c'est de l'incompréhension.
Quand on se trompe 3 fois pour la même chose, c'est de la connerie.
La 4ème, c'est une faute envers soi-même.

Pierre Fasquelle

*

Si le travail est la santé, confie-le aux malades.

*

Les futurs souvenirs se construisent aujourd'hui

*

Les gagnants ont un plan, les perdants des excuses.

*

C'est pour satisfaire les sens qu'on fait l'amour,

*

c'est pour l'essence qu'on fait la guerre

Raymond Devos

Silence mortel

L'horloge murale sonnait une heure et demie le matin. Fortuna se réveilla en sursaut. Une voix étrange venant de quelque part lui disait :
- Lève-toi, Fortuna. Va voir ce qui se passe dehors, j'ai besoin de toi !.
Irritée et angoissée, elle descendait à pas de chat l'escalier et ouvrit la porte d'entrée de la maison.
Fortuna ne connaissait pas encore bien l'environnement, puisque c'était seulement le deuxième jour qu'elle y habitait.
Elle vivait seule depuis que son compagnon l'avait quittée : Elle était veuve.
Le vent s'engouffre devant elle et semble constituer des voix. Avait-elle vraiment entendu des voix, imagination ou mauvais rêve ?
Puis soudain un silence mortel tomba sur elle. Le vent s'était arrêté de jouer l'imitateur de voix.
Seuls quelques pétales tombés à terre bougeaient encore comme de petits êtres en train de danser.

Un chat noir s'approchait et s'arrêta pile devant elle.
Son sentiment de peur monta en degrés.
Les yeux du chat vert brillant se reflétaient dans le candélabre.
Le chat ne bougeait pas.
Tout d'un coup, il tourne la tête un quart de tour vers

la droite. Puis son dos se courbe, il souffle fort et s'enfuit comme si sa vie en dépendait.

Surprise Fortuna regarde vers la droite. Elle ne voit rien d'étrange.

Toujours en pensant au chat qui semblait soudain fuir, elle se dirige vers le banc devant la maison. Elle s'assoit.

Qu'est- ce qu'il avait vu, ce chat?

Le banc se trouvait sur le bord d'un chemin de promenade, avec vue sur un ancien moulin. Malgré la nuit, elle constata qu'il n'y avait pas de vie, même les lames ne bougeaient pas.

Elle sait que le moulin a été utilisé pour traiter le papier, mais elle ne savait pas si le moulin était encore productif.

Elle s'interroge avec la curiosité qui lui est propre : aller voir ce moulin, qui est peut-être le mystère de ces étranges sentiments.

Avec prudence, elle se dirige vers la bâtisse, tout en regardant autour d'elle pour voir s'il y a quelqu'un.

À plusieurs reprises, elle s'arrêtait pour retourner vers la maison pour se mettre à l'abri. Mais sa curiosité gagnait sur sa peur.

Arrivée devant le moulin, elle chercha la porte d'entrée.

Elle la trouvait cachée derrière un gros buisson. C'était certain, il y avait longtemps que ce moulin était abandonné.

En écartant le buisson,e elle se coupe avec une branche. Son bras saignait sérieusement.

Elle était obligée de couper une bande de tissu en bas de sa chemise de nuit, qu'elle porta en-dessous de son

peignoir pour en fabriquer un bandage.
Elle n'était pas surprise que la porte de l'ancien moulin ne fut pas verrouillée, une simple pression suffisait à ouvrir la porte.
Un moment, elle pensait qu'à nouveau elle entendait des voix, ou plutôt une voix. Mais d'où venait cette voix ? Un vagabond ? Ce serait normal, puisque à l'intérieur du moulin il faisait moins frisquet qu'au dehors, d'autant plus que s'il y pleuvait, il fallait mieux être à l'abri.
Elle essayait de mieux écouter, mais la voix semble avoir disparu. Était-ce son imagination à nouveau ?

La curiosité de Fortuna gagnait à nouveau sur sa peur et elle continua dans l'obscurité. Le plancher craquait tellement qu'elle craignait passer au travers.
Elle rechercha un mur, pour essayer de se soutenir. Puis elle se heurta contre un objet rectangulaire et dur. Par le toucher elle essayait de découvrir ce que cela pouvait être. Il semblait que c'était un pilier d'escalier. Situation normale, puisque dans un moulin il y a très souvent plusieurs étages. En effet, il y avait un escalier.

Les yeux de Fortuna s'étaient doucement habitués à l'obscurité de la nuit, et elle pouvait mieux voir autour d'elle. Aussi sur une vieille table recouverte de poussière, elle découvrit un vieux journal, une boîte d'allumettes et une bougie.
Dans la lumière de la bougie, elle prend le journal, le secoua pour enlever la poussière et essaya de lire l'article en haut de la page.

"Accident dans le vieux moulin délabré, la fille tombe du premier étage."

Maintenant c'était certain, il semblait que ce n'était pas une bonne idée d'aller en haut par l'escalier. Même avec une bougie.

Puis elle revint vers l'entrée, elle se fit la promesse de revenir le lendemain, mais cette fois-là avec une lampe de poche.
Mais soudain, elle entend à peine à quelques centimètres de son visage un fort gémissement.
Elle sursauta de peur et tomba en arrière sur le dos. Quand elle ouvrit les yeux, elle regardait droit dans les deux yeux vert brillant. C'était une fois encore le même chat noir. Elle se dressait péniblement pour essayer de s'enfuir, mais elle sentit qu'elle était surveillée.
Peut-être le vagabond avec un énorme couteau, parce que il ne veut pas être dérangé...
Elle observa maintenant une silhouette à moins de deux mètres d'elle. Malgré sa peur, elle se retourna et tenae de prendre contact avec l'ombre. Sans succès.
Puis elle voit en un éclair le chat noir courir vers l'extérieur et dans la même seconde, l'ombre avait disparu.
Elle courait au plus vite vers la maison, sauta dans son lit sans enlever son peignoir en se couvrant pour ne plurien voir. Elle se sentait ainsi en sécurité, comme dans son enfance. Mais, quand même, si cette fois ce n'était pas une rêve ?

Après quelques minutes, elle tomba presque dans un profond sommeil. Mais sous ses couvertures, elle avait trop chaud , elle suffoquait par manque d'air.
Fortuna repoussa un peu les couvertures et regardait l'heure sur son réveil.
Il était une heure trente deux. Le dateur affichait le 23 juillet 2002.

C'était irréel. Toute cette histoire s'était déroulée en si peu de temps ? Avant d'aller au moulin il était une heure et demie, c'est-à-dire une heure et trente minutes. C'était seulement deux minutes plus tard !!
Pourtant, sa blessure, la robe de nuit déchirée, c'était bien réel !
Mais le journal ! Le journal datait du 24 juillet 2002. Ce journal, ce vieux journal ne pouvait pas exister. C'était le journal de demain !

À nouveau, elle entendait des voix, ou plutôt une voix. Une voix qui avait une similitude certaine avec la voix de son défunt compagnon et lui disait cette fois-ci claire et compréhensible :
- Viens maintenant, ne pars plus. Je t'attendais. C'est l'heure.
Puis il fut silence.

Un silence mortel.

Hot line

Popol se met en relation avec la hot line pour prendre conseil auprès d'un technicien de la marque de son ordinateur.

Le technicien :
- Comment puis-je vous aider ?
Popol :
- Je ne reçois pas d'image sur mon écran LED !
Le technicien :
- Êtes-vous, monsieur, derrière votre ordinateur ?
Popol :
- Non
Le technicien :
- Pourriez-vous vous asseoir derrière l'ordinateur ?
Popol :
- OK, j'y suis.
Le technicien :
- Dites- moi ce que vous voyez maintenant ?
Popol :
- Des câbles, que des câbles.

Napoléon est de retour !

Un soir, dans la salle commune d'un hôpital psychiatrique, l'un des patients crie :
- Je suis Napoléon ! Napoléon Ier !
Un autre fou lui demande :
- T'es sûr que tu es Napoléon ?
- Bien sûr que oui répondit le Napoléon.
- Et comment tu sais que tu es Napoléon l'empereur de la France ?
- C'est simple, Dieu me l'a dit lui-même !
Puis venant d'un homme très très barbu et aussi très très âgé au fond de la salle :
- Je t'ai rien dit, pauv'con !

Yaka XIII

Le rire peut être contagieux.
Vite, c'est peut-être une épidémie
*

L'homme reste souvent un enfant, seulement ses jouets sont sensiblement plus cher.
*

Partager ne provoque pas la pauvreté.

Chasse aux canards

Deux hommes décident de chasser les canards sauvages. Aucun d'eux n'a de l'expérience dans cette activité.
Quelques heures plus tard leur butin est toujours exempt de canards.
L'un regarde l'autre et lui dit :
- Vraiment, je ne comprends pas. Nous n'avons toujours pas choppé ne serait-ce qu'un seul volatile !
L'autre lui répond en secouant la tête :
- Je te l'ai déjà dit, je pense que le chien n'est pas lancé assez haut !

Anniversaire

Une petite fille demande à sa mère :
- Maman, quand je suis née ?
- Le 28 novembre ma puce.
- Wow, répond la fillette, c'est super ! C'est justement à mon anniversaire !

Les glaçons

Un homme rentre après une journée de dur labeur. Il trouve son épouse penchée au-dessus de l'évier. Elle pleure de grosses larmes.
- Qu'est-ce qui ne va pas ? Demande l'homme inquiet. Puis entre deux reniflements, sa femme lui répond :
- C'est que je voulais te préparer une boisson fraîche, puis les glaçons sont tombés à terre. Donc je les fais tremper dans l'eau chaude pour bien les nettoyer.
- Et alors ?
- C'est que je ne trouve plus les glaçons. Je ne me rappelle plus où ils sont passés.

Moitié sourd

Un fou va chez le médecin et dit:
- Docteur, je suis à moitié sourd.
Le toubib fronce les sourcils et lui répond:
- Nous allons faire un petit test, je vais dire quelque chose et vous me répétez ce que vous avez entendu. Écoutez bien :
- 88
Le fou lui répond :
- 44

L'homme à singes

Un jour un homme arriva dans un village au fin fond de la campagne sud-américaine. Il demanda au chef de village de bien vouloir réunir tous les villageois sur la place.
Après un court discours de bienvenue, il proposa d'aller en forêt et d'attraper les singes d'une certaine espèce. Il disait les acheter pour 10 dollars US chacun.
Les gens du village sentaient le bon filon, parce qu' il y avait beaucoup de ces singes dans les bois autour du village.
Aussitôt, ils avaient attrapé un grand nombre de singes qu'ils vendaient à l'homme. Ils n'avaient jamais gagné autant d''argent si facilement.
Mais arriva ce qui devait arriver, les singes diminuaient sensiblement en nombre. Les villageois estimaient qu'il fallait entreprendre trop d'efforts pour capturer des singes vivants. L'affaire n'était plus rentable pour seulement 10 dollars.
L'acheteur se montra très compréhensif et proposa de doubler la prime de capture et de payer désormais 20 dollars par singe.
À nouveau les chasseurs de singe se mirent à chasser. Puis peu de temps après le nombre de singes avait encore diminué. Il n'y avait quasiment plus de singes dans les bois autour du village. Même dans les

contrées plus éloignées, il n'y avait plus grand chose.

L'homme proposa alors de payer 30 dollars par bête. Mais hélas, le butin était maigre. On attrapait à peine trois singes dans la journée. Au début de la campagne, il n'y avait pas moins de soixante dix singes pour une journée. C'était plus qu'évident, la manne n'existait plus.
Mais dans un dernier geste de bonne volonté, l'homme proposa de payer soixante dollars pour chaque singe apporté. Comme ça, même avec trois à quatre singes, la journée était encore rentable.

Le lendemain, l'assistant de l'homme à singes se présenta aux villageois. Il expliqua que son patron était en déplacement d'urgence pendant au moins deux semaines.
Il vit qu'aucun singe n'était proposé. Visiblement il n'y avait plus de singes dans les bois.

L'assistant expliqua que son patron ne savait plus exactement combien de singes restaient en cage. Il proposa aux villageois son idée :
Je vais vous revendre chaque singe pour trente cinq dollars. Vos vendez à mon patron les singes pour soixante dollars, vous faites un bénéfice de vingt cinq

dollars par bête. Je vous demande seulement dix pour cent de votre bénéfice pour que je gagne un peu plus que ce maigre salaire qu'on me paye.

Les gens du village se mirent d'accord et amassèrent toutes leurs économies, pour réunir l'argent pour acheter les singes.
Les singes revenaient au village.

Ni l'homme, ni l'assistant de l'homme ne sont revenus au village. N'ayant plus d'acheteur pour les singes, les villageois décidèrent de lâcher les bêtes et de pleurer les économies envolées.

Yaka XIV

L'amour propre est un ballon gonflé de vent dont il sort des tempêtes quand on y pique. (Voltaire)
*
Aucune prévision ou planning élaboré ne peut remplacer le cul bordé de nouilles.
*
Faire des erreurs est humain. Les attribuer aux autres s'appelle le management.
*
N'ai pas peur que la fin du monde soit pour aujourd'hui, en Australie c'est déjà demain.
*
Le client est roi. Il a le droit de payer royalement.

Le cadeau

Pierre et Marc travaillent dans une grande administration. Ils sont d'excellents collègues mais aussi de grands amis.
C'est la pause café. Et comme d'usage, ils papotent devant la cafetière.
 - Dis donc, t'as un beau costume sur toi !
 - Merci du compliment, répond Marc. C'est un cadeau surprise de ma femme !
 - De ta femme ? Incroyable ! Tu en as de la chance !
 - Oui, t'as bien raison de penser que j'ai de la chance. Ma femme me l'avait mis sur la chaise dans la chambre à coucher.
Comme j'étais rentré plus tôt que d'habitude, elle m'avait dit qu'elle n'avait pas eu le temps de faire un emballage cadeau !

Histoire de chiens

Deux chiens se promènent sur le boulevard.
Ils s'arrêtent devant un parcmètre et commente :
- C'est honteux, faut-il, nous aussi, qu'on paye pour aller pisser ?

Solidarité

Le nouveau prof entre dans la classe et avec une humeur plutôt sarcastique, il annonce :
 - Les emmerdeurs et emmerdeuses dans ce local sont priés de bien vouloir se mettre debout.
Après un long silence, un élève se lève.
Le prof lui demande :
 - Alors, tu te trouves être un emmerdeur ? Ou peut-être un idiot ?
 - Non, quand même pas, mais je me lève au titre de solidarité avec vous. Je ne voudrais pas que vous soyez le seul à être debout !

L'âne

Jean :
 - Maître, est-ce une insulte si je vous traite d'âne ?
 - Certainement, c'est une insulte. Je n'apprécie pas qu'on me traite d'âne.
 - Et si on traite un âne de « Monsieur »
 - Tu peux dire à un âne « Monsieur »
Puis Jean satisfait lui sourit :
 - Merci Monsieur !

Raide

Petit Pierre aide son grand-père à amasser les feuilles mortes dans le jardin. Il voit qu'un ver de terre essaie à nouveau mais sans succès de se faire un chemin dans la terre asséchée.
- Pépé, demande petit Pierre, on parie que je peux l'aider à se faire un chemin ?
- Impossible, répond pépé, un ver de terre est bien trop mou pour faire un trou dans cette terre.
Pierre entre dans la maison, se dirige vers la salle de bains et prend la bombe de laque de sa mémé.
De retour, il asperge le ver avec la laque et attend quelques instants que la chose se durcisse.
Puis il prend le ver et le pousse sans grande difficulté dans la terre. Pépé émerveillé le félicite, ouvre son porte- monnaie et sort un billet de cinq euros.
- Tiens, dit il à son petit-fils, t'as bien mérité. Tu es un garçon facétieux. Donne-moi la bombe, je vais la ramener de retour dans la salle de bains.
Bien une demi-heure plus tard, un peu essoufflé, pépé revient et appelle petit Pierre. Il a de nouveau un billet de cinq euros dans la main.
- Mais pépé, tu m'as déjà donné cinq euros.
- Je le sais, mais ces cinq euros viennent de ta grand-mère !

Histoire de famille

Bernard entre dans son café habituel et commande cinq vodkas pour lui tout seul.
Le barman lui demande :
- Tu dois avoir une dure journée derrière toi ?
- Putain, mon gars, exclame Bernard, Tu t'imagines, mon grand frère a déclaré qu'il est homo !
Le lendemain, il revient à nouveau et hop ! Encore cinq vodkas.
Le barman toujours curieux :
- Et maintenant, c'est quoi ?
- C'est mon petit frère. Il a dit qu'il est aussi homo !
Le lendemain il est encore une fois de retour et encore une fois « hop » cinq vodkas.
- Mais il n'y a personne qui aime les femmes dans ta famille ? Interroge à nouveau le barman.
- Si, si, répond Bernard, ma femme !

Yaka XV

Avec deux pieds à terre tu n'avanceras jamais.
*
Le doute est le commencement de la sagesse.

Le porteur d'eau et les amphores

Il y a quelque part un endroit où tout le monde a droit à la parole. Pas seulement des humains, mais aussi les poissons, oiseaux, insectes, les mammifères, bref tous le animaux.
Mieux encore, les objets fabriqués avec amour par les mains-mêmes de l'artisan ont également le parole, puisque dans ce lieu de quelque part, on estime que certains objets qu'on a connus avec l'âme de bien faire, ont eux aussi une âme. Et tout le monde le sait, quand tu as le bénéfice d'une âme, tu as la capacité de parole.

Ce qui m'amène à te raconter l'histoire du porteur d'eau nommé Félicie.

Félicie est un homme vigoureux, travailleur et ayant une âme pure, il est le bien-aimé de beaucoup de monde.
Félicie occupe le temps qui lui est attribué dans ce monde à faire plaisir à ses prochains. Un plaisir utile d 'ailleurs, puisqu' il est porteur d'eau dans un quartier de la ville où les gens n'ont pas d'eau potable dans les tuyaux et aux robinets.
Il exerce son métier avec beaucoup de zèle avec l'aide

de deux amphores avec chacune une anse pour mieux les porter.

L'une des amphores est quasiment neuve, fabriquée par son petit frère contre sa volonté, puisque selon ce petit frère, il avait autre chose à faire que fabriquer des amphores pour son frère. En plus, c'est le problème de son frère s'il ne se fait pas payer pour porter l'eau.

Lui, petit frère, n'avait aucune envie de mouler la glaise à l'œil.

Bref l'amphore était bien fonctionnelle, mais c'était un objet sans âme.

L'autre amphore fut fabriquée par le grand-père de Félicie, un homme avec une grande âme. Ce qu'il faisait dans sa vie, il le faisait avec du cœur et de l'amour. Il aimait faire du bien autour de lui. D'ailleurs c'était lui qui portait l'eau pour les pauvres gens en premier.

Quand grand-père ne pouvait plus faire le bien autour de lui, il appela son unique fils pour que la tradition du portage d'eau se poursuive dans sa famille. Malheureusement, le fils estimait qu'il n'était pas fait pour cette corvée et qu'il pouvait abîmer ses beaux vêtements.

Il proposa d'appeler son fils à lui, c'est-à-dire le petit-fils Félicie. Ce garçon bon à rien, que son épouse avait nommé Félicie comme sa grand-mère. Pour un garçon, quand-même, c'est le pompon !

Bref, Félicie accepta. Désormais, c'était lui le porteur d'eau.
C'est donc évident que l'amphore du grand-père avait une âme, donc la parole !
L'amphore avait aussi quelques petites fissures, signes du temps passé. Rien de grave, mais il y avait quelques pertes d'eau pendant la route du portage.

Au bout de quelques temps, l'amphore de grand-père avait un peu honte pour toutes ces pertes d'eau, et voulait s'excuser auprès de Félicie :
- Pardonne-moi, mon bon Félicie, mais je commence à être vieille, c'est peut-être l'occasion de me remplacer par une nouvelle.
- Mais pourquoi ? Répondit Félicie.
- Parce que je perds tous les jours d'avantage d'eau !
Félicie promettait de donner sa réponse le lendemain.

Le lendemain, tout en portant de l'eau, il s'adressa à l'amphore, candidate à la déchetterie :
- Tu vois ? Sur ce chemin tout du long, il y a de très jolies fleurs. Ces fleurs sont toutes d'un seul côté. C'est-à-dire de ton côté. Tous les jours tu penses que tu perds de l'eau. Moi, je te dis c'est faux. Regarde, c'est toi qui arroses les fleurs, c'est grâce à toi qu'elles fleurissent aussi belles. Leur beauté est la nourriture de l'âme. C'est donc aussi grâce à toi que le bonheur existe !

À qui le tour ?

Me voilà de retour. Hier, j'ai été invité chez mon trois fois arrière-petit-fils pour célébrer l'Union Civique pour la Procréation (U.C.Pro.) mieux connu sous l'appellation « mariage » dans les années du début du 21ème siècle et avant.

C'était le 14 août 2263, nous sommes en plein milieu, ou presque du vingt-troisième siècle. Puisqu'il s'agit de mon trois fois arrière-petit-fils, c'est-à-dire l'arrière-petit-fils de l'arrière-petit-fils de mon arrière petit-fils, qui est lui le fils de mon petit-fils, lui-même le fils de mon fils. C'est-à-dire que je viens de faire un bond de 250 années aller et autant de retour.

Je ne sais pas comment cela est arrivé, mais ce dont je peux témoigner ici, *c'est arrivé* !!

Alors c'est hallucinant ce qui a changé. Déjà aujourd'hui le 14 août 2013, quand on y pense, si mon trois fois arrière-grand-père pouvait faire un tour chez moi aujourd'hui en partant de l'année 1763...

Il va voir des engins à 500 personnes qui volent au-dessus de lui à quelques milliers de mètres à une vitesse incompréhensible pour lui. Il découvrira les voitures, des carrosses avec des formes aplaties sans chevaux se déplacer sur des chemins larges et durs. Des gens se parlent dans une petite boite plate en se regardant dans une petite fenêtre. Pourtant la personne en question est à plusieurs millièmes de lieux ! Puis, bon j'arrête, j'avais oublié que toi aussi tu es de 2013. Pour toi, comme pour moi toutes ces choses sont banal !

Revenons à la vie de mon arrière-petit bis bis fils. Celui qui va se jeter dans un UCPro, parce que comme je l'ai expliqué plus haut, le mariage a été supprimé pour tous. Finies les anciennes coutumes, c'est la vie moderne. Il faut être le fils ou la fille de son temps. Tant qu'on ne veut pas procréer, il est inutile de se Ucéproer

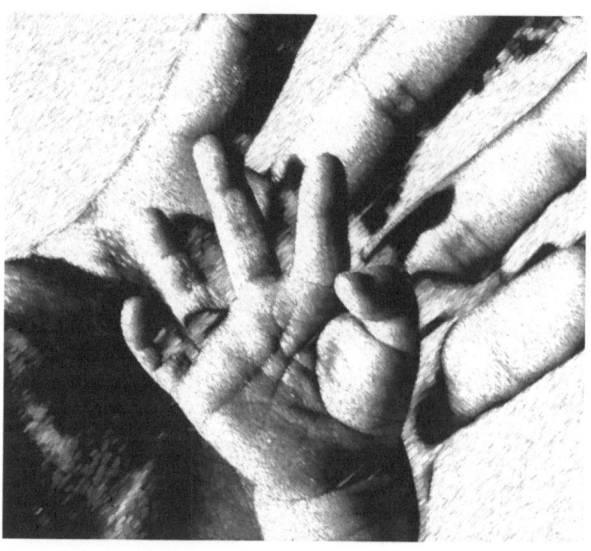

Une fois décidé, on se ucéproe puis on va faire des

prélèvements au centre des ucéproistes associés pour faire le mélange des cellules et de le faire fructifier dans un ucéproeur automatique. Quelques mois après, il y a une sonnerie de fin et le ucéproeur s'ouvre automatiquement pour que le couple puisse prendre la livraison du bébé humain. On le place ensuite dans un cocon avec nourrissage automatisé selon le sexe et le poids de l'individu.

Bien sûr, le sexe n'est pas interdit, au contraire. On estime que le sexe est un stimulant musculaire de premier plan.

Les parents du bébé travaillent. Homme ou femme peuvent tous faire le même travail, ils sont tous et toutes salariés au même tarif. Seul le grade peut augmenter le salaire. L'euro, le dollar le Yen et autres monnaies n'existent plus. D'ailleurs il n'y a plus d'argent, ni de monnaie. C'est la misère pour les pickpockets. Maintenant tout le monde possède à partir de quinze années d'existence une mini puce dans son index ou ailleurs ; cette puce est plus petite qu'un grain de sel fin. Et facilement injecté avec un stylet injecteur dès l'ouverture d'un compte à une banque régulatrice des échanges des biens et des services. Ton salaire est automatiquement placé sur la puce inviolable, et tu peux dépenser ou acheter directement en posant un de tes doigt sur une tablette chez le prestataire.

Bon, je n'ai pas tout compris puisque je ne suis resté qu'un seul jour.

Ce que j'ai remarqué par moi-même, c'est qu'il n'y a plus de voiture perso comme aujourd'hui. D'ailleurs l'usage du pétrole sous quelque forme que ce soit est

strictement interdit depuis l'an 2225.
Dans les maisons, pardon, unités de vie, il y a du chauffage l'hiver fourni par une centrale collective disponible pour tout le monde. Le chauffage individuel est prohibé aussi. La chaleur est pompée de la terre et à une profondeur aujourd'hui encore impossible à imaginer.
L'électricité vient de la mer et des océans, obtenue par des turbines dans les grandes profondeurs captant des forces de courant énormes. Même les centrales nucléaires sont interdites. Trop dangereux. Il reste encore des panneaux photo-voltaïques avec un grain de nostalgie, surtout en campagne où les humains vivent encore un peu à l'ancienne.
Chaque trimestre l'humain et certains animaux de compagnie doivent faire une visite de régénération médicale, ce qui évite des maladies difficiles et la plupart des épidémies. D'ailleurs seuls les bébés sains ont droit à la vie.

Les gens se transportent en cabine individuelle ou à plusieurs, gratuitement, ce qu'on appelle des giro-taxis. Il y en a à tous les coins de rue et dans les grands ensembles de cellules de vie.
On s'assoit puis il suffit de dire la destination. Par exemple : Cellule 412 voie CV256. C'est tout. Quelques secondes plus tard, vous y êtes. C'est par le transfert de particules m'a-t-on dit. Ne me demande pas comment cela fonctionne. J'en sais rien, mais ça fonctionne. Je l'ai essayé moi-même.

Il n'y a plus de président, prime minister ou roi,

désormais le monde est dirigé par un collège de sages de 6 personnes. 3 hommes et 3 femmes entre 100 et 120 ans.

Eh oui, tu l'as bien compris entre 100 et 120 ans. L'espérance de vie en 2263 est de 195 ans. Il n'est pas rare de rencontrer des « vieux » qui ont 230 ans ! La médecine a fait des bonds ces dernières 150 années. Plus personne ne connaît les mots « cancer » ou « sida ». Même la grippe n'existe plus. L'humain est devenu une machine bien « huilée » entretenue par une technologie avancée.

Pour la nourriture, la quasi totalité des gens est devenue végétarienne. Il reste encore quelques omnivores mais ils doivent se contenter de quelques poulets et du poisson. L'élevage des bœufs et autres herbivores a été supprimé à cause du méthane des « proutes » bovins. Seuls quelques troupeaux de moutons et de chèvres sont maintenus pour la production des fromages d'origine conservée.

Le lait de vache est remplacé par le lait de soja et les lactose-algues. Ces algues élevées en mer ont été découvertes par l'INRA après plusieurs inséminations croisées.

Toutes ces découvertes m'ont quelque peu choqué. La vie est devenue sous contrôle, l'humain maîtrise son destin. Il est devenu créateur... Effrayant !!

Je ne sais pas quand je retournerai vers cette année-là, peut-être jamais ? Ce voyage intemporel est déjà fort étrange. Surtout que j'ai été bien fatigué le matin.

Enfin, je suis quand même très content de retrouver ma maison, ma famille, mon chien et mes chats, puis mon morceau de poulet bien grillé et le faux-filet du

dimanche. Sans oublier la douzaine d'escargots que je me suis promis aujourd'hui.
En attendant je vais me taper deux œufs à la coque, puis un bon café pur arabica. Ces promenades en pleine nuit sans qu'on me demande mon avis me dérangent quelque peu.

Je pense que nous vivons pas si mal à notre époque. C'est vrai, nous voulons toujours plus que hier, pourtant imagines-toi seulement cent années en arrière, même cinquante.
Ne faut-il pas mieux se contenter de ce qu'on a ?
La science avancera sans aucun doute, veillons à ne pas écraser l'autre pour aller plus vite que le destin.
Regarde et tends ta main, il y a sûrement quelqu'un qui veut bien la prendre dans la sienne.

À chacun et chacune son tour !

Yaka XVI

Le Créateur donna à l'homme des cervelles et un pénis. Dommage que la pression du sang
ne soit pas la même
*
L'homme est créé en premier.
C'est-à-dire le brouillon de la femme.
*

Une tragédie projetée

À six heures et vingt minutes précisément, le réveil sonna.
Justin se réveilla de bonne humeur. Il faisait beau et le soleil traversait déjà les double rideaux.
Il aimait se réveiller un peu avant tout le monde. Il l regarda sa femme et l'embrassa légèrement en lui murmurant :
- Endors-toi encore un peu mon amour.
Comme il a l'habitude de dormir nu, il se mis directement sous la douche froide pour bien se réveiller puis se sentir frais et prêt à attaquer la journée de travail.
Justin est responsable du service finition d'action commerciale. Le FAC comme ils disaient au bureau. Son boulot était de superviser le bon déroulement des actions commerciales et provoquer les retombées.
Il déjeuna tranquillement, en buvant son cappuccino et une tartine de pain complet avec du roquefort et de la confiture de myrtilles. Il termina par un verre de jus de fruits de la saison.
Habillé avec soin, costume d'été couleur pastel, chemise en coton léger avec une cravate assortie nouée avec une certaine nonchalance tout en gardant le premier bouton ouvert.
Avec sa clef ,il zippa l'ouverture de sa voiture et se mit

derrière le volant en posant sa serviette de documents à côté de lui.

Tous les matins, il empruntait le même chemin, disons une sorte de raccourci connu par les riverains. Il y avait trop d'embouteillages sur la route officielle.
Avec ses doigts il tapotait sur son volant en mesure avec la musique de son poste radio. Encore une fois, il constata que c'était une belle journée.

C'est à ces moments que l'imagination a l'occasion de dériver dans une absurdité inexplicable.
- Bien,, se disait Justin, tout cela ne tient qu'à un bout de ficelle. Il suffit que je braque un petit coup à droite et « pam » je me plante avec une belle vitesse dans un platane. Puis je ne serai probablement plus, ma famille sans mari et père... Peut être Anne se remariera avec Pierre mon soi-disant copain. Mes enfants l'appelleront papa.
Puis pour le boulot, c'est encore plus facile. Le grand patron n'avait-il pas dit un jour lors de son discours d'efficacité trimestriel que personne n'est indispensable. Qu'à chaque poste il y a plusieurs postulants possible aussi bien que l'occupant actuel. Ces phrases font réfléchir.
Et puis Pierre venait trop souvent sous le prétexte qu'il est le parrain des enfants de Justin, certes choisi par Anne, mais parrain quand même.

En face de lui arrivait à grande vitesse un camion de belle taille. Justin le regardait arriver, il ne fallait que quelques secondes pour que les deux véhicules se

croisent à toute allure.
Et encore une fois Justin s'imaginait et se faisait peur en se proposant de braquer cette fois-ci à gauche. Le choc serait tellement grand, que ce serait difficile de reconnaître le corps de la petite voiture écrasée contre ce camion robuste et lourd.
Il voyait dans le même flash arriver tard dans la soirée, cause l'identification, la voiture de policiers à son domicile pour communiquer cette affreuse nouvelle à son épouse.
Les mains de Justin étaient devenues moites, ses muscles se ramollissaient dans ses bras.
Le camion était déjà passé et la route devant lui était à nouveau libre.
Justin happait l'air avec des secousses dans son cœur. Il ralentissait et essayait de s'harmoniser avec la réalité plus paisible.
Il se demandait ce qui lui arrivait.
Pourquoi toute cette imagination ? Est-ce la soif aux sensations ? Perdait-il les pédales ? Serait-il jaloux de Pierre ? Il se posait mille questions et toutes sans réponses.

Le soir à la maison il se mit à table et dîna sans dire grand chose. Il avait salué sa femme et ses enfants avec la tendresse d'usage. Après le dîner, il décida de faire un tour dans la fraîcheur de la soirée. Il aimait bien marcher le soir pour digérer sa journée.
C'était une belle soirée, le soleil s'apprêtait à se coucher et distribuait une lumière merveilleuse à faire pâlir des peintres d'arts.
Justin traversa le parc botanique, il aimait bien sentir

les parfums des multitudes de fleurs et plantes diverses.
En face de lui dans le sens inverse un autre promeneur, c'était un homme d'un âge moyen, habillé quelconque au visage ordinaire qui visiblement flânait par là.

Justin mit la main dans sa poche, ses doigts rentraient en contact avec le couteau laguiole à lame étendue. C'était un cadeau de son oncle préféré pour son dix-huitième anniversaire. Un joli couteau pliable avec un manche en cerisier sculpté représentant une patte de biche.
Il regarda l'homme, un désir fou lui irritait la gorge, le sang lui monta à la tête devenu toute rouge.
Et si je plante ce couteau dans le cœur de cet homme ? Délira-t-il.
Il trembla presque à l'idée de sentir la présence d'une force indescriptible lui donnant le pouvoir de vie ou de mort sur cet individu.
L'instant plus loin, il lâcha le couteau qui demeura dans sa poche et il se ressaisit. Soudainement, il avait honte de ses pensées. Qui était-il pour penser comme ça ? Justin souri -ait un peu timide à l'homme lors de leur croisement et lui dit :
- Belle soirée n'est ce pas ?
- Oui, certes, c'est une belle soirée. L'homme avait ralenti un peu pour lui répondre sans tourner le dos à Justin, - Bonne promenade !
- À vous aussi, monsieur, répondit Justin.

Ce soir-là, il embrassa sa femme pour la nuit, et

s'endormait dans ses rêves.

Il avait essayé de positiver ses pensées pour contredire celles de la journée. Quand même, un suicide et un meurtre, c'était trop !

Le lendemain tout était normal. Justin avait repris ses habitudes, était adorable avec son épouse et plaisantait comme tous les matins avec ses enfants.

Il avait décidé de prendre la route principale et il était parti même un quart d' heure plus tôt.

Un énorme camion venait d'en face, voulant doubler la voiture devant lui.

Justin sortait de ce virage avec peu de visibilité, en vitesse réduite. Soudainement il aperçoit le camion pile en face de lui. Le choc frontal était évident.

En un éclair Justin braqua son volant vers la droite, évita avec justesse le camion et traversa la piste cyclable à quelques mètres de la route réservée à l'automobile.

Quelques minutes plus tard, les pompiers commençaient à désincruster le corps de Justin de cet amas de tôle éclatée comme une tomate trop mûre contre le seul platane centenaire à quelques dizaines de mètres de la route.

En passant par la piste cyclable, il avait heurté un homme en vélo, projeté quelques mètres plus loin avec son vélo, dont le guidon s'était planté dans la poitrine comme un couteau. Plus jamais il ne pourra humer les parfums du parc botanique.

Ce soir-là, le soleil imperturbable s'apprêtait à se coucher, pendant ce temps la police sonnait à la porte du domicile de Justin.

Les décès d'Olivier

Il y a quelque part un petit village au pied d'une chaîne de montagnes. L'un des personnages célèbres et connu par tout le monde s'appelle Olivier, une sorte de vagabond et fou du village, qui était souvent invité par les agriculteurs à venir manger. C'était un peu leur porte-bonheur pour avoir une meilleure récolte.

C'était le tour d'Albert Frontignan d'inviter Olivier à partager un poisson pêché le matin même par le père d'Albert, le vieux Émile Frontignan.
Olivier, heureux devant ce grand morceau de poisson, préparé avec maestro par Colette, la femme d'Albert.
Il attaqua le morceau avec toute la ferveur de quelqu'un qui semblait être affamé.
Mais quel malheur, Olivier avala une arrête de travers et commençait à s'étouffer. Rien n'y fut, ils avaient beau taper sur le dos d'Olivier, mettre le doigt dans sa bouche, rien ! Olivier rendait l'âme quelques minutes plus tard avec un visage tout rouge.
Albert et Colette étaient tristes, mais surtout morts de trouille. Et si on les accusait de meurtre ? Ou de négligence ayant entraînée la mort ? Aller en prison ? Jamais ! Et les enfants, la ferme ?
Rapidement, Albert prit une décision. Son plan était clair comme la roche. Il savait que Dimitri son voisin

était à la ville, donc il a traîné Olivier jusqu'à sa maison, et le posa contre le portail de son domaine.
Dimitri était un rentier, et surtout prêteur sur gages. Un vrai gratte-sous sans aucun complexe. D'ailleurs, Albert avait du retard dans ses remboursements.
Dans la soirée, Dimitri revint en calèche et vit de loin une silhouette contre le portail de sa propriété.
- Ah, pensait-il, j'attends personne. C'est certainement un voleur qui veut me voler ma cassette. Peut-être même un débiteur qui cherche sa reconnaissance de dettes pour ne plus payer ! Il arrêta la calèche et se glissa doucement vers le portail, saisit un morceau de bois, sauta sur la silhouette et donna un énorme coup sur la tête.
Il regarda un peu mieux pour voir qui était l'individu et reconnu immédiatement Olivier. Le vagabond à qui il donnait parfois un bon bout de vieux pain destiné normalement à ses lapins et cochons, mais tout de même encore bien consommables.

Même sa servante en mangeait, et elle était bien heureuse avec ça.
Bref, il constata qu' Olivier était mort, bien mort.
C'était difficile de décider quoi faire. Finalement, il traînait Olivier à la rivière où il l'a mis contre un gros rocher. Il se promettait de ne rien dire à personne,

même pas à sa servante et encore moins à sa femme.
Le lendemain, il demandait à son jardinier Fortuna d'aller au village pour chercher du pain pour le déjeuner, et du vieux pain pour ses animaux. Fortuna porta sur son dos un grand panier en osier. Il n'avait pas le droit de prendre la belle calèche de son patron, aussi partait-il à pied tout en sifflant une belle mélodie. Il faisait beau et il aimait se promener au bord de l'eau. Il longea le chemin de halage de la rivière au lieu du chemin habituel, quand il a vu assis contre un rocher Olivier le vagabond.
Hey, Olivier ! s'écria-t-il, mais Olivier ne répondait pas Il est sûrement en train de roupiller, pensait-il, et il ramassait une pierre pour la lancer devant Olivier dans l'eau.
Mais, bon Dieu quelle horreur ! La pierre rata sa course et frappa Olivier en pleine tête, et Olivier tomba dans l'eau. Fortuna se précipita vers le bas pour tirer Olivier sur la berge, mais grande angoisse, Olivier ne bougeait plus ! Il était bien mort ! Probablement noyé parce que tombé dans l'eau par ce caillou qu'il avait lancé !
Il pesait le pour et le contre d'aller voir le prévôt et déclarer son forfait involontaire. Mais est-ce qu'on va le croire ? Il décida donc de ne rien dire et il traînait le corps en traversant le chemin pour le camoufler dans les buissons. Dès qu'il fut de retour sur le chemin, il aperçut au loin deux hommes qui arrivaient ! Il marchait très vite sans se retourner d'où il venait.
Les deux hommes revenaient de la ville. Ils avaient un gros panier de pain volés dans la ville à la boulangerie pour les vendre dans le prochain village où il n'y avait

pas de boulanger. Aussitôt qu'ils virent Fortuna, ils cachèrent rapidement le grand panier de pains dans un bosquet au bord du chemin et continuaient de marcher en souriant. Ils s'apprêtaient à revenir plus tard pour prendre le panier et faire leur commerce.

Une fois les deux hommes hors de vue, Fortuna décida de retourner pour voir si les deux hommes n'avaient en rien remarqué ce qui concerne Olivier.

Et ... à sa grande surprise, il trouva le panier de pains.

Ça... ça tombe vraiment à point ! pensait-il, et il chargea les pains dans son propre panier. IL mit Olivier dans le panier des voleurs, le couvrit avec du pain et des chiffons et rentra chez lui.

Un peu plus tard, les voleurs étaient revenus pour ramasser le panier avec des pains. Ils se disaient entre eux :

- C'est plus lourd que je pensais, nous avons fait une bonne prise. Mais quand finalement ils furent à la maison, ils ont découvert avec stupeur ce qui était dans le panier ...le cadavre d'Olivier !

- Oh, bonne mère que faut-il faire maintenant ?

Ils décidèrent d'attacher Olivier sur un cheval. Ils donnèrent au pauvre animal un grand coup sur la joue et tirèrent fort sur la queue. Le cheval était si effrayé qu'il se mit à galoper. Les voleurs couraient après le cheval en criant

- Au voleur, au voleur! L'un d'eux tira avec un fusil en l'air. Le cheval a été encore plus effrayé et a disparu à jamais.

Olivier et le cheval n'ont jamais été retrouvés. Seulement, si vous êtes en soirée dans les montagnes et que vous entendez le ploc ploc d'un cheval, les

gens se disent entre eux :
- Le voilà , c'est Olivier, le voleur de cheval ! C'est avec cet homme que nous avons partagé notre pain quotidien !

Yaka XVII

Si quelqu'un t'a fait du mal, ne cherche pas à te venger. Va t'asseoir au bord de la rivière et bientôt tu verras passer son cadavre.
(Proverbe chinois)
*

Tu peux prendre un homme tel qu'il est. Mais n'oublies pas de l'affiner, il bonifie avec l'âge.
*

Le micro-ondes est comme un homme,
ça chauffe bouillant en quelques secondes.
*

La différence entre un homme et un cochon est qu'un homme peut devenir un cochon, mais un cochon ne deviendra jamais un homme.
*

L'homme pense ce qu'il sait,
mais sa femme le sait toujours mieux
*

Quand tu trébuches sur un obstacle, beaucoup de gens te diront par où il ne fallait pas passer.

Écrire

Deux amis se promènent sur le sable en bord de mer.
Pour des raisons pas très claires lors d'une discussion enflammée, ils s'insultent copieusement jusqu'à ce que

l'un d'eux frappe l'autre dans la figure.
Triste, l'homme battu s'arrête et s'assoit. Des deux amis, c'est lui le poète. Il écrit dans le sable :
« Aujourd'hui mon meilleur ami me frappe au visage. »
Puis il court pour rattraper son ami. Ils s'arrêtent ensemble pour boire un coup dans la bouteille d'eau qu'ils ont apportée.
L'ami battu se déshabille et entre dans la mer pour prendre un bain. Mais imprudent, il avance trop loin et se laisse piéger dans un tourbillon.
L'autre ami, excellent nageur plonge dans l'eau et sauve son ami de justesse.
Il pose son ami contre un grand caillou et lui fait cracher l'eau de ses poumons.
Quelques temps plus tard, l'ami sauvé grave avec son couteau dans la pierre :
« Aujourd'hui mon meilleur ami me sauve la vie ! »
L'autre l'observe et lui demande :

- Pourquoi, quand je t'ai frappé, tu l'as écrit dans le sable, puis quand je t'ai sauvé la vie tu te fatigues à écrire en gravant dans la pierre ?
- C'est simple, mon ami. Quand quelqu'un te contrarie, écris-le dans le sable. Le vent et la marée effaceront le tout comme un pardon.
Par contre, ce qui est gravé dans la pierre, restera pour toujours. Crois-tu que je puisse oublier que tu m'as sauvé la vie ?

Chez le docteur

Le docteur demande surpris comment on peut se brûler les deux oreilles.
- Eh bien, dit la patiente, je repassais quand le téléphone a sonné et j'ai mis accidentellement le fer contre mon oreille à la place du combiné.
- Mais comment avez-vous brûlé l'autre oreille ? demanda le toubib.
- Ils ont rappelé !

Yaka XVIII

Qui se lève de bon matin pisse où cela lui plaît.
(proverbe Français)

La grenouille géante

Très loin, à l'autre bout du monde se trouve la Nouvelle-Zélande. Les premiers habitants du pays sont les Maoris.
Les Maoris très âgés, croyaient encore que les grenouilles peuvent faire tomber la pluie. C'est certainement parce que, si après une longue période de sécheresse la pluie tombe finalement, il y a tant de grenouilles qui sortent. Personne ne comprend d'où elles viennent.
Les grenouilles sont ainsi très honorées et malheur à celui qui les tuent.
- Ces grenouilles ont beaucoup d'eau dans leur ventre, disent-ils, si on les tue, il y aurait un énorme déluge comme jamais.

La légende des grenouilles est née il y a des lustres :
Il y a longtemps, avant que les humains, blancs ou noirs vivent dans ce pays, il est apparu une grosse, grosse grenouille sur la rive d'un lac. Elle était beaucoup, beaucoup plus grande que toutes les autres grenouilles. Elle avait l'air étrange et la bête semblait avoir une tell incroyable soif qu'elle n'arrêtait pas de boire jusqu'à ce qu'elle ait bu tout le lac. Et puis elle a sauté vers un autre lac qu'elle vidait aussi et il en fut ainsi de suite, jusqu'à ce que toute l'eau des lacs et

des rivières ait disparu.
Une fois tout vidé, elle s'assit au milieu d'un lit de rivière à sec et cria sans cesser :
- Quaak, quaak, quaaaak ! Cela signifiait qu'elle avait bu assez.
Vous pouvez comprendre comment tous les autres animaux dans ce pays ont été terrifiés, il n'y avait plus nulle part une goutte d'eau à boire.
Ils demandaient à la grande grenouille si elle pouvait redonner un peu d'eau, ils mouraient tant de soif ! Mais aucune réponse. Seulement un « Quaak, quaak, quaaaak ! » Ils n'ont rien eu. Puis ils se disaient entre eux :
- Nous devons essayer d' obtenir qu'elle ouvre sa grande bouche, pour que sorte un peu d'eau. Mais comment faire? Peut-être la faire rire ? Aussitôt dit, aussitôt fait. D'abord, ils ont envoyé le roi des kangourous qui a fait toutes sortes de sauts fous et enfin il a essayé de marcher. Uniquement sur ses avant-pattes si courtes. C'était un spectacle très drôle. Mais la grenouille dit :
- Quaak, quaak, quaaaak ! Mais elle ne rit pas. Puis un petit ours koala recroquevillé en boule chutait dans une descente et se mit à rouler avec toutes sortes de sauts stupides puis ils se sont retrouvés dans les roseaux secs où était la grosse grenouille. Mais qui a dit encore :
- Quaak, quaak, quaaaak ! Et toujours pas d'eau.
Un gros serpent noir montra aussi toutes sortes d'arts fous. Ils ont attaché leur long corps de la manière la plus étrange que vous puissiez imaginer et tous les autres serpents dansaient et dégringolaient autour.

C'était fort drôle à voir, mais la grenouille disait :
- Quaak, quaak, quaaaak ! Et toujours pas d'eau. Puis vinrent les cacatoès et perruches à leur tour.
Ils se rassemblaient tous ensemble au-dessus de la tête de la grande grenouille et ils racontaient des sketches et autres blagues drôles. Les autres animaux se tordaient de rire. Les larmes coulaient sur leurs joues. C'était tellement drôle, tous les autres animaux les imitaient. Puis un vieil oiseau savait d'anciennes histoires de fées. Il s'assit en face de la grenouille et lui racontait l'histoire idiote du serpent dévorant sa propre queue et qui se mangeait progressivement lui-même.
Mais la grenouille assise tranquillement dans les roseaux secs disait au plus profond de sa gorge :
- Quaak, quaak, quaaaak ! Mais toujours pas d'eau.
Les marsupiaux drôles, les porcs-épics et des fourmilliers essayaient aussi, mais en vain. Enfin, la journée était presque terminée. Un congre avec sa femme et sa famille arrivèrent et ils ont voulu tenter à leur tour de faire cracher l'eau à la grenouille.

Les animaux assemblés sur la rive de la rivière sèche allumèrent un feu. Ils demandaient au congre s'il y avait assez de lumière malgré le crépuscule pour sa performance ?
- Oh oui, déclara le congre, ça suffit amplement. Nous allons commencer dans quelques instants.
Il prit rapidement toutes les lames vertes d'herbe qu'il pouvait trouver et sa femme avait pris certaines herbes. Toute la famille congre s'ornait avec ces verdures. Puis ils élevèrent leurs queues et toutes ces

anguilles ont commencé à mener une danse folle autour du feu.
Ils acquiescèrent et se prosternèrent, l'herbe et les algues flottaient dans la brise du soir. Ils faisaient des grimaces à la grande grenouille qui cette fois-ci pouvait à peine se tenir. Puis enfin, la grenouille riait à grande gueule ouverte. Si grand ouverte qu'il s'écoulait plein d'eau avec une impressionnante force. Les anciens canaux n'avaient pas cessé de couler, avant que tous les lacs et les rivières ne soient à nouveau remplis.
- Voilà le travail, disait le congre. Mes anguilles et moi, nous allons retourner en mer. Si jamais vous avez à nouveau besoin de notre aide, appelez-nous !
Et aussitôt toute la famille se glissait au loin.

Maintenant que la grande grenouille avait redonné l'eau, les autres animaux regardaient la grenouille bizarrement : elle n'était même pas en colère parce qu'on l'avait fait rire et qu'elle avait perdu son eau.

A peine amaigrie, elle semblait toujours avoir toute une masse d'eau encore dans le ventre.
À partir de ce moment, les animaux, et plus tard les humains ont eu peur que leur pays soit inondé.
Plus jamais, ils n'essayeront de faire rire la grande grenouille.
Et si quelque part, même dans le monde entier, il y a des inondations, il se peut que cela soit à cause de quelqu'un ou quelque chose qui fait rire la grenouille géante.

Petit Pierre et les loups

Je vais vous conter maintenant une histoire qui se joue dans un petit village. Un village sans aucune renommée, sans célébrités, sans événements importants. Bref, sans importance.
Aujourd'hui, la vie continue sans sursauts. Tout y est d'un calme linéaire.
Le meunier mouline son blé, le boulanger pétrit sa pâte à pain, le fermier trait ses vaches et transforme le lait en crème fraîche, beurre et fromage, Le bistrotier remplit les verres avec le vin du pays. Tout le monde est content de vivre dans ce village sans histoires.
Tout le monde, sauf le petit Paul.

Petit Paul est berger et garde toutes les brebis du village. Il a deux chiens avec lui, Bob et Tay. Toute la journée, il est dans les collines et observe les chiens travailler. De temps en temps, il se lève pour envoyer Bob chercher une brebis perdue. Bob est le spécialiste de cette corvée.
Même aujourd'hui, il est dans les collines assis sur ses fesses en train de s'ennuyer. Il n'est pas satisfait de son sort. Il aimerait bien qu'il arrive quelque chose de passionnant, d'excitant.

Soudainement, il a une idée. Il se précipite rapidement

avant l'heure au village.

Dès qu'il arrive à l'entrée du bourg, il commence à crier de plus en plus fort :

– Le loup, le loup ! Le loup est de retour ! Au secours !!

–

Immédiatement tout le monde stoppe net ses propres occupations. Les villageois se munissent de bâtons, fourches, coutelas et même le fusil de monsieur le baron. Tout ce beau monde se précipite dans les collines.

Une fois arrivé, tout semble tranquille. Les brebis broutent en paix et les chiens sont couchés.

D'apres un tableau de G van Os (19ème)

- Peut-être le loup s'est-il sauvé par peur de ma voix ? supposait à voix haute petit Pierre.

On félicite le berger et chacun retourne chez soi. Pendant au moins une semaine, petit Pierre était la vedette du village. Il avait sauvé tout un troupeau de moutons à lui tout seul.

Petit Pierre était plus que ravi. Aussi au bout d'une dizaine de jours, il répéta l'opération, puis une troisième et même osa une quatrième fois.

Les gens commencèrent à s'habituer, et ne se précipitent plus pour voir les brebis. Puisque le loup se sauvait avec les cris de petit Paul, pourquoi s'inquiéter ?

Jusqu'au jour lorsqu'il était calmement assis contre un arbre dans un endroit stratégique, il observe et voit soudainement bouger quelque chose. Il se concentre et ... Mais non, c'est encore trop loin pour être sûr. Tout de même, on dirait que... Mais bon Dieu, oui, ce sont des loups ! Il en voit deux, puis quatre, puis sept !
Il court aussi vite qu'il peut au village et crie très fort :
- Au secours, au secours les loups ! Beaucoup de loups, il y a tout un paquet de loups. Au secours, aidez-moi !! Venez sauver les moutons, prenez les armes et venez avec moi, je vous en prie...
Personne ne réagit. Il n'y a personne qui vient avec lui. Pire, il n'y a plus personne qui croit encore petit Pierre. Même ses pleurs, ses prières ne servent à rien.
Abruti de douleur et de honte, il se mit dans un coin et pleura de tout son cœur.

C'est ce jour-là que le village avait perdu le gros de ses moutons. Les loups les avaient tués et dévorés.
Petit Pierre exprima son profond regret, mais les villageois regrettaient aussi de ne pas avoir cru le petit Pierre.

Voilà, c'est l'histoire du petit Pierre.
Pour la morale, c'est comme tu veux.

Jacques Cuissapoule et la grue

Il était une fois un seigneur qui a vécu en Italie. Don Labali était un grand seigneur, célèbre pour son amour de la chasse et ses délicieux banquets. Un jour, Don Labali prit avec son faucon une belle grue, il demandait à son cuisinier Jacques Cuissapoule de rôtir l'animal.

L'oiseau était presque cuit quand une belle jeune fille rendit visite à Jacques.

Jacques Cuissapoule était un fort bel homme et très populaire auprès les femmes. D'ailleurs il le leur rendait bien. Quand elle sentit la délicieuse odeur du fumet de la viande rôtie, elle profita de la faiblesse de jacques et prit une des pattes de l'oiseau.

La cuisson terminée, l'oiseau a été dressé sur un plat en argent et servi à don Labali.

Étonné, le seigneur appela son cuisinier :
- Cet oiseau n'a qu' une patte !
Sur ce, le pauvre Jacques répondit :
- Mais monseigneur, les grues n'ont qu'une patte !
- Quoi, une patte ? Tu me prends pour un imbécile ou quoi ? Je sais très bien qu'une grue a deux pattes comme tous les oiseaux !
Mais Jacques insistait sur le fait que les grues ont une seule patte et il ajouta :
- Si j'avais un oiseau vivant ici, je voudrais vous le montrer!
Le seigneur qui n'avait aucune envie de se disputer avec son cuisinier devant ses invités lui proposa :
- Excellent ! Nous y allons demain matin ensemble à la chasse à la grue, mais malheur à vous si j'ai raison!

Le lendemain matin, à l'aube, Don labali donna l'ordre de seller les chevaux.
- Nous allons voir qui est le menteur ici !
Jacques aurait aimer fuir mais il ne l'avait pas osé.
Quand ils atteignirent le fleuve, le cuisinier avait vu un troupeau de grues. Elles dormaient toutes debout sur une patte, ce que toutes les grues font quand elles se reposent.
- Don Labali ! cria Jacques. Regardez, j'ai bien raison. Les grues n'ont qu'une patte !
- Tu y crois vraiment ?S' Exclama Don Labali, tu vas voir !
Puis il tapa fort dans ses mains. Toutes les grues avaient sorti leur deuxième patte et s'envolèrent.
- Tu vois ? s'écria satisfait Don Labali. Tu vois bien qu'elles ont deux pattes !

La réponse de Jacques fut rapide :
- Mais Monseigneur, si vous aviez hier à la table tapé dans vos mains, la grue aurait certainement déplié aussi sa deuxième patte !
Lorsque Don Labali entendit cette réponse il en riait.
- Oui, mon brave Jacques, tu as raison. C'est ce que j'aurais dû faire !
Il donna une tape bien amicale sur les épaules de Jacques et il ajouta :
Devant un homme avec un esprit aussi intelligent, je m'incline. Mieux encore, désormais tu n'es plus seulement mon cuisinier, mais je t'offre également mon amitié !

Tu fumes ou tu ne fumes pas ?

Jean voyage en train. En ce temps-là, il y avait encore des compartiments fumeurs.
Confiant et avec une intime satisfaction il sort un superbe cigare et demande par pure politesse à la dame en face de lui :
- Ça ne vous dérange pas ?
- Mais non, je vous en prie, faites donc comme chez vous !
- Tant pis, murmura Jean et il remit le cigare dans sa poche.

Kevin chez la tata

Petit Kevin est en vacances chez sa tata. Le soir couché sur son lit. Il entend crier dans la chambre de la tata, veuve depuis deux ans déjà.
Curieux, il décide d'aller voir par le trou de la serrure.
Il voit sa tata nue sur son lit tout en gesticulant crier :
- Je veux un homme, Oh bon Dieu, je veux un homme.
Quelques jours plus tard, il entend un autre bruit. Il va voir à nouveau et observe que la tata n'est plus toute seule. Elle est en compagnie d'un monsieur également tout nu.
Il retourne dans sa chambre, se déshabille, puis se met au lit tout nu. Il crie :
- Je veux un vélo, Oh, bon Dieu, je veux un vélo !!

Yaka XIX

Celui qui a vécu sans qu'on s'en aperçoive,
s'il meurt, on ne s'en apercevra pas.
(Proverbe Africain)
*
La vie est un désert dont la femme est le chameau.
(Proverbe Arabe)

La suite

Ça fait des nuits et des jours
Que j'aimerais suivre la suite
Que j'aimerais faire un autre tour
Dans le passé en fuite

Ça fait des nuits et des lustres
Que j'attends pour te dire
Que j'aimerais être illustre
Le désir de grandir

Ça fait des jours et des nuits
Que ma vie respire
Que je sors le parapluie
Pour écouter le pire.

Ça fait maintenant belle lurette
Que je n'écoute plus chanter
de stupides chansonnettes
Des diables sans queue à tenter

Ça me fait grand plaisir
De te dire en complice
Que l'amour fait induire
En force mes paroles à dire.

Aventures en Tropiques

Teddy et Elsa étaient assis ensemble au bar peu après avoir profité de la belle journée qu'ils avaient passée ensemble. La scène de l'action se déroulait quelque part aux Caraïbes.
Le soleil venait de se coucher à l'horizon de la mer. Il régnait une délicieuse odeur de mélange de fleurs et d'iode.
A droite se trouvait le restaurant où ils venaient de dîner. Teddy aimait dîner tôt et par la force des habitudes Elsa s'était associée à cette coutume.

Ils n'étaient pas seuls au bar, il y avait un autre couple.
À plusieurs reprises, ils levaient leur verre comme s'ils cherchaient à converser.
Teddy et Elsa souriaient de retour, et en apportant leur verre s'approchaient vers le couple. Les présentations faites, Steven et Mary racontèrent qu'ils habitaient en permanence sur l'Île. Steven en était même natif.
Ils proposaient rapidement de goûter la boisson traditionnelle composée de rhum agricole cœur de chauffe au gingembre. Une boisson bien traître, puisque le taux d'alcool de ce breuvage est supérieur à 60°.
Ils décidèrent de s'asseoir ensemble à une table, plus confortable que de rester accouder au bar avec quelques verres dans le ventre.

Après avoir papoté agréablement ensemble, Mary propose d'aller chez eux, juste à côté de l'établissement. Il faut absolument que vous gouttiez à mon mix à moi.
Elsa protesta un peu :
- Tu ne crois pas que tu as assez bu ce soir Teddy ?
- Mais non, je ne conduis pas, et ce soir je m'amuse. Un petit verre, qu'est-ce qu'on risque ?
- OK, mais après, retour à l'hôtel !

Teddy souriait. C'est souvent qu'il avait gain de cause avec sa compagne.
Au bout de deux verres, (sur une jambe c'est difficile de marcher) ils décidèrent de partir. Elsa se levait en premier et tomba presque sur son homme.
- Aide-moi suppliait-elle, je ne tiens pas debout.
Teddy se levait aussi mais il ne tenait pas trop bien non plus. C'était comme si ses jambes se transformaient en marshmallows.
Steven se proposait alors de les aider et de les accompagner jusqu'à l'hôtel à quelques pas de chez eux. Il prêta ses larges épaules de sportif et les portait plus ou moins dehors.
Devant la porte d'entrée de leur villa un van était garé. Les side portes étaient ouvertes. Deux hommes sortirent du véhicule et attrapèrent le couple en les poussant assez brutalement à l'intérieur de la camionnette. La porte se referma rapidement, et le van partit .

- Où nous emmenez-vous, qui sont ces gens ?"
Teddy regarda autour de lui, mais tout était trouble. C'était tout juste s'il apercevait Steven discuter avec les deux hommes, leur donnant un petit flacon, sur lequel il vissa une aiguille. Quelques instants plus tard, on lui shootait le liquide dans le bras. Avant qu'il ne sombre dans un profond néant, il observa que sa chère et tendre subissait le même sort.

Un temps indéfini s'écoula et Teddy se réveilla doucement. Il ouvrait les yeux et en face de lui il y avait Steven. Elsa n'avait pas encore repris connaissance.
- Que me veux-tu ? Demanda Teddy. Il voulait se lever avec l'envie insupportable de faire la fête. Impossible. Steven et ses acolytes l'avaient solidement attaché à une chaise, tout comme Elsa.

Steven détacha Teddy de sa chaise. Il noua ses poignées derrière lui et faisait transporter sa compagne sur sa chaise dans la pièce à côté. Puis il ferma la porte.
Ensuite Steven saisit un revolver et l'appuya directement contre le front de Teddy
- Je peux te tuer tout de suite. Mais si tu fais exactement ce que je vais te demander, tu sauves ta vie et surtout celle de ta gonzesse.
Teddy s'efforçait de rester calme. Visiblement, résister ne servirait à rien. Il fallait mieux écouter ce que Steven voulait de lui.
- Je t'explique, reprenait Steven. Je suis en concurrence avec un autre importateur de cocaïne. Il

ne sait pas que c'est moi qui suis derrière tout ça. Alors tu vas le rencontrer à ma place et tu lui files cette mallette. En contrepartie, il te file une autre mallette avec des US dollars. Il doit y en avoir trois cents mille.
Il est à court de marchandises pour son commanditaire. Je sais que ce type ne rigole pas. Moi aussi je travaille pour lui.
Mon concurrent a demandé à l'un de mes adjoints de lui fournir pour trois cents mille dollars de cocaïne. J'ai fait savoir que je lui envoie un émissaire avec la camelote, pour faire l'échange.
Il connaît bien mon équipe, mais il ne sait pas qui je suis. Pourtant il me connaît trop bien. Dans le temps j'ai travaillé pour lui. C'est souhaitable qu'il ne sache jamais que c'est moi qui lui pique ses clients.

Teddy écouta le récit de Steven. S'il se révélait autant, c'est que ses intentions ne laissaient entrevoir qu'une issue mortelle. Il réfléchit quelques instants et tout en regardant Steven dans les yeux :
- Je veux voir et parler à Elsa d'abord.
Comme réponse, le tortionnaire frappa Teddy avec la crosse de son revolver et cria :
- T'as rien à vouloir, c'est moi qui commande ici. Tu verras ta nénette quand tu auras fait ce que je te demande de faire.
Et fais gaffe, pas de coups foireux. Tu m'amènes la marchandise, tout va bien. Tu rates ton coup, tu perds la drogue, ou le pognon, je trancherai la gorge de ta gonzesse. Quoique, après l'avoir baisée, ça va de soit.
Teddy n'a pas le choix, le plus tôt sera le mieux.

- D'accord, explique moi le topo.
- Bien, mon garçon, c'est raisonnable ! Puis Steven reprenait cette fois-ci sur un ton presque aimable :
- Cette nuit, à quatre heures, tu t'embarques dans un bateau à rames. Tu trouveras un téléphone portable avec un N° de téléphone en mémoire. Il y a un compas aussi. Tu navigues en direction Nord-Nord Est pendant environ quarante cinq minutes si tu rames dare-dare. Tu vas voir une île devant toi. Il n'y a qu'une seule plage dans une crique. Tu prends le téléphone et tu composes le N° de téléphone mémorisé. Tu fais sonner cinq fois, tu raccroches, puis tu fais sonner trois fois. Tu raccroches à nouveau et tu attends.
Il viendront te voir et tu fais l'échange.
Bon, t'as tout compris ?
- Je crois que oui, répondait Teddy.
- À la bonheur ! Tu vas dans la pièce à côté, tu te laves et tu te changes. Il y a des fringues propres sur le lit. Teddy partit avec le bateau à rames dans la direction indiquée. Trois quarts d'heure après, il aperçoit la petite île devant lui, il navigue sur le bord de la petite plage, tire  l'embarcadère sur le sable et regarde autour de lui. Il y avait un autre bateau, un zodiac avec un hors-bord. IL s'en approcha et constatait qu'il n'y avait personne. Il y avait une pochette avec quelques clefs ainsi

qu'une clef à bougies. De-là lui vint l'idée de boycotter le bateau. Il constata qu'il n'y avait pas de rames de secours. Aussi il prit la clef à bougies, démonta la bougie et tapa sur les contacteurs pour qu'elle soit hors service. Pas de bougie, pas de fonctionnement de moteur.

Satisfait de lui, il saisit le téléphone. Il composa le numéro par deux fois comme stipulé dans les consignes de Steven.

Quelques instants plus tard, trois hommes à l'allure lugubre s'approchaient, avec une petite valise dans les mains de l'homme derrière les deux autres.
Il s'arrêtaient à environ vingt mètres. L'homme à la valise invitait Teddy à s'approcher avec la mallette.
Teddy s'exécutait. De toute façon, il n'avait pas le choix.
Une fois approchés de moins d'un mètre, les deux hommes sautaient sur lui, le jetaient à terre tout en le maîtrisant et lui confisquaient la valise.
Teddy eut droit à un coup de bâton derrière la nuque et on le laissait pour mort au bord de la plage.

Comme il se réveillait, il constata que son bateau à rames avait disparu et que le bateau des criminels était toujours là.
Teddy réfléchit quelques instants. C'était impossible de retourner vers Steven. IL n'avait plus la marchandise, et encore moins le pognon. La vie d'Elsa et la sienne étaient sérieusement en danger.
Il enfonça les mains dans sa poche : il avait toujours le

téléphone.
Il souriait. La solution était dans sa main.
Il composa le numéro de secours de la police locale. Il tenta d'expliquer son cas en mauvais anglais. De l'autre côté de la ligne, une voix féminine lui répondait en parfait Français :
- Que se passe-t-il monsieur ?
- Vous parlez Français ?
- Mais oui, mon brave monsieur, ma mère est Française. Mes grand parents aussi.
Teddy expliqua en détails l'histoire. La dame l' assurait que les services se mettaient en route sans tarder. Un hélicoptère allait décoller pour venir le chercher, puis deux vedettes de la police maritime allaient sortir pour intercepter la barque. Pendant que en même temps une autre équipe s'empressait d'aller vers la villa de Steven et Mary pour tenter de libérer Elsa.
Quand Teddy arrivait enfin sur la terre ferme avec l'hélicoptère, Elsa était déjà là à l'attendre.

Les bandits avec la drogue et l'argent ont été interceptés, puis Steven a été tué lors de l'assaut avec les snipers de la police spéciale d'intervention de l'île.
Mary était appréhendée et mise sous les verrous pour complicité.

Quand à Teddy et Elsa, ils décidaient de retourner en France. Qui sait, ils profitent maintenant de Paris Plage. Certainement moins dangereux. !

Il est libre Max !

Bien, Lisez d'abord le texte avec toute l'attention que vous pouvez fournir. Les questions et les réponses seront traitées après.

Max Fallard était prof de français dans le collège Léonard Cohen à Plissy, une commune de banlieue.
C'était la première année pour Max. Les collègues l'avaient averti :
- Tiens bon, ne te laisse pas faire. Ils vont vouloir te provoquer. Reste calme. Compte jusqu'à dix, même vingt, avant de répondre !

Max traversait la salle de classe. Avec son pied, il poussa ce qui semblait être un sac à dos, couché dans l'allée entre les tables. Christelle le regarda comme si elle était personnellement insultée.
- Enlève ta casquette Karim, tu connais les règles.
Max lâcha un grand soupir.
C'était presque impossible de maintenir l'interdiction de porter des couvre-chefs en classe. Certains collègues de Max estimaient que c'était un gaspillage d'énergie d'appliquer les règles venues d'en haut.
Max militait pour une discipline maîtrisée. Le collège possédait un vaste local rempli avec du matériel informatique du dernier cri.
Il en était le prof responsable. Seule une discipline

entretenue pouvait éviter la vandalisme. En tout cas, il en été persuadé.

- Alors Robert, tu ne lis pas ? Y-a-t-il un problème ?
- Un problème ? Répondit Robert, Je n'ai pas de problème. C'est toi qui as des problèmes...
Et pour accentuer ses paroles, il glissa presque complètement sous sa table. Max compta jusqu'à dix et continuait sa promenade entre les rangs de ses élèves.
Priscilla était occupée à envoyer un SMS
Max posa sa main sur le bras de Priscilla et lui dit :
- Pas de téléphone portable, range-moi cette chose s'il te plaît.
- Mais c'est pour ma mère m'sieur !
- Après les cours. Tu auras beaucoup plus de temps ".
- Oui, mais je n'ai ..."
Max tendit la main vers le téléphone mobile. Inutile.
Priscilla continua quand même et en quelques secondes elle appuya sur la touche « envoi » puis rangea avec un geste éclair le téléphone dans son sac.
Elle regardait son prof avec un sourire séducteur :
- Ça va comme ça m'sieur ?

Max décida de ne pas répondre et continuait à exécuter sa tournée dans la classe.
Certains élèves lisaient, d'autres faisaient semblant, mais ils avaient au moins le journal en face d'eux.
Dofi semblait dormir. Probablement il avait travaillé jusqu'à tard dans la nuit pour livrer des pizzas.
Dofi d'origine Ghanéenne était plus âgé que les autres élèves de sa classe. Il avait déjà dix neuf ans. Dans

son pays d'origine il n'avait pas eu la possibilité de fréquenter l'école comme il aurait voulu.
C'était un bon élève. Mais il était aussi celui qui rapportait le plus dans la marmite familiale. Son père n'était plus présent, il était parti avec une blanche il y a quelques mois déjà. La maman avec ses six enfants était seule, sans travail. Ils vivaient avec les allocations et la paye de Dofi.

Ce matin à la gare Max avait pris une pile de « métro ». Un journal gratuit. Il estimait que son contenu était plus éducatif que les textes des livres scolaires. Toutes les semaines, il organisait un tour de table pour commenter l'actualité et autres articles de fond traités dans ce journal.
- Pas uniquement les pages sportives, Johnny. Lis la première page, puis la suite à la page quatorze. Comme je l'ai indiqué sur le tableau noir.
Tu peux garder le journal. Donc les articles de sport tu peux les lire pendant la pause !
Johnny lui jeta un regard foudroyant. En fait, il exigeait d' être appelé John. A l' âge de quinze ans, il mesurait déjà un mètre quatre-vingt-cinq, et il avait la forte posture de quelqu'un qui se rend régulièrement dans la salle de gym. En fait, il était le jeune sosie de son père, qui lui, s'appelle vraiment John.
John Preston. John est américain. Il était venu en France avec une copine pour traverser le pays en auto- stop. Au bout d'un certain temps, la copine était partie avec un séduisant français, propriétaire d'un van équipé comme un camping car. C'est quand même plus pratique de se promener avec son lit !

John avait rencontré la mère de Johnny dans le métro.
Elle chantait des chansons de ses compositions.

Il y a quelques semaines, Johnny s'était fait tatouer. Sur son avant-bras gauche, on pouvait lire : « I want to fuck you »
Même pas capable de s'exprimer en français.
D'ailleurs, Johnny prenait un malin plaisir à parler comme un américain. Il parlait l'anglais couramment grâce à son père.
Cette 3ème était aussi un groupe raisonnable, mais Johnny était en permanence sous tension. Un fusible dans un baril de poudre
Max marchait entre les tables.
Lise était bonne élève en presque tout, une fille sans problèmes. Elle échangeait parfois des bouts de papier avec Maria, sa copine. Mais Max les ignorait volontairement.
Puis les emmerdes commencèrent.
Tout à coup Max trébuchait. Il avait juste vu Johnny rapidement retirer sa jambe.
Il tomba en s'appuyant comme il le pouvait sur deux tables bordant le couloir des élèves. Il se levait avec difficulté. Une douleur irradiait la région de son coccyx.
- Tombé monsieur ? Johnny regardait Max avec un sourire moqueur.
Quasi toute la classe se mit à rire avec Johnny.
Max se traînait péniblement vers son bureau devant les élèves rigolards. Il soupira profondément quelques instants.
- Eh bien, dit-il, vous avez tous lu l'article. La première

question que je voudrais poser est ...
Il regarda autour de lui. Certains élèves le regardèrent comme s'ils voulaient dire qu'il fallait mieux abandonner la question.   Les autres continuaient à lire.
Johnny se penchait vers son copain Mehmet et lui chuchota quelque chose à l'oreille.
Max le regardait droit dans les yeux.
- Johnny, Quel est le message principal de l'article ?
- Baratin de chiotte répondit Johnny.
Max comptait jusqu'à vingt cette fois -ci. Il décida de ne pas réagir, au moins pas pour l'instant.
Il ignora le garçon, et reprit son cour.
C'était la dernière heure de classe de la journée. Max clôtura et avec un « à demain » unilatéral, les élèves partirent du local sans réponse.
Quand Johnny passait devant lui, comme d'usage en dernier, Max l'arrêta avec son bras.
- Non, pas toi !
- Ah, bon, et pourquoi ? J'ai autre chose à faire qu'à écouter tes conneries.
Max se mit en face de Johnny. Il regarda sa montre : Quatre heures et quart.
- Si c'est nécessaire, je resterais ici jusqu'à ce que l'école soit fermée.
Jimmy s'était légèrement reculé.
Max entama un monologue sur ce qu'il voulait à l'école, la formation, comment il voyait l'avenir avec ses élèves.
Johnny haussa les épaules et bougonna :
- Qu'est ce que ça peut me foutre ?
Max poursuivit la leçon de cet après-midi. Il expliquait

une nouvelle fois ce qui était prévu.
- ...Et le genre de réponses que tu as données, je ne peux vraiment pas accepter.
- Mais je pense que ce sont des conneries, répondit Johnny.
- Je ne t'ai pas demandé ton opinion personnelle, tu le sais très bien. Tu n'as même pas lu. Comment tu peux dire que ce sont des conneries ?
- Hé, mec, je ne comprends rien de ce que tu veux me dire. Puis bouges-toi, je me casse maintenant.
- OK Johnny, si tu ne veux pas ou ne peux pas comprendre, je suis obligé d'accepter. Tu peux partir de suite, mais pas avant de t'excuser pour ton comportement.
- Quoi ? Des excuses ? Pourquoi faire ?
- Parce que tu perturbes la classe. Tu es grossier, puis j'ai bien remarqué que c'est toi qui m'a fait tomber.
Johnny regardait Max avec un sourire de brigand.
Max comptait cette fois-ci jusqu'à trente et gardait le silence encore quelques instants.
L'élève récalcitrant s'avançait vers la porte et déclara solennellement :
- Je dois vraiment y aller.
- Pas question, tu restes là. D'abord des excuses !
Johnny faisait comme s'il ne l'avait pas entendu et s'avança pour quitter la salle. Max se posta devant lui. Il sentait que ses jambes étaient fragiles, le sang lui monta à la tête.
- Punaise, qu'est-ce-qu'il m'arrive, pensait-il. Quand même, ce connard va d'abord faire ses excuses. Il ne faut pas que je cède maintenant !
C'était tout ce qui importait maintenant.

- Reste calme, reste calme, se disait Max,

Johnny essayait de le repousser, mais Max était ancré sur le sol comme un socle inébranlable.
- Eh bien putain, mec», exclama Johnny, avec toi il y a toujours des conneries. Tu devrais la mettre en veilleuse. C'est mieux pour tes nerf et ta santé !
Max retenait le garçon comme il le pouvait. Puis il le repoussait vers l'arrière.
C'est là que Johnny tomba sur la table dernière lui. Il se blessa sérieusement à la tête. Il perdait beaucoup de sang.
Max courut vers l'infirmerie pour chercher de l'aide.

- C'était une façon très regrettable d'agir, commenta le principal.
Max regarda le principal du collège.
- Je ne pouvais rien faire. Il est tombé.
- Tu l'as jeté en arrière oui ! Il me l'a dit.
- Je l'ai repoussé à sa place. Nous n'en avions pas fini et ...
- Un bras cassé ! Le principal l'interrompait, J'espère qu'ils ne porteront pas plainte. Ce n'est pas bon pour l'école et encore moins bon pour toi !
- Il s'est comporté très agressivement, se défendait Max. J'ai réagi comme n'importe qui d'autre.
Le principal regardait avec mépris ses lunettes de lecture.
- C'est votre métier de maîtriser ce genre de situations. On ne frappe pas un élève. Vous allez devoir rencontrer les parents.
- Mais je n'ai pas frappé. Je l'ai poussé !

Ouais, je ne sais pas ce que ses parents font. Je ne connais pas trop les parents.

Max resta malade quelques jours.
Après le retour à l'école, il avait l'impression que ses collègues le regardaient différemment.
Aucun commentaire sur Johnny Preston, même pendant la pause-café, Max a été particulièrement surpris que le sujet ait été explicitement évité en faveur de thèmes tels que la météo, les catastrophes à l'autre bout du monde, les chiens écrasés dans le pays etc.
il retrouvait la troisième dans sa classe. Johnny Preston prônait son bras plâtre peint de tracés multicolores et le posait avec un coup très lourd sur la table.
Il était remarquablement calme. Probablement le calme avant la tempête.
Lorsque les élèves furent sortis de la salle de classe après la sonnerie, Johnny s'approchait de Max :
- Mon père veut vous parler.
- Euh ... ouais, c'est ... euh, eh bien, normal ... Je veux dire ... euh, les parents sont toujours les bienvenus, mais j'ai peu de temps. La semaine dernière, j'étais malade ... Je te donnerai un rendez-vous demain. Il va y avoir une réunion de parents, je crois.
Johnny hocha la tête en signe de « bien reçu »
Les jours d'après, la routine de l'enseignement ordinaire s'était rétablie.
Max était heureux, les élèves se comportaient mieux. Ce n'était pas encore parfait, mais il y avait un début.

C'était surtout Dofi qui avait défendu Max.
Max habitait à une quarantaine de kilomètres de l'école.
C'est pour cela que Max était tous les soirs pressé de rentrer. Il s'était engagé à prendre sa femme à son boulot, puis leurs deux jumelles chez la nourrice.
Ce qui réduisait les possibilités de rendez-vous avec les parents.
Puis un soir, une réunion des parents d'élèves était prévue par le principal. Les profs étaient tous présents par obligation.
Max aperçut le père de Johnny, qui était venu lui aussi.
- Merde, le rendez-vous ! Il n'y pensait plus !
John Preston avait repéré Max. Il lui faisait signe et s'avança vers lui.
- On a encore quelques minutes de temps avant que tout le monde n'arrive. Discutons un peu, voulez-vous ?
Max regarda l'homme. Il était impressionnant. Le torse d'un body builder, des muscles partout...
Max sentait la transpiration couler sur son dos. Le père de Johnny allait bientôt être là tout près devant lui,.
Il lui fallait peu d'imagination pour savoir ce qu'il risquait d'arriver.
- Je ne porterai pas plainte pour mon fils, déclara le père. Je crois que dans ce cas, c'est inutile et injuste.
- Je crois que je ne me sens pas bien, déclara Max.
Il faut que je m'échappe ! Le mot résonnait dans sa tête, mais en même temps il savait que ce n'était que temporaire.
Preston mit son énorme main sur le bras de Max,

comme s'il voulait en juger la fragilité.
En une fraction de seconde Max avait vu une ambulance en face de lui, un hôpital, les médecins, les infirmières. La grande angoisse....
- Professeur Max Fallard ?
Les mots émerg eaient d'un brouillard.
- Oui, c'est moi répondit Max, totalement soumis à la situation.
Il ouvrit les yeux et voyait à nouveau le père de Johnny. Il le tenait toujours par les bras.
- Oh la la, Monsieur le professeur, restez avec nous !
Je viens juste pour vous dire que mon épouse et moi aimerions vous remercier et vous féliciter d'avoir réagi avec fermeté aux agissements de notre fils.
Toujours une grande gueule, rien n'est bien avec lui !
Il était temps que quelqu'un lui donne une leçon de savoir-vivre. Vous l'avez fait. Il vous respecte maintenant. J'en suis sûr.
Moi, je suis son père. Je n'arrive pas à faire ce que vous avez fait. John Preston leva son bras et tendit sa main à Max.
- Merci, merci pour mon fils !

Max sourit un peu timide.
Quelques instants plus tard il se regardait dans le miroir du vestiaire des profs. Il regardait autour de lui, il y avait personne. Puis s'adressant à son reflet dans le miroir :
- Toi, alors ! Tu m'étonnes tous les jours !

D'après un pastel réalisée par le peintre Néerlandais Max Allandt (1875-1930)

Parader

C'est bien loin d'être un mythe,
Il faut bien que cela soit dit.
Même si tu cours après ta fuite
Sous les couettes de ton lit.
L'impression solennelle des paroles
Vidées de leur sens profond,
Transformées en histoires drôles
Brouillonnées au crayon.
Depuis les temps mémorables
Ne peuvent allumer l'artifice en bouquet
En passion de conter des fables
Au fin fonds des mastroquets.

C'est difficile de se tenir à distance
Levant la verre de l'amitié,
Souhaitant avoir de la chance
de ne plus devoir mendier.
Alors avancer, attaquer et posséder,
Passer en outre mesure,
T'auras le droit de parader
Devant les énigmes du futur.

Nahéma

Je m'appelle Nahéma Soidiki, C'est le nom qui figure sur mon passeport depuis que je suis adopté par Monsieur Soidiki et sa femme.
Mes parents ont été tués lors d'un pillage de mon village par des rebelles. J'avais huit ans environ. Je suis Bosicarienne.
C'est mon oncle, le mari de la sœur de mon père qui m'a sauvée et s'était obligé par tradition à s'occuper de moi.
Il voyait cela d'assez mauvais œil, il ne m'aimait pas, et je ne représentais pour lui qu'une bouche à nourrir.

A tout juste 12 ans, et comme beaucoup de filles de mon village, j'étais suffisamment modulée pour que les hommes remarquent la beauté de ma jeunesse.
Son fils, à peine plus âgé que moi, n'avait pas demandé mon accord pour me transformer en jouet.
Je ne pouvais rien faire, une fille sans protection ne parle pas.
Jusqu'au jour où l'oncle voulait aussi avoir sa part, j'ai manifesté clairement mon dégoût et j'ai hurlé de désir de vouloir partir, de mourir, de disparaître.
Ainsi, j'étais heureuse qu'il m'annonce qu'il ne pouvait plus s'occuper de moi, et que je serai adoptée par un couple de personnes riches et importantes.

La vérité était que je devrais travailler sans être payée.
Je devenais désormais leur fille adoptive.
Mon oncle avait gagné de quoi acheter quelque bétail,
Il m'avait en quelque sorte vendu. Pourtant, j'avais à peine 13 ans et déjà les fils de barbelé plein de tête.

Au début, mon nouveau père était plutôt gentil avec moi, c'était inhabituel. Jusque-là, avec mon oncle je ne connaissais que des gueulardes et le bâton.
Même Madame, ma nouvelle mère, très évasée et très occupée avec sa beauté pour plaire à son époux, me donnait des gestes d'encouragement et m'accordait de larges sourires.
J'étais chargée en premier temps de m'occuper des autres enfants du couple. Les deux aînés d'un premier mariage de Soidiki et la petite sœur qu'il avait eue avec Michèle, sa femme.
Les enfants étaient à peine plus jeunes que moi.
J'étais jalouse. Ils avaient tout ce que je n'avais jamais eu quand j'avais leur âge. Des jouets et des choses inconnues pour moi, venant d'une monde d'ailleurs.
Ils pouvaient manger à leur faim, boire à leur soif, s'habiller très fashion, de la marque quoi !
Rapidement mes parents m'ont séparée des autres enfants. J'avais une éducation à compléter, me disaient-ils.
En attendant des jours meilleurs de ma rééducation, je ne mangeais plus avec la famille, mais je faisais le service en aidant Gisèle la bonne. Je mangeais avec elle et les autres.
Il est vrai, que chez mes vrais parents et mon oncle nous mangions avec les mains et nous nous servions

tous dans le même plat, notre façon à nous de partager le repas.

Quelques temps après mon arrivée, mon père adoptif était muté à l'ambassade de Bosicar au Sénégal. Nous prîmes l'avion et après deux escales, nous sommes arrivés à Dakar.
C'était la première fois que je voyais un avion, et mieux encore volais dans le ventre de ce grand oiseau en métal. J'avais peur, et au départ je ne voulais pas entrer dans l'engin. J'étais persuadé que ce grand truc ne décollerait jamais du sol. Nous allions nous écraser contre un quelconque obstacle.
Rien ne fut comme prévu, l'avion se dressa comme d'usage et glissa sur les nuages vers sa destination. Jamais je n'oublierai ce moment.

A notre arrivée à Dakar, plusieurs voitures nous attendaient. L'une pour mes bienfaiteurs et le fils de Soidiki, l'autre pour les filles et moi-même. Nous étions habillés comme des princesses. Un monsieur en tenue militaire nous ouvrit la porte de la limousine et nous pria de bien vouloir embarquer. Il avait même enlevé sa casquette et m'appelait respectueusement mam'zelle ! J'étais aux anges. Mais pas pour longtemps.
La villa qui nous servait de demeure était immense. Il y avait une dizaine de chambres, un grand living, le bureau du maître, le boudoir de la maîtresse. Aux sous-sol, une grande cuisine et les chambres du personnel.
Il y avait trois bonnes et un maître d'hôtel qui faisait

aussi office de chauffeur. Le jardinier n'habitait pas sur place.

Pour les enfants, ils avaient engagé une gouvernante, qui leur enseignait en même temps que les matières d'école, les us et coutumes de la bonne société..
Moi, je n'avais pas le droit d'apprendre. D'ailleurs, j'étais désormais directement « au service » de monsieur avec le privilège selon lui d'apporter les boissons fraîches, de s'occuper de la garde-robe de ses invités, de nettoyer son bureau et l'intérieur de sa voiture.
Une vraie occupation digne d'une jeune fille de la maison, fille adoptive bien sûr.
Ma chambre que je partageais avec la femme de chambre de son épouse, était également aux sous-sol avec les autres membres de son personnel.
Nous avions changé de pays et moi de statut au sein de la famille. J'étais toujours leur fille adoptive pour la vitrine. En réalité, j'étais une bonne obligée à tout faire.

Nous sommes restés presque deux ans à Dakar. Je n'avais quasiment plus le droit de sortir. Quand monsieur n'était pas là, j'étais à la disposition de Gisèle. Je n'avais pratiquement plus de contact avec les enfants ou avec madame.
Aussi je n'avais plus le droit de les appeler affectueusement Papa et Maman. Désormais, c'était Père et Mère, avec l'obligation de vouvoyer.

Ils trouvaient que je n'aurais jamais la classe pour

faire partie de leur famille intime. Qu'ils s'étaient trompés. Que c'était trop tard pour parfaire mon éducation et ainsi rentrer dans leur moule.

Bien plus tard, je compris que la femme qui faisait office de bonne et cuisinière pour la famille, était aussi la maîtresse de monsieur. La relation avait débuté presque depuis leur arrivée à Dakar.
Elle était jalouse de moi et me voyait plus comme une future concurrente.

Gisèle est une femme assez belle et d'ailleurs un peu provocante avec ses yeux en forme d'amande aux couleurs de noisette grillée. Son décolleté méritait bien les honneurs qu'elle proposait.
Même le chauffeur-maître-d'hôtel profitait de ses largesses, quand monsieur était occupé ailleurs.
Gisèle jouait parfaitement son rôle de ma geôlière pour le compte de monsieur. Elle avait trop à perdre à ne pas exécuter ses ordres.
Lui, l'homme puissant, maître du quotidien et des destinées de chacun et chacune.

Au bout de quelques mois, il était nommé ambassadeur en remplacement de son patron rappelé au pays pour faire partie du gouvernement de son pays.
Nous sommes restés à Dakar un peu plus de deux ans en tout. Et après un court séjour au pays, Soidiki était nommé ambassadeur en France.
C'était une sacrée promotion, être ambassadeur dans la république Française lui donnait l'envergure de ses ambitions. Il pouvait désormais fréquenter ce beau

monde dont il rêvait depuis si longtemps.
Soidiki était un vicieux. L'homme si gentil quand j'étais une petite fille se comportait de plus en plus comme un égoïste, pervers et si content de faire étalage de sa nouvelle puissance.

A l'anniversaire de son fils Dahirou, il m'avait offerte pour ses quinze ans. J'étais obligée de partager sa chambre avec lui et réaliser ses fantasmes de gamin en chaleur.
Le fils incarna bien la pomme qui ne tombe pas loin de l'arbre.
A partir de ce moment je suis devenue son souffre-douleur, obligée de répondre à ses caprices. Il m'insultait et même me frappait. Cela faisait rire son père.
« Faut pas prendre cela au premier degré » me disait-il, il est très jeune et il a encore tout à apprendre.
Et moi ? je venais d'avoir seize ans. J'étais une vieille ?

La vie était devenue impossible, je me levais à cinq heures le matin et j'avais enfin le droit de me reposer après dix heures le soir, si toutefois le fils n'en avait pas décidé autrement.
Souvent je rêvais de m'échapper, de partir loin de cette famille de dingues. Seulement, je n'avais pas de papiers, mon passeport était dans le coffre personnel du père. Personne ne partageait la combinaison.
Chaque fois que j'ai osé le lui demander, il me le refusa. Je n'avais pas besoin de passeport, puisque j'étais la fille adoptive de l'ambassadeur de Bosicar en France.

Le jour où Lionel était venu parler affaires, et partager le goûter avec la famille, j'en ai profité pour partir. Tant pis pour les papiers. J'étais certaine que tout le monde était trop occupé pour faire attention à moi. J'avais dit à Gisèle, la cuisinière, que je ne me sentais

Composition d'après deux oeuvres de BERT (2012)

pas bien, mal au ventre. Je ne sais pas si elle m'avait crue.
J'avais couru presque une heure pour arriver à la route

départementale où il y avait un peu de circulation. Il pleuvait et il commençait à faire sombre.
Un type m'a emmenée et me transporta sans dire un mot à environ quarante kilomètres plus loin.
C'est là que j'ai été prise en stop par Lionel. Peut-être le hasard du destin.
Il s'est immédiatement imposé comme protecteur, j'avais déjà moins peur en sa présence. De toute façon, qu'est-ce qu' il pourrait m'arriver de pire ?

Lionel :

C'est clair, Il fallait faire quelque chose, Je ne pouvais pas déposer la jeune fille quelque part sur la route et continuer mon chemin comme si de rien n'était.
Elle était visiblement fragile, malgré la détermination qu'elle dégageait.
Aussi et sans réfléchir d'avantage, je lui ai proposé de venir avec moi, et de reparler de sa situation le lendemain à tête reposée.
Il était évident qu'en premier temps l'ambassadeur ne pouvait pas soupçonner que la fille était au secret chez moi. J'habitais dans un appartement assez vaste pour l'héberger, puis dans ma ville, il y a beaucoup d'immigrés d'Afrique et des originaires des Antilles. Personne ne se retournerait sur elle comme si c'était une curiosité.
La villa de Soidiki se trouvait bien à plus de cent soixante kilomètres de mon domicile. L'ambassade proprement dite à plus de deux cents.

Un moment j'ai pensé à me présenter à la

gendarmerie ou la police pour déclarer qu'elle était chez moi. Il était évident que cette solution n'était pas la bonne, puisque son père adoptif pouvait faire valoir ses droits. En plus il bénéficiait de son immunité diplomatique si jamais Nahéma aurait eu le courage de porter plainte.
Je lui ai proposé de rester et d'attendre ses dix-huit ans, l'âge de sa majorité dans quelques semaines.

Dès le début de son séjour chez moi, j'avais défini les règles à tenir. Il n'y avait pas et il n'y aurait pas de situation ambiguë d'homme - femme. Nahéma avait sa chambre, moi la mienne. Ces deux lieux seraient des lieux privés, et respectés par l'autre. Nahéma logerait chez moi comme si c'était une nièce, voire ma fille. Je ne voulais en aucun cas la considérer comme une copine.
J'étais plus âgé qu'elle, elle me devait du respect dans une sorte d'autorité de beau-père ou grand frère. D'ailleurs, moi-même j'ai un fils du même âge qu'elle qui vit avec sa mère.
Je suis divorcé depuis plusieurs années. Je m'étais marié trop tôt et déjà père à dix huit ans. Je ne voyais mon fils que pendant les grandes vacances. Sa mère s'était mariée avec un antillais et habitait à la Guadeloupe.

Nahéma accepta avec bonheur. Il nous restait à attendre qu'une solution se présente.
En pratique, j'allais travailler comme tous les jours, Nahéma se borna à faire un peu de ménage et m'épata avec des plats qu'elle avait appris à

confectionner avec Gisèle.
Le soir, je lui contai mes petites misères de la journée. Nous regardions les infos à la télévision ensemble et je lui expliquais et commentais leur contenu.
Je lui appris à compter, mieux parler, à écrire d'une bonne orthographe. C'était idyllique, nous avions quasiment oublié la véritable situation dans laquelle nous nous trouvions.
Jusqu'au jour de ce samedi matin. On sonnait à la porte de mon appartement. L'horloge dans le couloir marquait sept heures. Nahéma habillée en chemise de nuit était assise dans la cuisine. Elle déjeunait. Moi j'étais encore dans ma chambre où je m'essuyai de ma douche matinale.
Je lui dis d'ouvrir. Je m'entourai d'une grande serviette de bain et en sortant de ma chambre je lui demandais qui étaient les personnes.

C'était la police.

Joseph :

Je me prénomme Joseph. A l'époque j'avais 56 ans et j'étais commissaire de police judiciaire.
C'était à la suite d'une plainte déposée par l'ambassadeur de Bosicar que je me suis rendu au domicile de Lionel.
L'ambassadeur avait engagé un détective privé pour rechercher sa fille adoptive disparue sans laisser trace ou mot.
La police avait fait acte en main courante, mais n'avait pas effectué toute l'investiture souhaitée par ce

diplomate. Ce qui justifia selon lui le détective privé.
Il lui fallait près de trois mois pour trouver la trace de Nahéma en épluchant la vie de chaque individu ayant eu contact avec la jeune fille et la famille.

Suite aux renseignements obtenus, nous avions constaté que la mineure Nahéma était bien au domicile de Lionel..
C'était en effet elle qui nous ouvrit la porte d'entrée, habillée en simple chemise de nuit. L'horloge affichait sept heures du matin.
C'est aussi à ce moment que Lionel nous est apparu. Il était habillé d'une simple serviette de bain nouée autour de la taille, pieds et torse nus.

Nous étions immédiatement persuadés que nous étions en présence d'un couple établi.
Il y avait deux chambres avec les lits défaits, mais nous estimions que cela ne vaut pas grand-chose comme preuve. Puis dans la chambre de Lionel, il y avait bien un lit de deux personnes.
Nous avons fouillé l'appartement de fond en comble en présence de Lionel, après avoir demandé aux deux personnes de se vêtir d'avantage. La jeune fille a été entre-temps transportée au commissariat.

A notre demande, elle n'a pas été capable de nous fournir les papiers de son identité. Pire, elle refusa catégoriquement de nous parler.
Entre-temps, et après la fouille, le dénommé Lionel a été également transporté au commissariat pour interrogation.

Il refusa également de parler de la jeune fille.
J'ai été obligé de transmettre à mes supérieurs que nous étions incapables de nous imposer auprès de ces personnes.
C'est l'ambassadeur de Bosicar lui-même qui s'est déplacé pour identifier formellement la fille comme étant sa fille adoptive. Il a d'ailleurs apporté ses papiers parfaitement en règle.
Malgré les résistances de la fille, il exigea de la ramener à l'ambassade. Nous ne pouvions rien y faire, elle était Bosicarienne et sous la protection de son beau-père, lui-même représentant du gouvernement de son pays. D'ailleurs le préfet en personne nous a fait savoir qu'il fallait éviter tout conflit diplomatique avec ce pays en plein développement. Il y avait trop d'intérêts communs en danger de rupture.

Une fois la fille partie, il nous resta Lionel. L'ambassadeur n'avait pas porté plainte contre lui.
Déjà au départ j'ai senti une certaine pression autour de cette affaire, mais je n'aime pas que quiconque en dehors de ma hiérarchie se mêle avec ce que je dois faire. Aussi j'ai été heureux que les charges contre Lionel aient été annulées.

A peine une heure après avoir été transportée d'office vers le commissariat de police, mon soi-disant père était venu me chercher. Il était accompagné d'un monsieur qui se disait le représentant du préfet.
Immédiatement, nous sommes allés à l'ambassade. Ils avaient aménagé une chambre pour moi pour me rafraîchir et m'habiller d'avantage.

Soidiki m'avait confiée à l'une des secrétaires. Dès le

D.A.O. de BERT – "K & K" réalisé en avril 2013

lendemain, je devrais quitter l'ambassade pour retourner à Bosicar.
- Pour être entendue par la police de mon pays, m'avait-il dit.

Si la justice Française désirait avoir ma version des faits, il transmettrait le dossier à qui de droit.
Il était évident que je ne pouvais plus m'exprimer selon ma vérité. Cela me condamnait moi-même.
Pire, je risquais d'être réduite au silence définitivement.
Impossible d'accuser la famille Soidiki d'exploitation d'esclavage, d'attouchements sexuels et de viols par le père et le fils. Impossible de dire que j'étais leur chose et pas leur fille adoptive.
Je ne savais plus quoi faire. Je n'avais plus de nouvelles de Lionel, autre que :
- Lionel ? Eh bien, ton Lionel va moisir en prison. Il apprendra qu'il ne doit pas se mêler avec des choses qui ne le regardent pas. Je ne savais pas encore que c'était un mensonge.

Nahema

Dans les locaux de l'ambassade, une jeune femme me présenta mon témoignage pré-écrit. Un texte qu'on m'imposait et que je devrais signer sincère et en vérité. Ce témoignage a été obtenu en présence de deux témoins, suite aux questions d'un officier de police judiciaire de Bosicarien..
Je n'avais pas le choix. Le texte était plein de mensonges et de contre-vérités.

Soidiki était peint comme un bienfaiteur, soucieux de mon avenir. Mon éducation n'a pas été à hauteur de ses espérances.
Ma fuite provoquée par Lionel, après un rendez-vous

près de leur résidence secondaire en France, avait accentué ses douleurs, idem pour son épouse et ses enfants.

J'étais désormais devenue adulte et je pouvais aller comme bon me semble, ajoutait-il. De toute façon, il se ne souciait pas une seule seconde de ce qui pourrait m'arriver.

Au moment de partir de l'ambassade, l'officier me donna une enveloppe avec un peu d'argent de la part de mon père sans amour, sans foi ni loi....

Devant moi, il préleva à peu près la moitié et me donna le reste. Il paraît que j'avais de la chance. Il y avait de quoi vivre quelques mois en faisant attention aux dépenses.

J'étais seule, je ne savais pas où aller. Je ne savais pas où planquer l'argent, je pouvais facilement me le faire voler. C'était hors de question que je m'accroche à un homme. Leur regard en disait long sur leurs intentions.

Je ne savais pas où dormir, assise sur un banc, tout en croquant un bout de baguette, je méditais sur ma nouvelle situation.

Peu après, une jeune femme s'asseyait à côté de moi.
- Je ne te connais pas, t'es nouvelle ?
- Comment nouvelle ? Nouvelle de quoi ?
- Tu ne fais pas le tapin ?
- Le tapin ? C'est quoi ?
- Mais qu'est-que tu fais ici ?
- Je ne sais pas où dormir ce soir. Je ne connais personne. Je suis épuisée.

Il était évident que je n'avais pas envie de lui raconter ma vie. Au moins pas maintenant.

- Alors, tu ne cherches pas à travailler comme nous autres ?
- De quel travail me parles tu ?
- Toi alors ! Tu viens d'où ? Tu n'as pas compris ? Nous sommes des ... disons des travailleuses sociales pour déstresser certains hommes ! Des putes quoi ...
- Vous êtes une prostituée ?
- Oui, ma chérie, une pute indépendante. Pas de mec, sauf pour mon bon plaisir. Comment tu t'appelles ? moi c'est Vicky. Et arrête de me vouvoyer. !
- OK, moi c'est Nahéma, t'as pas d'embrouilles avec les flics ?
- Pas du tout ! Il arrive de faire une petite gâterie.
- Il faut que tu sois habillée comme ça ? Je veux dire aussi court ?
- C'est mieux, c'est un peu notre tenue de travail.
Viens avec moi. Pour aujourd'hui, j'ai assez travaillé. Je t'invite chez moi.
Je souriais et je suivais ma nouvelle copine, ça ne pouvait pas être pire qu'avec ce connard qui prétendait être mon père !

Vicky

Bonjour, je m'appelle Vicky. Je gagne ma vie en tant que péripatéticienne. Un métier vieux comme le monde, a-t-on dit souvent, mais aussi un métier répulsif malgré l'aspect matériel et parfois social.
Bref, je gagne en toute indépendance ma vie à régler le tensiomètre des hommes de tout poil.
J'ai rencontré Nahéma dans mon secteur de travail. Elle n'avait pas bonne mine et faisait pitié. Quand elle

disait qu'elle n'était pas du métier, je l'avais cru de suite. Ce qui s'est confirmé d'ailleurs dans les jours qui suivirent.

Je lui ai bien fait quelques propositions de collaboration, mais en vain. Cela ne m'avait pas empêchée de continuer à l'héberger gratuitement. Elle faisait adorablement la cuisine, était plaisante à converser sur beaucoup de sujets. Jamais elle ne me faisait de rapproches sur mon métier. Pas de questions embarrassantes comme le « pourquoi ? »

En un minimum de temps, Nahéma était devenue une sorte d'ange protecteur, Elle nous faisait penser à notre jeune âge, en ce temps-là, nous aurions pu avoir le choix, ou l'aide de faire autre chose dans notre vie.

Ce n'est pas que je me lamente, je me suis plus ou moins habituée et je me suis trop attachée à un certain confort et au luxe. Témoin ma collection de chaussures que je porte d'ailleurs rarement.

La seule chose qui me manque vraiment, c'est de ne pas avoir poussé d'avantage les études à l'école. J'étais plus souvent absente que présente. Et quand j'étais là, je ne glandais pas grand chose.

Pour beaucoup de mes camarades de métier, c'est la même chose. Je ne parle pas de quelques étudiantes, parce que elles, elles sont de passage. Et une fois réussis les diplômes, elles ne te regardent plus.

Tiens, je te donne un exemple :

Une de mes copines a été attrapée pour avoir consommé de la drogue. C'est vrai, ce n'est pas bien. D'ailleurs moi-même je ne prends pas de drogue ni je ne fume.

Bref, elle s'était présentée devant la juge qui n'avait aucune clémence envers ma copine. Une juge qui faisait, il y a à peine deux ans, encore la tapine à côté d'elle !
Elle l'avait mise en détention immédiate sans broncher.
Faut pas me dire qu'elle ne l'avait pas reconnue !

Bref, mes copines de travail ne sont souvent pas des fleurs en écriture et autres paperasses.
J'avais remarqué que Nahéma se débrouillait pas mal, elle savait écrire, avait une belle orthographe, comprenait vite les textes officiels etc.
Aussi en un minimum de temps, mes copines sollicitèrent son aide.
Et chaque fois, elle était gratifiée d'un peu d'argent.
Petit à petit, cela faisait une jolie somme.
Elle a eu l'idée de faire les choses selon les règles. Elle s'est inscrite comme entrepreneur indépendant comme rédactrice. Une sorte d' écrivain public. Aujourd'hui, elle a son appartement, pas loin de chez moi d'ailleurs, et a comme principales clientes les filles de la rue.
Elle est devenue notre porte-parole.
Aujourd'hui, elle a passé son baccalauréat en candidat libre et elle va entrer en fac pour étudier le droit.
Nahéma veut devenir avocate. C'est pour nous aider plus efficacement encore.
Je dis tout ça, pour témoigner que, comme Nahéma, notre exemple, rien n'est perdu dans la vie.
Donne un peu de tes capacités à l'autre. Aide un peu ton prochain et laisse-toi aider. C'est un gage de bien-être.

Lionel

Je crois que c'est à moi de clôturer ce récit.
En effet quelques années plus tard, mon fils qui était revenu en France métropole pour étudier le droit à l'université m'avait annoncé qu'il désirait me présenter le nouvel amour de sa vie.
Cette fois-ci c'est le gros lot, m'expliqua-t-il. Je l'aime, je veux vivre avec elle.
La fille était étudiante comme lui, stagiaire dans le même cabinet d'avocats.

Quelle était ma surprise de reconnaître Nahéma entrer dans mon appartement parisien au bras de mon fils.
C'était une surprise heureuse de taille !
Aujourd'hui Nahéma vit avec mon fils, ils sont avocats tous deux et dirigent leur propre cabinet. Puis, et c'est le plus important, ils sont papa et maman d'une superbe petit fille qui se nomme Emérancy comme la mère de Nahéma.

Yaka XX

Un orchestre ne se forme jamais si tout le monde se prends pour le premier violon.

D.A.O. de BERT – "l'oiseau" réalisé en août 2013

Mémo

Du même auteur :

Le dindon ou la Farce
Chroniques d'une vie d'homme
Edition BOD – février 2009
Tirage limité, épuisé

Mots cornés
Poésies
Édition BOD – juin 2010
Tirage limité, épuisé

Des mots en cafouille I
Histoires courtes
Édition BOD – juin 2013
ISBN : 978 232 203 0 149

Des mots en cafouille II
Histoires courtes
Édition BOD - août 2013
ISBN : 978 232 203 2 839

Courriel :

www.vandenheuvel.fr